HARRIS'S ARK

Harris's Ark

A History of a Small Group of People in a Time of Madness

Corinne A. Dwyer

NORTH STAR PRESS OF ST. CLOUD, INC.
St. Cloud, Minnesota

ISBN-10: 0-87839-300-5
ISBN-13: 978-0-87839-300-8

First Edition: September 2009

Printed in the United States of America

Published by
North Star Press of St. Cloud, Inc.
P.O. Box 451
St. Cloud, Minnesota 56302
www.northstarpress.com

To my daughters
Seal, Miranda, and Elizabeth
That their times be interesting . . .
but kind.

I

HIJACKING

TUESDAY, OCTOBER 8, 2013

THE DRIVE FROM ST. CLOUD to St. Joseph on County Road 75 after I'd picked up Beth from school had become so routine I found myself zoning out one Tuesday afternoon in October. Beth was trying to read in the front seat, and Andrea, sitting in her booster seat in the back, was playing with her stuffed koala. Then, Andrea, bored probably, threw her stuffed toy at her sister. The bear made a squeak when it hit Beth's book. Beth turned around and, with older sister indignation, tossed the koala bear back. Andrea squealed.

"Come on, you two," I said. "Knock it off. If that lands down by my feet, I won't be able to brake."

A semi pulling a tanker passed us as I refocused, trying to formulate supper from the contents of my freezer and refrigerator. It'd been a while since I'd gone shopping, and I couldn't remember what was left in the house. *A package of chicken maybe. Do I have rice?* Nothing was coming together in my head.

An older green Chevy pickup passed me and pulled in between me and the tanker. Good. One should never get too close to tankers these days. Three more vehicles—a pickup and a panel truck and a large semi-type tow truck—passed us and pulled up alongside the tanker. That maybe should have sent up an alarm flag, but it didn't. Again the koala flew into the front seat, hit with an abreviated squeak—something almost akin to surprise—and Beth immediately tossed it back. Irritated I glared at both of them, then went back to planning the meal that refused to come together. The pickup might have pulled in front of the tanker just as all of us slowed for the light.

The stuffed koala flew over the seat yet again, bounced against the instrument panel with a particularly plaintive squeak and fell next to my feet.

"See!" I snapped. "Now I have to fish it out of there." I tried reaching, but couldn't get around my pregnant belly. There really was no "around" at this stage. I worked with my toes to shove it over the drive-train hump.

"I could unbuckle and get it," Beth offered, sounding contrite.

"No, let me—"

Then my world went sideways. I think it started with the pickup in front of the tanker braking prematurely for the light. The tow truck, near the cab of the tanker, veered into the tanker's lane, forcing the tanker onto the shoulder. Metal hit metal—horrible sound. Horns blared. Brakes screamed. Black lines smoked on the highway in both lanes. The green pickup hit the breaks just ahead of me, fishtailing behind the tanker. I was half a second behind him slamming my foot to the floor, only to have it slip off the pedal when I stepped on the damned stuffed koala, which gave a sustained squeak. I yanked on the wheel, pulling the Prius to the far left beyond the tracks of burned rubber. We hit the shallow ditch, then bounced up into the left-turn lane.

I hit the brake again, connecting with the pedal this time, and managed to get the car stopped in the middle of the intersection of County 134. A red Ford Taurus flashed just past the nose of my car, its horn and squealing tires protesting my sudden intrusion.

The tanker, tow truck, and other trucks had screeched to a halt with smoking brakes right next to us. Men jumped out of the trucks. I saw two hunting rifles and a shotgun. *Oh, God, a hijacking.*

I hit the gas. No way was I going to put two little girls in the middle of a fuel-truck hijacking. On top of that, I was eight months pregnant. Risks compounded in my head. The Prius lurched through the intersection as I made a U-turn, heading back to St. Cloud, and I sped away. In the rear-view mirror, I saw the driver of the tanker pulled from the cab.

"Mom?" Beth said, her voice soft but in a high register. "What's—?"

Several shots rang out behind us. I jumped, close to panic. Beth started to turn around. "Eyes front!" I yelled and hit the gas harder. "It's a damn good thing you didn't unbuckle. Never unbuckle when the car's moving."

I know my tone was harsh, but there were some things, even in these dangerous times, that a ten-year-old really shouldn't have to see. I glanced at Andrea. Her face was frozen just at the edge of tears.

I WAS STILL SHAKING WHEN I REACHED our little farm on the north side of St. Joseph, having taken backroads home. I saw Frank's Mazda truck with QUILL CONSTRUCTION stenciled on the side parked by the house. I was glad. I pulled up next to it, turned off the engine and just sat, my hands still gripping the wheel. Beth silently got out and helped Andrea from her booster seat, then, holding her hand, headed for the house. I took a deep breath and followed them a moment later. They had found Frank in front of the TV and both started jabbering about what had happened when I reached the living room. Andrea was crying now.

Frank took the little girl into his lap and looked up at me.

"It was another fuel hijacking. Right in front of us," I said.

"I've told you to put lots of space between you and *any* semi," Frank said.

"I . . . I thought I had." I saw he had the news on. "What's going on?"

Frank hugged the girls and sent them upstairs to change clothes so they could help him with the animals before supper, the supper that was still a mystery to me. "It's not good. I swear someone's trying to see just how bad it can get. At this point I don't think there's one square foot of the planet not in some kind of dire circumstances. China's a mess, people rioting. More are protesting in Brazil. Mexico City just enacted martial law to control crowds and looting. Paris, Brussels, Tokyo all reporting riots. The Senate just voted to pull all our troops from the Middle East to help control rioting in New York and LA. That can't be a good sign. And the stock market took another nosedive, but I'm pretty sure it can't fall into negative figures, so it can't fall far."

I sat heavily on the sofa. Every day it was the same long list of misery all over the world. This had been going on for years, it seemed, but the last several months it was definitely worse. My stomach flip-flopped. I didn't know how much more I could take.

"I'm afraid Harris is going to call," I said.

Frank nodded. "I know. I'm scared too. The thing is all in the timing. Too soon, and there's risk; too late and there's far greater risk."

I thought about the tanker hijacking. "There's risk just living now. How's he going to know when to put out the word?"

Frank shrugged. He met my eyes again. "I don't know."

I levered myself to my feet. I had to come up with something for supper. But as I headed for the kitchen, Frank caught my hand. His palm was damp. When I looked at him, I saw that he was staring at the TV. I turned my head to look. An info crawl line moved across the bottom of the screen: NUCLEAR EXCHANGE IN THE MIDDLE EAST. JERUSELEM HIT.

I drew in a shocked breath, my hand going to my mouth. Then the phone rang. Both Frank and I stared at the cell phone on the coffee table through two more rings as it vibrated itself almost in a circle. Then Frank picked it up. He never said a word, just looked at me, and I started to cry.

2

THE SHELTER

WEDNESDAY, OCTOBER 9

ISRAEL WAS HIT WITH TWO NUCLEAR "DEVICES." Jerusalem was gone. When I saw the news on that crawl line that second Tuesday in October, I found myself wondering why it had been described that way. Devices. Could a device be as destructive as a bomb? Was this a sanitary way of "lifting" Jerusalem off the map without devastation, death, or suffering? It galled me that anyone—the TV personnel or the government that had issued the statement—could belittle the agony of a people by trying to camouflage the reality of what had happened, trying to sterilize the death and destruction, making it seem bloodless, pristine. A nation had been destroyed. Millions of people, momentarily terrified, had died in flaming radioactive horror. Countless thousands more suffered this day, burned, injured, lingering in pain and likely doomed. Let's not sweet-talk death.

I knew that the bombing in Israel could be just the start, the beginning of the end of all we knew. Violence in these tortured times could spread like a virulent virus. Where would the next breakout be? The global economy? Governments? At that point, when my mind was winding up into horrific scenarios, the cell phone rang.

The point of the call was that we weren't going to wait for Armageddon. Hadn't been waiting for nearly ten years. The family had been planning, and building. A shelter to survive the end of days. And now it was time to activate it, to go inside. I cried.

WE HAD BEEN CAUTIONED not to consider our move to the shelter exactly like a move from house to house. It wasn't. We could bring no furniture. Family treasures and special heirloom pieces had been cleared through Harris, Frank's older brother and the architect of our shelter plan. Most already were stored in the shelter well before that early October Tuesday. Yet, even unburdened with the task of transporting couches, big-screen TVs, or the washer and dryer, I was horrified to see how sprawling our lives were; it seemed

5

impossible to funnel them down small enough to fit into the shelter. Yet, slowly, with the inertia of our troubled lives holding us, moving began.

We started the move immediately. We skipped supper altogether. Instead, we told the girls to pack. We began filling Frank's truck. We gave the girls cereal and put them to bed about ten that night, but Frank and I worked through the night. Frank's truck, old and roomy though it was, bulged. The first frosty light of Wednesday morning found me in the garden, pulling carrots and beets as fast as I could spade and yank, filling boxes with green tomatoes, squash, and pumkins. I made no attempt to clean the dirt from anything, just heaped the boxes and crates with lumps of black earth showing the orange of carrots and dark purple-red of beets. The squash and tomatoes had vines attached. I filled the Gardenway cart, tied down the covering tarp and pushed it to the back of the truck. As I headed to the house, the fallen-over stems of my tuberoses—my favorite flower—caught my eye, and a surge of panic filled me. I couldn't leave them. I quickly dug them and added them to the produce under the tarp. An hour later, the truck creaked out of the driveway, past the swayback barn, the huge weeping willow with the broken top, and our picket fence that leaned in places and always needed paint.

M Y FIRST GLIMPSE OF THE SHELTER in nearly four years took me by surprise. I remembered the gravel road to it being longer and nearer the valley floor—I almost thought we'd taken a wrong turn. I didn't recognize the hills. I remembered the construction site as being nearly half a mile from the farm Harris had once owned. Now we stopped practically in the farm's backyard. As I looked for our shelter, all I could see was a bunker-like structure with old-fashioned cellar stairs. Behind it a hill rose, probably a hundred feet or so. The concrete structures I had seen in the construction phase had been so much taller. The only familiar thing was a huge sugar maple that stood at the end of the farm compound. The bunker lay in its shadow now. The hill had to be the buried silo-like shelter, but, where the unfinished shelter had resembled a open pit mine with huge silos in the middle, the completed shelter matched up perfectly with the rolling glacial moraines of Collegeville. The hill behind the basement bunker was clothed in grasses and hazel bushes, small birches, aspen, and hawthorne. A barbed-wire cow fence came up to the back corner of the bunker and extended up the hill that had to be part of the shelter. Truly, if I had not known something else was here, all I would see was the roofed over basement of an old barn nestled against a hillside.

STARTING VERY EARLY THAT WEDNESDAY morning, the five local families began bringing over as much as they could load into pickups and cars, then rushing home for more. Mike and Marie Deters made the trip from Edina in little more than an hour, their station wagon stuffed. The other two families from the Cities arrived in tandem an hour later. Anna DeSota, my baby sister, and her dark-eyed, six-year-old, Lynn, had their Subaru so crammed it scraped the dirt driveway as she drove in. Paul and Lori Fisk came with his window van pulling a U-Haul trailer. The van's radiator steamed heavily. Later, when we tried to move it out of the way, it wouldn't start.

Lori seemed unusually quiet through the unloading of their van. When it wouldn't start afterwards, she broke down in tears. Then Paul related several incidents on the highway before they got out of the Cities. There had been some kind of total societal breakdown. The bombing in Israel had blown open a floodgate that released a general panic. By the time he had received the call to the shelter, cars already crammed the highways as people abandoned the Cities, fleeing the dysfunction of their lives, but did they have a shelter awaiting them somewhere?

I quickly realized the futility of the exodus. Times were just as hard in Chicago, in St. Louis, in Memphis. What happened in the north happened as well in the East, the West, the South, in Canada and Mexico. All over the world. News reports all day had talked about people fleeing cities. I hoped they had relatives on Iowa farms or Montana ranches. People might be safe there, might find food and shelter.

Minnesota winter pressed hard against our balmy October Indian summer, crisping the nights and chilling the lakes. Without resources, winter this far north could be more than difficult; it could be deadly. Maybe that was why people left the Cities in droves, fleeing a much more ordinary enemy—winter without fuel oil, natural gas, or electric heat. Part of me, though, doubted the panicked mobs had thought that far ahead.

The Fisks had witnessed beatings and vehicle hijackings. Panic prevailed. They had seen a woman dead on the median strip. A group of men had even tried to stop them, but Paul swerved the van over the center grass and into the other lanes, which also headed west. Forced back over the median almost immediately to avoid collision with a truck that would not move over, Paul said he heard one of the men shout, "Now we got 'em!" But Paul had gunned the van through the grassy ditch. Wheels spun, and the van almost mired, but it never stopped. The men got as close as Lori's locked door before Paul got it back on the road and floored the gas. If the old Dodge van had given up then and not in the driveway of the shelter. . . . Lori cried again. The men unhitched the trailer and pushed the van out of the way.

All day we packed and dug and hauled. Evening pressed in on the day before Frank and I completed our last trip. The rabbits and their hutches, the chickens, and ducks and all the feed we had made up one load, our clothes and household goods plus the garden produce another, Mom and Dad Quill and their keepsakes a third, and the rest of our baggage the fourth. We were exhausted. My eight-months pregnancy felt like fourteen months. After the final load, I remained in the cab of our pickup while the unloading proceeded down that cellar entrance into the bunker Frank called the "woodroom." My belly and back were vying for some kind of pain award. I hated to tell them that my legs had won hands down. Right then, my ankles had swollen into barrels and throbbed horribly.

Harris and Jillian were trying to coax one of their ponies down the bulkhead into the woodroom, which, apparently, was the only entrance into the shelter. The pony had other ideas. It dug in its hooves at the top of the stairs and could not be budged beyond that point. Frank joined the effort. He shouted to Harris, "Put your jacket over her eyes."

My girls and I watched from the pickup. While Frank and Harris covered the little bay's eyes with Harris's sweaty jacket, Jillian positioned herself behind the pony's round rump. She placed herself about a foot out of kick range and was obviously loathe to move closer. The girls enjoyed the rodeo but were disappointed when, blindfolded, the little mare was led down almost placidly. The four other ponies were equally easy to handle.

Boxes and crates of stuff—some of it ours—were stacked outside awaiting transport after the ponies had been safely led inside. The Fisks, Mike and Wayne Deters, and the rest joined Harris and Frank and shouldered boxes from the pile of goods. Slowly, it diminished.

My girls—Beth a blonde, blue-eyed ten-year-old, and Andrea, a curly-headed, dark-haired cherub just turned four—fell asleep after the pony show ended. Beth snuggled against me under my arm. Andrea had her head in Beth's lap.

It had been a hard day for them, too. A lot of unpleasant choices had been made. Tears had been left with many things left behind. The worst had concerned Shep, our fourteen-year-old shepherd-collie, and Beth's new black Manx kitten, Silk.

Silk came. Frank led Shep behind the barn to the compost pile. I cried as hard as the girls over that decision even though I had allowed Beth to accept the kitten from a girlfriend a month earlier knowing old Shep's fate. Broken toys and torn books had not been so hard to leave behind after that.

What we were doing made more sense to Beth than to Andrea. And, comforting her little sister over every little loss seemed to make it easier for Beth. Maybe it was because the girls were so far apart in age, but they had always gotten along pretty well. Andrea hero-worshiped Beth. Beth was glad to have a little sister to tease or mother, depending on her mood. I hoped number three would fit into our lives as easily as Andrea had. How could anything fit in these times?

The sun angled toward evening. If anyone had noticed, which I doubted, it had been a glorious Indian summer day. Frosts had come only in late September that year so that the gardening was just finishing. Boxes of pumpkins, potatoes, and squash were among the piles the men carried into the depths of the shelter. Insects still buzzed, although most of the flies and mosquitoes had been decimated. Crickets chirped from the grass, and, when the men walked around the heaps of goods, grasshoppers flared from their shoes. The air was sweet-tart, like a tree-ripened apple.

The huge sugar maple just at the far edge of the woodroom's foundation glowed orange-gold. Leaves drifted down the cellar stairs as the men muscled boxes down. I promised myself I'd gather a few of those leaves and press them in a book. Who knew when any of us would have the chance to do that again.

The sky was that clean, brilliant blue Minnesota enjoyed on autumn days. No clouds. No lingering summer humidity. Beginning blue-indigo at the zenith, it gradually milked to robin's egg at the horizons. The multi-colored hills around us—yellow of ash, golden willow, and the brilliant reds of maples next to the deeper reds of oaks—set off the dome of sky with remarkable pleasures for the eyes. I made a point of fixing this scene carefully in my memory. I remember thinking: *Maybe I should write it down.*

James and DeeDee, the youngest Quill couple, pulled in with Wayne's Wagoneer and tailer. They had taken many trips also; their younger faces were nearly as tired as Frank's. This trip they had Wayne's Jersey cows and calves. The procession of bearers abandoned the crates of apples and boxes of household goods to help unload the moaning cows. Even blindfolded, the cows balked. Had they been

Holsteins, moving them would have been hopeless, but the fat brown Jerseys were finally shoved down the stairs. Their bawling faded down the passage. The calves were easier. Their rich scent lingered.

I had not been inside the shelter yet. Ever. Frank certainly had been through it many times. Most of the others had seen at least parts of it, although Harris, in his strange possessiveness, had appointed some sections with utmost secrecy and had escaped to the shelter often in the last three years to the deficit of his law practice and the eventual loss of his pretty little farm. But I had never been inside. At first Frank had coaxed me. I resisted, saying that the construction site was too dirty for baby Andrea. When she was older, and I slowly began entrusting her to sitters then daycare when I went back to work, he asked again that I see the shelter. I agreed but managed to put off the tour each time it came up. I guess I thought that, by not ever going inside, I could somehow keep us from needing it. That was silly. Like I could affect world politics? But going in could mean not coming out for a long, long time. The shelter had been constructed to contain our large, extended family for five to ten years—we hoped as long as necessary. Frank slowly came to understand my fears. After a while he stopped asking.

FRANK CAME OVER TO THE TRUCK and leaned on the passenger door. I could feel his heat through the open window; his exhaustion pressed against the sleeve of my shirt. He patted my arm and smiled. Then he turned and leaned his wide shoulders against the door frame and wiped his hot brow on his sleeve.

There hadn't been much conversation between us. And, though the tension of the day was probably measurable on the Richter scale, we shared a unified purpose. Any doubts we had about the shelter or about the sanity of trying to use it to save ourselves from the danger we faced just didn't seem important at the moment. What other choice did we have? If the shelter couldn't save us, what could?

We both knew these concerns pressed foremost in each other's minds. We both felt the loss of our lives and the trepidation of entering this strange subterranean world even if it might be salvation. All these things had been expressed repeatedly over the last five years. Voicing them now would not clear up lingering questions and doubts.

Together in spirit and cause, Frank and I looked out over the hills and meadows that swept away below us from the elevated site of the shelter. Evening began to slip over our long day of work. Shadows filled up the low spots and slowly stretched through the wooded hills like a dark mist, deepening the autumn hues. Evening sounds of crickets, katydids, and the muted songs of a few late-migrating robins rose up from the meadows. The moistness of evening mists from the pond and stream at the end of the road mixed with the occasional coolness of night breezes. The sun set with just a glimmer of rose and purple through the already stark branches of the aspen in the hedgerow to the west.

I was glad we were able to watch evening fall this last night as we had done so casually countless other evenings from the porch of our old white farmhouse. I gathered each detail and pressed it—like maple leaves—in my memory. I might not see another sunset like this in my lifetime.

Headlights, suddenly bright in the growing dusk, signaled the arrival of Wayne and Jeannie Deters' household goods. Their loaded Jeep Cherokee wheezed over the ruts. More unloading. Frank sighed and heaved himself into motion as Jeannie climbed out with her twins. As Frank neared her, she spoke to him, and he pointed to our truck with a swing of a tired arm. Jeannie, with a six-year-old hugged against each hip, came over and stared in the driver's window, her eyes wide, almost pleading.

"Is this real, Barby?" she said, her voice quavering. She was a worrier. I felt brave in her company. But, in comparison to her comely, perfectly made-up face and fashionable, blown-dry russet curls, I usually felt plain. Me and my ordinary face and thin, mousy hair that never held a perm. It was the mixture of feelings over the years that probably made it impossible for us to be particularly close friends even though we lived only three miles apart on the same gravel road outside St. Joseph.

I smiled with feigned lightness. "Real? Yes. But not hopeless. We're going to be okay, Jeannie. It might . . . even be fun."

She frowned.

"Come sit for a bit," I said. "Us pregnant ladies have done enough."

Her eyes slid to my full belly as she smoothed her silk top over her shapely waist and opened the cab door. At three months pregnant, she didn't show yet and could afford to be critical. I gathered a fussy Andrea onto my bulging lap while she helped Roland onto the seat and took Ronald onto her lap to fit in behind the wheel. Beth groaned and shoved over closer to me. She didn't like these cousins.

Together we watched the unloading of the Jeep Cherokee. The last of Jeannie's produce came first—boxes and baskets of late potatoes with black earth clinging to them, carrots and whole uprooted brussels sprout plants, crates of green tomatoes. How she gardened with long, shapely nails, I didn't know. My broken, bitten nails still had black rims from the morning's gathering in my own garden.

When Jeannie clucked her tongue at the under-ripe sprouts, I offered, "I ripened some in the basement one year because of that blizzard. Remember? Two years ago? They grew in pails until Christmas. Worked fine."

Jeannie's expression told me she knew I was humoring her. I shut up. I could see by the way she was clutching her boys that she was really suffering. Maybe she was giving up more than I was. I didn't know. I did know she and Wayne owned one of the cutest little farmsteads in the township. Immaculate. The house, barn, and six outbuildings all in perfect repair, all painted sky blue with darker blue trim and slate-gray roofs. Even the doghouse that never had a dog. The little place Frank and I left still had the original cockleburs behind the swayback, weathered barn after fifteen years.

The men finished with the back of the Jeep Cherokee, moving everything just as far as the woodroom entrance, and started on the boxes and plastic bags in the back seat. Jeannie's treasures began moving toward the dark cellar stairs. I saw her tense, and her breathing came in short little gasps.

"That box James has is photos and albums," she said in a tight whisper. "Every picture we ever took of the twins and our wedding and before—and after . . . and that box has my mother's tatted table cloth. It took her four years to make it, her fingers were so arthritic. That one's her silver. It came over from Germany with her grandmother. Frank has the box with my dad's carved decoys, and that bag has—"

"Sh-sh," I said softly as I pulled down her pointing arm. My throat had tightened too much to offer comforting words. This was meant to be our salvation, this secret underground shelter, this ark, as we called it when teasing Harris. But each of us, though among many of our family members, would be leaving great chunks of our lives behind. Jeannie's folks were long dead, but it didn't matter. She mourned. I mourned.

A vehicle roared up the driveway. Dust billowed up behind it and clouded into the yard when it slammed to a stop. A heavy-set but tall man with a shotgun jumped out of the ancient Suburban in front of Harris. My sadness froze. I could see that hijacking again. Jeannie inhaled sharply. The man never actually pointed the weapon at anyone, but its presence was implicit threat. Harris seemed not to notice it. He stuck out his hand, forcing the man to shift the weapon to his left hand. Harris shook the man's hand, stuck his grinning face into the station wagon and then chatted with the man, who I was beginning to recognize was Max Gertz, the farmer who had purchased Harris's farm when his obsession with the shelter ruined his law practice. In another moment, the gun was handed to Jillian, who looked at it with a mixture of revulsion and awe, and the farmer's arms were loaded with suitcases pulled from the Suburban's back seat. Harris climbed right into the car, while he kept up a joking chatter. A chubby, plain woman, her hair tied in a scarf, and two lank teenage boys emerged and helped carry their boxes inside.

I was surprised. Harris, so protective of his shelter as to keep whole sections secret from his own family, seemed ready to hand over the place to these armed intruders without a qualm. In a way, it frightened me; in a way, it made me very proud.

It was full dark, ten o'clock, when a caravan of two trucks and two cars pulled in, towing a horse trailer, two open trailers covered in canvas and sheets, and what looked like a boat trailer with boxes and trunks strapped to it. These were the northern families—my brother, Marty, my older sister, Emily, and the two Reinhart cousins. Kids, noisy, fussy and tired, piled out and were herded to the bright light of the basement entrance. Literally tons of boxes waited unloading, as well as the sheep, goats, pigs, ducks, chickens, and a few unidentified squawking crates. Donald Reinhart's oldest son, Pete, even carried in a cardboard box with a nervous fox terrier dam and her four whimpering newborn pups. Donald Reinhart's aged mother-in-law—frail and tight-lipped—was helped out and guided along the ant-like procession of workers to the tunnels below. She seemed to be angry and protesting the whole way.

I felt my throat tightening again as I realized the gargantuan effort the family was making to stem the death we feared otherwise. We all believed in the horrors of a nuclear winter, and an incident of hemorrhagic fever in Florida that took seventy lives and spread to O'Hare Airport in Chicago and Logan Airport in Boston before it was controlled had convinced us that a biological winter would be just as bad. Other unknown dangers loomed just out of sight: world war, total anarchy, military take-overs, invasion. I looked up at the steadiness of the autumn night. How could the night be so peaceful when there was so little peace in the world?

JEANNIE CLIMBED OUT OF THE TRUCK without a word and followed the last of the procession into the cellar, her two boys still pressed to her sides. For a long, silent moment, the yard stood empty. All the vehicles had been emptied and driven down to the Gertz farm to be parked inside the barn, all the piled goods removed to storage. The endless day neared an end. How close to the end were we?

Frank came out of the basement and, obviously tired, shuffled to the pickup. "Time to go in, hon," he said with forced cheer.

I could see that while his body had been pummeled this day, his spirits still buoyed on boyish excitement.

I glanced down the road quickly. "What about Andy and Bob and the rest of them—?"

Concern flickered in his eyes, but his voice didn't register that. "Oh, not tonight. With luck they got into the airport this evening, but no way will they get out of Minneapolis before morning."

"But . . . what if what Paul and Lori saw is worse? It probably is worse. How are they going to get out of the Cities?"

"Under control. Harris anticipated problems on the road. He actually has a helicopter standing by. The pilot and a companion will join us as payment. But he won't know the way until he picks up our people. Harris is flaky, but smart. Just so . . . just so the planet holds together."

"How's the news?"

Now his voice did fall. He paused long enough to swallow. "Not good. All communications between the U.S. and North Korea have broken off. No surprise there. The Russians have sided with China, though it's hard to say if North Korea or the U.S. is going to be the focus of their aggression. More bombs in the Middle East. Some in the Arab countries and Egypt. No one knows how much damage has been done. So far that's the only area of the globe bombed. That's all we know anyway. Maybe everyone will come to their senses before the rest of the world feels compelled to join the massacre. Who knows? I don't. I doubt even God does."

I sighed deeply and looked out the window again at the soft October night.

"What?" Frank asked.

I frowned. "All the others." I knew I shouldn't broach what had gone unmentioned all day, but I couldn't help it. "My cousins out West. Your Uncle Albert. Aunt Madeleine—"

Frank reacted as I knew he would, with testiness and frustration. "Oh, Barby, don't. Not now anyway. Everyone couldn't come. Some didn't want to.

Everyone was contacted. You know that. They opted out. I called Uncle Albert last week. He said he was going to climb to the top of the Empire State Building and 'watch the fireworks.' He said he'd watched the World Trade Center buildings come down and would watch the rest go down, if it came to that."

I tried to turn off the negative thoughts . . . or just stop voicing them, but I couldn't. Maybe I just didn't want to go into the shelter at all, and I was stalling. I said, "So, why are we doing this?"

Frank scowled, started to speak but closed his mouth. He leaned again on the pickup, his jaw working. He was trying really hard not to fight with me, and I felt bad. For a long moment, he was quiet. Then, in a voice I knew was in direct line to his most private self, he said, "I want to be able to stand before my Maker and know that I did every damn thing I could to protect my family. Just so I can say I tried. Just so I can have a little pride. But, you know, Barb, I believe in the shelter. I really do. If we have a chance in the world, we have it here. Now, come on. No more stalling. We *have* to go in."

We woke the girls. They slid out the driver's door as Frank eased me out the other. My legs had stiffened and were frightfully sore; the bottoms of my feet felt like bruises. The girls, familiar with the tunnel already from the afternoon moving, ran on ahead and disappeared down the cellar stairs. Frank tucked his hand under my elbow and, together, like a grotesque parody of a courting couple, we slowly made our way to the rectangle of bright yellow light that spilled into the yard. At the top of the stairs, I paused and tried to reach down for some of the brilliant maple leaves. I couldn't bend enough to reach the ground.

"What is it?" Frank whispered, suddenly concerned.

I found myself near tears. I couldn't help it, couldn't begin to explain. "The leaves," I said with difficulty, helplessly. "I want . . . I wanted to save some."

Without irritation or patronizing quip, Frank, who had put out gargantuan effort all day, stooped down and carefully, selectively, picked through the drift of leaves against the concrete curbing around the concrete basement. I half expected him just to snatch a handful and thrust it at me. He took time with his selections, discarding those with ragged edges or muddy color or damage from the passing of feet. The dozen or so leaves he gave me were gorgeous.

"Wait a minute," he said, vanishing around the corner of the foundation. "I saw these seedlings earlier," his voice came back. "They probably won't live, but . . . what the hell, let's see if we can pot them and keep them going. Didn't pioneers bring grape vines or apple trees all the way from Europe to plant in the New World? We've got a journey of sorts starting here, too. Let's see if we can do as well with maple seedlings."

I hugged Frank when he came back to me with four seedlings in his fist, their delicate roots balled in more fallen leaves. He wrapped his arms around me in a tight embrace. It seemed as if we could not let go. Teetering between the insanity of a world plunging to its death and an unknown future within the tunnels of our new and unfamiliar subterranean world, we found comfort only in holding on to each other. As rotten as the familiar was, it was hard to let it go. And, somehow, it seemed significant for us to reaffirm our now-comfortable relationship as we had once affirmed it with deep passion in a quiet spring meadow some fifteen years earlier.

"Someone's coming down the tunnel," Frank whispered and eased away, quiet passion easily giving way to propriety and embarrassment. Again he took my elbow, and we started down the stairs.

Harris appeared at the bottom step. He looked up and grinned his near-insane grin. "Finally, you guys are coming! What have you two been up to out here? Surely not trying for number four with number three still in the oven."

I really hated Frank's older brother at times. "Harris," I said caustically, "shut up. Frank got me some leaves and seedlings from that big sugar maple of yours."

Harris stopped giggling his "I got Barby" laugh and said, "I thought about doing that but got tied up with other things. I'll get you a pot and some soil for them. In the storage cellar, they should stay dormant until . . . spring. Now get your butts . . . and belly . . . down here so I can get the woodroom closed up and the tunnel sealed."

I felt every fiber of Frank's body tense, and his hand immediately reached out in a "stop" gesture. "Whoa. Seal it already? What about . . . ?"

"Just the tunnel," said Harris with a grin. "Security. All the trampled ground out there makes it pretty obvious something's been going on. I'm not sealing the wood-room yet. When Andy and the others get here, I'll give them instructions on the PA how to get in via the secondary route. But there's more people like Gertz out there who know what we've got here. I'm surprised he's the only one who showed up tonight. We've got to be ready if others do. This shelter is for *us*, not everyone."

It was clear Harris was ruler of our new world. That was okay. He knew the territory at least. He was also basically benign. Good attributes for starters, better than many presidents lately. And although I had always considered Frank to be the truly intelligent one of the family, especially in a practical sense, and definitely the most level-headed, he was not really the leader type. He would never take the wind from big brother's sails. I think Frank secretly knew how fragile Harris was. He would let him be leader and protect him in that role against all the others if need be. I had seen this happen before, and Mom Quill had hinted that it always had been this way. Frank would also keep Harris from straying too far into left field. That was good, too. I doubted anyone else in the family saw an order any different from this.

The tunnel off the woodroom was surprisingly long and angled steeply downward. Again I found myself surprised. The woodroom had been nestled against a hill, one I had assumed was the shelter silo destined to be our home. Was I wrong? I tried to hold down my panic by visualizing the early stages of the shelter when the place looked like a collection of enormous dinosaur eggs. I couldn't remember that the biggest one was so far from the woodroom. Spatial estimation had never been my forte. We passed doors along the tunnel's length. Most were identified as STORAGE. The two doors I tried were locked. There were dozens of them.

I looked back. I had to. I had see the way out. Harris stood at the door to the woodroom, watching us, maybe having an inkling of the difficulty I was having with this final stage of the move. Frank lifted my hand off his arm, and I realized I had been clawing his skin with a tightening grip. I apologized with my eyes.

"This isn't so bad, Barby," he whispered.

"I know," I said, but I heard the quaver in my own voice, the disbelief.

I drew in a deep breath, willing my fears away. I told myself that the tunnel was a long corridor—like in the St. Cloud Hospital basement—connecting buildings. A connection tube. Yes, I could visualize that. I was walking down a connection tube between the known world and the unknown. The picture worked. The panic didn't fade.

The end of the tunnel widened into a kind of cul-de-sac with four heavy steel doors. I could almost tell by the tracks what had gone through each. Most of the fallen vegetable leaves ended at the first door on the left, appropriately marked "ROOT CELLAR." Goat and sheep marbles were squished into the door straight ahead. It had no title but had to lead to the animal room. A linen napkin had fallen at the stoop of the door on the right, and, at the second door on the left, I saw three Fisher-Price "Little People." As I guessed, Frank reached for that doorknob.

17

The tunnel had been dirt quiet except for our footfalls, but when Frank leaned against the steel door, and it clanked open, an assault of noise hit me. Shouted orders, babies crying, children yelling and squabbling, boxes grating on the concrete floor—the racket of displaced life welled up discordantly from the floor of the living space.

The sight that greeted me was equally dismaying. The tunnel door opened at ceiling height so that it was several steps to the floor. Not many steps. The room was only about ten feet high. And, at a diameter of maybe sixty feet, it seemed a squat space. It was one big room filled up with the bodies and possessions of what seemed a crowd of people. Claustrophobia crawled at the back of my mind. Where was the huge shelter? Was this all the space we had? Around the perimeter of the living space, between the wall and a circle of pillars some ten feet into the space were curtained-off places. I could see into the nearer ones from where we stood. Each blunt wedge between wall and adjacent pillars was to be the space for one family. It was smaller than the average bedroom, but it had to accommodate beds for all family members, storage for needed clothing and personal items—everything we needed on a daily basis. My mind couldn't wrap around that. It wasn't enough space.

Dewey Reinhart's cubicle was just below us to the right. Bunks against one curtain slept Burt and Kurt, while little year-old Gertrude had a trundle bed that pulled out from the shelves at the back wall. Dewey and Melissa's double bed was pushed against the other curtain, and a long chest of drawers stood across the front of the space, just inside their curtain. The floor space was almost non-existent, yet Melissa had laid one of her hand-braided rag rugs down to brighten the room. It was a close fit for a family of five, which was what our family would soon be.

In all the noise and clutter, I searched for something familiar to indicate where our cubicle was. At the same time I was fighting down the panicky, claustrophobic feeling telling me to escape that place, to run up the long corridor and burst out of the woodroom into the cool Minnesota night. If Frank hadn't been right at my elbow and I wasn't so tired, I might have tried. But, even if I could have given in to the panic, I knew my legs couldn't implement escape. I was tired beyond imagination. I leaned against Frank and asked, "Where are we?"

"Far side," he said with some relief, as if he knew my fears and inner war. "Just left of the kitchen doors. It's a corner cubicle so we can push against the curtain a bit for space. All the bigger families have corners.

"Those curtains don't seem to offer much privacy."

Frank sighed. "This isn't the Radisson, Barby. It's not even decent Best Western or a lousy Sleep Six, but the curtains are more sound-proof than you might think. It'll be okay, which is more than it might be topside in a short while."

I let out a sigh of acceptance. Ten years and a lot of money and effort had gone into this shelter. I knew the outside world was falling apart so fast that it might not be livable come morning. This place, cramped and crowded as it was, had to be home now. I had no choice. "Well, let's get settled. I've got to get off these feet soon."

Andrea and Beth saw us coming across the floor and ran up to us.

"Can I have the top bunk, Mom?" Andrea pleaded in her sweetest voice.

I shook my head. "You'll fall off. Let Beth have it for now. We'll see later."

"See!" Beth jabbed at her sister. "Told ya!"

Before Andrea could wind up to a full-blown fuss, I intervened, "It's very late," I told both of them in my firmest, not-now voice as we walked across the squat room toward a closed curtain. "Go get your nightgowns on. Bedtime in—"

We reached our space, and I eased aside the front curtain. About the same arrangement as the Reinhart's cubicle, but, where Melissa had achieved a crowded order, our space was piled with boxes, crates, and bulging grocery bags. It looked like what it was—moving day. But I steeled myself to the mess. "Bed in ten minutes. Just get the boxes out of the way. There, that one has the sheets and blankets. Nightgowns? That one. Frank, where did you say the bathroom was?"

I turned to him. Frank stood in the curtain way. He was half-smiling, his face a mixture of exhaustion and gratitude. I realized that he had worried greatly about my reaction to the place, hoping I could tolerate it. And while the jury was still out on tolerating anything, I had no doubt that I loved his concern. I returned his smile. I would try, and he knew that now. He grinned and pointed me to the "BATH" doors adjacent to the kitchen.

I made an ungraceful passage around the corner of our cubicle and found relief for my full and compressed bladder. By the time I made a perfunctory wash up—though I still didn't worry too much about the soil around my fingernails—and waddled painfully back to our small space, Frank and the girls had achieved a rough order—good enough for tonight. The girls were in their bunks, though the foot of each mattress was piled with stuff. Frank sat on the edge of our bed, pressing the maple leaves between the pages of Aldo Leopold's *A Sand County Almanac*. For some reason this was always my book of choice for pressing leaves and flowers.

When I came into the curtained-off space, he stood up and laid the book on one of the shelves at the foot of the bed that he had filled with boxes and bags to get them out of the way. He gave me an affectionate hug and a little kiss on the cheek. I could feel his exhaustion, the heaviness of the day's work.

"You get some sleep, hon," he whispered. "I'll take care of the seedlings. Then Harris and I will be listening to the radio for news from Andy and the others. We might be up most of the night."

"Aren't you tired?" I asked with concern.

Frank gave a little laugh and kissed me again. "Don't worry," he said. "There'll be plenty of time for rest later. Lots of time."

After Frank left, I sat heavily on the bed, too tired to think. Now even too tired to panic, and that was a blessing. I remember easing my canvas shoes off my swollen feet, but, after that, nothing.

3
DAY ONE IN THE ARK
Thursday, October 10

MORNING CAME IN A FOG that consciousness could not penetrate. Some noise or disturbance half-roused me, and I muttered for the girls to turn down the television. I laboriously heaved myself over and lost myself in the enveloping mists.

Later—an inestimable time span—I again washed into semi-wakefulness on a tide of noise. I raised myself groggily and sat hunched over my belly at the edge of the bed. A painful kick in the ribs by my crowded unborn both straightened my posture and startled me into a surer awareness.

I looked about me with sticky, fuzzy eyes. The girls' unmade bunks and pawed-through bags of clothes seemed to fill our small cubicle. Frank lay sprawled on the bottom bunk on top of Andrea's disordered sheets, still in his sweat-stained clothes from the day before. A pale pink corner of Beth's sheet dangling down from the top bunk hid his face from my view, but I could hear his soft snoring and knew he was not going to be awakened easily for me to get news. I would have to wait to hear if Andy had made contact with us.

My few hours of sleep had not recharged my spirits enough to make me feel very agreeable. I frowned at the ugliness of our tiny space and compared the cramped disorder with the morning routine at home. Sure, there were usually hassles—Beth screaming that she had no clothes for school and Andrea requesting a seven-course breakfast that only ten minutes of careful negotiating could reduce to cold cereal or eggs and toast without a tantrum—but there was also the smell of tuberoses outside the kitchen door in the summer and the sound of Frank humming as he shaved. In many ways, it seemed both impossible and ridiculous for us to try to compress our lives into a space barely more than a closet. I resolved that Uncle Albert had it right after all. I wanted to go home, whatever happened. And what could happen to our peaceful little farm? The good Minnesota countryside would stand against the evils of the world. No harm could touch us if we held to the land.

The baby kicked again. Hard. I straightened, realizing I had drifted back into sleep, slumping over my belly. There were no tuberoses at home now. I had dug them for storage with my beets and carrots. For all I knew, there was no more home besides these cramped little quarters. Had bombs dropped yet? What was happening out there?

Sleep had left me now. The fog lifted, leaving only a deep exhaustion and achy legs. The curtain across the front of our cubicle was partly pulled back. It fluttered, and I became aware of a riot of noise just beyond it. Had I not noticed this before? It sounded like a pep rally for a large high school.

I levered myself up and drew aside the curtain. Between the family spaces around the perimeter of the large living space and the central columns with their additional cubicles was a clear circle of floor. This was the scene of a wild road race. Two ten speeds, three Big Wheels, two tricycles, and an unbelievable assortment of skateboards, wagons, scooters, in-line skates, and foot-powered kiddy cars, and a bright green pedaled John Deere tractor circled the course at top speed. I had never seen anything like it. With shrieks and whoops punctuating the hoopla, and several littler kids dashing precariously through the mob, the din, both on my ears and newly-awakened eyes, was awful. Yet, unbelievably, I seemed to be the only adult in sight. All the cubicle curtains remained closed.

In the few seconds I watched the children, I became alarmed by the intensity of their play—it wasn't really play. It was too frantic, bordering hysteria. The level of activity had reached pointless, repetitive movement. Only break-neck speed mattered. I saw one of the trikes go down and its six-year-old rider jump up and start running. An older runner grabbed the tricycle and took off on it, knees sticking out as he pumped.

It was a kind of musical-chairs madness fueled by the tension of coming to the shelter, of escaping the unsettling horrors of the world outside. For the children, the oldest of whom was twelve, this was a tension that they could never express, nor truly understand, let alone process. I felt my chest tighten as I watched them, and I knew I had to shut this activity down. I also knew that later the feelings had to be dissipated—somehow—if the children were to adjust to living here. Assuming we lived.

I waded into the thoroughfare, shouted roughly to Beth to stop and grabbed the handlebars of Harry, Jr.'s, ten-speed as he swerved to avoid Beth.

"Where are your folks?" I asked Harry, Jr., bringing my face very close to his to get his attention.

Flushed and panting, he stared at me and blinked mutely. He was so much like Harris, his superior intelligence often masked by utter denseness.

"Um," he said, blinking again. "Sleeping maybe?"

"I think most people are still sleeping. Yesterday was a lot of hard work. Maybe this noise better stop, huh?"

"Yes'm."

"Good. Put the bike away and help me with the younger kids. Beth, stop Andrea . . . nicely! Have any of you eaten yet?"

Harris, Jr., shrugged, surprisingly docile after such wild activity. He pointed. "Um, there were some donuts open in the kitchen. I had . . . a lot of us had some. But that was a while ago. Guess I'm kinda hungry now." He looked at me with expectant eyes, as if I had to somehow fix all this.

I glanced up at the big school clock mounted above the kitchen door. Eight-forty. "Anyone else hungry?"

Instinctively, I guess, I had hit upon something to redirect the minds of the frantic children. Food. I doubted any had eaten normally the day before, and sugary donuts could only fuel the aimlessness of their play. The promise of a meal focused all the children toward me, many just dropping their locomotion and leaving it lie. I was astute enough to see I was piping the right tune. "Hungry, kids? How about we go find some breakfast? What are you hungry for?"

Predictably, the requests were outlandish, weird. Tacos. Pizza, chow mein. One of the Reinharts suggested kangaroo stew. They began to shout each other down with wilder and weirder ideas. Jacob, Mike Deter's oldest son, screamed out, "Bomb burgers!"

I winced. Others started up with "atomic eggs" and "riot ravioli." I stopped them before I started crying. What had we done to our children? I was frightened for them.

"Let's have some . . . scrambled eggs and toast with cinnamon or maybe . . . pancakes with blueberry syrup! That sounds good. Come on! Everyone has to help!"

I could see I had only tenuous control. The children were beginning to race about again. If I wasted time, I was lost. As quickly as my sore legs allowed me, I made my way to the kitchen area and flung open the double doors onto a huge lunchroom with some thirty long tables. The children streamed in, hitting the tables and benches like playground equipment. They swarmed over and under them at top speed. The tempo—and the decibels—were rising exponentially. I hurried around a serving counter and through a set of swinging double doors to the kitchen, hoping food would calm them if I got it ready quickly enough. But then I had to pause.

The kitchen was daunting. Several bays of stainless steel counters faced me. A wall of ovens, stoves, a long grill, and two sets of double sinks lined the back of the room. Everything gleamed stainless steel. A battalion of shiny copper-bottomed pots and pans hung ready for service. A dozen skillets flanked them. Along a side walls and over each of the counters, cupboards reached to the ceiling. Through their glass doors, I saw ranks of glasses, plates, and serving ware. The end wall seemed to be all doors. While some clearly were humongous refrigerators, others were not. Passages to pantries, maybe, or storage rooms. I was both impressed with what I saw and deeply intimidated. I doubted my ability to fix a simple meal in this place.

Harry, Jr., had mentioned donuts. Six plastic bags of homemade donuts had been opened on one stainless steel counter. Many had fallen to the floor and were squashed by little feet. Bits and pieces and powdered sugar had spread like fungus. Kurt and Lisa, two of the Reinhart cousins, sat in one corner, a donut in each fist and powdered sugar all over them. They regarded me with caught eyes.

"I bet you two have had enough by now," I offered.

They seemed frozen.

"I'm going to fix breakfast," I said. I hoped I could in this industrial-sized kitchen. "Why don't we put the donuts away until later?"

Kurt opened his fists, letting his donuts crumble to the floor, and scrambled out. Lisa burst into tears, rubbing powdered sugar into her eyes along with her fists.

"Need some help?" an adult voice said.

I turned to see DeeDee's head poking in the door. She was wife of James Quill, the youngest brother, and a trim, pretty woman with dimpled cheeks and a turned-up nose. I saw her eyes widen at the huge kitchen as mine surely had.

"I sure could," I said, grateful. "How is it out there?"

"Bedlam," DeeDee shrugged. She was a two-year veteran kindergarten teacher. Not easily frazzled by noise. She looked at the little girl crying in front of me and said, "What's with Lisa?"

"Caught with too many donuts too late, I'm afraid."

Beth pushed past DeeDee. "Mom, Kurt just threw up all over the floor. Gross!"

"That doesn't surprise me," I sighed. "Beth, can you—"

"Yuck! No way, Mom!"

"Okay . . . then you help DeeDee find some food . . . some cereal . . . or maybe toast." I spied four six-slice toasters waiting in ranks on a counter.

I grabbed a roll of paper towels and went into the lunchroom. Sissy Reinhart, Lisa's mom, was already on her knees with a box of Kleenex tissues. Being no hero and not having a good working relationship with my knees anyway, I handed her the paper towels. She smiled up at me as she accepted them.

Sissy was a nice woman. I liked her. Not pretty really, with frizzy white-blonde hair with dark roots, a big frame, and thighs to fit a Percheron, she always had a ready smile and an easy manner. She was a waitress at a small café up north and worked hard. But what I admired most was that, when with the whole family, even though many individuals had masters degrees and professional training—lawyers, doctors, and the like—she never acted inferior. She offered her opinion right along with the rest, as if she had a Ph.D. in waitressing—which I could almost believe. One time, I watched her handle two recalcitrant truckers when I was visiting her. Instead of their walking out or giving her a fat lip (my worry), she sweet-talked those rough men into ordering pie. She got a ten-dollar tip from them on a thirty-dollar meal, too.

"Glad for the reinforcements," I said. "Lisa's in with DeeDee. She might just follow Kurt's example if being up to her ears in donuts is any clue. Sounds like DeeDee quieted her though."

"She cries easy," Sissy said with a shrug. "I'll see to her. We going to feed this bunch, then?"

"General idea. You get a choice: cook or jailer."

Ronald and Roland were leap-frogging from table to table. Sissy smiled. "No contest. I'll send DeeDee out to help you. Some eggs and milk into these kids, and maybe they'll calm down."

I shrugged. "Somehow I doubt it," I said with real concern. "The kitchen's yours, though. Don't let it scare you."

Sissy gathered up the soiled paper towels and Kleenex tissues while I tried to order quiet. I was ignored. DeeDee came out with Lisa and a two-pound sack of raisins. She was instantly mobbed by a ring of outstretched hands and eager voices.

Even my sister Anna's daughter, Lynn, begged for raisins, and I knew she hated them. Strange. DeeDee began doling out handfuls, and the noise level diminished at least by the muffling effect of full mouths.

"So, where's the coffee?"

I turned to the doors and my sister Emily. Besides being nearly five years older than I, Emily was taller by an inch, more heavily boned and had a darker complexion. She was a "tough cookie" as she like to say about herself, while I, in her opinion, was a wuss. I bought the "tough cookie" part. I liked to think I was maybe adopted or something and not really related to her at all. In my childhood, it made living with her domination a little easier. And, if our childhood rivalries had mostly ended, it was still true that I didn't care much for her.

"Sorry, Em," I said. "We're not up to coffee yet." I swept my arm in the general direction of all the children mobbing DeeDee.

She frowned and took a long drag on her cigarette. "So, how hard can a few kids be?" and she addressed the throng. "Okay, you kids! Pipe down! Off the tables and stop grabbing at DeeDee. Candy, I said *off* the table! Cathy, can't you do anything? Keep that baby on the bench."

What Emily did have was volume. Her voice boomed down all the children's chatter. Inside of a few seconds, order had been restored, and every child quietly sat at a table with a handful of raisins. Emily took another drag on her smoke and strode to the kitchen. I waved away the cigarette stink.

DeeDee whispered, "She has quite the touch."

I snorted. "Yeah, early barbarian . . . but effective. I'd like to think she traveled with Genghis Khan in a previous life. Before that she was maybe a velociraptor. Let's keep the raisins in front of them for a few more minutes until Sissy gets the eggs ready. We might have this licked for now, but I want to talk to you about the chil—"

A crash from the kitchen drew our attentions. We heard shouting, swearing. My heart sank. I had forgotten that Emily got along with Sissy even less well than with me. Both DeeDee and I were on our way to the kitchen when the doors burst open and Sissy stormed out. She grabbed Lisa by the wrist and called to her other two children as she strode out of the cafeteria. Lisa started to cry again, and Peter and Diane complained about still being hungry. Sissy kept walking.

I waved DeeDee to the rest of the children who were starting to climb on the tables to see what was going on. I headed for the kitchen. Just inside the door, a large crockery bowl lay smashed. Yellow streams of eggs oozed down the dented stainless steel front of one of the big refrigerators and made a puddle on the floor. Emily's wide back was toward me as she slapped hamburger patties onto the sizzling grill.

"What happened?" I asked with what I thought was control, but there could have been a bit of frustration in my tone.

"Aw, lay off me, Bar-by!" she said in that slightly muffled tone that meant she held her cigarette in her lips. "I ain't in no mood for your high and mighty say." She turned and took her cigarette between two hamburger-stained fingers. With them she indicated the spilled eggs. "Ding-bat was giving them hooligans scrambled eggs. Great stuff for ammunition, maybe, but kids don't eat eggs. Meat! Give'm a stack of burgers! That'll keep'm busy. Now if you want to help, get out some pop and find a couple boxes of chips." She took a long drag on the cigarette and pressed the butt between her lips again as she turned back to the grill. "Burgers'll be up in five."

Emily was a short-order cook. Translated, that meant her recipe list was as short as her temper and she loved shouting orders. Arguing with her would gain me nothing, except maybe a lump on the head. She threw things. Still, I couldn't see giving those children more empty calories to fuel their nervous energies. Maybe if I did it quietly, I could make the meal (somehow breakfast had been changed to lunch by Emily's edict) into something more wholesome.

With DeeDee as cohort, we checked out the doors adjacent to the refrigerators and found a pantry, a huge space easily double the area of the downstairs floor space of my farmhouse and crammed with row after row of floor-to-ceiling metal shelving neatly stacked with the labors of the family's summer preserving effort. I had not seen so much home-canned goods outside the state fair. DeeDee and I stared open-mouthed a moment, then met each other's eyes. DeeDee said, "We did all this?"

We had, of course. In response to Harris's urging, we had put in larger home gardens and canned and preserved like crazy. I'd contributed spaghetti sauce, pickled beets, and had frozen so much corn, green beans, and peppers I didn't want to think about it, and I was near the bottom of the home canners and freezers in this family.

We did not explore or linger. The rising noise level from the lunchroom reminded us of our purpose. Reading nearby labels quickly, we grabbed some jars of Grandmother Quill's home-canned green beans—now she was a champion canner.

From an adjacent room—even larger and smelling of rich earth and potatoes—we fetched carrots and celery—home grown by one of us. The storeroom was huge and filled with enough produce to supply Green Giant for a day at least. By the time Emily's burgers were ready, we also had added milk and some delicious canned peaches to the menu. The bliss of watching the children fill their mouths with food rather than hysteria was almost worth taking Emily's guff. I felt even more complete when I sent Beth with a tray of food to Sissy and her children.

Some of the other adults began to filter in. DeeDee's husband, James, the youngest Quill brother, showed up to eat, and Mike Deters, Jillian's older brother, silently floated in on the first waves of coffee aroma. He downed two steaming cups standing at the counter before saying a word. Others trickled in.

Everyone looked exhausted and moved stiffly. Some groused about the cubicles and cramped space. A few allowed to have been vaguely aware of the noise earlier but assumed someone else would deal with it. That annoyed me, but I wondered how much of that opinion was affected by my own state of mind, my own weariness. Still, I had to make them understand just how scary those children had been.

"Jeannie," I said, "your boys were—"

Lori Fisk ran into the cafeteria and grabbed the end of the table where I sat with Jeannie and Wayne Deters. Lori's eyes were filled with terror. "I can't find Charleen!" she shouted loudly enough for all in the room to hear.

Lori was on the edge of hysteria if not a shade or two into it, like maybe she feared she'd left Charleen in the Cities. Her husband, Paul, called for the fourteen-month-old toddler out in the open area. Without a word, the search began. Every cubicle was searched—boxes, bags, and drawers. Every storage room with a door the small child could possibly open was explored. At ten o'clock, half an hour after the search had begun, every possible hiding place, trap, or escape route had been investigated. No Charleen. Lori was frantic, Paul tight-lipped and pale.

We regrouped to air new theories as to the child's whereabouts, when the big steel doors under the sign "ANIMAL ROOM" on the opposite side of the big room from the kitchen banged open. We hadn't checked this because the doors were too heavy for a toddler to open. We had ignored those doors, as well as the HOSPITAL and SCHOOL doors for the same reason. The Gertz boys came through. One carried a brimming five-gallon pail of frothy milk, and the other a basket of little white banty eggs. Between them, obviously quite at ease and happy, swung little Charleen Fisk. Behind the three-some came Max Gertz and his chubby wife.

Lori screamed and rushed the boys. Charleen started to cry as her mother swooped her into her arms. A splash of cream hit the floor as the startled boys pulled back. Mrs. Gertz spoke up. "Dear, dear. I had no idea it'd be a problem. We got up earlier. Everyone was asleep, 'cept the children. This'n was crying. I thought maybe I could help out a bit and took her with."

"What were you doing in there?" demanded Paul Fisk, abrupt with worry.

"The beasts," Max Gertz said slowly. "The beasts needed tendin'. Cows gotta be milked. Our room's there, just at the door to'm. I could hear'm lowin' through the doors. Thought we could earn our keep tendin' 'em."

Still hugging Charleen to her breast, Lori turned and carried the child away. Paul, a veterinarian by profession, had a keener understanding of a milk cow's needs. He nodded at Max before he turned to follow his wife. The others moved off without comment, going back to their coffee or heading to their cubicles, leaving the Gertz family standing there. I couldn't let it end like that.

"Did you give some hay to my bunnies?" I asked, smiling.

Mrs. Gertz regarded me warily. But then her eyes slid to my belly, and she softened. "The Flems?"

I nodded. "Yes . . . the big spotted ones. The Californians are mine, too."

She nodded. "Used to raise them myself. Flemish giants were my favorites. Californians raise to meat faster . . . but the giants sure are pretty."

"Yeah," I said. "Everything okay with the other . . . beasts?"

Max frowned. He obviously didn't like being patronized, and I know it came out sounding like that. His wife said, "They need sorting out. You've got them Jerseys in with them ponies. They don't mix well. The goats were into the grain, and the geese and ducks are making a mess of the cows' water."

"Everyone needs bedding," Max said then. "Couldn't see no straw, and that alfalfa's too rich for them ponies. Makes 'em mean. Meadow hay's better."

"I see," I said. "Well, we all did get here in a rush last night." I instantly felt my face go hot. The Gertzes sure did arrive in a rush . . . with a shotgun, I remembered. "Um, I'm sure Harris will organize the animals when he gets up," I finished quickly.

"I'd a done it, if I knew where stuff was," Max said.

I could see he was a decent man. "I'm really glad you milked the cows and fed all the animals," I said. "No one's thought that far ahead yet. None of us are really farmers. And I can see little Charleen was safe. Her dad's a vet, so she loves animals. Lori was too frantic to show her gratitude, but I'm sure she is grateful. We couldn't find Charleen, but we ought to have known she wasn't in any real danger."

No real danger. My God. That was the problem all right. We had no idea what dangers we faced. Nuclear war wasn't real. How could it be? How could any mind fathom what those words meant? It wasn't possible. So we focused on the nearest real danger we saw—a little child lost. That was the enemy. That was real. That kept our minds off the void beyond the edge of the world where we could see nothing and could hope for nothing good. If we weren't just very careful, we could live our days in the shelter moving from one tiny danger to the next. That was the surest way for us to perish.

"Last call for burgers!" Emily hollered from the kitchen door. "Get 'em while they're hot! I ain't standing here forever."

I took a couple obedient steps in the direction of the lunchroom, then turned back to the Gertz family. "She means it," I grinned. "I bet you big young men could put away three apiece. Hope you folks don't mind an early lunch. My sister has a limited menu, but the food's good. Mrs. Gertz . . . Abby, isn't it? We could fry up some of your eggs there, if you'd prefer."

Abby snatched the basket from her younger son and thrust it at me. "Them's *your* eggs. I just picked them and fed the hens."

I heard anger in her tone, probably at the awkward way I had handled talking to them. I deserved that. But I thought I also heard regret. This was a farmer's wife. A thought occurred to me. "I bet you've raised better chickens than those little banties."

She met my eyes with a faceful of German determination and set lips. Max muttered something to her and pointed the boys at the lunchroom. Abby tightened her jaw and trailed after them. I followed behind, wondering what the issue was and how it could be solved for the kindly farm wife.

Farm wife. My mind caught on an image of *Little House on the Prairie*. I thought I understood. After Abby filled her plate from the stack of hamburgers and other food we had set out, I sat next to her. "What's the best chicken to have?" I asked softly, hoping not in involve her husband.

"'Pends," she said sullenly, not meeting my eyes.

30

"Well, let's say I wanted a good meat bird. What should I have?"

She paused in the process of bringing her burger to her mouth, then said, "Them big southern cross birds. Grow to fryer size in eight weeks, six if you push 'em." Warming to the conversation, she looked up. "Gotta watch 'em, though. They're dumb. They'll die by overeating or forget to take their heads out of their water."

I smiled. "Okay. What about eggs? What's the best for eggs?"

Abby chewed her bite of burger thoughtfully. She swallowed and said, "Best? I s'pose it's them skinny, ugly leghorns still. They lay their minds out. Nice clean white eggs. I prefer brown." She focused again on her food.

I could easily imagine that Abby Gertz had raised hundreds of birds to meat and butchered them in her own kitchen. She must have collected basketsful of eggs. I bet she had chickens on the farm she had left the night before. "So . . . what do you have?"

"Buff Orpingtons." She didn't meet my eyes, but by the quickness of her response, I sensed that she had really wanted to tell me this. Max elbowed her, and she bent over her plate as if eating were hard and important work. I was a little afraid to push anymore, so I leaned back and sipped my coffee. My brother Marty sat down next to Max and started asking him about pigs. The farmer began to wax eloquent about consistency of droppings as a clue to feed balance.

"They lay the biggest brown eggs your ever saw," Abby whispered, catching my eye. "Deep yellow yolks. In the spring they get broody. Them's nice quiet birds. I bought a dozen fifteen years ago. Been raising chicks from them each spring ever since. Never had to buy another bird. I sure hated to leave them pretty brown hens behind."

I smiled. "Maybe something can be done. I'll ask Harris about it."

"And the mister has some fine head of beef and some good pigs. Ask Mr. Quill about them, too, will ya?"

I nodded and got up. My girls were in the far corner with some of their girl cousins and a box of Barbie dolls. Harry, Jr., was trying to teach Jacob Deters how to play chess, and DeeDee was reading to a knot of the youngest kids. Bedlam would certainly break out again soon, I was sure of that, but, for right now, everything seemed peaceful. I headed for our cubicle in hopes of resting my aching legs.

4
REGROUPING

———

THE CURTAIN SEEMED HEAVY as I pulled it aside. Frank switched off the radio at just that moment. Then he flopped back on our bed and covered his eyes with an arm. I sat at the edge of the bed, waiting for him to fill me in. When he didn't, I said softly, "Bad news?"

"Uh-uh. Status quo for the most part. World's still out there. Few hours older is all. The president's been on with a speech about not panicking. Little late. Bastard. One commentator said we're looking at the complete breakdown of nearly everything—the economy, the government, transportation . . . civilization."

A chill touched my spine. "What . . . what does that mean exactly?"

Frank shot me an astonished look but modified it almost instantly. "I don't know. I doubt anyone does. I think it means we're doing what we should be doing right now. What was all the noise about a bit ago?"

Frank was one of those people who could sleep through the derailing of a cattle train. I doubted he'd heard the road race that had awakened me hours before. "Charleen was lost. Seems she was crying when the Gertzes got up. They took her into the animal room with them. Fed all the animals. Milked. Picked eggs. Lori about had kittens before they came out with Charleen."

"All's well that ends well." Frank's tone was low-key, unemotional. I knew he had listened with only part of his brain, and his response was pre-programmed based on my tone. Communicating with him could get difficult at times.

"I wish we could do something about Abby Gertz's chickens," I said.

There was a long pause that meant that Frank's mind had completely wandered away from me. I knew then that switching off the radio had been on purpose and

32

not just coincidental with my coming in. I needed to ask a question. That might pene-trate because it required an answer. Statements didn't. "Frank, can we do something about Abby Gerz's chickens?"

Frank's mind heard the question tone and knew it had to form a response. He pulled back from his thoughts. "What?" he said.

"She left behind her chickens. I could tell it was a big loss to her."

Frank's eyes flashed. "Chickens? What chickens?"

"Abby Gertz's."

His face screwed up. Clearly he thought I was in left field or something. Like how dare I worry over some stupid chickens when the world was falling apart. "Gertz? We gave them a place to stay, and she's bent out of shape about her *chickens*? What's *wrong* with her?"

To communicate with Frank in this mood, I had to speak plainly and soft-ly. I tried to do that, though his distracted anger usually pissed me off before I made that determination. Today I managed to stay calm. "I didn't say she was bent out of shape. I said she was sorry to have to leave them. She'd had the line for fifteen years."

Frank's eyes narrowed as if struggling to understand me. "Fifteen-year-old chickens? That's assinine. Chickens don't live that long."

Clearly I still didn't have his full attention. "No, Frank, not the birds, the line. You know, chick to hen to chick. She had Orpingtons. I've read about them. Great all-around bird. Lays big brown eggs—"

"A chicken's a chicken, hon. We have plenty."

"We have banties. Sissy *had* southern cross, but she butchered all of them. We have no way to replace them. And Abby misses hers. Couldn't we—"

"No!" Frank stood. At home he would have begun pacing, but there was no room here. I could see most of his mind was busy with problems other than chickens, problems he wasn't sharing. The talk about chickens was rubbing raw the little edge he had left for me. He sat down. In a harsh whisper, he said, "They came in here last night with a goddamn shotgun, ready to take the shelter from us if we didn't let them in. Now we're supposed to rush out and bring back their stupid chickens? Does that make any sense to you? What have they contributed? What rights do they have? None as I see it."

I drew in a deep breath. This wasn't the time to start a discussion on rights and privileges. I filed that topic for later. I had a point and needed to make it while

I had his attention. "They're farmers, Frank. Think about that. Think about the animals we have. Do we have beef cattle to supply us with meat or Holsteins for volumes of milk? No. We have cute little Jerseys that give a couple quarts of mostly cream. What do we have for pigs? Durocs for meat or Chester whites for bacon? No, we have Chinese pot-belly pigs. Pets. Ducks? Little white things with pompons on their heads. We have a couple dozen banties that lay three eggs to the size of a medium store-bought egg and are about big enough butchered to make a meal for two. We have golden pheasants, homing pigeons, five Shetland ponies, a few goats and sheep, and a goddamn fox terrier with pups."

Frank's jaw hardened to a tight line. "Make the point, Barb."

"We're backyard, hobby-farm farmers, Frank. We don't know thing one about real farming. We have designer animals in a world that's probably already forgotten what that means. Max Gertz is a *real* farmer. He has the know-how and experience to do things right with the right stock and the right feed. I've got this awful feeling that, if we alienate him and his family, if we don't welcome them and make them feel needed here, we're losing the greatest resource we have right now, other than the shelter itself."

For a long moment, Frank said nothing, but his mind hadn't wandered. He stared at me through set features and angry eyes. I held firm, hoping he had allotted me enough brain space to process what I had said. Finally, he said softly, "Maybe you're right."

I plunged ahead. "What did they raise? Do you know? Abby mentioned beef and pigs."

"Yeah. Cash crops mostly. Grains, corn, soybeans. He kept a few head of beef cattle and some pigs, too. And Abby had Orpintons? Damn. I think you're right on the money with this, Barb. We should have thought about all this from the beginning. You and I can raise a head of cabbage to perfection, but a field of oats? Wheat for flour? We'd have to reinvent agriculture."

I grinned. "So, do we get Abby her chickens?"

Frank's enthusiasm froze. "No. No way. We can't risk it."

"But you said nothing much has changed out there—"

"We're in for good, Barb. Until everything's over, we're not leaving here."

"But it's just down the driveway. Their barn's maybe a hundred feet from here. There's a truck and trailer right outside."

"Barb, this isn't negotiable."

"Why not?"

"Because Harris said—"

"'Harris said.' Frank . . ."

"What?"

I couldn't do it. If I tried to come between Frank and his big brother, there was no way to win. There had to be another way. I swallowed my anger and began again. "Look, you agree that having a real farmer is smart. Right?"

"Well, yeah, but—"

"And he might be valuable when whatever happens is all over and we have to try to live in the real world again. Right?"

He sighed. "Yes, but this—"

"Well, you tell me, Frank. Tell me how anyone, even a real farmer with experience up the wazoo, is going to get things moving again if he doesn't have real animals to work with? I'm not talking Abby's chickens here. I'm talking real beef cows and pigs that butcher out at a couple of hundred pounds instead of thirty. Forget about the chickens. Think beef and pork."

Frank drew in a long breath. "I'll talk to Harris, but don't get your hopes up. If he says no, and I can't talk him out of it, do you agree to lay off?"

I narrowed my eyes. "You'll give it a strong plug?"

"My best. You're right about this, and I know it. It's just that Harris has some security protocols he's going to fight to maintain."

I nodded. I knew I could be as tenacious as a terrier sometimes when I set my mind on something, but I tried not to do it too often. We had long since worked out the parameters of how to deal with compromise. I had stated my piece, and Frank had responded. He had to act his part now, or the topic could reopen. But, if he asked Harris, put in a good plug for my point of view, and still lost, I had to give it up. I didn't have to like it.

Frank stood again and headed out of the cubicle. He paused at the curtain and said, "Aren't you coming? This is your idea."

I shook my head and lay back on the bed. "I'm beat. I'm going to rest awhile."

He rolled his eyes and left.

W HEN I LAY DOWN, I had planned no more than a brief nap. An hour maybe. I awoke at four-thirty by our travel clock after mingled dreams of being a child again at my parents' home in Indianapolis, then giving birth to my third child under a bush on a burned hillside, and spending the rest of my life in dungeon caves and caverns. I half woke after this last series, turned over and dozed awhile longer. When I finally roused enough that sleep was behind me, it was ten past five. I was annoyed that I had slept the day away but felt more rested than I had in days.

It was strange waking up in an unfamiliar place and not being able to tell the time by the shifting sunlight coming in the windows. I would have been confused enough at home, thinking it was morning and wondering why I was dressed and the girls not in bed. One time, after a mid-day nap, I had leaped up and called them to get ready for school. They were watching late afternoon cartoons and teased me for days. But here in the shelter, no sunlight helped me sort my orientation from dreams. It was difficult to see that little clock and accept its time without solar confirmation. I had to get used to that. It might be a long time before I saw the sun again. And the clock couldn't tell me which twelve hours it marked. Depression slipped over me, tarnishing my rest.

When I moved, I found Andrea snuggled against my back. I was glad she was napping and covered her with the spread when I got up. The hall outside was nearly empty when I opened the curtain. Mary Sue Deters and Lynn DeSota were jumping rope on the far side, and a couple of the littler Reinharts watched them.

I was on a pretty urgent trip to the bathrooms, but, as I passed the open cafeteria doors, I noticed a few of the older kids, including Beth, playing a board game at one of the tables, while Jeannie's twins stood at the counter picking at the leftovers from lunch. Jillian, Marie Deters, Sissy, and Melissa Reinhart sat at the far table having beers.

In the bathroom, two little boys sailed paper boats in one of the sinks. It was awash. My need allowed me to ignore them as I hurredly entered the first of the three stalls. But, as I sat to relieve my battered bladder, I distinctly heard someone throwing up in the third stall. The toilet flushed, and a pair of feet walked to the sinks. I recognized DeeDee's shoes. I finished quickly.

DeeDee was leaning on the sink looking pale and shaky. The boaters had vanished.

"Are you all right?" I asked with concern.

She looked up quickly, eyes startled. "Oh, Barby! You scared me!"

"Sorry. Were you just throwing up in there?"

"Yes. Nerves, I guess. My stomach's been twisted for days."

"Nerves'll do that, and we certainly have had our fill of worries these days. No fever or headache or anything else?" For me, any symptoms that varied from perfect health lately triggered thoughts of swine flu, ebola, or worse.

She smiled and shook her head. "I don't have bubonic plague. I'll be okay after we're settled."

DeeDee was easily the prettiest of the Quill brothers' wives. Medium height with a tiny waist, she had shapely runner's legs, short chestnut hair, dimpled cheeks, and amazing blue eyes. Not the icy kind of blue, but a dark, almost purple blue that lit up with almost every color of the rainbow when she smiled. Everyone in the family liked her, and Mom and Dad Quill openly adored her as much as her kindergarten students did. When James had wondered if he and DeeDee ought to get married, his mom threatened him with expulsion from the family if he didn't propose that very evening. She was only half kidding. "Don't you dare let that sweet fawn get away," I remember her saying as we all sat around the dinner table on New Year's night. He equivocated, but before he could get anything said as to why, she banged her fork on the table and said, "Why is it that when each of you boys finally finds the perfect wife, it scares the bejeebers out of you. You boys keep trying to shoot yourselves in the foot." We all laughed, James proposed, and the young couple was married on Valentine's Day.

DeeDee said, "Have you heard about Andy and the others?"

Pleasant memories ended. My stomach tightened convulsively. "No. What's happening?"

"Andy, Bob, and Linda are together in Minneapolis now. The airport. They can't get out of the Cities yet, but they hope to this evening. Sue and Pete aren't coming."

I drew in a quick breath. "What do you mean 'not coming'?"

DeeDee shrugged. "They never left Phoenix. They decided taking Phillip out of his school was a very bad idea. It would upset him too much."

Phillip had Down's Syndrome. "How's Jillian taking *that* news?"

"Badly. I'd stay away from her for a while. She's in one of her blacker moods, and I've seen some dark ones."

"Haven't we all. Thanks for the warning. You should get some rest."

I was about to leave when I saw a question in DeeDee's face. "What?" I asked.

She hesitated, colored and looked down. In a soft voice, she said, "How do you feel about it . . . your baby, I mean . . . the one that's coming?"

In a lot of ways, that was an impossible question, requiring about an hour's response. I chose to give DeeDee the abreviated version. "I don't know. Excited and worried, I guess. At this end of the pregnancy, I mostly feel like I'd be glad when it's out. Why?" As I asked this, I added up the last few minutes and figured this wasn't a casual question. "DeeDee, are you pregnant?"

Her cheeks burned, but she nodded ever so slightly. That seemed to break the dam, and she started to cry. I wrapped motherly arms around her.

"I always wondered how women know they're pregnant. I remember you said with this one that you knew but hadn't taken a test yet. I didn't get that. I do now. I know. I'm not sure how I know, but I do. Oh, Barby, I'm so scared."

I squeezed her shoulders. "That's part of it, being scared. It gets better."

"But, look where we are." Anger filled her tone. "How can I bring a baby into this world? We're living in a tomb here. What life have I got to offer a child down here? And when whatever happens happens, what's there for us outside? No one knows. Either there's going to be nothing left or the same rotten world we left. Neither is any good for a child."

I waited until her sobs and questions had worn themselves out. There were no answers that I could give her that would help anyway. Finally, I said, "Listen, DeeDee, I don't think any woman ever thought the time her child came was perfect."

She snorted. "This is a hell of a long way down even from *normal!*"

I remembered that dismaying glimpse of the inside of the shelter from the top of the stairs the night before and compared it to the pleasant October evening scene I had left outside. I looked around a large but utilitarian bathroom with water all over the floor and remembered the way my space looked all crowded with beds and boxes and pawed through bags. Outside was a mess of a world that made little sense and held little kindness anymore. But that wasn't the point. "It isn't the world we live in that makes a life for a child," I told DeeDee with feeling. "It's the people around the child. Sure, I'd like to turn the clock back for my kids to a time when the big worries were whether the United States should get out of Iraq or how to avoid cocaine. My mother lamented one

38

day to me when I was in high school that she wished all I had to worry about was which prom dress to wear or getting an A in geometry. Her mother worried about being American enough not to look like a greenhorn. Her grandmother worried about coming over from the old country. Do you get the picture?"

DeeDee smiled a little and nodded.

"I can't change what will happen to my girls. I can't mysteriously make the world better. All I can do is help them live with what they have to face. But, in the end, maybe that'll be enough. Life's being good or bad has a lot to do with our attitude about it. You should know that."

"When I was Beth's age," DeeDee whispered, "my mom was dying of cancer. My dad was drinking too much, probably his way of coping with mom's illness. One night he missed the turn at the lake. The spring I turned ten, I had already lost both my mom and dad and gone to live with relatives who had too many kids to raise already. I wouldn't wish that on anyone."

I hugged her again, my throat aching. "No one can predict how their future is going to turn out, let alone the lives of their kids. Your child might have it as hard as you did. Probably not. Most likely, with your background as a teacher and all of us to support you, your child will have a great life."

I had gone too far. Why did I always take that last improbable step? DeeDee frowned and looked down. "Barby, I've been thinking . . . of aborting . . ."

I sighed. "You've got a lot to think about then. Marty won't do it. I know that. Too much Catholic in the background. And Jillian is preoccupied with her own problems just now. Take a little time to think through this carefully. Does James know?"

"No. I'm scared to tell him. I mean, the timing is so lousy and all."

"It could be better," I agreed. "That's the way it goes, though. Look when this one is going to be born. James should be part of your decision, one way or the other, though. Maybe things will be different for us in a week or so. Maybe you'll be different."

We talked a bit more; then DeeDee went to lie down. I sympathized with her. It had been hard for me when I knew I was pregnant this last time to accept the idea of bringing new life into the same old mess. But I had my other two to remind me that they were doing okay. If we were meant to die in the Ark, then we'd die together—Frank, girls, unborn, and me. But if we were going to live, then maybe the new child had just as much chance at happiness as the rest of us. I hoped this wasn't false hope.

39

I paused at the cafeteria doors, half hungry. The children were gone from the back table. Monopoly money and little red hotels littered the floor. The twins had left also. Jillian sat alone. The tray on the counter held little more than dirty, crumpled paper napkins and three pieces of limp celery. One had a bite taken out of it. I picked up the other two. Jillian looked up, so I felt I couldn't just walk out without saying something. I crossed to her table and sat down opposite her.

Jillian was more a striking than a handsome woman. She was tall, thin and angular with an aristocratic nose and a bearing to match. Most of the time. At the moment, her hair uncombed, her shirtwaist dress slept in, and seven beer bottles in front of her, she cut a far from regal figure.

"I heard about Sue. I'm sorry," I said.

"Yeah," she looked up with a sneer, "you've got your brother and sisters around you. Sue was my only sister, my baby sister."

"I know. We've all left relatives, though."

"Great bit of comfort there, Barby."

I bit my lip. I could see I wasn't going to penetrate her misery. "When are Andy and the rest going to get here?"

"Who the hell cares. This whole ark thing is a farce anyway. Four and a half fucking million he spent on this ridiculous tomb. And that's besides what the rest of the family contributed. Four and a half million. Harris built himself a fucking ark! What a joke. I could just barf."

I had no idea Harris had put so much money into the shelter. The fifteen families that had paid for the shelter had contributed a lot. Frank and I, like the rest of the families, had been asked to contribute a year's salary. We had second mortgaged our farm and borrowed from the girls' college fund to contribute our share, just a bit less than one-hundred-eighty thousand. Some gave more, some less. Harris had put in much more than his law practice and Jillian's physician salary defined.

I tried to think of something to say as Jillian stared at me, her deepset brown eyes studying me minutely. Then she snorted and shook her head. "Aw, go away, Barby," she said. "I just want to sit here alone for a while. I'd go to my cute little tent, but Mr. Hero is sprawled over the bed like a beached whale."

I got up. "Take it easy, Jill. I wish I could do something for you. Let me know if I can, okay?"

She just waved me away like a queen bored with a servant. I was not one of Jillian's favorite people. I knew that, but I admired her anyway. Not at the moment, maybe, but in general. She was strong and outspoken. I liked that. When she was in a better humor, she could be generous, understanding and, sometimes, even wise.

When I entered the big common hall again, Frank and Harris were walking purposefully toward the animal room. Harris looked bleary-eyed; his hair stuck up straight in the back, as if he had just pulled himself out of bed. Frank saw me and grinned. I smiled.

In our tiny cubicle, I changed my shirt and brushed my hair. Then I began to organize. I put infrequently needed things on the top shelf, Frank's and my clothes and toilet items on the next highest shelf, and the girls' clothes and playthings where they could reach them. Heavy boxes of books were shoved under the bottom shelf. Then I changed my mind and pushed the bunk beds against the shelves and arranged the girls' treasures where they could reach them through the head of the bed. That put Beth's fragile glass statues and porcelain dolls on a high shelf out of Andrea's reach. Beth would like that.

Under the double bed was good storage for other boxes. Again, I used a priority system and pushed the least necessary items deep and the needed ones just out of sight. I used a sturdy quilt as the spread on the bed, knowing this wide space would be used as often as a play area as a bed. My mother's knitted spread just would not hold up, and I'd hate to see it destroyed. With everything stowed (the ship image did come to mind) and the beds made, the narrow space began to look almost homey.

The chest of drawers Frank had set just behind the curtain seemed to cut the living space too much. I turned it and pushed it against the head of the double bed. To get into it, I would have to open the curtain from the outside, but the middle of the cubicle had more room, and I wouldn't have to ease sideways to get in and out. As a final touch, I laid a bright yellow throw rug down the center of the floor and taped a few of Andrea's recent drawings to the side of the chest of drawers as if it were a refrigerator.

Beth came in just as I finished.

"Wow, Mom!" she grinned. "This looks great!"

Appreciation by one's child was the greatest praise of all. I beamed. "Not too bad," I said. "Problem is, we've got to work very hard to keep it this way. This space is so small, like a camper, that any mess is going to look just awful. Try to put things away when you take them out."

"Sure, Mom."

"What have you been doing all day?"

"Nothing much."

"Where's your sister?"

"I don't know. Last time I saw her she was with some of the Reinharts."

"When was that?"

"Ten minutes ago, maybe. They were in Sissy's slice."

"'Slice'?"

Beth grinned. "That's what Harry and I decided to call the cubicles. We're cut up like pieces of a pie, aren't we? Each family gets a slice. Get it?"

"I get it."

She turned to go, then spun back. "Oh, almost forgot. Aunt Anna wants to know if you want to help her with supper."

"Run and tell her I'm on the way."

T HE KITCHEN WAS A DISASTER. No one had cleaned up after lunch. The grill was streaked with white globs of fat, part of a ten-pound lump of hamburger had been left open on the counter, and the pans we had used stood in the sink. On top of that, the children had invaded the room as they had before we fixed food. Chips and donuts, again, had been spread everywhere. A package of chocolate chips had been burst open on the floor, and evidence that Kool-Aid had been made, spilled and made again was all over the counters. Plastic tumblers is a rainbow of colors were everywhere.

My little sister, Anna, had a broom in hand but was obviously overwhelmed.

I let out a deep sigh. "We *have* to get organized," I said. "Look at that meat. What a waste! And kids just can't have free run in here."

"You're preaching to the choir," Anna said. "The question is, how do we get this mess cleaned up enough to fix some supper? It's already seven-thirty."

Born nearly six years after Marty, my younger brother, Anna had inherited my dad's thinness and mother's shortness. Even in adulthood, she would be the baby, the littlest, shortest, cutest of the Dunn sisters. She had one daughter, the only good outcome of a poor marriage, but Lynn was one of those little girls who just always seemed neat and careful. Anna had never had to cope with chaos in her tidy Minneapolis apartment.

I, on the other hand, had two children and a husband who were naturally chaotic. I had learned years before how to follow Plan B. "What were you thinking for supper?"

Anna shrugged. "I don't know. Mashed potatoes, broccoli, and pork chops sounded nice."

"It does, but not tonight. With the kitchen like this, we wouldn't eat until midnight if we try for that. We need something simpler. I seem to remember seeing some institutional-size Cambell soup cans under the counter over there. Pull out three and start them warming in that big kettle. Then get two loaves of bread and make PB and J."

"PB and J?"

"Peanut butter and jelly sandwiches. Make a mountain of them and set them out. Replenish the pile as needed."

"What are you going to do?"

I faced the kitchen and started to roll up my sleeves. "Order the universe."

"But you turned on the grill."

"I'm going to fry up the rest of this hamburger for the pets. We can't eat it, but it should be okay for them. And a warm grill is easier to clean than a cold one."

Anna smiled. "You'd think Em would know that. Thanks, Barby. I hesitated to call you. I know you're tired. But I just couldn't face this alone."

It took me more than an hour to roughly clean the kitchen. During that time, Anna came in for the soup and a stack of bowls, DeeDee got glasses for milk, and Connie, my brother's wife, came in for a cloth to clean up spilled milk, another loaf of bread, and a second huge jar of peanut butter. Emily came in puffing on a cigarette and told me I was cleaning the grill wrong, but she didn't offer to help, so when she took a large pinch of the cooked hamburger, I didn't say anything. When she left, I Lysoled the room to get rid of the cigarette smell.

By the time I had the kitchen finished, Anna and DeeDee came in with stacks of dirty bowls, plates, glasses, and spoons.

"This is our job now, Sis," Anna said brightly. "We left a bowl of soup and a sandwich for you out there. Go eat it. We'll clean this up."

The eating area was spotless. Even the Monopoly game had been picked up. Connie was wiping the last table top. I sighed. Feeling overwhelmed had faded. Maybe this could work if everyone chipped in. I sat down and ate my simple supper.

Anna, DeeDee, and Connie sat down just as I was finishing.

"Here's the plan," DeeDee said. "Either one of us volunteers to get up early and beat the kids to the kitchen, or we leave out food."

"That sounds good," I said, "but we better do both."

Connie began nodding. "Good plan. I say we put cereal boxes on the tables with bowls. My kids eat cereal dry all the time. Then we put three signs on the kitchen doors—"

"Three?" said Anna.

Ah, the ignorant bliss of a mother with one neat child.

"Sure," said Connie. "We could leave a menu for the adults and older kids, a big NO for the grade-school kids, and a Mr. Yuck for the little ones."

When Anna's brows drew together, I said, "You know, the nasty face with the tongue stuck out that they put on poison bottles. It ranks right up there with power outlet protectors."

Anna looked almost as lost. "Oh. I guess I never used either of those with Lynn."

"Well," said DeeDee, "we've got twenty-two kids here now and more on the way."

She met my eyes when she said this. I smiled. I hoped the calm I saw behind her smile was a decision, but even if it was just clear thinking, that was okay.

BY NINE-THIRTY, THE ARK had quieted. All the children were in their cubicles . . . "slices," as they had been dubbed. Beth and Andrea each lay on her own bunk reading with the high-intensity nightlights we had with us. I sat on the double bed with a magazine, trying to relax my jumpy legs so I could sleep, when I heard some talking outside in the central area that the children called the "donut" because the center column and the ring that the family slices touched left a donut-shaped open area. I was about to get up and see if Frank was with them when he drew aside the curtain and came in. He greeted the girls, kissed them good night, and motioned me out of the slice.

I eased myself up and followed him. Harris stood there with Max Gertz, my brother Marty, and the two Quill cousins, twins Dewey and Donald.

"Good idea, Barby," Harris grinned. "Seems Max here had fifty head of prime beef. Couldn't take all of them, of course, but we selected ten of the finest cows and their calves for the animal room. We now have some nice Duroc sows, too, and a serviceable young boar. With Abby Gertz's canned goods and prize-winning jellies, we're set for a year at least. And we have twenty-four of her finest Orpington hens and a couple of roosters. Twenty other birds, six pigs, and four steers are in the woodroom. We have to butcher them in the next couple of days."

Max Gertz rested his broad hand on my arm. "Thanks, missus," he said. "This has made my wife very happy. Me, too."

"What's going to happen to the rest of your livestock though," I said with concern.

"We turned the cows loose in the hill pasture with a wagon full of hay and a frost-free water tank," Frank said. "The pigs have the run of the farm with plenty of food in the barn. We've got all the chickens. That's it. Everything's accounted for except a barnful of alfalfa and a couple hundred bales of straw. And Max agreed to help us out with our animals so the feed lasts, and we make the best use of the animals we have. His boys have been in the animal room all day penning and organizing. James and Paul have helped with pens. Pretty soon we'll be in great shape for the winter."

I WENT TO BED THAT NIGHT feeling good in a few ways. There was still just as much uncertainty in my world, still just as much fear, and it clenched my stomach when I thought of what might be happening in the rest of the world. But I had affected my immediate surroundings, maybe just in a couple of small ways, but enough that I could fall asleep feeling I had broken even at least. I couldn't change what was happening in the larger world, couldn't make a dent in the insanity out there; but inside the shelter, I thought I had helped ease a difficult day's passage. Tomorrow I would try again. With DeeDee, Anna, Melissa, and Connie as allies, we would try to organize our microcosm into something we could begin to understand. I fell asleep planning, and that was a whole lot better than falling asleep filled with worry.

5

ANDY

FRIDAY, OCTOBER 12

M Y FIRST CONTACT WITH CONSCIOUSNESS the next morning was hearing children laughing and yelling. I thought the road race scene was being replayed, and I moaned, rolled over and covered my head. Then Frank nudged my shoulder, and I woke up.

"Andy called," he said.

I looked into his grim face and felt my stomach tighten instantly. "And . . ."

"Nothing . . . yet. Come on. We're all meeting in the school."

"School? We're in the shelter. What school?"

He rolled his eyes. "Come on, Barb. Just get up." Then he left.

I didn't like it when Frank was obtuse, especially when I was just waking up. I pushed myself into a sitting position and blinked. It was as if none of my organizing had happened the day before. Boxes of clothes were pulled out, pawed through and scattered. The bunks dripped sheets and blankets, and Beth's obscene, naked Barbies lay all over. I felt irritation rising. To top it off, Silk, the Manx kitten, was just completing a neat job in the box containing Frank's and my underwear. I felt tears coming as she carefully pulled my lace panties over the mess with feline satisfaction and hopped out.

I was suddenly claustrophobic. This space was too small, too cramped to contain the four of us. Four. In a few weeks it would be five. I couldn't do it. There was no way. No matter what we had to face in the outside world, I preferred that to this molish, cramped living in the Ark. This wasn't living. It was nothing like living.

"Barb," Frank said, using his firm, you-have-to-wake-up-now tone.

I looked up through a curtain of uncombed hair. I hadn't heard him come back into the cubicle. "What!" I said, knowing I sounded vicious.

Frank's expression turned quizzical. He sniffed the air. "What's that smell?"

"Silk just pooped in our underwear box. Why did you leave it out? And look at this place—"

"Forget all that," he said. "Come on. Andy's going to call back any minute. Here's some coffee."

He handed me an institutional-style white mug and immediately left. For a second or two, I felt like flinging the steaming mug across the cubicle. I felt like ripping the sheets off the beds and dumping the rest of the boxes. Instead, I took a sip of coffee and felt around with my toes for my slippers. Thankfully, they were just under the edge of the bed. My flowered robe lay at the foot of the bed. I took another sip of the strong coffee.

By the fourth or fifth sip, I was standing, my robe on and tied with the very ends of the sash around the top of my huge belly. I began to shuffle out of the slice. I didn't care so much anymore about how the place looked. The clautrophobia had receded, and the rawness of first awakening began to scab over. Thank God for caffeine.

After a trip to the bathroom, which was almost as messy and cluttered as our slice, I entered the donut area again, wondering where the schoolroom was. But that problem was solved immediately. A pair of double doors stood open part way across the donut from me. The kitchen doors and bathroom doors were side by side just to the left of our cubicle. The open doors were three slices further around to the left.

As I walked toward the doors, I could see chairs set up in rough rows with desks piled in three tiers along the wall. At the doors, I saw into the room—which was half again as large as the cafeteria room, the size of a high school auditorium—had a slightly raised stage area in the front. Two speakers and a microphone stood on the stage. Just visible beyond the retracted right-hand curtain, a spiral stairway wound up out of sight.

About a dozen adults sat in the front row. Six medium-sized kids played musical chairs in the back of the room, using a Fisher-Price phonograph. A tinny version of "Pop Goes the Weasel" played and was interrupted repeatedly, and the children squealed and tried to hip-check each other out of the chairs. As usual, away from Jeannie, Ronald and Roland were little demons. I distinctly saw Roland pinch five-year-old Jimmy Deters hard enough to make his face light up with pain, more than enough to win the seat from him when the music ended. The twins locked arms and laughed. Jimmy screwed up his face as if to cry and rubbed his thigh but just walked away, looking more ashamed than angry. I chose not to notice and walked to the front of the room.

47

I sat down in the end chair of the second row, next to Jeannie. "Anything happening yet?" I asked. "Did Andy call back yet?"

At first Jeannie seemed to ignore me, then she turned to me with a start. "Oh, Barby! When's breakfast?"

"I don't know. I just woke up. Why—"

"Don't fix hamburgers for breakfast every day, okay? Supper was such a disaster last night, too. I'm sure my boys are hungry. I thought you were nutrition conscious. You're a nurse. You should be."

I blinked and stared at her perfectly made-up face, false eyelashes and all. "Are you okay, Jeannie?"

She drew up her mauve lips into a pout. "Well! You needn't bite my head off. Call me when breakfast is ready."

With that she got up and walked down the whole row of chairs instead of crossing in front of me. At the end of the row, she glanced back, put her hankie to her mouth and ran from the room.

Melissa, just ahead of me in the first row, turned around and sighed. "Jeannie doesn't seem quite right this morning."

I said, "Maybe she's come down further than we have," but I felt badly as soon as I had said it. I drew in a long breath and let it out. "That was mean. I'm sorry, Mel. Everyone shows stress differently. Maybe this is her way."

Lori Fisk, two seat down from Melissa, turned and hissed loudly at us. "Come on. Quiet. Andy could call any time!"

It was too early, and I was irritated. I opened my mouth to retort when I saw a pair of legs coming down the spiral stairs. Frank. He stopped on the stairs as soon as he could see us and said, "Hear anything on the speakers yet?"

"No," several said, and I could hear impatience and pique in those tones.

"Throw the switch, Dewey," he called up the stairs.

Blaring static filled the room. I held my ears.

"We got sound," Frank called, "but you lost the frequency."

After a few moments with varying static, silence, and buzzes, we heard, ". . . like World War III."

Andy. They had Andy on the radio! And yet, my head had a hard time rejoicing. He was out there, outside the Ark. In danger.

"Have you found the pilot yet?"

Harris's voice. Loud with nearness. I marveled at his almost insane calm, as if all this was just an adventurous diversion, maybe some role-playing game cooked up in his aberrant mind.

"Heh, heh. Yeah, big brother. I found him. Where'd *you* find him, eh? Under a rock? He's stone drunk. Has been since yesterday. Seems he can't quite remember where he put his chopper either. Says it's safe . . . just a little lost."

"Are you safe?"

"Yeah . . . kind of. We're holed up in a restroom on the Blue Concourse."

"Is everyone with you?"

"Everyone but Peter and Sue, of course. I never really believed they'd leave Phillip in Phoenix. Everyone else is here. We're all fine . . . a little dinged up, maybe, and a week's worth of tired, but okay. I'm armed, and, so far, we've managed to defend this can, but—"

"Defend? You've had to defend yourselves?"

"Heh, heh, what'd you think? Did ya think this was a picnic out here? I told you it was goddamn World War III. Bob and I have had two firefights with the guys across the hall. We got water, you see, and a chopper pilot. They'd like to get their hands on both. There's been shooting all night throughout the airport. Seems to have settled down the last couple hours, though. No air-worthy planes left maybe. Some took off for who knows where. Some burned. Saw a 747 crash early this morning. Probably no air traffic controllers to bring it in. We thought the whole damn airport would burn. Seriously big fire."

"Jesus. Well, if you're armed—"

"Yeah, we're armed, but so's everyone else who's left around here. So much for airport security. I swear those assholes across the hall have heavy artillery. Damn near blew the door off this can about half an hour ago. We reinforced it with john doors."

"Do you have a plan to get to us?"

"Staying alive is our current plan. After that, we're looking at breaking out of here after dark. If dinglehoofer's memory isn't too soused, the chopper isn't far from here. Once we're off the ground, it should be a piece of cake getting to you. Any activity at your end we need to know about?"

"No. None. Looks like we located the Ark just about right. We even made a foray outside last night. Not a soul in sight."

"Not a soul in sight down here either, big brother, not if souls have anything to do with humanity. Since the balloon went up in Israel, it's been *The Lord of the Flies* the whole nine yards. I don't see any way back from this, Harris. Hope the Ark can keep us safe a long, long time."

"Forever if need be, Andy. Get here safely and help us make it work."

"That's the plan. With luck we'll be with you in about twelve hours. Keep your fingers crossed. Maybe a prayer or two. I'm not sure God's watching any of this—I wouldn't if I was God—but I'd sure like to get his attention if I could."

I had always shied clear of Andy Quill. He acted the hard-nosed cop too much, and Clint Eastwood with a New York accent always hit me wrong. It was as if Andy constantly played a part, a role, as if his image of himself and his real life were pretty far apart. If asked, he'd say he was with NYPD (usually that he *was* NYPD), giving the impression he was some hotshot cop. I figured a forensic specialist really didn't see enough street action to satisfy his heroic police fantasies. He collected fingerprints not felons. Spent his days in a lab. I figured these very same fantasies were what cost him his marriage. I wasn't feeling at all charitable this morning.

Some kind of commotion broke out up above the stage where Frank had gone. I heard Jillian's shrill voice but couldn't make out the words. Two books flew half way down the spiral stairs, hit the rail and thumped to the stage floor. A chair fell backwards above us; then somthing heavy hit the floor. I could hear the scuffing feet of a struggle, then silence.

When the disturbance began, Jillian's brother Wayne got up from his seat in the front row and climbed up on stage. Her other brother, Mike, was right behind him. The books nearly struck Wayne. The two men were at the bottom of the stairs and starting to climb when Jillian, escorted by Frank and James, came down the stairs.

"What's going on?" demanded Wayne, not of Jillian, I noticed, but of Frank.

"Difference of opinion," James said without humor, his mouth grim.

"Yeah? Like what?" said Mike.

"It's over, guys," said Frank, his voice half resigned, half irritated.

Through all this, Jillian had not spoken either by way of explanation or defense. She stomped slowly down the stairs and shouldered past her brothers. Then she continued right off the stage and out of the schoolroom. After a brief, silent showdown between the two sets of brothers, Wayne and Mike also left the stage and the room.

I sighed. Occasionally over the years, filial ties had drawn lines through the family. Sometimes it was between my family, the Dunns, and the Quills or the Reinharts and the Deters, but most often the conflict was between the Deters and the five Quill brothers. Jillian was often the spark. The scene that had just played out was mild, but it was capable of pulling back all the other battles, all the other confrontations from over the years, and escalating into something more terrifying than what Andy faced.

I feared that the dislike I saw in Wayne's and Mike's eyes would eventually have enough history behind it to blossom into hatred. But where would we put hatred in our crowded underground world? There was no place for it to hide down here, no way for it to dissipate. I worried, though, that the minor conflicts that every family, every community suffered would have more than sufficient space to heat up, boil, and overflow like a volcano . . . or a nuclear explosion. Was there really a way for us to hide from the world destruction? Or were we simply carrying on our own quiet explosions out of sight below the surface of the rest of the world?

I thought about that awhile. The shelter was a technological "safe place," nothing more. If what we wanted to preserve was the art, history, and accouterments of the society we had left behind, this was the perfect facility. But our home-grown vegetables, even stored in the perfect root cellar wouldn't hold produce much longer than one winter. We came into the shelter with our faded sheets, our favorite books, the odd but precious things handed down to us. We also came down with all the foibles and failures of our personalities, all the stresses and jealousies and petty snits. As a root crop, we were pretty delicate. Left to ourselves, maybe we didn't have the storage capability to last the winter. A potato was more durable. What would it take to make us fireside apples or hubbard squash?

There had been no selection process to weed out the spoiled fruit from the sound, either. Our only criterion for who was to come into the shelter was that we wanted to protect our family. What did that mean? Were we of such sound stock and righteous upbringing that each of us was the best example of humanity we could be? I sure didn't feel that charitable even towards myself that morning. I felt spiteful, grumpy and fat. I was angry at Jeannie and none too pleased with Lori either. Frank didn't figure high on my list of empathetic people after the way he had awakened me, and I was not particularly looking forward to a soap-opera succession of squabbles between the Deters and the elder Quill brothers. How was all this supposed to work?

Maybe we should have taken some sort of a compatibility test before locking ourselves away together. Someone—Frank or Harris or . . . someone—should have told us to watch out, think about what we were doing before coming into such close quarters together. We would be rubbing up against each other with no way to get away or cool off; we'd rub ourselves raw.

The idea of life in the Ark seemed totally futile to me at that moment. I couldn't imagine how I had let things go so far as to pretend that I wanted to live like this. There was no way it was going to work with the people we had in our extended family. How long would it be before the dislike that existed between any two of us would escalate beyond anything we could control as we tried to in our separate, busy, "outside" lives?

I sat in the schoolroom long after everyone else had left, sat and pondered in circles until the circles closed in on me, and I found myself weeping silently. The tears seemed to wash me empty—empty of thought, of feeling, even, for the moment, of caring. I sat in the schoolroom until Andrea came to me asking for something to eat.

I looked at her round, cherub face framed in dark curls. In her innocent eyes I saw something I had been missing in my wandering, circling thoughts. It wasn't just for ourselves that we had come into the shelter; it was also for the children. Whatever we had to endure made so much more sense if done for our children than simply for ourselves. For Beth and Andrea, I would even learn to get along with Jeannie. Maybe that's what I had to hold onto, to keep fixed in my mind. The day began to look a little more livable.

6
WAITING

―――――――――

No one took charge of breakfast or, later, lunch. After Jeannie's comments, I sure wasn't going to run things just so she could criticize me. I was a nurse, not a cook. Let someone else take over kitchen duties. At lunchtime, I made sure my girls had a sandwich each and some milk. The kitchen was, of course, a huge mess. Again. This time it involved honey. While I was busy with my lunch, Marie Deters came in looking for food for her kids. I showed her where the peanut butter was.

"I sure hope they don't get into it down here."

I assumed by "they," Marie referred to the Deters and the Quills. "Yeah, me, too," I said. Marie, a gentle, pretty woman with soft, curly hair and a trim figure, was hard to read sometimes. She could be a Deters and side unilaterally with her husband, Mike, or she could take a kind of us-against-them women's position, which linked her with me. But even when she did this, I was careful; she could switch sides at a moment's notice.

"Do you know what the fight was about?" I asked, hoping Marie had toggled to the women's mode just then. I liked her a whole lot more when she allied with the rest of the wives than when she sided with the Deters.

"Mike didn't exactly say," she told me. "Something about going for Gertz's cattle, I think. Jillian objected. At least that's what she told Mike."

I nodded and got the milk out for her. Suddenly Marie faced me and put her hands on my shoulders. Her hazel eyes bore into mine. "Barby . . ." she said, then hesitated.

"What is it, Marie?"

She turned and leaned on the counter, near tears. "We have to make this work. We can't let them fight."

My fears weren't solitary musings, then. I rested a hand on her arm. "Yes. We have to make this work. We also have to be patient. I feel maybe when Andy, Bob, and Linda get here, we can settle in. Everyone's so tense with them out there . . . and maybe in great danger. Jillian's furious that Sue and Peter didn't come. But there isn't one of us who isn't worried, grieving or just plain scared. It's going to take time to overcome that."

Marie sighed, tears slowly spilling down her cheeks. "I know. I know."

"With everyone so upset, tempers are brittle."

She nodded, her gaze sliding around the messy kitchen. "When I'm depressed, cleaning sometimes helps. This mess might be just what we need."

She rolled up her sleeves and began to run dishwater. My heart sank. I knew I was going to help her. I saw no clear way out of it. And it wasn't as if I minded, exactly; it was just that I knew I'd end up with a sore back, aching feet, and another label I maybe didn't want. It had been too easy to be labeled a cook after helping with a couple meals. But Marie seemed fragile, and I felt a need to build ties where I could. If many small dislikes could blend into hatred, well, maybe a number of small kindnesses could grow into something just the opposite, something from which we could build trust and cooperation and love between those of us who hadn't really explored those possibilities before.

It was when I lifting yet another plate from the dishwasher almost an hour later that I noticed the bruises on Marie's upper arms. Just above her elbows and rolled-up sleeves on each arm was a darkened purplish circle.

"Marie . . . how did you bruise your arms like that?"

She quickly tugged her sleeves down, getting soap on them in the process. "Bruises? Oh, those! I was lifting a box to one of my high shelves, and it slipped. The bruises don't even hurt anymore."

"There are some step ladders in the pantry. I saw them yesterday."

"That's good to know," said Marie with a smile. "I'll get one next time I need something out of that box. Thanks."

Except for her nonchalant attitude, the situation seemed off. The kinds of marks I'd seen were consistent with abuse. But I knew Marie had some calcium absorption issues, and that could account for easy bruising. And I didn't want to upset Marie.

By LATE AFTERNOON, the waiting for Andy was getting to everyone. Wayne and Harris exchanged words and stalked off, Harris to the radio room, Wayne to his slice. Jeannie stayed away from all of us. DeeDee tried reading to a group of little kids, but she couldn't keep them from fighting for more than a couple minutes at a time. Jillian came into the cafeteria once, drunk and loud, then retreated to her slice.

Tempers were fragile at best. Mom Quill, usually a paragon of patience, snapped at her grandchildren like a bitter old fish wife. Kids squabbled whenever two came together, and not one couple, including Frank and me, could maintain pleasant humors with each other. It was as if all the places in all the relationships that could break down easily were buckling under the tension of the waiting. Frank and I had a spat about money—money!—as if that mattered anymore.

By seven-thirty, when we figured Andy was likely to start to think about leaving the Blue Concourse men's room, the tension became palpable. The men had wired the donut so that everyone could hear if Andy called in. I had herded Beth and Andrea to bed about then and lay down on the double bed to listen. The donut settled into quiet; all the children sent off to their beds. Yet, the quiet was not peace. It was as if I could feel all the eyes of all the relatives staring up at the ceiling, hear all the ears straining for word that Andy's group was safe, feel all the tension in the shelter like sandpaper against my skin.

At eight o'clock, the radio crackled. Both Beth and Andrea, whom I thought for sure had fallen asleep, leaned up and looked to the curtain. I sat up. Andy's voice filled the silence briefly. "Here we go, folks. Wish us luck."

After a brief pause, we heard Harris's choked voice say, "Luck."

I lay back down. Andy had survived the day at least. I tried to calculate how long it would take a helicopter to fly from St. Paul to where we were. I could drive to the airport in about two hours. Maybe it was an hour by air. But that didn't get them to the helicopter. As Andy had said, once they were airborne, there shouldn't be much of a problem. It was that race from the concourse to wherever the helicopter was hidden that would be really risky. What if the helicopter was gone? What if the pilot was killed as they tried to get to the aircraft?

"Mom?"

I looked up at Beth.

"Mom, can Andrea come up on my bunk with me?"

I heard the tremor in her voice and looked at Andrea, who sat almost huddled in her bunk, her big brown eyes huge with baby concern. "Do you want to, sweetie?"

The frightened stare eased. "Yes. Sure!"

"Okay," I said, moving over to help her climb the ladder to the upper bunk. "Snuggle down together. Andrea, you stay near the rail, not the back. Try to keep real still and go to sleep. I don't think Uncle Andy is going to get here much before morning. No point in waiting up."

"It's pretty awful out there, isn't it?" Beth whispered as she settled her little sister in next to her.

"Right now it seems to be. Don't worry. It'll get better. Soon, too, I hope."

Whether she believed me or not, I didn't know. She lay down with Andrea and said no more. I couldn't separate her tension from the rest weighing in on me. I felt as if I were under water, drowning slowly, gulp by gulp.

I FELL ASLEEP SOME TIME NEAR MIDNIGHT. I woke with a start, looked at the travel clock and sat up. Four-thirty. Frank was not in our slice, hadn't been in at all, I thought. I listened. Nothing. I got up and slipped out of the curtain.

The donut was deserted, and the bathroom was quiet except for a dripping faucet. I peeked into the cafeteria, but the lights in there had been turned off. I headed to the schoolroom. James sat in the second row, his feet propped up on the chair ahead of him, sound asleep. I climbed the steps to the stage and walked to the base of the spiral stairs. Looking around as I tried to decide if I wanted to climb those steep stairs, I noticed the wall phone at the back of the stage. I walked over and lifted the receiver from its cradle. After a moment just holding it in my hand, I slowly brought it to my ear.

I don't know what I expected to hear, wanted to hear, whether the sound of the dial tone would bring comfort or tension, or if no sound would elicit fear. I do know it was hard to listen. With the receiver at my ear, I actually heard a typical dial tone and knew then that it made me glad. The world lay outside still. I replaced the receiver on the unit and walked back to the base of the stairs.

I could just make out the murmur of voices coming from above. With care and a hand on each rail, I ascended round and round until I came to a room above the stage. At the far end of the room, which was very similar to the schoolroom in size, a tight knot of people sat in front of the radio, which I could tell was more sophisticated than a ham or short wave. It had a kind of NASA look to it. Harris, Frank, my brother, Marty, Don and Dewey Reinhart, and Grandpa Quill huddled together. Harris's hand was keyed to the mike. I expect he'd had his hand ready for hours to answer Andy's call.

Frank turned as I reached his chair. "You should be sleeping, Barb," he said. His tone was soft and reassuring. I instantly saw him hovering over me, a baby bottle in hand, taking a late night feeding to one of our daughters when they were small and I was exhausted. There was so much warmth and love in that tone.

"Andy okay?" I asked.

"No word. We'll wait up. You sleep. When they get here, we'll all need to crash."

I gave him a kiss and squeezed his hand. "Okay. I don't want the girls to wake up alone. Wake me if he arrives."

"Watch yourself on those stairs," Marty said as I turned to go.

"I'm a big girl," I said with typical older-sister hautiness but grinned when I met his eyes. Ever since he had first equaled my height in high school, he had taken on the role of big brother even though he was two years younger than I was. And he made such a nice big brother that we just left the arrangement that way. For me it was a way to make light of the fact that our dad always described Marty as his "first-born son," as if Emily and I didn't really count because we were girls. As a little girl, this unfeeling description—truthful though it was—had stung painfully many times; maybe it had hurt Emily, too. I didn't know. She never confided in me. I had often taken out my anger and frustration on Marty because of my feelings. Then he grew too big to beat up. That was when, between us, we came to an understanding of our father's limited outlook and realized what good friends we were despite him. My confidence improved after that time.

Going down the steep spiral stairs was not as easy as going up. After a few steps, I turned around and backed down as if on a ladder. I bumped into Jillian at the bottom.

"Ouch! Damn it, Barby, why are you doing it like that? That's the stupidest way to come down stairs I ever saw."

She was drunk. I could see it in her bleary eyes and the way she weaved in place. "You obviously don't remember being eight months pregnant then," I said and walked past her.

She huffed a laugh and muttered just loud enough for me to hear, "I was never a whale, not even the day before I delivered."

I should have been livid, and I was hurt, but I had this vivid picture of her a few days before she went to the hospital with Harry, Jr. She might not have been a whale exactly, but she got stuck in the couch, two easy chairs, and couldn't get into the driver's seat of her Porche. She needed help any time she sat down. At least I was still moving.

I turned at the door and saw her stumble and curse her way up the stairs to the radio room. I was grateful to be on my way out.

The girls still slept when I lifted the curtain of our slice. I sat on the bed and closed my eyes, trying not to think too hard about Andy and the relatives with him. I looked at the girls asleep side by side on Beth's upper bunk. They looked very comfortable. When had society decided that all little children needed beds of their own? It wasn't that many years past when two, three, and even four little children had to share a bed together. Was that so bad? If the girls were content to sleep together in the upper bunk, we could put the new baby in the lower one. That way, our slice would not be further crowded by a crib or trundle bed. All the baby's diapers and little clothes could fit on the foot of the lower bunk. It would save a lot of space.

The baby. Suddenly, I realized that I couldn't feel the baby moving. My hands flew to my belly as panic surged through me. When was the last time I had felt it move? I couldn't remember. Last night? Yesterday morning? I lay down and tried to wait for the movement that almost always came when I abruptly changed postions. Nothing. Panic climbed to my throat, creating sobs and choking me at the same time. With the difficulty of the move and the tension, had something happened to the baby? Had I stressed it in some way? I covered my mouth with shaking hands, trying desperately to hold the tide of panic back. A new wave of fear hit me when I realized that I couldn't picture myself with the baby in my arms. I had been able to picture Beth almost from the moment I knew I was pregnant. Andrea within a month. Why couldn't I picture this baby in my arms? Now I was sure something was wrong.

"Barby?"

I jumped.

"Barby, it's me. Connie. Are you all right?"

Before I could answer the whispered inquiry, Connie poked her head in at the curtain. I struggled to sit up, my hand still pressed to my mouth.

Connie came in and sat at the edge of the bed. "What is it, Barb?" she said with a quick glance at the peaceful girls.

I shook my head. In a way, I couldn't express what I was feeling; in a way, I was afraid of trying, afraid that words would breach the dam with no way to staunch the flood I could feel ready to burst behind the hand pressed to my mouth. I didn't meet her eyes.

Connie was beginning to look concerned. "Do you want me to get Frank?"

"No," I said quickly. Frank couldn't help, and he had his own heavy concerns right now. He'd just get Marty to examine me. All well and good. Marty was a fine general practitioner. But inside of twenty minutes everyone would know that Barb had lost it, had gotten all upset because she couldn't picture her baby in her arms. That sounded so lame. And, anyway, Marty's "privileged information" just didn't extend to his family, especially his older sister, the one who was supposed to have her act together. "No. I don't need Frank. I'm fine. Um . . . a little tired is all."

Connie didn't move. I had hoped she would go back to her slice. She didn't say anything, but her soft, slightly pudgy hand sought mine and squeezed it. I looked into her face then, intending just to smile bravely, thank her for her needless concern and say good-night. But I saw something in her face I hadn't expected. Understanding.

Connie was a sweet, gentle woman who put up with a lot with Marty's erratic country-doctor schedule. She stood shorter than I, and though certainly not fat, her figure had rounded with children and time. She had spent many nights alone, including the night her first child was born, because Marty was away helping someone else. Jillian thought Connie was a pushover, a sponge that absorbed difficulties mindlessly. I had given her more credit than that, figuring she loved Marty enough to put up with the life of a doctor's wife. But what I saw in Connie's eyes just then was not long-suffering acceptance, not mindless sympathy for whatever troubled me; what I saw was a real knowledge of what I was feeling. The little bit of composure I had regained evaporated instantly, and I drew in a quick breath.

Connie's hand slipped to my belly. "Do you remember when Marty and I moved to Hibbing?" she said, keeping her voice low so as not to wake the girls.

I swallowed. "It was the summer Cookie was born."

"That's right. I was six weeks to delivery. It was also six months after my dad had died and nine weeks after my mother's funeral. Marty was just out of residency. He went ahead to Hibbing to find us a house, while I packed up our apartment in Minneapolis. I also had to sort through my mother's things in Burnsville, garage sale what we couldn't keep and box up the rest."

I nodded. "I had forgotten all that. It must have been hard for you."

She coughed a soft laugh. "Hard? It was impossible!" She looked quickly at the girls, afraid she had awakened them. When they didn't move, she said in a lowered voice, "I had no brothers or sisters, no aunts or uncles living . . . it was like all my connections in the world had been severed when my parents died. There was nothing that stood between me and eternity anymore, no one to keep me from . . . flying off into space. My parents and I had been really close. Then Dad died, but Mom was so looking forward to the baby we just continued with our plans for her to come stay with us when it came, only permanently stay. But, suddenly, everything changed. My mother would never have a chance to see her grandchild. The position in Hibbing came through, and we had to move. I had never even been to Hibbing. I felt as if I were moving to the moon . . . alone. I felt so utterly and completely alone.

"Well, one afternoon I was packing up dishes—my mother's and my own— and it suddenly struck me that I hadn't even thought about the baby in days. And then I couldn't feel it move. I panicked. Dropped Mom's Christmas platter and broke it into a million pieces. Mrs. Jenkins, from next door, came in and helped me sweep it up. Then she sat me down and read me the riot act."

"Riot act?" I said. "Are you talking about the same Mrs. Jenkins who was about a hundred fifty years old? The one who was maybe three-foot-nine?"

Connie giggled. "Yup! *That* Mrs. Jenkins. High school teacher in a former lifetime, she used to say, before she married Hal. She was more likely a drill sergeant in a previous existence or a general. Anyway, she sat me down and told me to stop feeling sorry for myself. Her Hal had been a doctor in the thirties up through the sixties. Mrs. Jenkins said the job of a doctor's wife was one of the hardest and most important in the world. The important part . . . I don't know; the hard part I believed even then. Then I told her I couldn't feel the baby moving and thought maybe it had died. She dismissed that as nonsense with a snort. She gave me a glass of cold water to drink. I drank it, and, in a couple of minutes, the baby moved."

"Seems she was a pretty level-headed old lady," I said.

"She was that." Connie smiled with memories. "Especially since she knew what really was worrying me. I think maybe it's the same thing you're worried about. I was near enough to delivery that I had gotten past being afraid of that. I was fat and clumsy and hot. I was tired of being pregnant, eager to get on with it, ready to go through *anything* just so I could have my body back. And, before my mother had died, I had been planning what it would be like to have a little bitty baby to care for. I had spent hours sitting in the rocking chair pretending I had a cute little baby in my arms. What really scared me in the apartment that day was that I could no longer picture that baby in my arms. Dear Mrs. Jenkins saw that."

"A glass of water won't fix that for me," I whispered, tears coming to my eyes.

"No . . . but maybe this will . . ." and Connie crooked her left arm as if a baby was snuggled against her breast. She began to rock gently as she sat on the edge of the bed and started to hum.

I watched her, half-embarrassed by being witness to such silliness among adult women, half-mesmerized by the rhythm and authenticity of her actions. She smoothed an imaginary blanket and kissed an imaginary head, until, like watching a mime pushing against an unseen wall, I began to see what was not there. Then Connie reached over and placed the baby in my arms.

Without any practice—or, should I say, with the practice of two children behind me—my arms folded around the infant in just the way her arms had. But it wasn't emptiness I cradled; it *was* a baby, the *idea* of the baby within me. All the hopes and expectations flooded back into me and pushed back the panic, washed it away with my tears.

Connie hugged my shoulders. "When things get really hard, as they were for me that summer and now for us all, it's hard to believe in something so wonderful as a newborn child. The thing is, we *have* to believe. Belief in the everyday miracles is the first best way to get through these hard times and trust in the bigger miracles—like maybe we can get through this in one piece. Those are about the exact words Mrs. Jenkins used, too, though she wasn't facing the end of the world. I don't think it matters if it's the unknown we're staring down or something known, like the grief and trepidation I was feeling then, or the cancer Mrs. Jenkins was facing. We have to hold out hope for the small miracles and not worry about the big ones. We're not responsible for them anyway."

I had misjudged Connie. I had missed the strength within her disguised as simplicity and gentleness. I saw for the first time in the six years I had known her how powerfully she lived her life. I was more grateful to her just then than to anyone else in my life, but all I could do was hug her and whisper a tearful thanks into her ear.

Her expression told me it was all she had been able to do in thanks to Mrs. Jenkins, and that maybe passing on this insight was part of the obligation incurred.

Connie left soon after, and I lay down to sleep. The baby started kicking then as if rejuvinated by the surges in my emotions. It kicked and wiggled and did flips for almost two hours before it settled down again. It kept me awake the whole time, but I didn't mind. I enjoyed that small miracle all I could that night. When the baby stopped its gymnastics enough for me to slip into sleep, my dreams were filled with miracles—wild fanatastic ones, like the world waking up to peace. Near six-thirty I roused enough to go to the bathroom and return to bed. The girls still slept. I tried really hard not to think; this time I was successful and fell back asleep.

7

DAY THREE

SATURDAY, OCTOBER 12

I WOKE FROM A WONDERFUL DREAM of tending the garden among my tuberoses and lupines. It was one of those bright, color-filled dreams that sooths the soul and makes one smile upon awakening. I wondered if the sky was Minnesota blue this morning or overcast with autumn storms. And, still within the aura of the pleasant dream, instead of fussing about the limitations of our new existence, I tried to picture the day outside, picture it and make it pleasant, even if, in reality, it was not. I saw the boundless blue of a perfect autumn sky and the sun sparkling across the frosted fields of our little farm outside St. Joseph. The big willow tree blew gently in the breeze and the picket fence was as straight as an arrow and sparkling with a new coat of paint. It was a scene I wanted to hold with me always. Then thoughts of Andy intruded, clouding the sky of my perfect world and washing it of all color.

The travel clock showed me it was only eight-thirty. I knew I should try for more sleep if I could, but I figured both that thoughts of Andy would prevent it and that I could get a nap in later. I slowly eased myself up.

Frank was curled into the lower bunk. At first my thoughts blossomed with the idea that he had sought sleep because Andy had safely arrived, and the shelter's company was complete, but, as I studied his face, I saw no peace in it, even in sleep. I did not believe Andy had come. Frank simply had succombed to exhaustion. I sighed and worked my way to my feet.

The girls still snuggled together in the bed above Frank as I drew aside the curtain. Though no children played in the donut, I could hear that some had awakened. A child cried. It sounded like Charleen Fisk or maybe little Gert Reinhart. But it wasn't a hurt cry, just fussiness. I headed in the opposite direction, toward the bathroom.

Though I had washed up each day at the sinks and given each of the girls a face-cloth bath before bed, I felt the need for a real shower. Beyond the four toilet stalls, I found a small dressing room and doors that led to two shower stalls and two tubs, each in a narrow cubicle with a curtain as a door. Two showers?

I had only come into the bathroom basically on emergency missions to relieve my bladder. Now I took the time to inventory the space. Four toilets, two sinks, two washers and dryers, and the skimpy bathing facilities. Suddenly this all seemed woefully inadequate. Fifteen families needed a lot of bathing and washing of clothes. True the kids weren't playing outside, but there was plenty of muck and smell to be had in the animal room. How were we going to keep our bodies and clothes clean? And more family members were coming. Had no one given this any thought? Could there be another bathroom somewhere I didn't know about?

A man's pants and sweatshirt lay on the corner of the bench outside one shower, but I couldn't tell whose clothes they were. I felt a little uncomfortable about disrobing with one of the men showering, but then I realized that we likely were going to live together for a long time, and I better get used to sharing space and privacy. I peeked into the unused shower and saw that there was a tiny anteroom where I could hang my towel and clothes if I wished. They might get a bit damp from steam, but I would have the privacy I wanted. I entered and pulled the curtain closed.

I took a quick shower and slipped into one of my three enormous house-dresses, which were about all that still fit comfortably. When I came out, the men's clothes were gone from the bench, but the other shower still ran, and steam rolled from under the curtain. I thought maybe my companion had heard my water start and taken the pants and sweatshirt into his anteroom; wet footprints confirmed this.

Thoughts of Andy made me too nervous to want any coffee, so I skirted the kitchen without a glance inside and went directly to the classroom. Just as I reached the wide-open double doors but, thankfully, before I entered the room and got in his way, James Quill ran out, his eyes wild. I jumped back, protective of my protruding belly. He saw me and broke into a wide grin.

"He's here!" James shouted. "I just heard him on the intercom! Andy's here!"

With that, James ran out into the donut area, shouting out his news loudly enough to wake everyone. He swung himself around one of the center columns and clicked his heels for good measure. My heart soared on James's enthusiasm.

It's impossible to know how deeply one has been affected by tension until that tension is removed. I felt lifted on relief. Even with my belly, I could almost dance a jig. Tension and worry had been incredibly heavy burdens, yet even tremendous joy weighed nothing at all.

Marie and Jeannie Deters came out of their slices asking questions. Marty and Connie were laughing and hugging each other. Mike and Wayne grabbed James and made him repeat his announcement.

"Well, come on then!" said Mike, like Bob Barker on reruns of *The Price Is Right.* "Let's go welcome him in!"

He and Wayne, followed by the swelling group of relatives, trooped to the stairs. Children skipped ahead. Everyone was shouting and laughing and crying all at once. I followed when Beth and Andrea, in nightgowns, joined the parade.

As we began to cross the floor, Frank stuck a sleepy head out the curtain of our slice. "Barb! Hey, what's happening?"

"James heard Andy on the intercom. He's right outside!"

"What intercom? The only intercom is in the woodroom. Andy knows not to go there. Where's everyone going?" Frank's eyes opened wide. "They're not going to open the woodroom, are they?"

"Well . . . I don't know," I said. "I guess so. Where should Andy be, then?"

"Wait for me," Frank said, ducking back inside.

I heard boxes scrape the floor as he dug for pants and a shirt. Something hit the floor. "Damn!" he said, his voice muffled by the curtain. "Who else was on the radio? Harr—rriss—ss!" This last was bellowed loud enough to flutter the curtain.

Harris came out of the showers just then, his sweatshirt quickly soaking through from not toweling himself before dressing; his dripping hair had already darkened his neck ribbing. "What the hell is going on?" he demanded. He blinked at Frank through steamy glasses. "Sounded like the roof fell in. What gives?"

"Who was supposed to be monitoring the short wave?"

"James and me," came a voice from behind us.

We all swung around. Donald Reinhart strode through the classroom toward us. He looked more than irritated, maybe a little sheepish too.

"It's not Andy. I . . . I thought it was at first and told James to get you, Harris, but . . . it's not Andy."

"What do you mean?" Harris glared. "Who was on our frequency?"

"No . . . not on the radio. Someone used the woodroom intercom. I thought it had to be Andy, so I sent James. But I talked to the guy . . . and it's not Andy."

"Shit!" said Frank with a meaning as much dread as disappointment.

He and Harris exchanged horrified glances, then broke into a run for the stairs. Donald started after them, but Harris turned at the bottom step and shouted, "No, Don! Get back up to the radio room. Andy could call any time. Someone has to be there. Don't leave your post!"

I stood in the middle of the floor with Beth and Andrea while the men ran off in opposite directions. My joy evaporated as the realization that it had been premature began to sink in. I watched Donald circle up the stairs and, with a mental thud, knew we were still on hold, still waiting for our company to become complete.

The heavy steel door at the top of the stairs clanged shut. I spun to stare at it, suddenly realizing that, if it wasn't Andy in the woodroom, it was someone else. At the same time that fear clutched at my heart, a kind of territorial anger began to brew. I headed for the stairs leading to the long sloping hallway, my pace lengthening and quickening as concern and threat vied for position. The girls ran with me.

I slowed a little on the stairs and, at the top, had to tug hard to get the heavy steel door opened, but finally we were in the hall. Before the door closed, I stopped and hugged my girls against the wall. Something had gone very wrong.

Angry shouting, children screaming, and the heavy sounds of a large scuffle filled the dimly lit passage. I could distinguish no voices or individuals from the racket and mass of movement at the end of the long, shadowy hall, nor do more than shelter my babies with my arms. For a long, panicked moment, I could do nothing, think nothing, nor respond to what I saw and felt. The noise and confusion and uncertain danger were beginning to overwhelm me when a single blast of a gun cleared away everything except the need to protect my children. With the numbing echo of that shot still clogging my ears, I backed quickly into the shelter, paused on the landing just a moment, then herded Beth and Andrea, who were both upset, down the stairs.

Andrea was crying, and Beth asked repeatedly what was going on. I made— could make—no response. I took them into our slice and stood behind the curtain, my heart thumping in my throat. An eternity of minutes followed, time when my brain ran reckless with horrible scenarios of what could have, might have, must not have happened at the end of the hall. Each passing moment was a torture I thought I could not abide, then endured. Moment after moment after moment.

The heavy steel door at the top of the stairs banged against the railing. I jumped and peeked over the edge of the curtain. I thought at first the battle was approaching because a mob of people flooded in and shouted, ordered, reprimanded, and cried down the stairs. But I saw Jeannie, Connie, Wayne, Harry, Jr.—one by one, the mass resolved into the people I knew. Frank appeared at the top of the stairs, held the door and waited. A few moments later, Harris came in. Then Frank let go the door and began to follow his brother down the stairs.

Harris stopped midway down and shouted out, "Everyone to the classroom! Now! I have a few things to say! No exceptions!"

EVERYONE, EXCEPT DONALD Reinhart and Harris, were in the classroom when the girls and I came in. I could get no clear idea from anyone as to what happened. Connie was crying. Jeannie was unresponsive, and Marty said, "Damn fools!" over and over, but nothing more. I didn't know if he was referring to the people in the woodroom or us. I could get nowhere near Frank. He stood near the stage with the two Deters men and James. They were gesturing wildly, arguing loudly, but I couldn't piece together their abbreviated sentences to figure out what had happened.

Harry, Jr., appeared at my elbow and said through a handkerchief, "Do you have some tissues, Aunt Barb?"

His nose was bleeding, and the polyester handkerchief was not doing a good job of absorbing the flow. I immediately sent Beth to the lunchroom for tissues, sat Harry down and tilted his head back to see how badly he was hurt. Harry wasn't exactly a frail child, but he was subject to sniffles, allergies, and nosebleeds. This incident seemed to have been the result of an injury, however, as his left eye was darkening and the bridge of his nose had swelled.

"What happened, Harry?" I said, almost pleading.

"Some guys tried to break in. Uncle Mike shot one. The rest took off."

I was disgusted almost to the point of retching. I had to close my eyes and breathe deeply, then forced myself to ask, "Mike didn't . . . *kill* the man, did he?"

"Naw, it was just a flesh wound."

I almost laughed, even upset as I was, at Harry's cop-movie assessment. As a nurse, I had see lots of flesh wounds, especially at Hennepin County Medical Center when I was doing my emergency room stint. Knifings and shootings in the drug districts accounted for a nightly parade of flesh wounds, all of which bled profusely and were often excruciatingly painful. Such injuries might not be directly life-threatening with modern medicine, but the healing and rehabilitation a person had to endure could span months. A direct, penetrating wound—untreated—was serious and possibly life-threatening. We had no way of knowing if help was available to that man on the outside.

The idea that one of us was able and willing to shoot another human being for possession of the shelter truly appalled me. Even though, just minutes before, I had sweated out the possibility that the place could be taken from us and fervently hoped that would not happen, I was dismayed that we had come to shooting someone, and so soon. We had to do better.

"How did you get the bloody nose?" I asked Harry, Jr., quietly.

"I ran into the door just as Uncle James was opening it. I think those guys pushed it in when he got it unlocked."

Before I could pump Harry, Jr., for details, Harris came into the room from backstage. He was dressed in dry clothes and had a cordless microphone in his hands.

"Sit down, please," he said, and his magnified voice blanketed the noise. Not everyone actually took seats, but attentions were focused on Harris, and the din subsided.

"We have to establish a few ground rules around here," he said forcefully, "and the first one is to never, *never* leave this complex without notifying someone who knows how things work."

"You, then," frowned Mike.

"Me or Frank. Yes, that's right. Andy would *never* go to the woodroom. His instructions specifically direct him to the secondary entrance—"

"Just how many goddamn entrances are there?" Wayne said.

"Four," said Harris, with what I thought was a trace of reluctance, "but two are mostly escapes for us . . . if we need them. Anyway, don't go wandering around this place looking for them. No child should leave the main complex—the habitation silo, the bathroom, schoolroom, and the lunchroom of the kitchen complex—unless with an adult. No adult shall go beyond the kitchens, pantries, vegetable room, hospital, or animal room without authorization. This place is just too damn big to wander without knowing what you're about. And going outside is the biggest danger of all from here on out. I want you all to understand that."

"Just what the hell *is* happening outside?" demanded Emily.

Harris looked at her, considering what to say. "All right," he said quietly, "I'll tell you what I know. Mexico invaded Texas. It's getting rough down there. There've been at least two nuclear exchanges between China and Cambodia. North Korea has been threatened by the Chinese, too. The Middle East is too hot to know much about—"

"What does that mean?" Wayne said.

"Lots of fighting from some reports; no confirmation of any further nuclear explosions since the first few but a high likelihood that more have fallen."

"How do you know all this?" Connie said.

"For the last eight years—yes, that's even before the shelter got started—I've been setting up a complex radio network with operators around the world. We use both ham and short wave, as well as Internet, as well as land lines."

"You have phones in here?" Wayne asked.

Harris forstalled complications by immediately saying, "Coming in, yes. The phone's right over there at the back of the stage." He pointed to the small wall-mounted black phone I had found. "But you can't call out on it. See, I figure that's traceable, and we sure don't want to be traced. But its my old number, and should someone specifically call *me*—really though, I just thought we needed to know if the phone lines went down. The other communication systems are far more important. There are fifteen hundred ham, shortwave radio and Internet contacts who converse with us around the world; two hundred or so have shelters of varying degrees of complexity."

"Shelters like ours?" DeeDee asked.

Harris nodded. "A few. We've shared ideas and concepts. Some were incorporated as we were building this. Of course, there are those folks out in Utah and east Washington State that have complexes that make this seem like a rustic cottage in the woods by comparison, but we've got all the important stuff—the air systems, back-up power, protected water, and about twenty years worth of supplies—"

"Twenty years?" I said, this knowledge more frightening than comforting. "Are you saying—"

"No, Barb," said Harris firmly, "but *if* we have to, we could."

"How long do you *think* we'll be in here?" I asked.

69

Harris ran a hand through his damp hair and stared at me with exasperation all over his face. The room had gone quiet. He let the mike down and said, "I have no idea. I hope not more than one year and pray not more than five, but if the planet gets too hot, it could be a lot longer than that . . . it could be . . . forever."

Numbness crept through my arms and legs, and I sat heavily.

"But you said we had supplies for twenty years," DeeDee said, her voice a little high, and her words running together. "Twenty years. Twenty years isn't forever. How can we live here forever, Harris? How?"

He held up his hand, palm open and pushed down air several times in a "wait" and "be patient" gesture. "If the worst happens, and it becomes a nuclear or biochemical winter out there," Harris said, "we have the capability within the shelter to grow our own food . . . with hydroponics. According to my figures and the equipment we have—some of which I got from those crazy folks in Utah who live in a mountain—we could support two hundred people here indefinitely."

He let that sink in—and it was a little like oil mixing with water—then said, "But every time we break security, we risk *everything!* There has to be some order After we get Andy here, we'll start posting jobs and schedules."

"Schedules?" Paul Fisk said. "What kind of—"

The microphone again was at Harris's lips. His voice boomed. "We have to stop thinking of ourselves as little units and start acting like *one* unit. You may have wondered why there are no private rooms for families, or, if we had to live together in this hall, why the slices are made only of canvas. There's a very good reason for—"

"Harris! You guys up yet?"

It was Andy, loud and clear on the speaker system. Don Reinhard answered, "You bet, cuz! Where are you?"

Harris and Frank ran for the spiral stairs. "The rest of you stay down here," shouted Frank.

"Well," Andy said, "don't exactly know. I think we might be as far as Elk River, maybe Big Lake if we're lucky."

"So, you'll be here in an hour maybe," Harris's voice said.

"An hour? Cute. If we had the chopper we might be able to get there in an hour. No chopper."

"What do you mean?" Harris said.

"Well, it met with an accident, you might say," Andy said. "Dean did all right by us, big brother, once he sobered up, that is. We just ran into a little bad luck. That big explosion when the 747 did a nose dive . . . well it wiped out one of the two choppers Dean had stashed; the other was just lifting off when we got to it. I almost shot it down I was so pissed. Anyway, what we have is a couple of ornery horses and a wagon. Nineteenth-century stuff. Got them off that old-timey museum farm on Highway 10. That's when we knew we'd gone too far north. We've taken backroads since. We're not sure where we are. We're beginning to have respect for the folks who settled this country, though. It's a damn bumpy long ride, and we even have paved roads."

"But are you guys okay?"

"Oh, sure. We haven't seen more than a dozen people since we left Highway 10. We keep moving when we see someone, but, so far, no one's bothered us, not even when we took the horses and wagon. Food and water are going to be a problem from here on out, though. We figure we're about three days away from you, what with this team and wagon. Any suggestions?"

"Can't you find something faster?"

"We'll keep trying. Every now and then we get a glimpse of I-94. All six lanes are bumber to bumber heading west, but it's moving pretty slowly down there. It'd take us a week to reach you even if we had a Corvette. Some people gave up, it looks like, abandoned their cars and headed out on foot. And there's shooting down there. I kinda figure we're safer away from the highways. With so many people on the move, vehicles are not exactly parked on the side of the road unless they're belly up."

"Six lanes of cars belly up? That can't be."

"Well, some are grid-locked in so tight, a traffic cop'd need a week to sort it out. Some cars are just boxed in and abandoned. Doesn't take much to grid-lock a highway, you know. But some cars are still moving."

"What have you got for food?"

"We chewed field corn this morning and got water from an outside house faucet. I figure we'll have to do that the whole way up. Last night was chilly, too. So far, it's warming up real well, but this morning there was ice on a pond we passed. We might have to break into a farmhouse and hole up a day or two if the weather gets too bad. Our wagon doesn't have a cover. I have no idea if people are still living in the farms we pass. I expect some are. I also expect they're well armed. But there are enough really abandoned houses what with the banks foreclosing so many farms. I doubt anyone still hangs around some of the really old places we've seen."

"Sounds risky."

"In a word. But the highways are worse. There's more shooting down there then here in the boonies. We voted and decided to do it this way. I'll call you every morning at ten or around then when I find a high enough hill."

"If we knew where you were, we could come and get you," Donald said.

"Heh, heh," said Andy. "Now you don't want to be doing that, cuz. We're coming along just fine, but it's pretty scary out here. Ain't no people hanging around, that's true, but there's a kind of tension in the land that scares the shit out of me. It's like waiting for the second shoe to fall. You guys are safe right now. Stay that way. If the second shoe does fall, you can't help us. We've been left pretty much alone, I think, because this is a pretty sorry-looking team. NYPD Mounties have better looking livestock. People want to move fast; these two skinny fleabags ain't that. Hell, walking's almost faster."

Andy signed off to save batteries, and Harris called an end to the meeting.

I SPENT CONSIDERABLE TIME that evening, when I wasn't thinking about Andy, worrying over the fate of the poor fellow injured by Mike. I couldn't tell from the description of the events if the young man had had a minor wound or something much more serious. It bothered me that we had caused someone harm, and it bothered me that the young men probably hated us, as well. We weren't monsters, were we? The situation simply had escalated too quickly; people had became frightened and acted rashly. That's all it was, wasn't it? Just some unfortunate circumstances, an accident . . . wasn't it?

8
THE FIRST CASUALTY

T HE MOOD THAT DAY—AFTER THE SHOOTING incident and the news that Andy and the others were traveling by horse and wagon—remained very depressed. We all knew intuitively that maintaining a tense anticipation of Andy's arrival was too expensive, too difficult. We downgraded the sharp fear and worry to a numb sullenness. Few adults spoke to each other, and, when they did, it was in low tones, respectful of the general depression. Even the children seemed affected. Beth and Andrea lolled around in the slice all day, doing little else than picking at their toys and books and each other and complaining. It was a pissy, whiny, unpleasant day.

I spent most of the afternoon brooding about Mike's actions. From the bits of information I gleaned, the seven local men who came to the woodroom pushed the steel door as it was opened and threatened Mike, Wayne, and James. They were not armed but indulged in some shouting and shoving. Our people tried to force them to leave. Then the situation worsened, quickly escalating to the confrontation that resulted in Mike's shooting one of the men. It made me crazy to think that Mike carried a gun with him here in the shelter. Harris had confiscated it and three other weapons after his speech, but no one had made an exhaustive search, so I doubted that all weapons had been removed from everyone.

I could understand that Mike acted in our defense. At the very least I could accept that he had responded to the startlement and fear of finding men other than Andy and our people. But though I worked my way through the events over and over, I could not justify the shooting of an unarmed, frightened person. Would it have been so awful to allow seven more people inside? Were the men trying to take over or just looking for a refuge? What kept coming back to me with the regularity of a drum beat was that what Mike did tainted all of us. If the world emergency ended very soon, would we all be put on trial for "war crimes" for what had happened? What if the man died? Would we be tried for murder? I knew with certainty that our actions had been wrong when I secretly began to hope that we would have to remain in the shelter for a long time, long enough or through serious enough world events that all on the outside who knew what happened would forget or die.

Toward evening of that wearisome day, I was coming from the bathroom and saw James, Marty, and Donald going into the animal room. All by itself, that was not remarkable. People went in and out of the animal room all day, what with milking, feeding, and watering, and the children visiting pets, all of which—including Silk—had been relegated to that quarter. What drew my attention was the secretive, almost furtive manner of the three men. James, in particular, looked all around before slipping in after the others. It was when he was taking that last check that he spied me at the bathroom door. When our gaze connected, he froze, flitted his eyes all around again, then beckoned to me.

The entrance to the animal room consisted of two sets of double doors with a short walkway in between. The first set from the living area was steel, heavy and able to be bolted from the living area side. About fifteen feet beyond was another set of doors constructed of heavy wood. The hall between them was a kind of mudroom where manured boots, coveralls, and farm tools—rakes, hay forks, and shovels—were hung from hooks on the metal walls. James waited for me there.

"What's up?" I asked when the heavy steel door was closed softly.

"We're going after those men."

"What! Why? Wasn't Mike's shooting one of them enough? What are you going to do? Kill *all* of them?"

"Shh!" said James. "Come on, Barb, you don't really think we'd do that, do you?"

I blinked, realizing that I had let my fears and the depression of the day speak for me. "What then?" I said.

James took a deep breath. "Come with me," he said and pushed through the wooden doors into the animal room.

The warm scents of hay and cows that had been hinted at in the mudroom filled my nose as we entered the barn-like room, which seemed as large a circular space

74

like our living quarters. I walked with James past the penned-off stalls of the Jersey cows, Shetland ponies, Nubian goats, and several pens with Gertz's steers and pigs.

James seemd reluctant to say what was on this mind. Twice as we followed the circular pathway to the far side of the animal room he paused and half turned to me.

James was a shy man, the baby of the Quill family in more ways than one, but I liked him. While Harris was genius of nature—in a bizarre sort of way—and Frank was practical to the point of being methodical at times, James was a quiet, well-read intellectual. Both Andy, the cop, and Bob, a career naval officer, were a little too macho for my tastes. Harris and Frank had avoided that extreme, but it seemed to be James who viewed himself most comfortably as a person. As a kindergarten teacher like his wife and a librarian, he had chosen professions still outside the norm for males but perfectly suited to his quiet nature. This was where his strength lay. Still, there were times, as now, when the magnitude of *what* he wanted to say got in the way of actually *saying* anything. I would never have suggested it to his face—he would have been insulted—but, in this area, he showed great similarity to his eldest brother, whose bizarre reasoning so often blew past his ability to explain this thoughts to others.

I took James's arm and smiled reassuringly. "I don't believe you mean to hurt those men. But what *are* you planning to do?"

We were standing opposite a set of doors on the other side of the circle from the ones leading to the family area. The animal room was laid out pretty much like the living quarters, so that the pens were blunt-ended slices positioned around the perimeter like the dwelling slices were. We had walked around one-half of the circle. The pens in the other half stood empty, so that the Ark could hold a great many more animals than it did. In the center of the room—the center of the donut, so to speak—was feed storage. Piles of hay bales, sacks of grain, watering buckets, several large bins, and other assorted equipment to tend to the animals were stacked in this fenced-off central area. From behind a large stack of cracked-corn sacks, Marty and Donald came into the walkway. Marty handed James a jacket, all the while keeping contact with my eyes.

"What we're going to do is go after those guys," said Donald, his voice perfectly level, "and bring them back here. There's just the seven of them. Four were college students, probably from St. John's. I doubt any were married or had families in the area. Just seven young guys who couldn't get home."

"Mike was wrong to shoot that one," said James, conviction and emotion heavy in this voice. "The men weren't armed. They were just scared. If Wayne hadn't ordered them off the premises and just listened to them and if Mike hadn't had that damn .38 with him, we would have been fine. They weren't really even fighting, just pushing in. They were scared. Scared kids. It's got to be pretty terrible being sent from the place that might be the only way to stay alive. I just don't feel right about sending them away."

"I agree," I said, then added carefully, "but have you given consideration to the fact that they might just be pretty angry about what happened, that they might just be armed now and not so ready to talk first?"

"Yes," my brother said, "that's why we've got to go now and not tomorrow. We'll go and apologize and invite them into the Ark."

"I don't suppose Frank or Harris knows anything about this."

James began to blink rapidly. "You're not going to tell them, are you?"

"No," I said. "I agree with you about this. Actually, I think Harris and Frank do too, and, had they been at the door first, the men might just have been welcomed in the way the Gertz family was. But what you're doing now is very risky. If something happens to you three, it'll make Mike and Wayne's narrow-minded position here all the stronger. It could make the others believe that we surely do have to defend the Ark with force. Then we'd be like the people out West. I'd hate to see that happen. And we need your medical skill, Marty. As tempermental as Jillian is, she's not much help right now."

Marty squeezed my shoulder. "We're going to be very careful. We'll be fine."

"How are you getting out? I heard Harris tell Frank he sealed the woodroom door so that this sort of thing wouldn't happen again."

Donald pointed at the doors just behind us. "That leads to the manure pile, but there's a long hall past that. I followed it earlier today after Harris told us of the four entrances. It leads to a series of heavy doors and eventually reaches the outside near the Gertz's barn. We're going out that way."

For a long moment, I paused. Then I leaned up on tiptoes and kissed Marty on the cheek. "Be careful," I said. I turned to James and whispered, "Let me know when you get back because I'll be worrying until you're all safely inside again."

I watched the men go through the steel door into a dim tunnel rich with the sharp scents of manure and urine. After the door closed, I found it difficult to leave. If there ever was an inquisition after all this craziness ended, at least I could say I had sided with the ones who opted for humanity. The feeling of self-righteousness was short-lived, however, pushed aside by the thought that I might have seen these three compassionate men for the last time. Marty was a doctor we needed in our community, Donald a decent and fair-minded man. James, I was sure, still did not know he was going to be a father.

Beth's little Manx kitten, Silk, came partway down from the top of the feed sacks and purred at my shoulder. I lifted her down and cradled her in my arms. "What do you think, Silk? Are people all crazy, or what? You're the lucky one. Beth says you're getting good at catching streams of warm milk straight from the cows. Plenty of milk, a warm dry roost at the top of the grain, lots of attention from the children—what could be better?"

I looked around at the dozens of animals we had brought with us into the shelter. The little Jerseys lay in thick beds of clean straw and munched on their cuds. The goats and sheep stood at their grain box, while the goat kids in the next pen played king of the hill in their hay rack. The lambs, well fed and content, napped in the one after that. The ducks swam in a children's plastic swimming pool, and the chickens clucked quietly from their pen. None of the tension and anguish we felt in the next room was at all mirrored in this one. In many ways, these animals were probably being pampered as they never thought possible. They were warm and dry and very well fed. That the world was falling to pieces and men were risking their lives meant nothing to them. If they never saw the outside world again, I doubted any of them would even notice, let alone miss the sun or long for their meadows. People paid a very high price for their intelligence and awareness. A very high price indeed.

ANDY RADIOED IN about nine-thirty that evening. His spirits seemed to be flagging. It had rained through much of the afternoon, he said, a cold, sleety rain with a wind. They were soaked and weary and just beyond Becker—still a long way away from us. During the early afternoon, before the rain set in, someone had shot at them. They had escaped unharmed and without further contact, but they were a little spooked and had decided to push on through the night just in case they were being followed. I heard a tone in Andy's voice that had not been part of previous radio contacts; he was no longer enjoying the adventure. He wanted to be done with it and get to the shelter where it was safe. Maybe he had finally realized that marathon machismo was a little tiring, that Clint Eastwood had gone home between takes.

I put the girls to bed after Andy's call. As I tucked them into Beth's upper bunk, Andrea asked, "Why can't we hear the rain here?"

"We're too far underground," I said, and tried to smile with the answer.

"Grandma said she knew it was raining," Beth said. "How could she know that if there aren't any windows and we're under the ground?"

Again I smiled. Grandma Quill had been forecasting for many years. She wasn't much better than the meteorologists, except in hindsight. "I bet . . . she could feel it in her bones. Lots of older people can do that. She does have a little arthritis."

Beth said, "When Uncle Andy gets to the Ark and there's no one outside with a radio, then how are we going to know when it rains?"

I paused, my smile faltering, a little taken aback by the depth of meaning in Beth's statement. "Oh, I think Uncle Harris has some weather equipment somewhere that'll let us know."

My response seemed shallow to my ears, but Beth accepted it as if she understood past the words to the comfort I wanted her to hear. I knew I couldn't maintain the easy smile any longer and turned from the bed to lower the shade of the lamp on the shelf. I spent a few minutes quietly ordering the lower shelves so I could stay in the slice until the girls fell asleep. When I heard Andrea's soft snoring, I finally turned to leave. As I snugged the blankets to their chins, Beth whispered, "One of the radio stations went off the air today."

Though I felt a tightening in my stomach, I forced my voice to remain casual. "Oh, which one, dear?"

"The one I listen to in St. Cloud. They were playing the Heather Lively's song, 'Time to Run,' and the station just went dead. All I could get was static."

"Well, maybe your batteries are getting low, dear."

Beth didn't contradict me. I could feel in the space between us that she knew I was trying to minimize the event, that I knew there was nothing wrong with her batteries. I was proud of her. After I turned down the light, I reached over Andrea and patted her hand. "Don't worry, sweetheart. It might be that all the stations go off the air before they come back on, but they'll be back. Then the Heather Lively will have had time to come up with about forty new hits for you to listen to."

Beth smiled. "I don't think I'm going to listen to the radio any more right now. I don't want . . . I don't want my batteries to get too low."

I held back the tears and smiled bravely. "Maybe that's a good idea. We don't have a lot of spare batteries. Good night, dear."

As I left the slice and walked toward the classroom, I realized how adult that brief conversation with Beth had been. A lot of subtle communication filled our few words about rain and the radio. I tried to believe that this disheveled time might not wreak unilateral harm to the children, that for some, like Beth, it might be a maturing time when they could begin to see and respond to the adult world. I tried to be positive about that, tried to convince myself that acting like an adult at ten wasn't all bad, but when the crying started, I could hold no wonderful platitudes against the flood. Ten-year-olds were children. They should not have to be dealing with adult concerns or have to learn to protect their younger siblings. They should be riding their bikes on sunny country roads and opening their minds to the wonder and beauty of nature and human achievement through the centuries. They should be wide-eyed and innocent, creatures of joy and art. When, in what time in human history, would this be allowed to be true? Like all other parents through all time, I had only the future to look to, but mine had no visible horizon.

NEAR ELEVEN, I HEARD DeeDee calling for James. There was an edge to her voice I knew was worry. She hadn't been privy to the rescue party, then. Sissy joined her, and a search was launched by Mike and Wayne. Connie, however, remained in her slice with her two little girls. The fact that she was not a part of the searching adults let me know that she knew where the three men had gone.

Beth and Andrea were sleeping peacefully when I checked them. Though I hated to leave them for too long, I slipped out of the curtain again when the search migrated to back to the classroom and sidled over to Connie's slice. There was no way to knock against a curtain, of course, so I whispered, "Connie? It's Barb. Can I come in a minute?"

She didn't answer right away. I was just about to return to my slice when the curtain moved, and Connie peeked out.

"I saw them leave," I said in a low voice.

She drew in a quick breath and reached for my arm. When the curtain was carefully closed behind us, Connie whispered, "You're not going to tell, are you?"

"It's making me crazy to see DeeDee and Sissy searching and calling when I know where their husbands are."

"Me, too," said Connie, dabbing at her eyes with a tissue. "But Marty said to wait until midnight."

The search party migrated back through the donut. Someone, maybe Don's twin brother, Dewey, suggested the animal room.

"Oh, oh," I said, "that's the way they left. This might make it hard for them to get back in. And, Connie, they'll know you knew Marty was gone too because you're not out there searching just like the rest."

Her eyes opened wide. "You're right! I hadn't thought about that. What should I do, do you think? Should I go tell them I just realized Marty was gone too? Wait! I'll just say I thought he was in the radio room like he was most of yesterday."

I nodded and said, "That sounds plausi—"

The animal room door clanked open again, and Dewey hollered, "We found them!" He sounded particularly anticlimactic.

Connie and I were sorely tempted to poke our heads out and ask what that tone meant when the rest of the search party came into the donut. DeeDee's voice was clear and easy to pick out. "If you ever go off and play poker again without telling me . . . James, I swear . . ."

Connie and I clamped hands over our mouths and laughed. It was the first laugh in weeks, it seemed, because it felt strange, almost sinful, and damn good. Marty came in, followed by catcalls, and the giggling ceased immediately. Though he was smiling and trying very hard to look sheepish at having been caught with his hand in the cookie jar, so to speak, there was an edge of pain at the corners of his eyes and around his mouth when he faced us.

"What is it?" Connie asked in a whisper.

Marty waited a moment for the people to move on into the classroom, then sat at the edge of the bed. Connie sat next to him and slipped her hands into his.

"The man's dead," he husked. "I can't be sure, of course, but I think his companions killed him before they left."

"*They* killed him?" I said. "What—"

"Let me finish this all of a piece, Barb, because it's not easy. James said when Mike shot the one, they all took off over the fields rather than down toward the road as they would have if they'd had a car. So we followed that way. Ended up at St. John's University. We didn't look to see if the monks were still there, but the place looked mostly deserted otherwise. We went into Sexton Commons and poked around. Nothing much was left—no food at least."

"Sexton Commons?" I said.

"Yes. Well, the pizza place was burned and Brother Willy's Pub was looted bare. No one was around. We searched the neighboring dorm one room at a time and came upon the man in an upstairs dorm. He had been shot in the head."

"What!" Connie and I said on top of each other.

"From what I can piece together, the men who had been here went back to Sexton Commons and holed up in their dorm room. When they left our place, I distinctly saw the injured man hold his side, and the dead man was wounded there—a bad wound, but not fatal if he had gotten some attention. I suspect he was shot by his companions . . . out of compassion."

"They killed him so he wouldn't suffer?" I asked, horrified.

Marty shrugged. "There was no sign of a struggle. The man lay in bed, nice and comfortable. He was curled as if asleep or trying to rest. But his wound had bled through a heavy dressing. Maybe his friends thought there was no way to get him to treatment and ended his life so he wouldn't die of infection. Maybe they needed to move on and were afraid to leave him to starve or try to carry him with them and slow themselves down to a point of not finding sanctuary."

"That's horrible," Connie said.

"Yes," said Marty. "Anyway, James, Don, and I decided to come back. The university is too big a place to think about searching, especially if people there are armed. I don't think we'd been back for three minutes when they found us. Don had a pack of cards and whipped them out as soon as we heard people. How long had they been searching?"

"Ten. Fifteen minutes, maybe," Connie said. "I was starting to get really worried, hon."

He rubbed her arm. "Sorry, Con."

My cue to leave. "Well, I better get back to my girls. I feel awful about that man, Marty, but I'm thankful you three are back safe."

"Me, too." He smiled and stood as I left the room.

Outside the curtain, I paused and closed my eyes. I took several long breaths to calm the feelings surging through my brain. When I opened my eyes and started to walk back the few steps to my own slice, I caught sight of Sissy sitting on the floor in front of a slice down the curve of the circle from me. I didn't think she was at her own curtain. She looked stunned. I hurried over.

"Sissy? What is it? Don's safe. And a little poker won't hurt—"

She stared up at me with frightening eyes, eyes filled with awe and shock and . . . grief. When her gaze slid to the curtain opening, I yanked the heavy cloth back and looked in. The slice was dim; at first I saw nothing, didn't even know whose slice it was. Then I saw Sissy's mother, Ma Anders, on her bed. She appeared to be sleeping. A tray of food—soup and tea—rested on her bedside table, untouched. It looked as if Sissy had brought her supper, assumed she was asleep and left her. Checking now, it was quite obvious that she was dead. I covered her snow-white head with the handmade quilt folded at the end of the bed.

I sat down next to Sissy and wrapped my arms around her. She started to cry immediately.

"I'm so sorry, Sissy," I said. "Maybe the move was just too much for her. The excitement and fear."

Sissy shook her head. She wiped her nose on her sleeve and said, "No. Nothing like that. When we came into the Ark, she wanted to leave. She demanded that I take her home right away. She didn't want to live in this squat, loud, ugly place. I wouldn't hear of taking her home. She's been in her slice the whole time. I'd bring her food, but she didn't do much more than nibble and sip tea."

"She can't have died of starvation in three days—"

"No. I know that. But I think she willed herself to die just the same. All the way down here, she was ragging on Don to leave her by the side of the road and pick up some nice young person instead. I think that's why—"

"I know about the guys' trip outside," I whispered.

Sissy began to cry again and clung to me. As long as we were alone in the donut, I stayed with her, holding her as firmly as she held me. Finally, Don came, and I told him what happened. He took Sissy back to their slice while I found the others in the classroom and told them.

I'LL GIVE HARRIS CREDIT. He had planned well for this kind of eventuality. Ma Anders, at eighty-seven, was the oldest to come into the Ark, but the elder Quills were pushing seventy-five. Harris had set aside a small room off the root storage area. There was Minnesota soil underfoot instead of the terrazzo that covered all the other floors, including the animal room walkway. All four walls of the fifteen-foot by twenty-foot room were panels with typical Minnesota scenes of woods, fields, and prairies. I had seen this kind of painted panel in wallpaper stores. It had always looked excessive to me, or just plain cheesy—it had been popular in the late eighties, and, thankfully, it's popularity had been brief. But here on the walls of our little cemetery, the panels were so right that they brought tears to my eyes.

As per Harris's instructions, we encased poor Mrs. Anders in a black body bag for her coffin and actually buried her the next morning in the soil of that paneled room. To bury one of us so soon after coming to the Ark, even if Mrs. Anders was nearly ninety, began our fourth day on a new level of depression. The shelter felt more than ever like a prison, like a tomb. And, even though I was exhausted from a sleepless night, every time I dozed, the images in my dreams were bizarre and frightening. The only thing that might improve our morale now was the safe arrival of Andy and those with him, but he had not called that morning as planned. Besides the grief we all felt at the loss of Mrs. Anders, many of us, I was sure, were gearing up for more loss if Andy didn't arrive soon.

9

SUNDAY

OCTOBER 13

I F A DAY COULDN'T "DAWN" FOR US in the shelter because there was no sun to see, I wondered that morning of the fifth day what term for a new day's arrival would apply. Children outside the curtain began to play tag and jump rope, responding to their inner clocks that told them a new day had started. Children had awakened me most days. Maybe I could say that the fifth day rustled awake or that the morning sounded. I had a strong desire that morning to slip outside and take a look at the horizon.

It was Sunday. I wasn't an overly religious person. Who was these days? Yet I found myself missing the quiet hour at church I sometimes fit into the middle of an otherwise hectic weekend. It often calmed me and replenished my well of coping when coping seemed difficult. I couldn't do that anymore; there was no church room in the shelter. Maybe it was because we had buried Mrs. Anders the day before, I don't know, but I felt a need for connectedness with the higher power who had seemed to have turned a deaf ear to the events on Earth. Or maybe God was winding up to deliver a new flood, a nuclear or biological flood. All that had been promised to Noah was that great "waters" would never be used again to cleanse the Earth. Was that semantics? It sure looked like the world was going to be destroyed again even if the medium was now radiation or war or disease. The images forced me away from sleep; they also forced me away from thinking about God.

At breakfast on that morning of the fifth day, Harris announced that we had four steers, six hogs, and twenty roosters to butcher in the woodroom. Not exactly community worship. This news was met with utter silence and blank stares.

"It's gotta be done," Harris said flatly. "We need the meat, and we don't have the feed to keep them."

Wayne set down his coffee mug and ran a hand over his thick brown hair. "Shit," he said. "They're Gertz's animals. Let him butcher them."

Harris turned to his brother-in-law, his expression open, almost inquisitive. "That's fair . . . if Gertz and his family eat the meat by themselves. But, since it seems to me we're *all* going to share the food, we all ought to share the work."

"No. You've got that all wrong," said Mike, with a knowing glance at his brother. "We already contributed our share when we paid for this place. He paid zilch. Butchering the animals isn't even a small down payment. He's got two strong farm boys. Let them do it."

"Farm boys" had been said like an insult. I bristled at the slur. I knew the two Deters men well enough to know they seldom backed down once a clear stand had been made, especially if the issue was money. And, though they had not unequivocally stated that they would not help, I saw a stand-off forming. The truly unfortunate thing was that the Gertezes weren't even allowed an opinion; they were in the animal room doing the milking and cleaning and feeding—of our animals as well as theirs. Was that just part of their share also? Did Mike and Wayne want to make the farm family our slaves in exchange for living in the shelter? In my opinion, a very unfair decision was about to be handed down. I opened my mouth to object, but Marty beat me to it.

"I guess I don't mind helping Gertz butcher the animals that'll be used to feed my children." Then Marty turned to Connie and said, "What do you think, sweetheart? Would you help me?"

"I'm not big on the killing and skinning part," she admitted, "but I'll sure help out with the cutting up and packaging. Sissy, you're really good at estimating portions. Do you want to help me cut up and package the meat that we'll all enjoy?"

"Sure," she said. "Barb, you'll help, too, won't you?"

I grinned. "Count me in if I can sit at a counter to work."

James, Donald, and Dewey volunteered to help Gertz with the initial killing and skinning out in the woodroom. Even Emily and Anna were willing to help with the work; some of the older children got into the cooperative spirit and said they'd watch the littler children while we were busy. In fact, by the time the Gertezes came out of the animal room, everyone except the Deters brothers, Jillian, and Jeannie seemed to be ready to give them a hand. Harris suggested that Mike and Wayne monitor the radio.

The farmer and his family wouldn't have any idea what had just transpired unless someone told them, and I doubted anyone would.

I saw a look of pride on Frank's face and almost awe on Harris's when the whole block of us approached the Gertzes with the idea of butchering the animals in teams. I saw Max Gertz's face blossom; the wariness and distrust that had been in his eyes seemed to ease, at least for the moment. It was worth the sore back I knew I'd likely have at the end of the day.

Actually, there was no sore back. When Max Gertz was faced with the committed Quill-Reinhart-Dunn army, he rubbed his stubbled chin with the back of his hand and grinned. "I never expected so much help," he said. "'Course we hardly need all of it today. I'd like to get the beef hung today if we could, and it'll take a few men to do that, but ain't nothin' for you ladies to do with 'em till the meat's aged a bit. With all this help, we could do the chickens and even hang a few of the hogs, but we still should be done by noon."

I got to clean two meaty roosters after they had been rough-plucked out in the woodroom. Each was about as big as a small turkey, with a wide breast and heavy thighs—nothing like the scrawny birds I had butchered on our farm in past years or, heavens, purchased in the supermarket. And, though I had never had a problem with squeamishness when it came to preparing meat for the table, until that morning, I also had never really worked efficiently. Usually, I got tired before the job was done, then hesitated the next time there were animals ready to butcher. In the company of other women, some of whom had skills considerably greater than mine, I began to learn some of the finer points of an essentially lost art of self-sufficiency.

Abby Gertz hovered over Melissa, DeeDee, and me as we worked, but she managed to clean four birds to each one of ours. With Sissy's help, she washed and packaged the beef and pig hearts and livers as the men brought them in. I couldn't believe how efficiently Abby worked, while keeping up a delightful chatter at the same time. She brought in the animals' pancreases, brains, tongues, and kidneys, and cleaned and packaged them herself because Sissy seemed unwilling to handle these parts. But, when she brought in a steaming pail of white ropes, even I was dismayed.

"What in the world have you got there now?" DeeDee asked.

Melissa, who had been raised on a farm, giggled.

"Sausage casings," Abby said flatly.

86

"Sausage cas—oh, God! Those are intenstines!"

Abby grinned, showing a two-tooth gap on the upper right side back of her bicuspid. "And just what'd you think was wrapped around your weiners? We've got enough beef and pork to make some fine breakfast sausage—all kinds of stuff if you like. I've got my mom's recipes along with, and she was a prize sausage maker. But we got to put them sausages into something, don't we?"

Poor DeeDee was city born and bred. She had a good heart and had worked hard cleaning the chicken Abby gave her, but I could see she was losing it. Abby could too because she put a clean dish cloth over the top of the bucket. DeeDee left after her chicken had been safely encased in plastic. Then Abby gave Melissa, Sissy, and me a broom each and showed us how to scrape and clean the intestines to make casings and slide them down over the broom handle as we went. After I got over the smell, it wasn't difficult work at all, and the company made the time fly.

Suddenly I was a firm believer in quilting bees, corn shucking bees, and barn raisings—activities people could do together. Why, in the last century, had we abandoned this kind of thing? Pride? Autonomy of families? Or was it the slowly invading technology that promised to "make life easier" but separated people in the process? Maybe the developments of the last one hundred years had made life and work easier; I was beginning to see that it was at a price. I began to believe that the term "nuclear family" had a double meaning, as if it were partially responsible for the world's brewing disaster.

Max Gertz was about right in his time estimate. We were done the butchering and cleaning of the chickens by two o'clock. Harris had a huge walk-in cooler straight out of a butcher shop—one of the appointments Frank knew nothing about—and that shortened the effort considerably. After the steers and hogs were halved and hanging on hooks in there, the job was done for the day. The cutting up and freezing in the room-size freezer would take place over the next several days, one slab of meat at a time. I looked forward to our artfully creating roasts and chops and steaks.

After the last hog was hung, the men came streaming back into the kitchen wanting food. They had worked hard at their part of the task. Abby offered to fry up some of the fresh pig liver. Everyone—most were in the lunchroom, probably because it was the center of activity that day—except her sons and husband, groaned. Max laughed at us and teased that we were "chicken-livered city folks who didn't know what eating high off the hog was all about." We ate peanut butter sandwiches and

Campbell's chicken noodle soup as Abby filled the kitchen with the meaty aroma of liver and onions.

I looked around. People were laughing and chatting. There had been a change, as if some bonding had occurred. Abby sat where she pleased now, not right next to her husband, and the two lank Gertz boys were joking with James and Paul Fisk instead of bending silently over their food. But a division had occurred also, and it worried me. The Deters men, Jillian, and Jeannie were not with us. I thought maybe Harris had been wrong to let them off from helping with the butchering to tend the radio.

After lunch, the mood in the Ark faltered. No word had come from Andy. As our minds lost the calm that comes from completing a block of work, we turned inevitably back to the worry that seemed integral to our lives. We were still connected to the outside world, and that connection held us to the trauma it suffered.

"I'd like to go out and just see what's happening," Connie said as she, Melissa, DeeDee, Marie, and I sat together sipping coffee after the lunch dishes were done. I was beginning to warm to our industrial-sized kitchen. The dishwasher was huge and powerful and, after a good rinse, washed everything beautifully.

"Yeah, me, too," said Melissa.

I knew what they were feeling. I felt it too. I had awakened that morning with those feelings. Connie wasn't contemplating a foray to the outside like the men had made, but she was voicing a kind of growing claustrophobia, bred from being in the shelter for five days. We all knew that five days amounted to nothing. There was a possibility, though I tried hard not to think about it, but a real possibility that we would be in the shelter for the rest of our lives. For me, that was almost as fearful a thought as dying.

"I wonder if we should have sun lamps or something," I said.

"What do you mean?" Marie asked with an ironic smile as if I wanted to work on my tan.

"Well, you know, in the winter when people suffer from seasonal affective disorder, it's due to a lack of vitamin D from the sun. A little time under sun lamps each day cures them."

"I don't think that's our problem yet," DeeDee said. "It's this horrible waiting and wondering if Andy and the others are okay. I keep thinking of those two kids with them. Ben and Wendy are only twelve. I bet they're scared to death out there. And Linda's life might have been tough moving all over the country with Bob, but—"

"Oh, I don't know," Connie said. "I think Linda's plenty adaptable. She waited out the eight months Bob was in Kosovo, didn't she? And Bob was abroad when the Soviets took umbridge to the oil dealings after the Iraqi wars. It looked like he'd have to go fight again. She waited out the invasion of Iran while coaching Wendy's volleyball and T-ball teams, toting her to dance lessons and teaching full time."

"Hmm," mused Melissa. "Sounds to me like she was maybe trying awful hard to keep her mind *off* what Bob was doing."

DeeDee, Connie, and I nodded and sipped our coffee. I sighed. It didn't matter what we knew of Linda or the two children or even Bob and Andy. They were either going to make it or not going to make it with what they had in them. And, if they lacked the wherewithal to face what lay ahead of them, they either were going to come up with what was needed or fail to do so. My only useful concern was whether or not we who were waiting had the reserves to continue to wait, especially if Andy and company never came.

M EAL PREPARATION GRADUALLY was getting organized. That evening, the fifth night of our confinement, we made our first "real" meal. DeeDee, Connie, Melissa, Marie and I managed to sit around sipping coffee and commiserating together long enough that supper time approached, and the children began filtering into the kitchen area looking for snacks. We shooed them all away and set about making a bona fide Sunday dinner. Abby came in and suggested we use some of the fresh chicken.

It was like a church social. We cut up four or five of Abby's big birds, coated them with flour and bread crumbs and popped them in the huge ovens arranged on the institutional-size roaster pans. Then we peeled a couple big buckets of potatoes from Mom Quill's generous garden stores and set them to boil in three big pots for mashed potatoes. We fixed honeyed carrots, broccoli with cheese sauce, and halved acorn squash with butter and brown sugar. I think the squash came from my garden. And, when the preparations of all this were in hand, Abby brought in a bushel basket of rosy apples and started peeling them.

"Sauce?" I asked.

She grinned at me and shook her head. "Pies!"

"Do you have that kind of energy?" DeeDee asked, mystified.

"Pies don't take but a bit," said the farm wife. "When you get the chicken turned, you just start measuring the flour out, and we'll have eight pies quick as a wink."

"Eight!" I said, now in awe myself.

Abby frowned. "Ten would be better. Then we might have some for tomorrow."

We really needed Abby among us. All the rest of us led lives revolving around jobs juggled with our homes and children. I shuddered to think how many of my suppers back home had started with fast food, pizza, or Stouffers. Abby's life moved from the fixing of one meal after another for her hungry husband and two growing sons, as well as farm work. As I watched her and listened to her, I realized that she had a menu in mind for the next day that best used what we might have left over from today. She mentioned chicken salad sandwiches for lunch and mixed vegetables for our supper Monday evening. Leftovers in my house tended to turn green and threaten to sprout new life forms before I sadly tossed them out and vowed—again—to do better.

"Now, when them potatoes are ready," she said, wiping her hands on her apron, "just mash up the first two pots, not the third. If we don't need 'em tonight, we can have fried potatoes tomorrow for lunch, maybe potato salad for supper if you want. DeeDee, just reach right into that bowl and work the shortening through the flour with your fingers. A little flour don't hurt nobody, and the grease might stop your fingers from cracking so bad. You want it to look like sand and pebbles when it's right."

I liked her. I liked Abby Gertz a lot. She was a country catalyst reshaping our city thinking, our my-family-first thinking, into community thought. One of the reasons meals had been so dismal so far was that none of us had any idea how to plan to feed forty-some people. We had to learn to think in larger amounts, more complex proportions, greater lead time. Abby seemed to have had experience in this or just was a little ahead of us at guessing. Whatever it was, she was making it work. When the chicken had turned golden brown and filled the kitchen with a tempting fragrance, the rest of the meal was also ready, and Abby had her pies made. She popped them in the oven as we called everyone to supper.

As I watched people rush into the lunchroom and joyfully fill plates with the good food, I saw a rekindling of our wonderful mood of the morning. The chatter around the tables was lively, punctuated with laughter, especially from the children. The food on the counter disappeared, and the tension within each of us slipped a notch.

Mike and Wayne had been replaced by the Reinhart brothers on the radio. I was grateful—if annoyed—to see that they fit themselves in as if they had been a part of our work. Jillian wasn't there, however. Although her absence didn't seem to concern Harris, who obviously enjoyed the feast, it gave me pangs of disappointment. Jeannie was with Wayne and her two boys, looking like a fashion model. Her low-cut emerald dress sparkled, molding to the roundness of her barely pregnant belly. She even wore heels. Wayne had guided her in and seated her as if they were eating out in a fine restaurant. Something was seriously wrong with that woman.

When the plates had been cleared away, Abby and DeeDee brought out pairs of steaming pies on trays, their aroma quickly filling the room. Melissa was right behind them with a huge bowl of mounded whipped cream straight from our cows. A line formed quickly though I wondered, having seen the piles of food disappear, where anyone was going to put even a sliver of pie. Nevertheless, I joined the queue and accepted a big slice of warm apple pie spiced with cinnamon and nutmeg with a generous dollop of whipped cream slowly melting into it. It was pure heaven.

As the pie disappeared into appreciative mouths, Mike stood up and tapped his glass with his fork to get our attentions. Not much happened. He cleared his throat loudly, and soon the pie-muffled exclamations of delight began to subside.

"Thank you," Mike said. "I just wanted to say that this was the most wonderful meal we've had here yet. Truly delicious. And though at the moment I can't envision eating again for a week, I would like to encourage our fine cooks to hang in there and maintain this quality from here on out. *This* is how we would all like to eat."

I felt an instant and profound irritation.

"Eat like this every day, and you'll blow up like a balloon!" James quipped.

Everyone laughed.

Mike waved this comment aside. "We have piles of good food. We shouldn't waste our eating pleasure on canned soups and peanut butter sandwiches."

"You *did* want some of that liver," Don grinned. "I bet there's some left, Mike."

Mike paused and gave Don an indulgent look. "That liver would make a fine sausage or wurst if someone cared at all. I would be more than willing to eat it in that form. Anyway, I want to personally thank the ladies for their efforts and ask them to take on the job of our cooks permanently."

Mike started clapping, probably expecting the rest of us to join in. Some of the children did, but I was beginning to do a slow burn deep inside, and I wasn't alone.

"Why does it have to be us women?" DeeDee asked.

Mike, still standing at his chair, hesitated a minute, then said, "Because this was a great meal, and it just happened to be produced *by* women."

"What have you done toward meal preparation?" DeeDee challenged. I could see she was even angrier than I was.

Mike chuckled. "Me? Oh, you wouldn't want me to help out. I can't cook."

"Okay, then," DeeDee said and stood up. "I vote that if women are the ones who cook around here, then men ought to be the ones cleaning up afterwards. There's a dishwasher to fill in there and some pots to scrub with your name on them, Mike."

Mike's cheesy grin faltered. "Now, wait a minute. You wouldn't want me to clean up either. I mean, I drop things, break plates all the time. Don't I, Marie? And I assume you'd like to find things for the next meal."

"Can you clean toilets then?" Emily said. "That job needs doing too."

Mike flared. "Now just a goddamn minute. I compliment the cooks of this great meal, and you want me to clean toilets? See if I thank anyone again!"

He sat down amid a volly of comments from both men and women. Harris stood and raised his arms. After a few minutes, he finally achieved enough quiet to speak.

"Mike has brought up a very important issue. I'd like to expand on it for a minute. Mike, please sit back down. I'd like you to hear this. Wayne, you too. Thank you. And, Emily, I guess I'll have to ask that you sit down, too. I know you're all angry, and that's a shame. It's spoiled a fine supper. Mrs. Gertz, your pies were pure heaven. And thank you all who worked on this meal for your extraordinary efforts, not just today, but all week as well."

"Say what you have to say," said Wayne, scowling.

"Yes. Yes. It's just this. In a community this size, there's no room for men's work and women's work. I thought American society had gotten past that anyway. And, I think, maybe Mike's choice of words was more unfortunate than purposely unkind. Oh, sit down, Mike, and listen. I don't think there ought to be *any* permanent jobs, especially not cooking and cleaning. Those jobs are just too big. Everyone should be helping with meals and cleaning up our common areas—like the bathrooms and the donut. We should all help out with the animals, too. Anything else is grossly unfair. That's how I see it. And I'm just as guilty as many others who have let a few do the work for all of us. I haven't lifted a finger except to bring food to my mouth and push my chair back when I'm finished. I'm afraid my concern for Andy has pushed most else from my mind. What we need is *not* a permanent kitchen staff. What we need is a *temporary* kitchen foreman, someone who doesn't necessarily do the work, but recruits the people who will. I would like to offer that job to Mrs. Gertz not because of her pies, or, certainly, not because she's a woman, but because she seems to know how to do what we need done and have yet to learn. Understand, Abby, I'm not making you a cook, and you can turn this job down now or at any time it makes you unhappy, but I would be very grateful if you'd take it for a little while . . . until Andy gets here, maybe, and we can establish some kind of order and routine for our lives. What do you say?"

Abby had turned beet red. She giggled and hid her face in her hands. Max elbowed her, and she flicked her eyes up to Harris. "Sure. Why not."

He smiled warmly. "Thank you, Abby. Now, I want you to recruit helpers from among everyone, man or woman . . . or child. Whatever. Make the jobs small, if need be, but get everyone to help on a regular basis. And I caution the rest of us, especially the ones, like me, who have yet to contribute much, to not casually refuse Abby's assignments. The job of cleaning the toilets is still open."

Harris also dealt with the issue of the care of the animals. "Max Gertz and his family has been good enough to get us properly started with the animals, but, surely, their entire care and feeding should not rest on his shoulders. Max, if you would be so kind as to take charge—for a short time—of the workers dealing with the animals, I would be most grateful. See to it everyone, including the kids, helps out with them. Set up milking details and feeding and clean-up squads. Then assign the next foreman of animals when you're tired of the job. Again, we will all take it seriously if someone refuses to perform an assigned task. We'll also need a general cleaning detail foreman. Who wants that job?"

The room remained very quiet.

Harris smiled. "Since no job will be permanent and since everyone will get a chance to do everything, Marie, will you be cleaning foreman for a short time?"

Marie, taken unawares, blinked at him and nodded.

"Good," said Harris. "Get everyone to help out keeping the living spaces in order. The lunchroom, the donut, the bathrooms and the classroom. Make sure everyone contributes. Those toilets really are a mess."

Harris displayed some real leadership in defusing an explosive situation. He'd empowered Abby rather then put her into a menial role. Abby was foreman, not kitchen maid. So were Max and Marie. And, while I knew that Wayne and Mike looked on this transaction as a well-worded con job, that Abby had been snookered by semantics, I knew she felt she was being honored. I thought maybe Harris had let it have separate effects, as a kind of Soloman pronouncement, splitting his message in two. Picking Marie for cleaning foreman also had its purpose. She was part of the Deters side. Harris had gotten a tacit agreement to conform from Wayne and Mike because they would have to support one of their own. And while I could envision Mike trying to get Marie to give the worst jobs to James and others who had spoken out against him, like Harris had said, everyone would have to do everything eventually. It should work itself out.

10

FAMILY CURTAINS

MONDAY, OCTOBER 14

I SHUFFLED OUT OF BED WONDERING where Frank and the girls were and feeling more than a little foggy, as if I had gotten too little sleep. Maybe my tension-filled dreams had preventing me from getting the rest I needed. I felt almost drugged, though I had not taken even the mildest over-the-counter preparation of any kind in months because of the baby.

I saw no kids in the donut, though a bike and two pairs of roller skates lay on the floor. I felt slightly dizzy when I bent over to grab the handlebars of the bike and stand it up so someone else wouldn't trip over it. Mother compulsion. I set the kick stand and put the skates in the basket before heading for the bathroom. Both showers were occupied so I washed up at a sink. For a couple of minutes, I stared at my image in the mirror, thinking I was looking drawn, maybe a little haggard that morning. I shuffled out, heading toward the kitchen.

I could smell coffee brewing and . . . was that bacon and eggs? I turned into the lunchroom, but I got no further than the door before I stopped. Each one of the thirty or so long tables was covered with a tablecloth and decorated with a couple springs of parsley in a glass of water. A few tables actually had flowers, late-flowering mums that one of us had to have brought into the shelter at the move. At least half the people were seated and eating. I could see bacon, eggs, pancakes, and toast. A big urn of coffee stood on the counter with cups ready to be filled. Pitchers of orange juice and frothy milk stood on each table.

I skirted the counter and bumped into the kitchen. DeeDee giggled when she saw me. "Well, finally up, are you? We were about to send a posse, Barb."

"Um . . . I just—why didn't someone come get me?"

Abby turned from the stove with a stack of pancakes piled high. Her hair was tied back and covered with a pretty blue scarf. She smiled and ushered me back out into the lunchroom. "You're not on the schedule this morning. Grab yourself a cup of coffee and some milk for that little baby you're growing. I'll bring you out some breakfast in a jiffy."

I was bewildered, and I suppose I looked it. Frank and the girls waved from the end of one table in the back, and I made my way over to them. Frank was laughing. "See, Barby, you don't have to be mommy to everyone. Abby's been up and hustling since five."

"Are you kidding?"

"Nope. She's got a menu and schedule for the next three days. Beth and I have to clear the tables after breakfast."

A plate of food materialized in front of me. I stared at the steaming eggs, pancakes, and two thick slabs of lean side pork, then turned to look up into Abby's rosy-cheeked, grinning face. The pride in her eyes glowed.

"This looks wonderful, Abby, but it's too much—"

"No, it ain't. I've been watching you. You don't eat near enough. That there bitty baby inside you's doing its biggest growing 'bout now. In a place like this, you just better have the strongest, healthiest baby you can. You need lots of protein and energy. Good healthy food. None of that store-bought, city stuff. That side pork is better for you than bacon, too. Less salt and stuff. Hope you like it. And if'n you want more coffee, you just let me know, and I'll make you some decaf. Get started now, 'cause you're the last to eat breakfast this morning."

I gaped at her broad back as she strode back to the kitchen. Frank pressed a thumb to the bottom of my chin as if my mouth hung open, and Connie, facing me at the next table over, giggled.

"See," Frank said again, "you don't have to be mommy because Abby Gertz is a professional. Seems in a previous lifetime, she was head cook for St. Joseph's Lab School."

I turned to him. "Really! That explains a lot. Whew! She sure took charge fast."

"Yeah, but you missed the really great part."

"Great part? What?"

"Wayne and Mike put the tablecloths on the tables and found the decorations."

"You're kidding."

"Nope. She's got everybody scheduled. She even has a job for you later. She said you've been working too hard as it is, so when the tablecloths are washed after lunch today, you have to fold them. That's it. She did say that you could talk to her if you didn't like that job."

I couldn't believe how well Abby seemed to be doing.

"Yeah," Frank continued, "about the only one who's giving her trouble is Jeannie. She was supposed to serve plates after people sat down, but she walked out without saying a word."

"How did Wayne take that?"

"He wasn't here. He'd eaten already and gone to shower."

I thought about Jeannie a few minutes as I began to eat. The side pork was wonderful, crunchy and chewy like bacon but flavored like pork. The eggs were just the way I liked them, with firm whites and juicy yolks, and the pancakes were the lightest and tastiest I had ever eaten, better even than my mother's had been, and that was saying something. But even though I enjoyed each bite, Jeannie was on my mind.

"Frank . . ." I began in between bites, "remember how Jeannie was all dressed up last night?"

"Yup," he said, sitting backwards on the bench so he could lean against the table and sip the good coffee leisurely.

"Don't you think she was . . . a little overdressed?"

Frank huffed a laugh. "Jeannie's always overdressed."

"I know, but . . ."

He frowned, closed his eyes a moment and set down his coffee cup. Then he leaned close. "Now, Barb, you know how you react to Jeannie. Don't make an issue of this. Sure, she's been flakier than usual since we came down here. She's always been fragile. Maybe if you women gave her a little support, she'd open up and relax a little."

I could tell by Frank's quick tension that he was not going to react well if I continued this particular line of conversation. Maybe the Deters/Quill controversies were getting to him, and he thought I was adding to them. I turned back to my food and sopped up yolk with a forkful of pancakes. The food was good, but, unless we all started exercising or working very hard, it was way too much.

Frank and Beth got up to clear the tables. Andrea slipped over next to me.

"Hi, there, little girl," I said and hugged her. "Did you pick out those clothes all by yourself?"

"Yes, Mommy," she said, hold out her shirt for me to see. It had the cartoon character Dora the Explorer on it that Andrea had enjoyed watching on Saturday mornings. Andrea's pants, hand-me-downs from Beth, were a little big and needed folding up at the cuffs, which I did for her, only then noticing that she had mismatched socks, and her sneakers were on the wrong feet.

"Are your feet comfortable in those shoes?" I asked.

"Uh-huh."

"Why do you have on one orange sock and one yellow one?"

"Well," she said with authority, "the orange one matches my shirt," and she brought her foot up next to Dora's orange shorts, "and the other one matches my barrette," and she tried to bring her other foot up while curling down her head.

"I see," I smiled. "You must have worked very hard to get everything to match that well. Good work, sweetie. If your feet start to get tired, though, change your shoes around. Okay?"

Andrea skipped off to help Frank clear the tables. It was nice to be able to trust her out of my sight, to know that all the places she could decide to go were safe with family members nearby. I trusted that, if my children were acting out or doing something unsafe and neither Frank nor I were around, someone would bring them back gently into line or let me know. I could go about my day as I needed, knowing that even if I had not seen my girls in a little while, they were okay, most likely being supervised by a cousin's mother. It was the first immediate gain I had found in the shelter.

AFTER BREAKFAST, I resolved to see if Jeannie was all right. In a lot of ways, she seemed to hold herself above the rest of us. She always seemed to be just a little bit better dressed, a little more formal, a little separate from the rest of us. And, even if I tried not to react overtly to this kind of thing, I always reacted badly. But the high-fashion make-up and the gala dress of the evening before stretched over her expanding belly were inappropriate to our surroundings, and, for all that Jeannie strove to show she was better than we were, she was never inappropriate. I suspected that reality had slipped just a little for her.

Maybe she needed some help. The problem was that I couldn't approach her myself, not directly anyway, because Jeannie really didn't like me much. If Marie seemed to waffle at times from being a Deters to siding with the rest of the women, Jeannie never did.

The only person to help me who Jeannie would not dismiss outright was Marie. Also being a Deters wife, Marie spent more time with Jeannie than the rest of us did. Marie seemed to be siding with the women these last few day, and that made her accessible. I had not seen her in the lunchroom, so I went to her slice. I took hold of the curtain edge and called out, "Marie? It's Barb. Can I talk to you?"

I heard a box or something drop and Marie gasp. Then she hurredly said, "Uh . . . just a minute. Oh!"

Another, heavier object thumped to the floor. I thought maybe she needed help and pulled aside the curtain. The scene that met my eyes was not anything I expected.

Marie stood in the middle of the small square of floor. She had curlers in her hair and wore only bra and panties, but that didn't shock me. At her feet was a box of books and another of bandages and medicines. That seemed okay, too, although it seemed like a lot of bandages and ointments to keep in one's slice. What did shock me, however, was the series of dark bruises on her thighs and upper arms. These were not the result of a slipped box; these were the result of abuse.

I closed the curtain behind me. Marie's hands had flown to her mouth when I opened the curtain. Now she slowly lowered them and looked down at the floor in shame. "This isn't what it looks like, Barby. It's—"

"Tell me first what it looks like," I said.

She met my eyes but said nothing.

"How long has this been going on?" I asked, but began adding up missed cues that numbered the problem in years, the latest being the tugged-down sleeves in the kitchen just a few days before.

"Umm . . . it . . . it just started. The stress of coming in here. When everything settles down and Andy gets here—"

"Come off it," I said, almost shouting, my anger at what Mike had done to her rising to a scream in my head.

Marie broke immediately, sank to the bed and began to sob. I closed my eyes, then sat near her, resting my hand gently on her bruised shoulder. "Oh, Marie. All these years . . . I never knew."

"No one did," Marie sobbed. "I didn't want anyone to. I'm so ashamed, Barb. Promise you won't tell anyone. Promise me that."

"I can't . . . I *won't* promise that," I said, indignation rising.

She sat up, wiping her face with her hands. I handed her a tissue from the top of the dresser. "Mike's not bad," she whispered. "He's a good husband. He can be so affectionate at times, so loving . . . especially afterwards."

"Beating you isn't affectionate."

"I bruise easily. I always have. Something about poor calcium absorption. He's never broken anything or hit me in the face. Nothing like that."

"That doesn't make any of this right, Marie."

Her face scrunched up, and she shook her head.

"Does he hit the children?" I asked this in a whisper because I feared my own anger if I brought the words all the way into voice.

In the same kind of husk, she said, "No, Barb, of *course* not! Never!" But I had seen that look in her eyes, that truth quickly covered over. Then she said, "Listen, since we've come here, he hasn't hit me, not even once. With so many people around, he's probably afraid someone'll hear him. It's only the last couple of months that've really been bad. It was the uncertainty, the tension. But it's over now. He's stopped. I think it'll be better here. Please don't tell anyone, Barb. Please promise me you won't."

I almost succumbed to her tears and misery. Almost. But there were at least a dozen darkened splotches on her body. A promise on my part played into the cruelty she had already suffered. It freed Mike from accountability. "I can't make that promise." But who would I tell? Harris? He might be the head man, but he was too preoccupied right now, too caught up in worry over Andy. And Frank would get too angry and react badly. "I won't tell anyone right now," I said, "but it's got to stop. For good. Forever."

"It already has," Marie said, suddenly hopeful. "He hasn't hit me since we've come here. I told you. It's over."

"We haven't been here a full week," I said. "That's a long way from forever."

Marie closed her eyes and nodded. "But it'll be better. You'll see. He won't hit me again."

I LEFT MARIE, FEELING AWFUL. I felt abused myself to know that this was happening in our family. I thought of their three children. What messages had they already absorbed? Jacob, ten, was a nice enough boy, a little bossy maybe. Mary Sue was sweet, an ingratiating little eight-year-old, eager to please. Jimmy was a shy five-year-old. Many kindergarteners were shy. Then I remembered the way Jimmy had responded to the musical chairs game when Roland pinched him. Instead of being angry, he had appeared ashamed. Why? Was there more going on in that family?

MARIE AVOIDED ME AT LUNCH, and, shamefully, I avoided her, too. I didn't know what to say. I didn't know how to face her with the knowledge we shared. And, even though I hated myself for doing this, I just plain didn't know what else to do. I did watch for her children, however, and tried to study them, looking for signs of abuse. But, other than bruises, which I didn't see, I had no way of separating.

Jeannie came in toward the end of the lunch hour with her boys. I stared. Ronald and Roland wore matching blue suits. They had on red ties and dress shoes. Their hair was slicked back. They looked absolutely miserable and embarrassed. Jeannie wore a sequined, low-cut evening gown stretched over her tummy with silver hose and four-inch spikes. Her hair had been piled high, and her face made up like a cover girl. She reeked of expensive perfume.

With a palm on each boy's reluctant back, she forced them across the room to the counter where food was laid out for self-serving. She rapped her knuckles on the counter and waited.

Abby came out of the kitchen, drying her hands on a towel. She stared at Jeannie, as shocked as the rest of us in the lunchroom.

Jeannie smiled. "Well, let's see here. Ronald, you like sliced beef. He'll have sliced beef on toast. No mustard. Roland will have the sliced turkey with extra mayonnaise. I'll have the turkey also and a small salad. Blue cheese dressing on the side. They'll have small milks, and I'll have the iced tea. Sweetened. Do you want chips, boys? Sure, give them chips. And, for dessert, we'll have chocolate sundaes. Thank you."

Abby didn't move, but her jaw had fallen, and her hands in the towel had stilled. The lunchroom had gone absolutely silent. Jeannie turned and marched her boys to a table, sat down and began polishing her fork. She held up a finger and said, "Oh, miss. Some water here, please," then went back to polishing her fork and humming.

I knew Jeannie had gone over the edge, but, for the life of me, I had no idea what to do about it. I leaned over to Beth and whispered, "Go get Uncle Wayne, hon. He's in the radio room."

Beth bolted from her seat and dashed out of the room. I looked for more immediate help. Connie and Marty sat at the table next to Jeannie. Marty had frozen with his fork midair. I met his eyes and pleaded silently. He nodded, put down his fork and slid back his chair. My heart pounded as he walked over to Jeannie.

"Why, Jeannie," he said brightly, "don't you look nice. Ready for lunch?"

Jeannie smiled up at him. "Dr. Dunn! How nice to see you again. It's such a lovely restaurant, isn't it? I hear the chef is absolutely gifted. The recommendations have been impressive. Do you come here often?"

Marty met my eyes. He was over his head, and we both knew it. I waved my hand at Abby, signaling that she should bring food to Jeannie and the boys. Abby hurriedly prepared plates of fried potatoes, hamburger patties, and mashed hubbard squash. She caught DeeDee at the kitchen door and told her to help her take the plates to Jeannie. DeeDee frowned, began to object until Abby whispered in her ear. DeeDee's eyes snapped to Jeannie, did a double-take, then slid her gaze past her to me. I shook my head.

DeeDee brought a plate, and Abby had the other two. Without a word, they set them down in front of Jeannie and her boys. They turned back to the kitchen.

"Just a minute, Dr. Dunn," Jeannie said, "Oh, miss, come back here, please."

Abby turned back, looking scared and deeply embarrassed.

"This is *not* what I ordered. What is this garbage anyway? I think it looks like . . . leftovers. Please take it away and bring me a proper lunch."

"Them's good fried potatoes," Abby said defensively. "And DeeDee said those hubbard squash came from *your* garden."

"Please!" Jeannie said. "I don't want an argument. I want the lunch I ordered."

Connie and I both stood up at the same time. Because I was behind Jeannie and couldn't be seen by her, I signaled to both Connie and Marty that I was going to try to get my hands on the boys, and they should try to take charge of Jeannie. Neither looked ready, but I approached Jeannie and said, "Hi! So nice to see you, Jeannie. The rest of the children have a separate menu and meal being served in the kitchen. It's kind of a party. Why don't you let me take the boys to the party. Then we can see about getting you what you ordered."

Her carefully lipsticked mouth began to form an objection, but Roland said, "Please, Mom. Can't we go? Please."

"Well . . . well, all right, dears. You two go to the party."

102

I ushered the boys away from the table. They went willingly. Ronald looked back once, and I saw tears in his eyes. They knew then, knew their mother was not quite right. When I aimed them, not for the kitchen, but out of the lunchroom altogether, neither boy objected. I took them into the schoolroom and sat down with them.

"What's been going on this morning?" I asked Roland. Ronald was sobbing.

The little boy screwed up his face. "I don't know, Aunt Barb. Mom made us get all dressed up. I don't know why. We didn't want to, but she made us."

Wayne came down the spiral stairs at a gallop. He paused when he saw me with the boys. "Hi, guys," he said. "Where's your mom?"

"Lunchroom," I said.

Just then we heard a shriek from that direction and turned to see Jeannie run drunkenly across the donut. She seemed to fall into their slice across the way. I turned mutely to Wayne, who looked horrified.

"Marty could give her a sedative—" I began.

Wayne let out a bitter laugh. "I doubt it could take the edge of the other stuff."

I stared. "Other stuff?"

Wayne sighed and met my eyes. "She's been doing stuff—uppers and downers—for years. Is Marty in the lunchroom?"

"Yes."

"Good. I think I'm going to need him. Do me a big favor, Barb? Get my boys out of that get-up and watch them?"

"Sure, Wayne."

JEANNIE WAS MOVED into the room behind the fourth set of double doors that opened onto the donut, a set we had not yet needed. This was the hospital unit. Marty and Jillian consulted on how to control Jeannie's withdrawal discomfort. Wayne admitted that she had been taking uppers and downers for a long time. At first it was just a sleeping pill a couple times a week, but, over time, a dependence had developed. It seemed that what I thought of as superior coping skills all through the years was drug-assisted living. I must say that I never knew, never even suspected. This made me concerned for her current pregnancy. If this had been going on since the twins had been born, she easily could have harmed her fetus.

Jeannie had used alcohol, cocaine, amphetamines, and a variety of prescription drugs. Being a medical secretary had apparently given her ready access. I remembered how confused and overwhelmed Jeannie had felt after the birth of her twins. Those first months had been difficult. I'm not sure I could have coped well with two collicky babies screaming most of the day and night for three months. As they grew, they were active, mischevious boys who I always thought would make me nuts. Obviously they had done a job on their mother. She never asked for help, never let any of us know she needed any and turned down offered assistance. Apparently, coping challenged her far more than any of us knew. Now, with no access and no more stash, Jeannie would have to learn how to cope without drugs, and that likely would be difficult for her if she had never learned to deal with her life in the first place. The good news was that, should her unborn child have escaped serious harm, it now had a chance to develop normally.

I felt sorry for Jeannie. As Connie and I cleaned up her slice to get the boys to bed that evening, we realized that the clutter of boxes and suitcases was how all our slices had looked the day we had moved in. Jeannie had not progressed beyond that point; she had done nothing. We arranged the slice the best we could, gave the boys games to play on their beds and waited for Wayne to return from the hospital room.

When Wayne finally came in, he said little beyond the most profunctory thanks, but his face said more. The very real concern for Jeannie was there, and worry tugged at the corners of his mouth. But there was also a kind of relief there, too, as if he was glad the family knew, glad he didn't have to carry the burden alone anymore, and glad help could be gotten for Jeannie and the baby. I wondered if maybe exposing Mike and Marie's difficulties might not do the same: get the problem out in the open so that healing could begin.

As Connie and I let the curtain fall behind us, Wayne was telling his boys that all would be well, that their mommy was going to be okay. I profoundly hoped so.

11

FOGGY

FRIDAY, OCTOBER 25

━━━━━

I WAS QUICKLY DEVELOPING A DREAD of mornings, of waking up in the shelter. That backed up into a fear of going to sleep. And, since sleep in the later stages of pregnancy had become difficult for so many reasons anyway, I found myself restless until late at night. That made me dread morning even more. Andy's absence compounded the unpleasantness of waking up—thoughts of him were the first I had upon achieving consciousness and clenched my stomach like a vice. Fear that he and the relatives with him were dead began to settle like ashes on all our hearts.

Harris mentioned continuation of the fighting in Texas, but details were fuzzy. We all worried about Jillian's sister, Sue, and her family in Phoenix, Arizona, and hoped they were not in immediate danger, though it seemed like no one on the planet could really expect to escape danger in some form or another, even those of us in the shelter.

The Middle East seemed to have been blown off the map. No one had word of what happened there. The fear we all felt seemed universal. The few times I laboriously climbed to the radio room, I heard nothing but fear in the voices. Reports of complete break downs in civil order abounded, spreading across the planet like a pandemic plague, and everyone, one way or another, was trying to hide from it.

Harris seemed to spend a lot of time telling other ham, short-wave, and Internet people that we were okay and hoping to get the same information back. Still, behind each affirming response was a "so far" attitude. Those who had planned, as we had, those who had seen the inevitability of world chaos and prepared what shelter they could, looked about themselves with shaky hope. No one knew who or where or what kind of shelter would prove effective in the days to come. A concrete bunker that could withstand anything less than a direct nuclear blast might not be protection against radiation or disease. A hideout that kept people far away from disease exposure might not work if invasions and war found them. I hoped Harris had considered all possible ends to the world short of an asteroid strike.

Civil breakdowns had occurred in England, France, Morocco, Iceland, Tokyo, Jamaica, and New Zealand. But no nuclear blasts, no invasions or war. Survivalists in those places were justifiably relieved. But all operators spoke in awe edged with horror of how quickly the general breakdown of their governments and society had progressed. In most places it had taken just one day. Wednesday. Harris had anticipated perfectly, calling us on Tuesday evening. That Wednesday we came into the shelter eclipsed Black Monday, the start of the Great Depression. Commercial radio and television stations operational that day reported wholesale looting and many deaths as the cities all over the country emptied, as all of society melted down. We lost our last local radio station on Sunday, although Harris's much more powerful receivers still pulled in viable stations from Cincinnati, Chicago, New York City, and outside Atlanta.

Harris's log book of radio and Internet connections around the world enumerated check-ins. He had maintained regular contact with many people for years. After that Tuesday, some never contacted him again; others checked in on a varying basis. Harris spent hours each day trying working his way down his lists and reacted badly when one or another operator could no longer be raised or missed a schelduled contact time, which he marked down in his log. As each station or email contact failed to check in, Harris marked it until five were amassed. Then he stopped contacting them. We lost two to three a day.

Life in the shelter was slowly becoming organized. Maybe that was an improvement; it was hard to tell. On the one hand, days seemed to run together in sameness, but we assigned clean-up squads to monitor our common areas. Abby scaled down the caloric and fat content of food, but we still ate tasty meals. An effort was made to use produce dug from gardens just prior to coming into the shelter so that fresh, perishable food was not wasted. Abby combined this with processing. She would bring in all brussels sprouts, serve them one evening and freeze the rest for later. Tomatoes, brought in green from late gardens, found their way onto the tables as decorations until they ripened. She spent considerable time in the storage area, checking and organizing foods we had so diligently grown but heaped in when we arrived. When Max pronounced the hanging meat ready for packaging,

Abby organized teams for that work. She saved out roasts and chops each time we carved up a side of beef or pork for cooking that night, saying that soon all we would have would be frozen and canned foods.

As head of animal care, Max Gertz organized teams, often older children, to feed and water the stock and pets. Crews of adults cleaned up every morning, trucking the waste and dirty straw in big wheelbarrows into the next room. Max organized this work, as well as the waste. Soiled straw from the cows and ponies was piled in a steaming heap. Duck, chicken and geese droppings went into a different pile and was sprinkled with lime. The brown waste pellets from the rabbits, sheep, and goats went into a different area. The waste of the cats and dogs found storage in a huge plastic bin in the back. Max wanted to use each waste product differently and didn't want them mixed. I wasn't sure where we'd be using any of it, but organizing this seemed to make Max happy.

Classes started for the children in the schoolroom. DeeDee and James were the main teachers, but Melissa Reinhart had been a school librarian and joined them. We were all supposed to contribute. I spent a couple hours each afternoon reading to the littler children from the large store of books we had squirreled away over the years and I sometimes held classes in health.

As days in the shelter slowly marched into the second week, each of us had a schedule. Our days filled with activities that had to be performed at specific times. I kept a list taped to the dresser for each of us, but I could not seem to get enthusiastic about anything. So much of it seemed like make-work to me. Maybe that was because there was never enough to do to occupy my mind, not for very long, anyway. A fogginess seemed continually to drag at me, and it seemed to be getting worse. The vice of tension in my stomach tightened by increments each day, and after two weeks in the shelter, I had constant headaches.

I had never bought into the idea that coming to the shelter was an adventure. Most of the children had, the Reinharts might have, and certainly Harris had. He often mentioned "the big adventure of survival beyond the point when that was no longer possible in the larger world." Maybe it was. I began to doubt that survival was possible if we didn't survive within ourselves first, and, to do that, we had to have a purpose beyond staying alive. I was convinced of that. In the outside world, just being alive wasn't enough, so why would it be in here? Living wasn't the same as surviving. In the foggy depression of my mind, these thoughts haunted me at waking and made the idea of staying asleep in the morning almost enticing. I struggled in the morning to get up, and it was getting harder each day.

On Friday morning, two and a half weeks into our self-entombment, my mind was filled with half-thoughts, hinted threats, and quickly forgotten insights on our plight. I felt my mind was beginning to atrophy or was so enveloped by tension and fear of what was happening to our world that it was ceasing to function properly. Everywhere that weight, that pressure seemed to suffocate me. It frightened me, but not enough to force a solid hold on consciousness. I drifted into unpleasant dreams I couldn't remember, filled with hollow voices and words that seemed to echo in the increasingly empty corridors of my mind. I dreaded the coming morning heralded by the lights coming up in the donut, dreaded shuddering into wakefulness only to discover that, yet another morning, I was a prisoner in the shelter. I missed the sun, the woods, the earth. I missed the weeds in my garden, slippery winter streets, and going to work in the dark. I felt beleaguered, aimless, crowded, claustrophobic and desperately alone. I began secretly to hope that something would happen, anything, just so I could find the strength within me to wake up a bit. I also didn't seem to be able to take a deep breath anymore no matter how I positioned myself against the bulk of my unborn child.

I finally woke almost hearing something, as if the dreams and terrors holding my mind hostage were scuttling away. I listened intently for a few minutes and decided that the skittering sound I thought was mice in the ceiling was probably a dream sound. There were no mice in the shelter that I had seen, not even in the animal room. Max Gertz and Harris had discussed this at supper one night. Harris had told him the shelter was sealed tightly enough to exclude insects and mites, let alone rodents. Maybe that discussion had triggered the dream.

I fought the thick fog of sleep, laboriously got up and put on my robe and slippers before I shuffled to the bathrooms and waited my turn at the shower, grousing along with Don and Connie that Jillian and Emily were taking too damn long. The water was lukewarm, and the lights all seemed dimmer, almost like the brown-outs that had plagued us in the months before coming to the shelter. No one else seemed to notice, so I feared it was the fogginess heavy on my brain. It felt like a hangover.

I rinsed my hair and watched the suds cascade down the hill country of my breasts and belly, tumbling to the tiles and foaming like the spray of a high falls. This should have made me smile, led to pleasant memories of family trips to Yellowstone and Yosemite. I should take joy in those memories. I didn't. Even memories seemed tired lately. They should be jewels to treasure and enjoy endlessly. They weren't. They were scabs I had picked at too often, and the wounds were sore and infected.

I waddled back to our slice in my used nightgown because I had forgotten to bring clean clothes with me, my hair wrapped up in a lavender towel from the bathroom. I felt out of breath and heavy, each step like wading through dry sand. I felt as if I had struggled all day instead of being up a scant hour and managed only a toilet trip and a shower. That little effort had tired me. I was exhausted, more worn out even than the end of moving day when we came to the shelter.

Emily strode across the donut, seemingly on her way to the lunchroom, which had become the hang-out area for all of us. She was muttering, looking furious.

"What's the matter?" I asked, pausing at my slice's curtain.

"They're gone, damn it! Someone . . ."

"Who's gone?" I said, feeling a tickle of alarm deep in my belly.

She spun and strode over to me and glared into my face, our noses nearly touching. "Was it you? Was it you that took them?"

Spittle hit my face, and I stepped away from her and wiped my face with a corner of the towel. Besides being alarmed that someone might be missing, I was now annoyed with her aggression. "Took them *what*?" I said.

"You never liked cigarettes. Maybe it was you. When I was in the shower."

"Cigarettes?" I said, relieved. "You're upset about cigarettes? What's the matter . . . are you missing some? A pack? A carton? What?"

For a second Emily looked like she was going to slap me. Then she frowned. "No, it wasn't you. You're too terrible a liar to act so clueless. Had to be a smoker."

Still not really sure what was going on or, certainly, the scope of the theft, I offered, "Mike and Wayne do. Melissa does sometimes. Marty . . . no, he quit last year."

"I've been missing cigs and packs from time to time since we got here, but no one touched a carton I hadn't opened. But now . . . now someone's taken all three cases of cigarettes. They cost me over fifteen hundred dollars."

"Three cases! You had three *cases* of cigarettes here?"

"Until someone swiped them. Yeah. And I want 'em back." Again her face pressed too close to mine as she yelled this.

"Well, I didn't take them, Em. Neither Frank or I smoke. Three *cases!*"

Emily blew her breath out in a loud *humph* and spun on her heels, continuing her march to the lunchroom. I stared after her, allowing myself the smallest of smiles—I really hated the smell of cigarette smoke—when Connie came out of her slice.

"Barb, come here a minute."

I wanted to go lie down, but I walked the few steps to her slice instead and met her concerned eyes with question.

"My candles are missing and my hurricane lamp," she hissed.

"That's odd," I said and pointed in the direction of the lunchroom. "Emily was just saying that all her cigarettes are gone."

"I know the candles were there last night because I lit one."

I went to check my own slice while Connie headed to the lunchroom. I could hear Emily's loud, accusing voice. I had one ornate lamp with a candle inside, a wedding gift from my great aunt Bea. The lamp sat on the shelf where I had put it, but the candle inside was gone. As I checked through the rest of my things, I discovered that my perfume and Frank's shaving cologne were also missing. I was just about to continue searching when I heard a commotion out in the donut. I feared Emily might have found her thief. I spun quickly enough to feel a little dizzy and hung onto the curtain a moment before I pulled it aside.

Emily, Connie, Don, Dewey, and Melissa headed toward the schoolroom. I figured that they all had experienced thefts and were going to ask Harris what was going on. That seemed logical. But, before they reached the doors, Wayne opened them and came out. I was well behind the others, so I couldn't hear what Wayne said to the group of angry people, but I could see his face; it was lit up and excited. That certainly didn't seem a likely response to a group of indignant relatives. Like a moth to a flame, I fixed on that expression and hurried over as quickly as I could, hoping something good had finally happened, something to snap my mind out of lethargy. Again I seemed to be moving in slow motion, like trying to run under water.

"What's happening? What?" I said when I joined the others.

Wayne turned and held the door for Harris. He held up his hands as Emily loudly accused him of stealing her cigarette cache.

"Someone's here," Harris said, completely ignoring Emily. He repeated it three times before everyone heard him and stilled their own concerns enough to listen.

"Is it Andy?" Don asked eagerly.

Harris sighed. I could see his sorrow at that question, but it vanished as he lifted his head to speak. "No. It's not Andy. From what I heard on the intercom, it's a group of several adults and some kids. We need to decide what to do. Go get everyone else. Everyone. Meet here in the classroom in five minutes."

He ducked back inside the room. I turned but realized I had no one to go get; the girls were both in the classroom already, and Frank was up in the radio room. I found myself standing alone in the donut, thinking back to the previous time when people had come to us asking for help. I said a prayer that we would be more receptive this time and promised myself I would speak up in favor of letting them—whoever they were—come into the shelter. What had been done before needed atonement.

I looked down, surprised to see my faded plaid bathrobe over my flowered flannel nightgown, and I realized I still had my hair wrapped up in the lavender towel that, loosened by being in place too long, flopped on my head like a too-large turbin. I thought I should go get dressed, but then I decided not to take the time for that. I didn't want to be late for this meeting. Anyway, what difference did it make? Why should I bother to get dressed at all? I opened the classroom door and walked in.

DeeDee and James were busy shoving the school desks to the side of the room. I sat heavily on a folding chair near the wall, hoping my head would clear.

"How do you vote, Barb?" James called over, grinning.

I knew why he was so eager. It had bothered him horribly that one of us had contributed to the death of someone who simply had asked for help. This time he planned on speaking up early and loudly.

"I say let them in," I said, then added, "Does it seem foggy in here today?"

DeeDee sat down next to me. "Everyone seems to be moving at half speed. It was hard to get out of bed this morning, too, but we both have excuses." She giggled.

DeeDee had finally told James about the baby, and, together, they decided to keep it. I had seen pregnancy break apart as many marriages as it cemented together in recent years due, I supposed, to the abysmal economy. I was happy to see this couple tighten their union with the prospect of the child . . . even at the edge of the world.

The classroom quickly filled from all quarters. Abby and her helpers came from the kitchen smelling of bacon and cinnamon from breakfast preparations. Max and his crew came in fragrant from the animal room, and the rest—in various stages of dress and undress—came from the family slices. When everyone had assembled, the room seemed almost crowded, the air suddenly very close.

Frank, followed by Harris, came down the spiral stairs. Don handed Harris a microphone. He tapped at it, then, satisfied it worked, said into it, "We need to make this choice together. I've just been talking with these folks. There's two families out there: a husband and wife with their two kids and a woman with three small children. The guy's a carpenter and a teacher, his wife's worked in a daycare. The other woman met up with them somewhere on the road. She's in a bad way, kind of in shock maybe. She lost her oldest child."

"How'd they find us?" Marty asked.

Harris hesitated. "Jim Stone worked on the shelter. He did some framing for the firm that poured the foam and concrete."

"I thought no one knew what they were working on," Mike said, frowning.

"Guy must be smart," Harris said and shrugged. "No one was supposed to know. We were calling them experimental silos then. The firm I used came out of Mankato, too. If this guy came all that way—"

"How *did* he make it to us?" Wayne said, his tone suspicious.

"Yeah," Mike added. "How'd this joker make it, and Andy didn't?"

I think maybe this was the first time anyone had voiced the idea that Andy and company were truly lost to us, probably dead. I felt the heaviness in my heart gain weight. Grief swallowed Harris's face for a moment. Then he shrugged and shook his head.

"Maybe he knows about Andy," Melissa said, her tone compassionate.

"How the hell would he know anything about Andy and Bob?" Mike said, his face almost a sneer.

Melissa looked abashed. "I don't know. I just thought . . ."

Mike was a lot closer to me than to Mel. I heard him mutter, "Don't strain yourself," so Wayne could hear. Wayne snickered.

"What about my cigarettes?" Emily said.

Harris looked at her and blinked. "What about your . . . what?"

"Cigarettes," Emily said again, her voice in a higher register, her fists finding her hips and planting themselves there.

"Yeah," Wayne said, "mine, too. And we're missing candles, a box of really good cigars, and all Jeannie's perfumes. Some of those are really expensive."

"I'm missing candles, too," said Connie.

Harris scowled and raised his arms high. "Wait a minute. What the hell's this? There's people out in the woodroom who want to come inside, people whose fate we have to decide . . . and you're talking about stuff that's gone? Cigarettes? I think you need to focus here, folks. Where are your priorities? Let's decide on these intruders first."

I don't know why Harris used the word "intruders." It seemed out of character for him. It *did* refocus everyone, though. The sides in the debate were predictable: Wayne and Mike adamantly didn't want anyone to come in; James, Marty, and Don did. Jillian suggested they might be contaminated. I put in a pitch for humanity, but I thought my words sounded hollow, as if my thoughts couldn't make it out of my head.

"Maybe we could look them over first," Emily said. "See if they're worth it, if they could contribute something, as Barb said."

As I had said? What had I said?

"Contribute what?" Marie said. "All we're doing is sitting around. Who needs more than a backside to do that?"

That was fairly astute for her, I thought. I just wondered whose side she was on. *Whose side was I on? What* had *I said?*

"Right," said Connie. "We should let them in. It's only Christian."

"That's not what Marie meant," said Emily. "What she meant was, who needs them to help us sit around? We're crowded enough as is."

"No, we're not!" said Melissa. "We've got lots of room. And that's *not* what Marie said."

"Those rooms are for Andy, Bob, and the pilot," Jillian said firmly.

Melissa hesitated, then held up her chin. "I was thinking of my mother's room, actually. There's other slices empty in the inner ring, too. They're small but—"

"We've got to vote on this," Harris said, his amplified voice blanketing the discussion. "Let's have a show of hands. All in favor of letting these people in?"

Even without counting, I could see it was a clear majority.

"Opposed?"

Mike's, Wayne's and Jillian's hands flew straight up. Emily's followed. I smiled. Humanity would take the place of selfishness this time. Reason had replaced emotion. No one would be shot. People would not be turned away. It could not make up for what had been done before, but, maybe, in a small way, it was penance for our sins. On the other hand, as with the Gertzes, maybe we were having a discussion of whether or not to let in our most valued participants into the Ark adventure. Maybe without these people at our door, hat in hand, there was no way we could survive at all.

"Okay," Harris said. "They come in. Now, this time, let's not go trooping out like a fire drill. Five people. Frank and I and . . . Don, Connie, and . . . Marie—"

"No," said Mike. "Not Marie."

I snapped my eyes to her face, and, by will alone, forced the fog to lift a little. Marie had not spoken. Mike had. That was not okay.

"Let Marie speak for herself," I said into the silence.

Mike glared at me. I'm sure he heard something in my tone, almost as if he could see the bristling at the back of my neck. "I said," he repeated slowly, "that Marie wasn't going. She's not been feeling well. I want her to stay here."

My neck hairs prickled again. "Great," I said. "Let *her* say that."

Marie, deeply embarrassed if her red face meant anything, said, "I'm not feeling great. Maybe I should stay behind . . . but I'd really like to go. I'd be honored, in fact."

"You're welcomed to," said Harris, his expression quizzical. He looked from Marie to me to Mike. His mouth began to form a question; then he shrugged.

"I'll stay," Marie said and smiled softly. "I think Mike's right."

Mike grinned a victory. I just smiled. Marie had had the chance to pronounce her acquiescence to Mike's will, when before she'd had no choice but to accept it. I knew this was just the tiniest beginning of independence for her, but it definitely was that.

"They might need a doctor," Marty said. "Let me or Jillian go."

"You go," shrugged Jillian. "I think I'm going to take a nap."

She appeared colorless today. I didn't think she was drunk or hung over exactly, but she had no spirit, none of the fire I had admired so often in the past. Instead of standing larger than life, she seemed to have shrunk into herself.

With the delegation formed, we all trooped into the donut, following Harris and his welcome committee to the exit stairs. His foot up on the first step of the short ascent to the hallway door, Harris turned to us. "Wait here, all the rest of you. I don't know any reason there'd be trouble, but Frank can lock the door if there is. With that locked, the people can only get as far as the hallway, no further."

He climbed a couple more steps and turned again. "I don't expect any trouble, though."

It was then I began to worry. And why not? We were vaguely aware of the horrors outside, yet insulated from them enough to know only the larger events—the news headlines, so to speak—those three adults and their children had probably experienced a lot. Maybe they could bring those horrors with them somehow.

My slice looked dim when I entered it, and it was as if I looked for clothes in the dark, even though I usually only relied on the general lighting system. Was it just my fogginess, or were the lights actually dimmer? I thought about that. Harris had handed off the question of missing items. Had he known what was going on? In the short inventory listed by victims of thefts, all somehow had to do with air quality. Was there something wrong with our air supply? With the filtration systems? With the power supply?

I finally found the enormous tentlike thing I sought and slipped it on. Even this was getting tight around my gravid middle. Shoes had been a problem for months, not so much because my feet had swollen—they were actually better than just before coming to the shelter—but because I could no longer reach my feet to tie shoes. My slippers were more comfortable anyway, as long as I didn't stand too long—they had no arch support. I slipped them on by feel, reaching with my toes under the edge of the bed. Then, sitting, I brushed out my hair. I had let it sit too long and it had gone all frizzy in the towel. I usually combed it out wet.

Suddenly I was exhausted. I was out of breath, sweating a little and totally lacking the wherewithal to stand. I wanted to go back into the donut and wait with the others, but I couldn't. I flopped back on the unmade bed and closed my eyes.

Breathing become even more difficult as I lay on my back because of the pressure of the baby against my diaphram, but I couldn't seem to gather the strength to turn onto my side or sit up. I thought I should just rest a moment, then ease up, but, when a few minutes had passed, I realized I couldn't move. Couldn't. Now I panicked and began to struggle, but I could barely flinch my arms at the elbow. Breathing became gasping, and I knew I was in trouble. I had to turn over, had to get help or I would pass out and maybe stop breathing. There were people in the donut, but I couldn't make my voice work. Spots began popping in front of my eyes, and I seemed to be growing distant from myself. My ears roared with static. With what seemed a gargantuan effort, I reached for the head of the bed. Then the ceiling tipped.

12

BONUS

―――――

A BLUR OF SHADOW AND LIGHT SWAM in front of my eyes. Sounds, also fuzzy and muted, held no meaning. I sensed an urgency around me, felt it in a kind of tumbling, falling movement. I resisted the crash, then fell into a soft void.

A clock ticked. The crisp measurement of seconds penetrated the marshmallow world and opened a pathway back to hard lines and clear sounds. I drew in a deep breath. Oxygen. I was breathing oxygen through a mask. My hand came up to explore the plastic cap over my nose and mouth. A hand took hold of mine, and I struggled to open my eyes. Frank's green eyes met mine. Concerned lines in his face reshaped into a smile.

"Wha' hap'ned?" I mumbled through the plastic mask.

"You passed out."

Not Frank. My eyes focused past his left shoulder. Jillian reached for my wrist. Then she lifted off my mask and twisted down the valve on the oxygen cylinder.

"Did I fall?"

She gave me a quizzical look. "No. You pulled a bunch of books off the shelf above your bed. Mel heard the crash."

"The baby?"

"Fine, Barb. Just fine. You've got maybe a week to go. Nice strong heartbeat. Probably a boy."

"Why?"

She frowned and leaned a little closer. "Why what?"

"Why did I pass out?"

"Too much carbon dioxide in the air and some other contaminants. Carbon monoxide among them. The air filtration system was screwed up. It would've killed all of us in a couple days, except that it affected you, and the welcome wagon people felt better after being in the woodroom. We added it up."

I heard something in her voice. "Was anyone else affected? Charleen, maybe?"

Jillian exchanged glances with Frank. He nodded. Jillian turned back to me and said, "She was unconscious. Lori thought she was asleep. And we didn't even notice that Mom and Dad weren't in the schoolroom for the vote. They were unconscious in their beds. But they're all okay. Everyone's okay."

I said, "Ma Anders?"

Jillian shrugged. "Unlikely. That was only the third day. The air's only been bad the last thirty hours or so. No, old Mrs. Anders died because she wanted to die."

Frank leaned over me and smiled. "Marty thinks this air problem is partly to blame for everyone's depression the last few days. But the problem's solved. There was a stuck gauge. We fixed it. The filtration system kicked in right away when the gauge was fixed and has been humming ever since. Everyone's better. How are you feeling?"

"I have a headache," I said. "Not much else. And the baby is really okay?"

Jillian rolled her eyes. "Yes! Fine. Relax. We all have headaches. They should go away by tomorrow. Now, don't get up without help the first time, just in case you're dizzy."

She left. I thought maybe she had some of the crispness back in her step.

Frank squeezed my hand. "I best get back to the radio room."

"Sure," I said. "No word from Andy?"

Frank should his head. "Nothing."

My mind, clearer then than it had been all day, remembered events earlier that morning. "Oh, so it was because of the air system that Emily's cigarettes were confiscated. But why the candles and perfumes?"

Frank's face blanked. "Confiscated? Whoa! You think Harris was behind that? Not. He's missing stuff, too. When could he have taken anything?"

I frowned. "Harris didn't do it?"

Frank swiped two fingers across his forehead, then kissed them. This was some quasi-Boy Scout sign he liked to use. "He's just as bewildered as the rest of us."

I thought about that a moment. Something didn't ring true. Then I remember about the people in the woodroom. It seemed my memory had no protocols for importance. "We let them in, didn't we? The people? We gave them sanctuary?"

Frank smiled softly and slid his gaze to my left. A privacy curtain blocked most of my view, but I could see the hump of feet under covers in the bed next to mine. In a low voice, Frank said, "The other couple's okay. Getting settled in Ma Anders's old slice temporarily. They're caring for this lady's three little children. DeeDee offered to, but neither the Stones nor the little kids would have any of it. They've been through hell together, I'd say. God, it must have been awful. Anyway, we don't even know the woman's name. She's not talking yet, suffering from exposure and dehydration . . . shock and grief, too. Marty's got her settled in here for a day or two on IVs. The Stones—you'll like them—they'll be in with her baby. Little thing can't be more than six months old."

I felt tears come to my eyes at the thought of trying to survive in a hostile world with three little babies.

Frank squeezed my hand. "If her story ever comes out, I'll just bet none of us will like hearing it. But we'll need to. We should all be grateful for the shelter even if nothing worse happens out there."

I nodded. Frank produced a nurse's call button from under my pillow. He leaned close to whisper. "We put you between Jeannie and the new lady. Mom and Dad are in the last two beds past Jeannie. Marty asks that you stay put for the rest of the afternoon and . . . maybe tonight, too . . . and keep an ear tuned. Jeannie's doing pretty well, of course, but Marty fears that having these new folks here might upset her . . . threaten her or something. And the new lady needs to be monitored in case she has medical problems we don't know about yet. Use the call button if either of them needs attention."

I couldn't tell from Frank's voice if my confinement was really for the good of the other two women or a precaution for me executed in a way that he and Marty knew I would tolerate without question. I balked at the idea of spending the night in the hospital ward, but Frank promised to spend the rest of the day with the girls. He had spent so little time with us since coming into the shelter, I thought there might be some advantage to my remaining in the hospital room for that reason alone. I agreed to spend the night, and Frank seemed relieved. As he got up to leave, I had him pull back the privacy curtains separating me from the other women.

Jeannie said, "Wait a minute! Frank, pull that back. Further. All the way to the end. This may not be much of a room, but it's mine. Leave me alone, Barb."

Frank returned the curtain to its original position and grinned at me. "She's getting better, don't you think?" he whispered. "Before she was shrieking obsenities."

"I heard that!" said Jeannie. Then she switched on her reading light, aimed it at the curtain separating us and put her hand in front of it. Both Frank and I could clearly see the shadow of her extended middle finger. Yup, definitely dealing with things better. Before, she'd likely have dressed up and ordered caviar. Non sequitor.

Trying not to laugh, Frank went to the other curtain and began to push it back. A glance at the woman in the bed next to me sobered him. His face quickly slid to an expression of compassion and empathy for whatever had befallen her. Then Frank leaned down and kissed me before leaving the hospital.

I couldn't see the woman's face, but I could tell from her shape that she was not a heavy woman, maybe not quite as tall as I was unless her knees were pulled up. As the hospital room became quieter, so that the only sound was the crisp crinkle of paper as Jeannie occasionally turned a magazine page, I could hear the new woman wheeze as she slept. I turned onto my side and watched her. Every now and then, her shoulder shuddered, and she moaned softly. An IV dripped slowly, glucose maybe or Ringers lactaid. That would figure if she were dehydrated and maybe malnourished as well.

Tears burned in my eyes again as I imagined the poor woman exposed to the elements in a hostile countryside. I tried to imagine being outside with my two girls, what I would feel if I had to travel on foot for any great distance. It was difficult to imagine. Then I tried to picture being refused help, being turned away from shelter, and soon I lost the ability to form any picture at all. Tears slowly fell to the sheet.

Near noon, Abby wheeled in a food cart, and suddenly I felt ravenous. Jeannie received her tray first and complained about the offering. Abby just told her that was it until supper. She served the senior Quills, then came to me and smiled.

"Feeling better, missus?" she purred.

I had repeatedly tried to get her to call me Barb, but she didn't. She called DeeDee and Mel by name. I smiled anyway and said, "Much! How's your day going?"

"Now the air's fixed, great! I had no idea how slow I'd gotten." She drew in a deep breath. "Now I seem brimful of energy. We got the rest of the meat made into sausages this morning. That electric stuffer Mr. Harris has is just so quick, it'd like to send sausages right outta the kitchen. Poor DeeDee screamed when it snaked across the counter at her 'fore she noticed. We got the links twisted off just in time. Made six different sausages, including a right spicy one, my ma's favorite."

I marveled at Abby Gertz. Nothing seemed to faze her, not being in the shelter, not having her lifestyle ripped away from her, not giving up her home and farm life. She had adapted about as well as I could imagine anyone could, better than many of us who still groused about lives left behind. I never heard Abby complain . . . not since her regret at leaving her chickens, and that seemed so long ago.

"Should I wake the poor woman, missus?" Abby asked as she set down my tray of thick soup and meat sandwiches. The aroma alone made my stomach gurgle.

"I don't know," I said. "I think sleep is important . . . but she needs food, too. Why not gently see if she'll wake up."

Abby walked to the bed and leaned over the figure. She rested a plump hand on the woman's shoulder and squeezed gently. "Miss? You'll be wanting to eat something, maybe? You want your dinner now or later? I'll come back if'n you want."

The woman moaned and shuddered under Abby's hand. She stepped back. Slowly the woman in the bed stretched out and turned over. She was considerably taller than I thought. Bony shoulders poked out of the covers and hunched forward as the woman slid her hands back to push herself up.

"Let me do that for you," Abby said quickly and elevated the head portion. When she stepped back, I got a look at the woman for the first time.

She was African-American. That didn't bother me, but it did startle me at that moment. She was painfully thin. Out in greater Minnesota, sustained by big gardens and meat animals, we had been protected from the privations in the big cies. Life there, even Minneapolis and St. Paul, had been hard for some years—cutbacks in funding for most things, including welfare and schools and city services, had been drastic, frightening, deadly. It had worsened all year. The unemployment rate in cities had reached close to twenty-seven percent just before we were called to the shelter, and I was certain the numbers had been played down. People had been starving, dying.

This woman, obviously, had experience city life firsthand. Her eyes were sunken, her hair a shapeless, kinky mat. The long-fingered hand that tried to wipe sleep from her face was attached to a bony arm.

Abby, chattering on about needing food as well as rest, busied herself with adjusting the hospital table and setting out the food for the woman. She fussed about the pillows needing fluffing and plumped them at the woman's back, adjusting the bed twice to get the perfect position. Then Abby put the napkin under the woman's chin and pushed the table closer. "There," she said with German satisfaction, "you eat up now. I'll be back for trays later. Holler if you need anything. And don't you be afraid to ask for more, miss. We got plenty."

Through all of Abby's mothering ministrations, the black woman had said nothing. She regarded Abby with a kind of catatonic wariness, like a wild animal caught and resigned to its cage but far from tamed. No emotion flickered over her face or changed the expression in her withdrawn eyes. But, as Abby turned to leave, the woman seemed to struggle to speak. She husked, "My babies . . . ?"

Abby rushed back to her side and patted her hand. "Now don't you worry none, miss," she said soothingly. "Your children are just fine. We fed them big bowls of soup to warm 'em up and gave them nice fresh milk. Now they're having steamed meat and potatoes. Dr. Dunn said not to feed 'em too much too fast, but them children are getting all they can hold. Don't you worry. And the Stones are with 'em the whole time. Soon as you get some food in you and some of that good milk, they'll bring in your bitty baby to nurse. Do you both good to cuddle up warm and full."

Abby left, pushing the cart ahead of her. I watched the new woman as I began to eat Abby's rich beef soup. For a long moment, the woman didn't move, just stared after Abby's retreating back through the open hospital door. I saw a tear slide slowly down her mahogany cheek. I pushed back my table and slipped out of bed.

I took her hand as I sat down on the edge of her bed. "It's okay now," I whispered. "This is a safe place . . . well, as safe as any place can be nowadays. Your children are being cared for. Whatever you faced out there is over now."

Slowly, her eyes turned to meet mine. She seemed to search my face a moment, then looked down at the tray before her. A bony hand came up from under the table and wrapped around the spoon handle. A little awkwardly, probably due to weakness, she plunked the spoon into the soup and lifted a dripping portion to her quivering lips. She sipped the broth from the meat and let the spoon return to the bowl. It seemed to take effort for her to swallow.

I pushed the bowl closer. "Do you want help?" I asked.

She looked at me and shook her head. "I can do it," she said weakly. Her gaze slid to my belly, and she added, "Go eat your own meal. You got need, too."

I returned to my bed and pulled my table close. As I ate, I watched her. She drank all the broth from her soup, gulped down every drop of the rich Jersey milk and struggled to chew a bit of the sandwich, but she was so weak that she had to give it up even though the meat was falling-apart tender. She seemed to look at it longingly a moment. Then she leaned back against the pillows and closed her eyes.

The woman was haggard and emaciated, her hair tangled and ignored, but I didn't think she was much older than thirty-five. Though she was obviously weak physically and spent emotionally, I sensed a strength in her. She would have had to be strong to cope with three little children and make it here from . . . anywhere.

Abby came back to collect the trays. She loaded the elder Quills', then Jeannie's tray onto her cart. I could see that Jeannie had eaten precious little and had made a mess of her tray, too. I was ashamed for her. Abby rolled her eyes in Jeannie's direction when she took my tray and shook her head in disgust. I quite agreed. When Abby saw how little the black woman had managed to eat, she clucked her tongue.

"I shoulda guessed you'd be weak after all you've been through," she said apologetically. "Tell you what, miss, I'll stop back in a bit with more broth and milk. Would that suit you? Rest now. In a couple days you'll be fit as a fiddle."

After Abby left, I saw that the woman seemed to be sitting comfortably, her eyes open. I introduced myself. She pulled the sheet up to cover her breasts that had begun to leak through her hospital gown and regarded me soberly. "I'm Romala Magillicutty," she whispered. After a pause she said, "Where am I?"

"This is a shelter . . . um, out past St. Joseph and near St. John's University. Where are you from?"

"Minneapolis," she said. She looked away then and seemed to shut me out.

I imagined there were painful memories involved that prevented her from friendship so soon after coming to us.

The Stones came in a little while later and introduced themselves. They were a handsome couple, also African-American, with two boys ages five and seven. Jim Stone, about thirty in age, had a ready smile and very white teeth. Agnes, a couple years younger, I guessed, was more reserved, a little on the chunky side with very light skin and straightened brown hair. I liked both of them instantly.

Agnes had brought Romala's baby and pulled the curtain so the woman could nurse the infant comfortably. Jim Stone sat on a chair at the foot of my bed.

"You're Frank's wife, right?"

I smiled. "Yes. Barb."

He nodded thoughtfully. "Second oldest brother, right?"

I grinned. "What are you doing? Memorizing the lot of us?"

"You bet. Come from a big family myself. Thirteen of us kids. I'm second youngest, so some of my brothers and sisters were grown and married before I got to grade school. I have nieces and nephews older than me." For a moment, just a moment, though, I saw his concern for his family. I hoped they had found shelter. "You can tell a lot about a family if you know the order of the kids and how they relate to each other. Let's see now . . . you're Emily Johnson's sister. She's eldest. Then you've got a brother who's the doctor. Then there's you and that gal with the pretty, dark-eyed little girl . . . um, Lynn? And her daughter is . . . Anny?"

"Pretty good," I said. "only I'm older than Marty, and Anna is my sister. Lynn is her daughter."

Jim turned a dimpled smile on me. "Aw, come on. You're not really older than Marty, are ya? You don't look it."

He was a real charmer. I sopped up the flattery like gravy. When a woman was a big as I was with pregnancy, people tended to offer little by way of compliments. They'd say well-meaning things like, "I bet you'll be glad to get your figure back," or "looks like a big baby," or the ubiquitous, "due real soon, right?" All called attention to one's girth and awkwardness.

Jim Stone's line of conversation was intriging and fun, but he was making small talk, avoiding saying anything about the ordeal he, his wife, and the poor woman in the next bed had faced. And, except for the one unfiltered look, nothing about his fears and concerns. I wondered why. He didn't look as if he had faced the nighmare that Romala had, so I thought I'd try to draw him out.

"Frank said you were from Mankato. How long did it take you to get to us?"

He scooted his chair closer. "Has she said anything?" he whispered.

I whispered back, "She told me her name."

Jim sat back and blinked. "Yeah? That's more than she told us. Poor woman. Kept muttering about her oldest son getting shot by someone while he was looking for food because she was too weak to go any further. He just didn't come back one evening. She found him in the morning. The kid was only eight. Damn heartless bastards!"

His eyes apologized for the profanity, but I shook my head and said, "I agree. I don't believe anyone should be turned away from shelter in these times."

He let out a long sigh. "I don't know what we would have done if. . . . Anyway, thanks, Mrs. Quill."

"That's my mother-in-law. I'm Barb. So, Jim, tell me about your family."

"We've got these two boys, William and Charles . . . only if you call them that, they'll likely sock you. Billy and Chuck, they'll accept."

Together we laughed, then he grew more serious. "The firm I worked for was out of Mankato. We lived in Uptown. Until yesterday, we hid out in our basement, hoping the insanity would ease up. We had no lights and no heat, but we wrapped up in blankets and kept real still. I had an old van locked up in the garage, but I kept all the gas, the battery, spark plugs, and tires—about anything I could pull off it—with us in the basement to keep anyone from wanting it. We didn't dare leave. It was awful those first few days. Most people were trying to get out of town. Then there was looting and shooting. It was like the gangs gone rampant. Then it got real quiet. That's when we took off. Four in the morning. We got out of Uptown without a hitch. Once we got started, the trick was to keep going. The highways are jammed with cars . . . not traffic, mind you, just abandoned cars. It looked like a freeze frame of rush hour. Biggest mess I've ever saw. I left the highway as soon as I could and drove as fast as that old van could go. Scariest two-hour drive I ever hope to take. We parked outside and rang your bell."

"I'm surprised you lived in Minneapolis and worked out of Mankato. That's a long commute."

He shrugged. "Money's money, but I only worked there summers. The rest of the year I taught in the Cities."

"Taught? You're a teacher?"

"Yeah. Math. Sixth grade. Aggie taught science at Edina High School until cuts two years ago. She's been working mostly in a daycare since then. Had to make ends meet. Got any use for a couple pretty good teachers?"

I grinned. "What? You didn't see the horde of kids we've got?"

Agnes came around the curtain then, having heard us, and we all laughed, then grew quiet as Romala's baby began to fuss. I figured she was switching it from one breast to the other, and the baby's protests ended abruptly, confirming that guess. "When did you find Romala?" I asked softly.

Agnes looked confused. I nodded toward the curtain. "Day before yesterday. She came into our house and poked around upstairs. Anything worth taking was already gone. She was weeping over her eldest son and hugging the other three about hard enough to squish them. The baby was crying, the other two were all eyes and scared. We did what we could for her, but she needed help. In a way, it was her coming that forced us to leave. Jim knew what this place was, but we didn't intend to come up here until it got a lot more desperate. Travel seemed risky. Getting out in one piece was about as much luck as anything else. Anyway, we hoped you'd take us in."

I smiled. "I hope you'll be happy here."

Jim grinned, his even white teeth flashing. "This is quite the place."

Another thought came to me. "While you were traveling here, did you see any other travelers?"

"After we got out of the Cities, we didn't see any other cars moving at all. It was real spooky, I'll tell ya. I-94 filled with cars bumper to bumper in all four lanes plus the shoulders and none of them moving. Still makes my skin crawl."

"Not cars, Jim," I said. "We're missing some relatives who were traveling by horse and wagon. Did you happen to see anything like that?"

Jim shook his head. There was a commotion beyond Romala's curtain, then the curtain opened, and Romala unsteadily approached my bed, her baby in the crook of her arm and her IV skidding after her. Agnes Stone took her hand to steady her and slipped the baby out of her arms. Romala's eyes fixed on me.

"What's wrong, Romala?" I asked.

"Saw 'em . . . I saw them. The last town, I think. Not far."

Jim stepped close. "No. I'd've noticed if we passed anyone driving horses."

"No," insisted the woman. "Not on the road. Farm house. Red barn with a gray-and-white silo. Big trees out front . . . um . . ." She ran a hand over her face and closed her eyes. "There was a white picket fence along the driveway and the road. Big oak tree and . . . and a willow with a broken top. The horses were tied to the willow."

I felt adrenaline sweep through me and all but kick me in the stomach. I grabbed the call button and pumped it for all it was worth, maybe a dozen times.

Within moments, both Marty and Frank came running into the hospital room. "What is it?" they said almost together.

"Andy!" I said. "Frank, Andy is at *our* farm!"

13

RESCUE

———

M Y ANNOUNCEMENT CREATED AN INSTANT BATTLE. James and Dewey, of course, wanted to rush right out and get Andy and the others. It would take them little more than half an hour to make the round trip. But Mike didn't believe it was Andy at all.

"I mean," he said after we all met in the classroom, "why the hell would he hole up in St. Joe when we're just ten miles further down the road? That doesn't make any sense. I don't think it's Andy. If you ask me, I think that poor woman made it up."

"Why would she do that?" I snapped. "She described the farm perfectly."

"I don't know. Maybe she thought she saw them after you mentioned the horses. Maybe she's so screwed up she thinks her imagination is real. Maybe she want- ed to give us back something for our great generosity. Or . . . or maybe she did see a team of horses, but it wasn't Andy at all. Maybe it's even the people who stole the team from Andy . . . and *killed* them all. We could be risking both the men who go and maybe everyone here in the shelter. We could be going after murderers."

"Takes one to know one," Dewey said, only partially under his breath.

That would have caused a fist fight if both men hadn't been tackled by other brothers. It took four of them and a slow shuffle back and forth across the room to hold the two men apart.

"The fact is," Emily said after a semblance of order had been restored, "that it might *not* be Andy. We do have to think about that."

"And it could be that Andy or one of them is hurt," said James, "or just plain exhausted. What if they forgot the way up here?"

Frank shook his head. "Andy's been here before. Several times. Last summer when he was up here, he knew the way cold. We needed him to know that, and he

126

did. Maybe Bob doesn't remember the way, and I doubt Linda or Emily would, but Ben's been up here with Andy. He should remember. No, that's not the problem."

"Wait a minute," I said. "When I came at the call. I ddin't recognize the place. I hadn't been up here since the shelter looked like a collection of dinosaur eggs. Not even the farm looks the same. The road used to go down into the valley, not up a hill to the woodroom, and the hill behind it looks like it's been here since the glaciers."

"Maybe," Harris said. "Ben hasn't been here for . . . a while. Maybe it does look too different. But Andy was up here last summer. He knows how it looks now."

"And it still might not be Andy," insisted Wayne.

"If it isn't Andy," I said, "then it's someone else." I said this with firmness, with a conviction I didn't need more words to express.

"Maybe with kids," James said, picking up my cue. "Maybe they *are* strangers, but they might be nice folks just looking for a way to survive. Don't we owe—"

"We don't owe anyone jack shit," said Wayne. "This is *our* place, built with *our* money for *our* safety!" He poked a stiff finger to his chest with each assertion. "We sure as hell don't have to go out looking for stray people to share it with."

"Not even if it really is Andy?" James said.

"Andy should have come *here!*' shouted Wayne, his finger now aimed at James. "He *knew* there were risks. He *knew* that. He knew he was going to be on his own *until* he got *here*. If we go out, we risk the safety of everyone. Isn't that right, Harris?"

Harris had said precious little so far. He had laid out the situation right after everyone had met in the schoolroom, but then let the discussion work on its own. Maybe he knew it would work its way back to him; maybe he was willing to let everyone have a say. But I knew Wayne. He wouldn't have asked Harris's opinion if he wasn't reasonably sure that Harris would side with him. The leer at the corners of Wayne's mouth confirmed to me that he was sure. He knew something that most of the rest of us didn't.

Harris drew in a long breath. He looked around the room, then said, "Well, there are risks . . . more than expected. When we were going out to let the Stones in, I took some outside readings. It . . . it seems there's been an increase in atmospheric radiation levels. That increase has grown more dramatic in the last few hours."

"Radiation!" The word was repeated around the room as if the Black Plague had visited us. The plague was a lesser risk; it only claimed maybe half the human population in the Middle Ages. Radiation wouldn't be as negligent.

"How bad is it?" Connie said, her voice quiet with respect.

"Well," Harris said, equivocating not so much because he didn't want to alarm us as maybe not really wanting to talk about this subject at all. "Well, it's not so bad *yet*," he said with a shrug. "Not much more than the fallout here when Chernobyl went up. The problem is we don't know where it's coming from or how bad it's going to get. The levels could spike fast and without warning. If the wind was coming from the west, I could accept that this was the fallout from the exchanges between the Soviets and the Chinese. But the wind's out of the southeast today. I don't know what that means."

James stood up. "So what? What has this got to do with going and getting Andy. Today. Right now."

"Don't be a damn fool," Mike said. "You go out there and . . . maybe you don't come back."

"We're arguing the wrong issue," Dewey said. "It's not over whether we should go out or not? That was settled about the time Romala Magillicutty said she saw a team of horses. We're going. The only relevant issue now is how to do it."

Mike started to say something, but James stepped in front of Harris and said, "Dewey and I are going regardless of what anyone else feels about this. Even you, Harris. We're going. Tell us how to do it as safely as possible."

The following shouting contest involved nearly everyone in the room. A line of non-combative brothers and cousins stayed between the factions. Finally, Mike and Wayne threw up their hands, calling the rest of us damn fools, and stalked out.

From then on, the discussion swung to tactics. A plan formed. Even if the pilot had brought someone with him, which he had been allowed to do in exchange for bringing our people to the shelter, the numbers involved still should be small enough to cram into one van. James and Dewey would be the rescue team—that went without saying—and DeeDee and Mel seemed to accept it, if with tight lips. They would take Wayne's van because it was in the most reliable condition and race over to Frank's and my farm, which was the only one with a red barn, big trees, and a white picket fence on the way to the shelter from St. Joe. They would park some ways from the house, maybe on the road out front, and honk their horn. Depending on who came out, they would either stop or floor it away from the place. That was the really scary part to me; I wasn't so sure those particular two men would drive off even if faced with armed strangers. Anyway, if it was Andy at our farm, they would load everyone up and head back.

"What if they don't recognize the van or come out?" James said.

That seemed to pose a problem for a little while, until Dewey suggested they paint a sign on the side of the van.

"Wayne isn't going to like it if you paint up his van," Connie said.

"Who gives a shit?" said James. "Yeah, we'll paint 'Andy, is it you?' or just 'Andy.' Have we got some spray paint around here?"

Dewey started to chuckle. "No! No! I got it! We'll paint 'Harris's Ark.' Andy will recongnize that, of course, but other people might just think we're a bunch of loonies in a van, that the van is the ark."

It was perfect. In the years of construction before we needed the shelter, especially when Harris had seemed obsessed with the place, the family had often teased him, calling it Harris's Ark. No one would know that outside of family.

Harris said he had two radiation suits to help make the trip safer for the two men. I think DeeDee and Mel really like that idea.

"Why only two?" Emily asked. "Why not a dozezn . . . two dozen?"

Harris spread his arms wide. "*This* was supposed to protect us from radiation. The shelter. I only stocked two radiation suits because that's all I could think of our needing. We're not supposed to be opening up the shelter every other day, you know. I'm hoping that *if* it is Andy and the others at the farm, this will be the last time we go outside until the world is safe."

T HE MEN LEFT at about two that afternoon. Most of the rest of us walked to the woodroom with them. Marty recommended I not go, that I return to the hospital ward and rest. I couldn't. In a way, I guess I was hoping for a glimpse outside because, when the massive steel door was opened and I peered into the darkness of the woodroom, I was unaccountably disappointed. I drew in the slightly sour smell of split oak and a stale manure smell from the animals that had spent a short time there. I felt the chill of autumn air, too, but the door clanked shut before the men had made their way up the cellar steps to the outside. I felt an urge to follow them, to go outside, but I couldn't do that. Instead, I returned to the main area. Several people, including DeeDee and Mel were going to wait in the hallway, ready to open the door when word came from Harris.

It should not have taken much more than half an hour to make the round trip to our farm, maybe an hour and a half if much loading had to be done or any of them had been injured. Two-thirty came up very quickly, then passed. Three o'clock slipped by. Three-thirty crawled slowly toward us, each second a resounding *tick*. Then it, too, met silence. Four o'clock loomed, paused pregnantly, then passed. Four-thirty. Tension wound up with each passing moment like a watch spring tightening.

Sitting in the schoolroom, we formed a depressed, tautly anxious company. I chewed my lip and watched the clock, counting out each little step forward of the second hand. Then started again. I soon felt I had been sitting in that room for days.

I jumped when a hand rested on my shoulder. I turned to see Jim Stone. He crouched beside me, his finger across his lips, eyes furtively scanning the other semi-comatose waiting people. I frowned in question.

"I'm going after them," he whispered.

"No," I whispered back in alarm.

He closed his eyes and shook his head. "I got to. I don't know what's wrong, but something is. It's too long. It's been just too long. Maybe I can help. One thing for sure . . . I know those two guys aren't armed. I am."

Alarm must have lit up my eyes because he squeezed by hand. "I'm not going to shoot anybody, but if there's been trouble, maybe I can tip the scales. Okay?"

"You don't have to do this just because we let you come in here, you know. Regardless of what Mike said, it wasn't generosity. It was simply the human thing to do."

Jim smiled. "So's this. I just wanted you to know I went after them."

"What about the radiation?"

"It's no worse . . . well, not much anyway."

He stood up and walked out of the room.

"What did Jim want?" Frank said from the front of the room, straightening in his chair, his face haggard.

"Oh," I said, "he was . . . thanking us for taking in his family."

"He doesn't have to thank anyone," Don said firmly. "We should take in anyone who asks. Anything else and we compromise our own humanity."

I could see the young intellectuals of our company had spent a fair amount of time setting their priorities. I smiled. "He knows that, Don."

Frank eyed me as if he understood what I wasn't saying, but he didn't press the issue. Don was satisfied that Jim Stone knew how we felt.

Five o'clock came. And went. Soon it seemed like hours since Jim had left, and still nothing. I was exhausted and so emotionally spent I finally left the schoolroom and returned to the hospital ward.

Jeannie saw me coming and said, "About damn time *someone* thought I might want to know what's going on. Andy here yet?"

"No," I said wearily. "I'm sure they'll let us know when he does come."

I climbed into my bed and covered up. When I was settled, I noticed that Romala was watching me. When our eyes met, she smiled a little.

"How are you feeling?" I asked.

"Better. I ain't got no memory of much before this morning, though."

I panicked. "Even the horses you saw?"

She smiled. "Oh, I remember them 'cause my Benny pointed them out to me. 'Look at the big horseys,' he says. 'If we had 'em, we coulda been out of the Cities months ago.' So, I looked, and I remembered. There was something inside me that told me it was important. I looked, and I knew I *had* to remember. I s'pose that don't make sense to you, but I've always been able to kinda 'know' stuff. Aunt Selma said it was a gift or something; I never seen a whole bunch of good come from it, not for me anyway. Didn't do me no good to know where to look for my Albert."

Albert had to have been the child who was killed. I knew it from the far-off glaze that slipped over her features a moment. Romala withdrew back within herself.

I knew this woman had a lot of healing to do. For a little while, I thought about her grief and the ordeal she had faced, but my thoughts kept sliding back to wondering and worrying what was going on outside. And worry was so tiring.

I WOKE WITH A START, and my eyes snapped to the clock on the wall. Six-fifteen. I struggled out of bed. When I started out of the hospital, I nearly collided with Abby and her supper cart. The clatter of the cart must have been what had awakened me.

"Oh, missus! Heavens, you gave me such a turn. Where're you going?"

"I wanted to know what was happening. Has anyone heard from Andy yet?"

She clucked softly. "No word yet, missus. Everyone's so tense, too. Mr. Harris wouldn't come out of the radio room to eat, and even your mister is too upset for supper. Emily and me, we fed the kids, but no one else seems to have any appetite. I don't know whether I should keep it warm or pack it all up and serve it again at dinner tomorrow. What do you think I should do?"

131

"Keep it warm a bit longer, I think. If the rescue party gets here, appetites will come back really fast. Give them until . . ." God, so many hours had passed. I couldn't imagine what had happened. ". . . give them until seven."

I looked at the plate of fried chicken, baked potato, and steamed squash. It looked good, but I knew I couldn't fit a bite past the lump in my throat. "Put mine back too, Abby. I'm sorry, but I just can't eat until I know what's happened out there."

I hurried to the schoolroom. Not much had changed. People still sitting about looking anxious and ill-tempered. Not much point waiting there. I left immediately and headed for the bathroom. The lunchroom was noisy when I passed. Children raced about, teasing each other, bordering hysteria from the look of them. After a brief stop in the bathroom, I went back to the lunchroom and called to Beth and Andrea, who were tugging at either end of a naked Barbie doll.

"Andrea won't give me my doll," Beth said, her face flushed.

I recognized the gymnist Barbie as Beth's doll. "Why not, sweetie?" I asked Andrea. "You have Barbies of your own."

"Mary Sue has them," Beth said. "She took most of mine, too. When I went to her slice to get them back, Uncle Mike told me to go away."

I didn't like the sound of that. Mike might not be happy when opinion turned aginst him, but he couldn't take it out on my girls. "We'll get to the bottom of this," I said. "You just come with me so you can show me which dolls are yours."

I spun on my heels and crossed the living space to Mike and Marie's slice with Beth and Andrea galloping at my sides.

I don't know what I was thinking. Why was I so upset about some silly dolls when all that was on my mind was the unknown dangers and happenings outside the shelter? Yet I was absolutely furious, angrier then I had been in a very long time.

At the closed curtain of Mike and Marie's slice, I shouted out, "Mike! Why can't my girls get *their* dolls that *your* daughter *stole* from them?"

I heard a scuffle inside the slice, and Marie began to cry. Suddenly the situation seemed to flop from one of dolls to something much more insidious. I made a decision that was probably rash, probably based in the anger that had propelled me across the living area. I took hold of the curtain near the top and yanked it wide.

Mike stood over Marie, his hand raised. Little Jimmy sat far back in his trundle bed, his face streaked with tears and his thumb in his mouth.

132

"Stop!" I shouted.

"How dare you!" Mike shouted back, coming toward me aggressively. "This is *my* slice! How dare you come in here without being asked."

I thought he might hit me and almost backed up, but something within me stopped me. I would not back down from this cowardly wife-beater. I stood my ground, my two girls pressed behind me, even when Mike came within a foot of me and shouted into my face, spittle flecking my cheeks. "How dare you interfere in my life!"

"I don't give a shit about your life," I said. "You're interfering in Marie's life. In your children's lives. This must stop. You must not do this ever again."

Then I stepped around Mike and grabbed the other end of the curtain where it attached to the column and yanked it with all my strength. The curtain ripped free and heaped onto the floor. I turned again to face Mike and saw beyond him a gathering crowd of people coming from the schoolroom and the kitchen.

"This must stop," I repeated. "You must stop abusing Marie and your children. The curtain is pulled on your dirty little secret. Never again. You must not ever hit them again."

Mike turned the most incredible shade of crimson I had ever seen outside of cartoons. He broke into tears and collapsed. For a long moment, we all just stared at him, aghast, I guess, by his reaction. Marie slipped her hand into mine.

"I have to go to him," she whispered.

"Don't you dare!" I said quickly, then saw her face. She was as much in pain as Mike and almost as red-faced. I patted her hand and whispered, "Just don't let him think you agree with him. This behavior has got to stop now."

My anger fizzled. Was this the right way to attack the problem? I had no idea. The shocked faces of the relatives gave no indication how they felt about the situation . . . or if they even knew what had been going on. I felt embarrassment also, a shared shame that such disgraceful behavior was part of our family. I wanted to be away from there, away from Mike and Marie and the knowledge of what had happened. But, truthfully, I just plain didn't know how to leave.

Jillian arrived from the hospital. She took one look at the scene and said, "Accident prone, indeed! Damn it, Mike. Well, get up off the floor, both of you. Now that this is out in the open, you'll have to find another outlet for your anger. It's about time you got some backbone anyway, Marie. Took the curtain down, huh? Good. Leave it down. Privacy, obviously, has been misused. Having none now might make it a more valuable thing later."

We left Mike and Marie alone. I sincerely hoped they could find a place from where to rebuild their lives in a healthier manner. I hoped, too, that we would all have to be a part of that healing. I walked my girls to our slice, thinking that, if there was any survival for any of us, even within the shelter, we had to change. Not just Mike and Marie and Jeannie. To make our effort worthwhile, we had to try to become better people.

I headed to the lunchroom, then. Melissa was talking to DeeDee and Abby. Her thoughts dovetailed into mine. "We've got to dump what's grown stale, even cancerous. We have to stop thinking of ourselves and start to think about our community."

DeeDee nodded and added, "We're not saving many separate selves."

I said, "A group of separate individuals is doomed to fail in this ultimate test of communal living. Only together, only as a single, dedicated entity, can we make the shelter work."

A little later, I ducked under the curtain of my slice and sat at the edge of the bed. Quiet settled in around me, throughout the entire room, in fact. The little travel clock's ticking found my ears again, and I suddenly remembered that Andy and the others were still missing. I snapped my head around to see the clock's face. Seven-thirty. James and Dewey had been gone for five and one-half hours, Jim for over two. Where were they? What was happening? What could be taking so incredibly long?"

Beth was reading *Green Eggs and Ham* to Andrea, and they seemed content to stay in our slice. I walked toward the schoolroom, drawn there by the knowledge that word would come over the speaker system there first; relief for my stretched nerves would be soonest there.

I had just reached the doors when the speakers crackled. "So," James's voice blared, "hope you all saved supper for us. We're plenty hungry. And, by the way, put plates out for about thirty extras."

14
ARRIVAL

FRIDAY EVENING, OCTOBER 25

F OR THE FIRST TIME IN THE NEARLY TWO WEEKS of our confinement in the shelter, I felt euphoric joy. The tension that had so dominated all of us evaporated in the happiness we heard in James's voice on the speaker. In its place grew an expectancy that bubbled up into giggles and grins as we waited on the floor of the living space at the foot of the stairs, watching for the steel door to open. Everyone seemed to be feeling the same way. We were like kids on Christmas morning, held back those last few delicious moments before being allowed to race down the stairs. The last wait was always excruciating, awful and wonderful at the same time; then it too was over.

The big steel door at the top of the stairs finally banged open, and Harris stood above us, his silly grin careening over his face. He gave us a thumbs-up, and we cheered in one voice. We surged forward, eager to culminate our relief with sight of our lost family members.

People began to file in after Harris and slowly descend the stairs, and, for me, the euphoria quieted. There was no joyful mirror in the faces of those coming down to us to match the crazy laughter of our crowd. Instead, I heard echoes of the confusion we had felt when first coming into the shelter and saw in the faces of the many strangers the pain of passage they had endured in their time after the fall of the world. That pain demanded a quieter greeting, joy, perhaps, but something that respected their suffering. We could see that the people coming down the stairs were burdened enough without carrying our joy, and those of us on the floor all felt this, drew in our exuberance and held it patiently in our hearts.

Some of the people descended the stairs clutching bundles they probably had carried since leaving their homes, and those bags and suitcases, though cumbersome for some, were far smaller than the car and truck and trailer loads of possessions we had brought in. I remembered wondering how we would funnel down our lives small enough to fit into the shelter; these people would not have that problem. Some carried only the shadows behind their eyes. Theirs were the heaviest burdens of all. I saw loss and grief in those shadows and wondered if the shelter had enough space to hold them all.

A young woman slowly inched down the stairs, one hand on the rail and the other clutching a baby blanket to her breast. She paused in the middle and turned to go back up, as if something or someone had been left behind. The young man at her elbow—her husband, I assumed—folded himself around her and helped her continue down, his head bend to her ear and one hand on the hand that clutched the blanket. A boy, hardly older than Beth, looked out of sad, deepset eyes as he walked down the stairs alone, his clothes ragged, his hand wrapped in filthy cloth. I did not know the details of his recent life, but I read in his face and aloneness more pain than I hoped my children would ever have to endure.

There were stories of misery in almost every face, of loss and privation, stories that had to be told, recorded, remembered in hopes of not forgetting or repeating what we all had experienced.

Andy came in, wrapped in a blanket and supported heavily on either side by James and Jim Stone. His face had lost that annoying cock-sure macho leer and was pale and drawn. A bandage around his head had stained through with blood above his left ear. He had been injured then. That began to explain what had happened.

Bob Quill came in, supporting his wife, Linda, with his daughter, twelve-year-old Wendy, holding Linda's other elbow. Bob looked good; he even grinned for us, but in his face also, I saw less of the macho that had kept me at a distance from him in the past. In its place I recognized a kind of open confidence, as if new convictions had begun to order his life. Linda looked tired. Wendy had that aura of burgeoning adulthood that Beth was showing.

Andy's son, Ben, also twelve, came in with Dewey and Mel. He was joking and laughing as we had been just moments before in direct contrast to most of the people's expressions coming down the stairs. I wondered if a new kind of macho had formed in this boy, the kind that fears to show fear or pain. At first I wondered how a twelve-year-old could go through even the events I knew about that had happened to them—the armed defense of the men's bathroom at the airport, the cold and rain while traveling to us, not knowing if they would reach us—and not have that record impressed on him. Then I realized that if that passage was not visible in his face, as it was on so many of the other young faces of those who made their way down the stairs, it didn't mean it didn't exist. Ben had to have suffered, had to have been afraid at times and must have faced the possibility of dying. Those tracks were etched indelibly someplace. Hiding them with laughs and bravado and shrugging them off didn't make them go away. I feared for Ben.

The procession down the stairs seemed to go on forever and stopped just at the bottom, with the rest of us in a semi-circle around them. Young people in shock by the switch in their lives, older ones looking like the immigrants their relatives had been a hundred eighty years before, crying children who had been cold and hungry for too many days, a young girl with a poodle in her arms—so many people, so many stories. In numbers, they were more than half our own company. That would take adjustment, an adjustment we likely were more willing to make now than had they come when we had just arrived.

We had not been as cold as these people had been nor, certainly, as hungry, but we also had suffered. We had been made to look at ourselves and analyze who we were, and I had no doubts this process of deconstruction and rebuilding would continue, that it was, in fact, only in its earliest stages. We had seen ourselves as less than perfect, far less than ideal, perhaps barely worthy of salvation. With no illusions that we had cleaned up all the ragged edges in our lives, we were ready, as we made an avenue for the new people to the lunchroom, to face the future with these refugees, merging their endurance with our vision. It would take time—probably a great deal of time— but I was confident that, if the world allowed us, we could come to a better definition of humanity within the walls of the shelter. There was hope for all of us.

When I felt this hope swell within my breast, I knew then where my joy had gone. Though respect for these people's suffering restrained it from oozing into giggles and laughter, it still could not wait patiently in my heart after all we had worried. Hope had more dignity—a more respectful tone—and a built-in patience that effervescent euphoria just couldn't manage.

T HE FIRST ORDER OF BUSINESS was food. We had been informed by James that many had not eaten in a couple of days. Some inadequately for a lot longer than that. We also needed to find places for the new people to sleep. As that process began, Abby heaped platters of food on the counters and front tables.

I watched the blank eyes of some of the new people come to life at the sight of the steaming platters and tureens. The slow progress of the newcomers across the donut quickened. Dirty hands reached for Abby's hot buns and grabbed plates but forgot forks and spoons. DeeDee and Abby stood ready to assist. I saw DeeDee's face fill with tears as she tried to help a parentless child with his plate. The young boy, maybe eight, repeatedly filled his plate to overflowing with coleslaw; it was the first bowl on the counter. After several gentle attempts, she abandoned the effort and simply prepared another plate for him from the many foods available. Then she sat with him until she finally convinced him that he could have all he wanted of any of the foods. He reminded me of a dropped-off puppy that had appeared at our farm early in our marriage. The poor thing was barely alive, dehydrated and painfully skinny. I found him eating spoiled squash out of the compost heap. He ate it, not because dogs were fond of squash, but because he knew it was food. In all of his many years with us, Shep forever whined and sulked when I walked to that compost heap, as if memories of that desperation and privation still haunted his canine mind. I was sorry now that Frank had laid him there just before we left the farm. I grieved that he had not come with us. He should have.

As I waited with the rest of the family, who stood back to let the newcomers have the food to themselves as much as they needed, I began to understand the levels of caring in how these people approached abundant food. The young man who had prevented the woman from returning up the stairs prepared a plate for her and sat her down before going back for a plate for himself. Even as he sat, his eyes eager for the feast in front of him, when she seemed slow to eat, he pushed his plate aside to butter her roll and help her cut her fried chicken. The little girl with the poodle, as thin and hungry as a Dickens character, paid no attention to anything but the meat. At first I thought she was instinctively going for the highest protein source. But she carried the plate to a corner and sat down on the floor with her little dog, feeding him bite after bite of chicken breast with her fingers and eating none herself. Abby saw her doing this and brought her another plate of food divided so that the child could see one side was for her and the other for her pet. She began to eat only when the poodle refused any more.

Our children, fed earlier, seemed fascinated by these new people. When we finally sat them down with desserts, even the youngest of them hesitated, sat quietly and ate in silence. Though I often heard complains from these same kids, though the size of cake and pie slices had to be precise to keep them from comparing pieces, these same children had learned dramatically that such behavior was not acceptable. It was as if that old refrain—"There are children in India who would love to have what you have."—that my mother had used to shame my sisters and brother and me into cleaning our plates had suddenly become very immediate and real for our children. I vowed never to say anything similar ever again; the reality of hunger was too painful to be part of casual behavioral control. And it was too close to home.

Finally, with our own children busy, the rest of us slowly began to move to the counter for our supper. Many of us ate very little that night, both because we dared not take food from those many hungrier mouths and because we were too emotionally spent to need much food. Abby made a point of assuring us quietly that there was plenty left in the kitchen and more ready to be cooked if that seemed necessary. But she didn't eat either. Instead, she circulated among the tables of the newcomers and refilled plates and bowls as they were emptied. She didn't even ask if a person wanted more. I wondered if I should tell her that overfilling a stomach long deprived of food was maybe not a good idea. I caught Marty's eye at the next table and nodded toward Abby. He seemed to understand but shook his head. I wasn't sure if he meant that it wasn't a problem or that I shouldn't interfere. A moment later, however, I saw that Abby had taken a plate from a young man who could eat no more, assuring him that she'd save his food for him until later. Marty smiled.

EIGHT CHILDREN HAD COME without parents. As accommodations were being arranged for families and couples, and as the people began to move from the lunchroom toward the slices as space was found for them, these children stood silent, little waifs waiting for the adults in charge to dispose of their lives. That had already been done, of course, and to their detriment; in this new world we were beginning, we had to do better by them. James and DeeDee approached the seven-year-old boy who had heaped his plate with coleslaw. He looked up at them with a kind of pained hope, his eyes empty saucers. DeeDee cried and hugged him. Clearly her unborn child now had an older brother.

Connie reached toward the little girl with the poodle, but the dog snapped and growled. The girl turned away and hugged the little beast. Two sisters, one fourteen and the other maybe eight, faced Connie with faint smiles, and the kindly doctor's wife melted immediately, took their hands and led them to her slice. As I walked over to the parentless children, I saw Melissa also try to reach out to the little girl with the poodle. Again the scrappy little dog bared its needley teeth and issued forth a growl far larger than its miniscule body. Melissa pulled back her hand and stood uncertain a moment as the girl turned away. She took the boy with the injured hand to her slice instead. Sissy eyed the poodle from a distance and steered clear, selecting instead two brothers, both under ten, who held onto each others' hands as if afraid to let go.

Paul Fisk appeared at my elbow. "A pretty little girl."

"Yeah, but I don't know how to get past her little monster. It might be all of three pounds, but it'll take my hand off."

Paul laughed. "That's what it wants you to believe. He's a good actor. He's protecting her, of course. Lori wants to take the other girl with us. She's closer to Charleen's age. That little girl with the poodle would fit right in between Andrea and Beth. I suggest you approach the dog and not the little girl at all. If that doesn't help, I've got some tranquilizers that will."

I walked toward the little girl, trying not even to look at her. When I was near, I awkwardly crouched down and extended my hand to the little dog. The toy poodle stared daggers at me but didn't bare its teeth.

"Hi, little guy," I cooed. "You're going to need a place for you and your little friend to sleep, you know. This might be a strange down here, but it's safe, at least."

The little girl, a thin child hardly more than six, looked at me. I smiled, trying to keep my gaze more on the dog than her.

"What's your dog's name, sweetheart?" I asked.

I inched closer, no mean trick in a crouch with my belly over-balancing me, until the palm of my hand was just at the little dog's black nose. It sniffed at me, and I hoped it would be satisfied.

"Prince," whispered the little girl.

"And what's your name?"

No response. I eased my fingers under the dog's chin and scratched it a bit, then reached around the girl's shoulders with my other hand. The poodle watched me with the wariness of a fox, but it didn't offer to snap. Nor did the child resist. I guided the little girl out of the lunchroom and toward my slice.

It was nearly midnight, long after the children were asleep, before I lifted the curtain to our slice and eased my tired legs inside with hopes of rest for myself. All the new people had been fed, cleaned up a bit and settled in temporary slices or bedded down in the lunchroom and the hospital wards. Some had taken up quarters in the unused stalls of the animal room, including the Gertzes, who willingly gave up their slice to a family with six children. Their generosity moved me deeply.

At least a dozen of the people new to us had lost immediate family members; the young couple had lost their three-month-old son to exposure. Many of the people had been gathered as Andy traveled from Big Lake to St. Joseph, but a few had met up with him while making journeys of their own. The furthest from home was a solemn-faced young man from Iowa trying to get to his family near Virginia, Minnesota. We agreed to feed him and let him rest, then fill his backpack with supplies if he insisted on continuing his journey.

I sat heavily on the edge of the bed. Beth and Andrea were asleep in the top bunk. In the bottom one lay the little girl with the poodle. At no time that evening had she let the animal out of her arms. The tiny white dog still had pink ribbons in its topnot and showed a recent clip, but its coat was dirty and the ribbons ragged. Huddled in the arms of the little girl, whose name I hoped to learn soon, the dog watched me. I still could see the wariness in its glittery eyes and a protectiveness far larger than its small size. I wished there were a way to tap the courage that small beast had grown into; I thought we could all benefit from it.

Frank had said he would be in later, after all the new people had been settled. I had to get off my feet. Still, I found sleep wasn't what I needed. I lay on top of the covers on the bed, listening to the relaxed breathing of the children, holding silent communication with the dark eyes of the little dog.

The room grew quiet slowly. Once in a safe and secure place, the need to talk had opened up many of the shadowy faces of the people who had come with Andy. That talk lasted until well after midnight. Tears lasted longer. My own included. I thought maybe I was weeping for joy because Andy and Bob and Linda and their children were finally safe, finally with us, but that wasn't all of it. I also cried in sorrow for the suffering of the people who had come. Especially the children. I cried for the suffering of those who hadn't come to us, as well. Perhaps we had grown too comfortable in our existence, perhaps we had grown too selfish and proud. But, for many of the people who experienced these times, we had also grown incapable of dealing with this depth of hardship. For those found wanting, the climate all over the world had grown harsh. I mourned for the losses in my species. Yet, behind all of that—intimate and global—I cried for something within myself. I found I couldn't identify this, certainly couldn't define it, except that it was definitely a mourning, not joy, and it welled up from my very soul. In another way, though painful, the tears I shed seemed like labor tears, the final release of sorrow before real joy could begin. I hoped so. I desperately needed relief from the anxiety I had been feeling.

I ROSE TO WAKEFULNESS on torrents of noise, reminding me of that first morning in the shelter, but when consciousness firmed, I heard nothing. I listened. All was quiet. The travel clock said six-thirty, and I noted the still-dim lights in the donut that had not yet brightened with artificial day. We followed an autumn schedule of light so that brightening should not occur until after 7:00. Harris had even programmed a gradual lightening that last half hour of night to mimic the dawn. By the darkness in the donut, I knew I could sleep another hour before activity woke me. Of course, once my bladder knew I had awakened—even though I had not moved a muscle—it let me know how full it was, and sleep was history. I moaned, at least mentally, and fought gravity to rise.

Sitting up, I saw that Frank actually lay next to me—the first time in the shelter—and my girls were curled mostly as I had tucked them in. The girl with the poodle, however, sat in the far corner of the head of the bed, staring at me with frightened eyes. The poodle, held tightly in her thin arms, let out a soft growl.

I made no move toward the child but smiled and whispered, "You know what? I bet Prince needs to go potty after all the meat he ate last night. You think so? Let's you and me take him to a place where he can go."

The little girl seemed to shrink further into her corner, and the little dog moaned another soft growl. I wasn't sure what I had said that had scared her. "Don't you want to let him go potty?"

The little girl shook her head.

The poodle whined.

"I think he needs to," I said. "Come on. You can take him. It's right over there," I said, holding the curtain aside and pointing across the habitation done to the animal room doors.

The girl looked out, her eyes on the stairs. I thought I understood.

"We're not going outside. We have a room *inside* for the animals. We have cows and ponies and chickens and ducks and rabbits. There's four cats and a mama dog with puppies. All inside. Come on, I'll show you around, and Prince can go potty. What do you say?"

The little girl eased off the bed. I held the curtain aside for her, then climbed to my feet and followed her out. Though I feared wetting my own panties if I delayed my trip to the bathroom too long, I walked with her to the animal room doors. All around the donut, sleeping bodies lay singly or in clumps. Our living space looked crowded with the newcomers, but I remembered Harris saying that the shelter could support two hundred people. We weren't nearly half that. My own count indicated that the slices around the donut and in the center had overfilled with the inclusion of the new people. Where would another population the size of ours be housed? But, though I considered this, I didn't worry about it. The shelter had provided well enough for us so far. I trusted that what Harris said was true. What choice did I have anyway?

I opened the animal room door as quietly as I could and let the little girl and her pet inside the mudroom. The young husband and his wife lay against Max Gertz's crusty boots. The man opened his eyes and half sat.

"I'm sorry," I whispered. "The little dog needs to go potty."

He didn't look irritated. In fact, he didn't look anything, his face remaining entirely expressionless. Poor man. I ushered the little girl through the wooden doors. I knew some of the people had taken temporary residence in the unused animal slices, so I held my finger to my lips to let the little girl know to keep quiet. Mentally, I shook my head and told myself how stupid it was to caution a child who hadn't said two words to keep quiet.

We walked to the stall where a compost bin was set up. Five fifty-gallon drums were arranged on stands and had cranks to turn them. Theoretically, we should be composting food wastes to make rich soil for later use. In actuality, the succession of food was such that plate scapings and food that had ceased being usable as leftovers went to the pets and pigs and rabbits and chickens. Not much was left for composting after that, except bones, and they were set aside in a kind of dryer awaiting grinding into bone meal. So far, all that had been fed to the composting drums was some floor sweepings. Inside the stall, the floor was dusted with sawdust, and a pooper-scooper stood ready.

I closed the stall door behind us and smiled at the little girl. "Put him down now and let him go potty."

Obediently, the little girl set the dog on the sawdust. Roaching his back and daintily stepping through the bedding, Prince tottered a few steps away from the little girl and lifted his leg on one of the compost barrel supports. Even for so tiny a dog, he peed a long time. Then he tiptoed a few more steps and squatted. After he had completed his job and was safely back in the little girl's arms, I scooped up his leavings and deposited them in a bucket that would be emptied later in the animal waste bin the in the next room.

"Now it's our turn," I said to the girl, directing her to the animal room toilets. I rejoiced mentally when she offered no objection and entered the room.

"Do you need help?" I asked, trying not to pee down my legs.

To my horror, the child shoved the poodle into my arms and went into a stall. Great. Not only could I feel a drop of pee trickle down my leg, but the little dog glared up at me with abject hatred. I crossed my legs. It growled. I squirmed. It growled again. I moved my hands the least bit, and it bared its teeth. I figured if it did bite me, I'd pee all over the floor, and, if the little girl didn't hurry up, I'd puddle the floor anyway. I could smell that she was going to be longer than a quick pee, and I knew the exact limits of my bladder. One kick from my unborn baby and my slippers would be soaked.

With the poodle growling and baring its teeth the whole time, I sidled to the sinks and deposited the animal into one. It snapped at my thumb as I pulled my hands away, and needle teeth snagged a bit of skin. Another drop of pee trickled down my leg. I made my way to the nearest stall as quickly as I could. I barely had time to pull my panties down and sit before the floodgates opened, but the relief that washed over me afterwards was worth the nipped thumb.

Upon leaving the stall, I saw the little girl with the poodle in hand facing a startled-looking Abby Gertz, who stood halfway into the bathroom. The poodle snarled viciously, it's tiny, glittering eyes bulging.

"Easy. Easy," I said, imposing my bulk between the little beast and Abby. Oddly enough, the dog stopped growling.

"My, my, my," said Abby. "That bitty dustmop thinks he's a German shepherd, don't he?"

"Apparently," I said, turning to look down at the little white bundle, who looked up at me solemnly but without snarling. "We were all on a potty run. Surely you're not getting up for breakfast duty already."

"Actually, I am. With all the new people, I thought we'd need to eat in shifts, and I want there to be plenty for them poor new folks."

"You can't fill up the hollow places in their eyes with food, Abby," I said, and regretted it immediately as Abby's face fell almost to tears.

"I know I can't, missus," she said softly, shaking fingers quickly covering her mouth. After a moment, she got control of herself, removed her hand and said, "I know I can't, but I don't know what else to do. I'm not a doctor type. I get around them sad faces and can't get a word outa my mouth past the lump in my throat. I just want to sit and cry for them, but what good would that do? What I *can* do is feed 'em. I figure, if that's what I can do, I'm going to do it good."

I smiled warmly. "You already do it well, Abby. Right now, I think good food, friendship, and shelter is about all we can do for most of them anyway. Time is the only thing that will heal them."

"How much time, missus?"

Not an easy question. "I don't know. For each of them it'll be—"

"No. How long must we stay in the shelter?"

A much more uncomfortable question. "I don't know," I said in a whisper, the words spawning strings of thought I found disturbing and different from the concerns that had crowded my mind for so long. With Andy and the other relatives away from us, our minds had been tricked into believing *that* was the big concern, the big issue, and yet, now that those concerns had ended, I found my mind had been harboring other worries all along.

I ushered the little girl back to bed and lay next to Frank, thinking.

15

ORDER

TUESDAY, NOVEMBER 5

———

E VERYTHING ABOUT OUR LIVES changed when Andy and the people with him arrived. We no longer had to worry about where these relatives were or how they were going to get to us. This was good. With that debilitating weight lifted from our minds and shoulders, an era had passed. But, with its passing, when the nervousness in my stomach didn't go away, I realized that thoughts of Andy in the days past had only mirrored the larger worry, the greater concerns we had for our world. The tension did not diminish one iota, and I felt incredibly cheated by that. Yet our lives changed after Andy came.

We, of course, began to learn the stories of our relatives. Andy had been hurt, and the radio he used to contact us had been destroyed by the same bullet that grazed his temple. The radio probably had saved his life. But none of the others remembered the way to us. Bob and Linda had only been home one time during the construction of the shelter, and they said that they had intended to go to see it, but that Linda had fallen ill on that occasion. They didn't even know where Harris's farm was. Young Ben had been to the shelter once, but as a ten-year-old, and he only remembered the dinosaur-egg stage and didn't remember the way. Having gotten as far as St. Joseph two days after last talking to us and even searching some of the roads around St. Joseph for several days in an effort to find us, they could go no further and holed up in Frank's and my farm. That was as far as Bob and Linda's memories carried them. Upon questioning, it turned out they had actually come as far as the crossroads below the shelter, not half a mile from us, but had turned back, loathe to leave the shelter of the farm and not sure the muddy dirt road led anywhere. Rain had obliterated all recent tracks by then. They prayed each night that someone from the shelter would come looking for them.

Andy, with his head wound and concussion, was not the only one of the new-comers needing medical assistance; a number of people had bumps and bruises, cuts and infections and frostbite that needed attention. Being a nurse, this gave me and others something concrete to do for a few days. We filled the beds in our tiny infirmary and brought in cots to accommodate others needing attention for injuries and malnutrition. I gratefully tackled cuts, infections, and frostbite, giving each meticulous attention. With Jillian and Marty calling the shots, I revelled in shift hours and regular rounds of meds. These were things I knew well—as Abby knew how to fill empty bellies—things on which I could focus my weary mind, filling the nasty places where worry festered with a kind of gauze pack of purpose. For a few days it worked.

Our living space had to be adjusted, of course, because we just couldn't allow people to sleep in the animal room or on the floor in the bathroom. A small shifting of how the slices were arranged yielded some space, and the center of our living area, formerly used for luggage storage, had an expansion feature that Harris activated. This yielded nearly twice as many small slices for single people and the childless couple. These adjustments proved insufficient. Harris, with the aplomb of someone who had thought of little else for five years, had us move the tables and benches out of the cafeteria into the donut, clustering them around the kitchen and bathroom doors—kind of an alfresco arrangement—and, with panels already in place, half the cafeteria was changed into a dormitory for unattached people with little or no belongings. He and a few men disappeared into the hall to one of the STORAGE rooms and emerged with enough bunk beds to accommodate everyone. He even came in with a divider screen to separate women from men for privacy.

As the infirmary became my focus, food preparation became the purview for a whole squad of people with Abby at the helm. A detail of men went out to retrieve more of Gertz's cattle, and for days the smell of blood seemed to permeate the room. Fourteen head of cattle were rounded up; one butchered to supply our immediate needs, the rest accommodated in the animal room. Five more pregnant cows were added to the herd we had amassed, and half a barn of alfalfa and several tons of grain and corn moved in as feed for them. None of the pigs turned loose into barnyard could be found.

With all this outside activity, three more people were found and taken in. A woman with a six-month-old baby, the wife of a man who had worked on the project with Jim Stone, was found in the woodroom one morning. Her fists were raw from pounding on the door, her face haggard and streaked with tears. She and her daughter were alive and reasonably healthy, but, at the bottom of the road, a small plane lay in smoking ruins. The body of her husband, a plasticine expert, lay on the road. We buried him next to Ma Anders. The third newcomer—now there were several levels of newcomers—was a teen-aged boy. Beth thought he might have gone to her school. The seventeen-year-old had wild looking eyes, and I didn't like the way he carried his mouth. I would have called him a thug. Perhaps before the world fell apart he had been. When the men found him curled up in Gertz's barn, he was a shivering, frightened, hungry kid. The men left a camera and sensors in the barn in case someone else got that close to us unaware.

News from the outside remained depressing. We lost the Internet connection one morning. For Harris, that meant the loss of dozens of contacts. I was surprised it had lasted so long; the commercial radio stations had been gone for almost two weeks already. Ham and short-wave radio people disappeared more slowly. Some told us they were abandoning their stations to find food; others just stopped transmitting. We maintained contact with about a dozen survivalist groups, most para-military outfits or religion-oriented enclaves. Harris called them regularly but had to filter through the dire predictions of all-out war and the end of the world to catch any real news. Several of the para-military groups related shooting intruders. We were saddened by this, believing that people were just looking for help.

Those who came to us told us about their journeys. Most said that whole towns had been abandoned, with the people heading south for fear that winter in Minnesota would bring hardships they could not survive without electricity and heating fuel. They were probably right; almost no one had wood-heating systems of any kind anymore. Bob and Linda said that St. Cloud, Waite Park, and St. Joseph had all been deserted as far as they could tell. Other towns around us—Avon, St. Stephen, and Holdingford—probably had suffered in the same way. The person who had shot Andy never showed himself, though Linda had cowered in fear every night after that, afraid they were being watched.

With the countryside essentially emptied of people, we knew few more would be coming to us by the time snow locked the land in cold and prevented much travel. Several inches already lay outside, and Harris hoped for more so our tracks to the Gertz farm would be hidden. We had found ourselves in an interesting philosophical position.

Security demanded that we not advertise our whereabouts, but we intended to take in anyone needing our help. We believed that many needy people shivered and starved in hiding places as near as St. Joseph, certainly in St. Cloud, but we could not go out and find them. Some worried that too many people would come if we sent a van out. Others argued that, even if we sent out a van, people might fear to show themselves. The condition of many of the children—like the little girl with the poodle—confirmed that fear would keep many, probably the most needy, from responding to the van. She had been found in a house Andy's people had broken into as shelter for the night. She screamed every time any of them looked at her, and the little dog snapped and growled. It had cost a few minor bites to get them to come when the group left.

Reluctantly, with the pain of waiting for Andy so much in the forefront of our minds and not wanting to revisit that each time someone went out, we voted as a group to remain within the shelter, taking in only those who came to our doors. It was not a comfortable choice, but we accepted it as the only one we could reasonably make. We did set up a video camera in the woodroom and a motion alarm system that kicked in with any movement larger than a mouse. Several cameras were set up outside the shelter, also, aimed at the road, the lower meadow, and the hill behind us. In the next week, we took in a Siamese cat and two stray dogs—a mixed-breed collie that wagged her tail furiously and whined pitiously when she saw us and a purebred airedale, who looked as shell-shocked and wary as some of the people who had come. Some food, some soft words, and a hefty dose of tranquilizer finally got the airedale inside. Some worried the big dog would hurt the children, but Paul assured us that the airedale's aloof behavior was really pretty normal for the stoic breed, that he would warm to us in a few days.

The young man in search of relatives in Virginia, Minnesota, left us at the end of the week. Jim Stone gave him his van. We supplied him with water, gas for the van, blankets, cooking gear, guns and ammunition, a CB radio, and as much other stuff as he asked for and could fit in the van. We also gave him our warm wishes and promised to let him back in if he decided to return with or without his relatives. Like a man going off to war and facing near-certain death, he thanked us grimly and marched away up the long hall to the woodroom. I hoped he would return to us safely, but I didn't let my heart believe too hard that he would.

For three more days, no other person or animal arrived needing our care. The cameras in the woodroom, in the barn, and those set up outside, showed no animal life at all. A storm blew in one evening, a typical, early winter storm that started out as rain and changed over to sleet, then thick, blowing snow, filling in our recent tracks outside and obliterating any sign of life. One outside camera set on a post at the edge of the woodroom was able to pan one hundred and eighty degrees, showing the Gertz's buildings down the road, the entire valley below the shelter, and part of the road leading up to our shelter. Had this camera been set up when Andy's company searched the roads for us, it would have caught the team of horses. All the cameras had television connections in the radio room, but a wide-screen TV the size of a dining-room table was set up in the donut connected to that rotating post camera. Quickly the most fascinating thing for us to do was watch the Minnesota countryside develop its repertoire of cold and snow and wind. That television had a crowd around it all day long and half the night. It was hypnotic. All the next day, while the wind blew and snow fell, we watched the scene outside. I felt such a sense of longing that my soul ached each time I looked at the screen. On the other hand, for the first time since coming into the shelter, I felt some of the oppressive tension begin to ease. Something about looking outside, about knowing what was outside, gave me respite. Need for that brought me back to the screen often.

Two days later, the morning broke clear. That Minnesota blue sky brought out more smiles than I'd seen in weeks. The fields and woods had filled with snow, and cold had seeped into the land. Nothing dripped. Though early, we could get cold even in early November in Minnesota. James confirmed that it had dipped to fifteen degrees. This meant that anyone without shelter was likely dead from exposure. Minnesota winters were unforgiving. With no plows clearing roadways, we knew it would be highly unlikely that anyone else would come to us. That saddened me, and I saw a mirror of that awareness throughout the shelter that morning. From the moment of the call, our world had begun to collapse, closing in on itself. We lost our community immediately, lost contacts through radio and television and Internet, lost the network of people like us who had headed for shelters, until, finally, the scope of our world was the range of the camera that showed us the countryside full of snow.

Nearly six inches lay out there—six inches drifted to feet in places. Roads would no longer be passable without plows. And who would plow? The young man who had headed north could no longer return to us. We believed that, with Minnesota winter raging outside, our isolation was effectively complete. No one could reach us now. Yet, that very afternoon someone did.

16
LATEST ARRIVAL
LATER THAT TUESDAY, NOVEMBER 5

L ABOR STARTED FOR ME ABOUT TEN that morning. Since I had been through this twice before, I knew I had a good while before I needed to go to the hospital. I didn't tell anyone. I wanted to spend some time with the process, maybe be alone a little while with the effort the new baby and I shared. Each contraction felt intimate, an effort neither the baby nor I really made but one that affected both of us. Only later would the tightening in my belly push all the way into pain.

I took a long, warm shower, longer than the ten-minutes Harris had levied. I spent time straightening the slice. I dug out the box of baby clothes I had shoved deep under the bed and lovingly lifted out each tiny outfit, remembering my girls in each piece. It was hard to believe they were ever so small. When voices outside my curtain reminded me I was far from alone in my reverie, I hid the box again under the pillow. Labor wasn't meant to be a spectator sport even if partners had become part of the process.

Frank and I had decided that the new baby and the little girl with the poodle, who we had dubbed Jane for lack of knowing what her name was, would share the lower bunk. Jane was a small child and didn't need the whole length of the bed. As the foot was closest to the head of the double bed, that would be the new baby's place. Frank and Jim Stone had constructed a small crib that fit there. I made that bed up for the first time, laying in the baby sheets and blankets and a few small stuffed toys I had used when each of the girls was small. It gave me great pleasure and a sense of preparedness.

I went to the animal room. I had no clue why this seemed important, but I was giving my emotions free reign that morning, and that's where I felt drawn. As I walked past the pens of cows and goats and ponies, I drew in the rich scent of the animals and hay and sweet grain and manure. Children, even some of the new ones played here often, feeding the ponies handfuls of hay and giggling when they reached over their stall gate with nimble lips to nibble the offering. The collie, now washed and brushed, walked with me as I strolled the circle, wagging her tail as furiously as before. She had been called Lassie, of course, and was one very grateful refugee. The fox terrier dam and a small herd of pups just learning to romp barked at the collie from their pen. The little Reinharts often sat with them, cuddling the pups and rolling in the hay.

Further down, I saw the airdale, named Rex, in a separate pen with a warning sign. I peeked in at him. He saw me, of course, followed my movements with his intense gaze, but he didn't wag his tail. Suddenly the airdale leaped up and came right up to the fence toward me. I almost pulled back, but there was no way he could hurt me unless I stuck in my hand. He poked his nose between the boards. In a way, it was a very aggressive move, but I thought that might just have been his way. On a hunch, I lifted my hand to the end of that nose. He sniffed and gave the smallest wag of his tail. I began to talk to him, and he made some soft growling noises in the back of his throat that I knew was terrier talk rather than aggressiveness. As I looked into the dog's brown eyes, I could see that he had made peace with us. I would tell Paul.

After the airedale pen, I came to the one with the two huge draft horses, big gold-and-white Belgians that Andy had taken from the Kelley Historical Farm in Elk River. They dwarfed the Shetlands. The gentle giants looked tired and thin, but I knew they would get the best of care. In a few weeks these standing skeletons would likely fill out into the sleek, powerful animals they once had been. Chances are they had been abandoned before the final Tuesday. Funding for such places had long since dried up. If Andy hadn't taken them to pull the wagon they likely would have died.

Finishing the circuit of the animal room, a slow walk of about fifteen minutes and two contractions, I stood again near the Jersey cows and ponies, listening to their contented mutterings and smelling the richness of their odor. I'd always loved the smells of the farm. No children played in the animal room then because we had regular school hours now that we had so many qualified teachers. As I thought about it, I remembered that Jim Stone should be teaching math about then, and he was their most animated and beloved teacher. With little fear of discovery and still in a mood to allow my emotions free reign, I pushed through the doors on the other side of the animal room, immediately being assaulted by much stronger manure and ammonia smells. Large metal gateways contained the growing pile of manure and bedding waste the crews under Max

Gertz' direction built each day. I followed the narrow passage past these bins, looking for the passage James, Don, and Dewey had followed to go out for the wounded man.

I had to hold my nose due to the strong odor, my eyes burning from the ammonia, but I made my way down the passage, stopping when a contraction came hard enough to impede my walking. I had no idea where exactly I should go, and several passages broke off from the walkway. I stayed on the main route. When I had progressed what I thought might be the diameter of another silo, I paused and looked around. Lighting in this section was much dimmer than either the animal room or the living area. Dim fixtures spaced at intervals cast an uninviting thin light, probably on purpose.

The temperature had fallen slightly as I had progressed across this room. To me that indicated that I was headed in the right direction. I almost stood before a pair of heavy steel doors before I realized I had crossed the space. I rested my hand on those doors before opening them, and, as I had anticipated, they were very cold. Unlike other doors that separated rooms—like the big double doors leading to the animal room from the donut—these doors looked heavier and had large latches connected to a double-bar locking mechanism that was massive and looked secure enough to keep out a bulldozer.

With some trepidation, I grasped the latch on the right-hand door because I could see the left one was also attached to a steel framework bolted into the ceiling and floor. What I was about to do violated the strongest rules imposed on all who lived within the shelter. I was about to breach the security of our locked world. I gave that some thought. From when we arrived, ours was to be a sealed, separated environment. It hadn't been. Almost immediately, we found reason to breach those locks, to reenter that more familiar if dangerous world outside. With Andy and other relatives missing, even after we locked the doors for the first time, we planned to unlock them. Maybe that was the mindset that allowed us—forced us—to maintain a connection with a world that had ceased being hospitable, the condition that made it virtually impossible to ignore the need we found out there. Until Andy was with us, we couldn't hide beneath layers of concrete and lack of knowing. Fortunately for us, perhaps, Andy's separation from us had lasted long enough that we grew to understand that we could never sever our outside connections. With time to think, time to form policy, most of us had realized that total isolation was buying into the madness rather than protecting ourselves from it. Odd juxtaposition of thought and ideals. For better or worse, that was our world, and our connection to it remained as intimate as the marriage bed.

Perhaps that was why I felt such an overwelming draw to the outside with my child about to be born. For a moment, I desperately needed to know firsthand what lay beyond the locked doors. I needed to feel the cold wind and touch the snow—to connect with the larger world into which my child was really being born. Some of the tension that remained after Andy and the others came to us seemed to be connected with knowing if the Earth still could support life. I know this dramatic fear had little basis in reality. Of course the Earth still could. Of course, no matter what human beings did to it, it would heal, given time. Sixty-five million years before, when a meteor wiped out the dinosaurs and three quarters of all life, the Earth had healed, filling up again with a vast array of beings, though different ones. Theoretically, if even a few rats, cockroaches, and crabgrass remained, all forms of animals—herbavores, carivores, and omnivores—and all manner of plants in all environments on the planet would regenerate. Though humans might be able to inflict more harm and devastation than a comet, the Earth would again heal. It might not allow intelligence to conquer strength and diversity as it had in our present eon, but, that really wasn't our concern.

Our concern was whether the Earth would heal *soon*. Within our lifetimes. Would we who huddled in the shelter ever live outside again? Would I live again on my little farm with the cockleburs behind the swayback barn? I don't know if I wanted to know that outside was pretty much as we had left it or if the air smelled of devastation and we were right to remain inside. To bring forth new life, I needed to know that life had a world in which to live. It was a mother thing, a hormonal, instinctive kind of thing, and the pressure of it forced my hands against those latches even as my brain tried to convince me it was a very bad idea. This wasn't about reason. It wasn't even about risk. In some long forgotten, animal part of my brain, I realized it was a deeply instinctive need to know if the environment would sustain my child. I had no control of those basic urges and felt overwhelmed by them.

I remember putting my hands on that cold latch. I remember straining upward with it, pitting my strength against the security of our world even as that same pushing forced downward in my uterus. Something changed then. I vaguely remember feeling wet down my legs and thought my water had broken. Then reality and dream began to mix.

Heart pounding, I watched the heavy bars swing inward, releasing the lock. I could still feel the heaviness of the door. I waited out a contraction and let my eyes adjust to the darkness beyond. For a moment, I wondered why it was dark. A flash of panic allowed me to believe that Harris had tricked us all. Every day we watched that television in the donut. Every day we watched as winter filled up the valley. Was it all now trickery, some video loop to calm us while protecting us from a larger disappointment that the outside world had changed? I rejected that as soon as it came into my head. I realized then that the door I had opened was not the door to the outside. A dark tunnel smelling of cold and decay yawned ahead of me. Cobwebs and roots hung from the ceiling.

Suddenly I feared going into this tunnel, feared returning to the world outside. I feared the door would somehow close behind me or that something lurked in the darkness. Cold wrapped around my ankles and sent shivers up my legs as I stared into the tunnel, trying to decide what I should do. I squinted, trying to see another door up ahead. Instead I saw a bend in the tunnel. Though the arched concrete passage looked more like a cattle culvert than anything, though the only lighting came from the naked bulb behind me, though I feared being shut out of the only safety present in my life and knowing that life outside the shelter was dangerous now, with winter building up its reserves for its truest onslaught, I finally made what seemed close to a decision to continue.

I shivered with waves of cold that accentuated the contractions when they came. I closed my eyes, thinking about the walk from the house to the barn on our farm before a path was plowed. In the early years of our marriage, when we kept rabbits and a couple sheep, and four Toulouse geese that paraded the barnyard like sentries, I always managed to need to go to the barn before Frank got around to plowing it. He'd gripe that I was trying to make him feel guilty—and maybe I was a little—but he knew the animals needed feeding first thing in the morning and late in the afternoon. Almost invariably, about the time I made it back from the barn, he'd be pulling on his Sorels to go plow and gave me a look that said, "You could of waited a few more minutes." I could have, I suppose, but that would have spoiled the *Little House on the Prairie* feeling that I always got when trudging through knee-deep snow. I felt . . . partnered with winter, in a way, as if, though a huge, white, scary monster, it was my friend. I could go to the barn and back through deep snow, high winds, and punishing cold, and it wouldn't "get" me. I needed that reassurance again.

Images from my childhood mixed with images from much later winters of my children spread-eagle in snowsuits that took forever to zip up properly. I chuckled, then sobered as I wondered if I'd even get the chance to put this baby into a snowsuit before he or she had grown too old to need one.

I found myself blinking in the blinding light and only then realized I no longer stood in the dim passage with my hand on the massive door. I was outside. Wind grabbed at my hair and the thin housedress. I couldn't see much besides woods from this vantage, but the naked aspen and birch were creaking in the wind, rubbing branches as if to stay warm in the cold. I stood ankle deep in a drift of snow near the entrance opening, which looked like a natural, rocky hollow stuffed with sumac. In another couple years they and the thin birches would merge to completely hide the opening.

My heart thumped in my throat. I didn't remember walking through the tunnel. I didn't remember giving my feet permission to continue on as memories of past winters flooded me, but there I was, standing in snow at the end of the tunnel. I didn't get a *Little House on the Prairie* feel at all. I got a very distinct, falling off the edge of the world feeling, and I didn't like it. This was foolish, dangerous, and I knew I had better get back inside. I turned, but, before darkness sliced off my vision, my traitorous eyes begged one last look at the world without being separated by walls and cameras and TV screens. Then, holding my belly, I lumbered back down the tunnel toward the door, hoping with all my hope that it wasn't closed, locked tight against me.

The door was far from wide open. I panicked when I saw it, thinking it was closed, but then I saw one of my slippers squashed between the heavy steel panel and the vault-like jam. I looked down, surprised to see I wore only a cotton sock on one foot. Had I done this on purpose? Can the body function on its own, making decisions, however foolish? I pushed with all my might against the inertia of the heavy steel. Even then, I managed to move it only enough to force my body inside, not taking my slipper from its place until I knew the door couldn't knock me down outside and lock behind me. Only when I was safely inside the hall did I toe the slipper from the jam and let the door close with a heavy clank. It locked itself down tight before I could attempt to do so. Again I was washed through with the knowledge of how stupid I had been, how great a risk I had taken by breaching the shelter's security. This door had one job to do, and it would have successfully withstood any miniscule attempt I could have made to reenter the shelter if it had succeeded in locking me out. I figured from that outside view, I would face an hour's walk through snow and cold to get to the woodroom, then who knew how long before someone noticed me on a monitor. In the clothes I was wearing, I'd freeze.

I started walking, intending, of course, to return to the animal room and the living area, but time and again, I found myself faced with the massive metal doors solidly bolted and barred against the world. I could feel myself panicking and walked faster, though the contractions continued, trying to get away from that door and the darkness.

A powerful contraction hit me, one that meant that labor had advanced. My abdomen tightened so quickly, it made me grunt and pulled my attention down into my body. The force of it reshaped my abdomen into a conical volcano threatening eruption, and, with a warm splash, my water broke, soaking the insides of my legs and spattering onto the floor. I remember thinking that I wouldn't have to try to explain the soaked socks now. I doubled over, then sank to my knees in the amniotic fluid. Then I lost any awareness other than the pain.

Sometime later, I felt someone lifting my arms and saw a number of people standing around me, but it was too dim to recognize where I was.

"What happened?" I murmured.

"Looks like you're about to have a baby," Marty said. Though he should have been joyful and teasing, his tone sounded grim.

The next I remembered was being in the hospital with Jillian inches from my face. Her expression was even more serious. She was pushing my shoulders down.

I lay back, now able to let the contractions work their way through me. They were close, easily just five minutes apart, and strong. This kept my awareness very close to my body. I did breathing and counting and tried every relaxation technique I had learned with the other two deliveries. It was kind of working, but I was impressed with the pain that got around the breathing and counting. Then I'd tense, and the pain screamed into agony. This delivery was certainly moving along much faster than either of the other two, but time does weird things when women are in labor. My mind was focused tightly around my belly, as if my total concentration was part of the birthing, part of the tightening that would eventually push my baby out. I didn't even notice when Frank arrived until he slipped his fingers around my fist.

I gripped his hand like a vice and willingly shared some of the pain I had to endure to bring our child into the world. He accepted my white-knuckled grip and reminded me to try to relax. Within minutes, he took over as coach as he had with the other two births and guided me through the breathing and counting. He pressed chips of ice between my lips and held a cool wet cloth to my forehead as the succession of contractions grew stronger. His soft voice played background music to the percussion in my belly, and I struggled to listen, not really needing to understand what he was saying.

I knew Jillian and Marty came in from time to time, but my focus was such that their presence didn't impact much of my brain. I vaguely felt their concern. Wrapped around my belly with the contractions tightening through it, my awareness didn't let in much other than Frank's hand and Frank's voice. And yet, I was vaguely aware that more, many more faces and bodies pressed close to the curtain pulled around my bed. Our whole population knew I was in labor; my delivery had become a group event. I didn't know how I felt about that. At the moment, I spared no brain cells to form an opinion.

Then I reached transition, and not even Frank's voice could penetrate the intense contractions and pain. I waited for the desire to push, knowing that, with the pushing, I would finally be able to partner with the process of birth rather than struggle to stay out of its way. Time meant nothing anymore. Events outside the curtain of the hospital ward meant less. The larger world didn't factor in at all. My entire existence, my whole world had narrowed and shrunk to my belly. Not even the baby, just a few layers of skin and muscle away, mattered. Labor wasn't really about the baby just now. Labor was about work, about pain, about a process over which I had no control whatsoever. All I could do was endure, and each new contraction made me doubt my capacity to do that.

I dozed between contractions. How one can slip into sleep for one minute, fight through pain for five minutes, then just go to sleep again, I don't know, but I did.

The first pushing impulse made me grunt, but it felt good. It was as if my mind unwrapped from the constrictor pressure of the uterus and took charge of the birthing process. I could push. I could do something. Pushing was something I added to the squeezing of the uterus, something separate yet partnered with that process if birth were to occur.

I remember hearing Jillian ask, "Do you feel pushy yet?"

She had so often accused me of being pushy, of sticking my nose in where it wasn't wanted. Maybe I did that; mostly I thought I meant well. "Yeah," I said, panting between contractions that seemed now to heap up against each other with almost no time in between.

"Okay," Jillian said. "You're totally effaced and dilated. So, push."

"Don't I have to move to a birthing table?"

"If we had one. We don't. Just go for it. I'll catch the football."

Football? Oh, brother! Jillian ought to know she couldn't be cute right then. It missed entirely. I might have uttered a very uncharacteristic and vehement oath. But Jillian had my attention only a moment, then was gone from my horizon. She chattered on, giving me directions. As if she were in charge. She wasn't. Of course, I had no more control. That aspect most impressed me with the other births and with this one in renewed form. The doctor was exterior to the birth, except maybe with a cesarean. But the mother wasn't in charge either. Neither was the baby. None of us guided the overall process of the birth, yet it followed a very careful choreography. If that didn't enlighten one to the existence of a higher power, I don't know what could.

As each contraction threatened to overwhelm me, I pushed back at it, and the pushing itself brought the contraction under my control. I was using it, directing it, making it work the way I defined. Now the birth was something *I* did.

This last phase always went quickly for me, and something in the process of pushing greatly reduced any sensation of pain except for a burning at the vagina as it stretched for the crowning of the child. Very quickly, that burning began to eat into me, but I pushed again, harder, and the pressure eased.

Time changed for me again. I couldn't tell if it slowed or speeded up, but I felt a change. Jillian's face hovered between my knees, and she seemed to be saying something. I didn't, couldn't hear. Every fiber in my body worked to complete a process that swirled around me like a winter blizzard. Then, in the midst of the storm, a quiet place opened up for me. It was as if I stood again outside the shelter with the snow melting around my ankles. I looked down across the meadows below the hill, admiring the pristine beauty of winter. Sparkling snow set off by the dark trunks of trees against the perfect blue of the sky. Far more dramatic than the softer, subtler tones of the other seasons, winter had its charms. I feasted on the sight of the countryside, letting my eyes rove along the edge of the wood on the other side of the meadow. Then I saw them. Four deer. Looking round and gray in their winter coats, four deer stood at the edge of the meadow, probably wondering why hunters hadn't tried to blast them to bits. I could see their breaths puff from their nostrils, and they pawed at the ground with a kind of impatience.

"Push!" Jillian's command broke through the dream, dissipating it.

Faces hovered over me—Frank's with intense concern, Marty, almost as grim.

"Come on, Barb, push!" Jillian said. "One more really big one."

I could feel the roll of thunder building within me, and I pushed with it. I strained every muscle in my body and held my breath with the effort. I closed my eyes but could still see the baby slip from my body, slip from the simple shelter of my belly into the complex and less comforting larger world. The protectiveness that had been intrinsic to my belly in all the months I carried the child swelled, burst into the void of the world beyond the shelter. I couldn't protect any child there. I couldn't even protect the deer at the edge of the woods.

"Barb. Barb! How you doing, there?" Marty's voice penetrated the strange mixture of reality and dream.

"The baby?" My voice sounded spent, out of breath, weak.

"He's fine. A big, healthy boy. Looks fair, like Beth."

Frank's face hovered inches from mine. "He's wonderful, hon. Nearly nine pounds, and did you hear that healthy cry?"

I had heard nothing. Then Frank's face twisted in my vision, and his words sank somehow below my understanding. I stood again in the crystal snow looking down across the meadow at the herd of deer. Five now stood at the edge of the woods, five deer wrapped in the insulation of hollow hair and sheltering branches waiting for the meadow to be safe.

17
THROUGH THE GATE
THURSDAY, NOVEMBER 7

A S IT TURNED OUT, I BLED BADLY with that birth. I didn't come to myself for some time. When I did, I had never felt so weak and like an invalid as I did then. I found myself with an impressive number of tubes running into me. Frank dozed, his head bowed to his chest and his chair propped up against the wall at the foot of the bed.

The lights in the hospital had been turned down. I thought maybe this meant it was night in the shelter, but I wasn't sure. On the one side of me, Romala McGillicutty slept. A glass bassinet filled much of the space between our beds. At first I assumed this was her baby, but, when I ran my hands along my own stomach and realized I had been delivered of my baby, I turned to see if another bassinet filled the space between me and Jeannie. There was nothing there.

I know I would have panicked under normal circumstances, but maybe my body knew it didn't have the reserves for that kind of thing. Instead, I closed my eyes, just kind of quietly wondering about where my baby might be. I thought to look beyond Romala's bed. No bassinet there.

Slowly, I moved in the bed, trying to get a look at Romala's baby. With unbelievable soreness, I eased my legs over the side of the bed. With them halfway to the floor, I looked at them for what seemed like the first time in months. I even waved at them with a wiggle of my fingers, then toes. They didn't look as shapeless and swollen as my imagination had molded them. I slid them down to the floor and eased my bottom out, being well aware of the episiotomy. Raising my trunk in the bed hurt in my belly and left me dizzy a moment, and I sat at the edge of the bed unfamiliar with the feeling of not having my baby resting there, almost propping me up. Not that I was skinny or "had my figure back." I'd have to lose thirty more pounds before I even got close.

I peeked into the bassinet. A fair-faced, golden-haired cherub slept there. I fell in love instantly. This was *my* son. I wouldn't make the mistake of calling him my "first-born son" as my dad had when my younger brother was born—I knew the price of that on my dear daughters—but, for the first time, I kind of understood what my father had felt. I sighed. It irked me how, when we're young, we think we know everything, only to find out that we don't know half as much as we thought we did or how the actions we once condemned in others became less condemnable as we grew older. I figured by the time I was eighty, I would understand at least twice as much as I did then. I smiled.

"If you're planning on calling him Frank, Jr., forget it."

I looked over at Frank, who had awakened and was watching me. He lowered the two front legs of his chair and came to sit next to me.

"He's perfect, Barb," he said, slipping his finger under the miniature, perfect little hand. His hands looked so huge and the baby's hand so very tiny.

I looked around at the collection of intervenous tubes and drip pouches headed into my arms and said, "I take it all didn't go as planned."

Frank kissed my forehead. "You're fine, hon. There were . . . some difficulties, but Marty and Jillian have been so thoroughly bored dealing with frostbite and bruises that they went into high-action, super-doctor mode. I never had any doubt that you'd pull through, but, well . . . they'll give the four-alarm version when morning comes."

"So, how long . . . ?"

Frank snugged the blue blanket up to the baby's double chin. "You've been out of it for almost two days. You lost a lot of blood. They've been pumping stuff into you full bore. You'll have to stay here for a few more days, but you're going to be fine."

He was making too strong a case. I knew he'd been worried. But, to force him to devulge what happened probably bordered cruelty. I'd wait for Marty or Jillian.

Sitting up began to tire me. My belly hurt. That hadn't been true of my other two deliveries. With Beth and Andrea, as soon as I had delivered, I felt great. Well, the episiotomy always hurt some and made me sit carefully, but otherwise, I'd felt fine. Something really must have gone wrong for me to feel so beleaguered. If I had been semiconscious for two days, I knew it was serious.

I let Frank assist me back against the pillows. He kissed me again and said he'd go to our slice so the girls wouldn't wake up alone. When he left, I eased my less encumbered hand down to my belly. There, I encountered a bandage. It's position and length, and the rough row of stitches I could feel through the gauze let me know what Frank had not been able to tell me. I knew I had delivered the baby vaginally; there was no reason for a line of stitches on my belly unless heavy bleeding had forced Marty and Jillian to open me up and repair or remove my uterus.

Though on the one hand, I forced myself not to get upset about that until I had confirmation from the mouths of the doctors, I also began to find a way to accept what had happened. Frank and I had already agreed that more children was not a good idea. He had already had a vasectomy since the middle of the pregnancy. If now I no longer could bear children, nothing had changed.

I tried really hard to buy that reasoning, but it didn't much work. What did work, however, was looking at my son through the plexiglass bassinet. For the next two hours while the lights remained low, I stared at him, watching him sleep. The only other image I let into my mind was the one of the five deer in full winter coats at the edge of the woods. I'm not sure I really understood that image, but it comforted me.

When lights gradually strengthened, activity in the shelter increased as well. I could hear kids, who always preceded adults into wakefulness. They were playing in the donut. Even my infant began to stir. Almost as quickly, I knew Abby had started breakfast. I smelled sausage frying. Soon after, Jillian breezed into the hospital.

"Well, well," she said with a smile as she came to my bedside. That she came to me first let me know I was the sickest patient. "It's about damn time you woke up."

"Frank said two days," I said, my voice still not quite my own.

"About. You gave us a few scares. Nothing Marty and I couldn't handle."

"What happened?"

Jillian sat at the edge of the bed. She smiled again. Then she looked at the baby in the bassinet. "Your son is a big kid. He's eight pounds eleven ounces and twenty-one inches long—a football player if ever I saw one. When he delivered, he tore the placenta loose too. Fortunately for him, the final delivery went quickly enough that he was never at risk, but you hemorrhaged." She paused, squeezed my hand and said, "We had to open you up, Barb. It was touch and go, and the only sure way to stop the bleeding was to take your uterus. Even then, we weren't sure for a little while we had closed everything down fast enough. Your veins collapsed. But we already had a line in and . . . we pumped you full of blood and fluids, and began to gain ground. By then, of course, you were in shock and had slipped into a coma. It was pretty tense around here for a while, but the coma began to lighten last evening. I'm not surprised to see you awake this morning."

"Did you take my overies, too?"

She grinned. "Nope. You still should have about ten years to menopause . . . just no more kids."

"Frank and I had already decided that."

Jillian nodded. "He said. I hope that makes it easier for you, but you should not be alarmed if a period of depression follows this. Your body's been through considerable shock, and it needs to heal from that. Take it easy on yourself mentally as well as physically. And, by the way, you're here for the next four or five days."

I looked over at the infant. "Can I nurse him?"

She shook her head. "I'd like to keep up with the intervenous antibiotics for another day or so. After that, you can. But we have a breast pump you can use to keep up the milk supply."

After she took some vitals and left, I lay thinking. I must have come close to dying; in another time and era, I would have died. I would have died had the child been born outside the shelter right now. Though, during its construction, I had resisted coming inside, seeing into it, thinking of it as home, if the shelter had not been part of my life, that life might have ended. If the family, in its foresight and perhaps bizarre imagination, had not conceived of the shelter and actually constructed it, even if that cost was astronomical, I might not be alive.

Deep inside, I knew I had come through one of those mythical passages that change the meaning of all that came before and everything that would come for me.

A little later as Frank had time, he and the girls came to visit me. Andrea was excited about the new baby and chatted on endlessly about how she was going to take care of him. Jane, our adopted daughter with the poodle, said she'd help since the baby would sleep at the end of her bunk. She even set Prince on the foot of my hospital bed, and the little beast tottered up to lick my hand. He had come to accept us as family, and, though Jane had no memory of what came before she arrived in in our midst, she had begun to talk. Beth, however, hung back. I knew something troubled her. I had Frank return the two little girls to their classes and had Beth sit at the edge of my bed.

"What is it, sweetie?" I said. "Were you worried about me?"

She smiled. "Well, yeah, but . . . I have to tell you something else."

I waited.

"You know right before Andy and the others came, when Aunt Emily and the others were missing their cigarettes and candles and perfume and stuff?"

I had no idea where this was going. "Yeah. What about that?"

She shrugged. "Well, Harry, Peter, Diane, Cathy, Jacob, and I did that."

"Did what?"

She met my eyes. "We took the stuff."

I felt my eyes open wide. "You kids took it all? Why?"

That opened a floodgate of information. "Well," Beth said seriously, "we had all come into the Ark to get away from what was bad in the outside world. We watched Aunt Jeannie go nuts because of drugs, and we just thought that the Ark should be a place where people could start over again."

"I thought it was a place where we could survive the bad times outside."

Beth shook her head. "That's not enough." She smiled then and gave me the most knowing, the most adult look I had seen on her young face. "We started thinking: what if Aunt Jeannie goes back to her drugs when we get out? Would the world be any better? Would she? When she went nuts, all you guys worked to make her better, to help her get over her drugs. We thought we should do the same thing. We gathered up every cigarette in the place and flushed every one. Really, Mom, my hand got tired from flushing them. They made the place stink, and none of us kids wanted them around. We thought we should make *everyone* adjust a little, then, and took all the perfume and scented candles—anything that spoiled the air for the rest of us. Then you fainted from the bad air, and we knew we'd done the right thing."

"Does anyone else know?"

Beth nodded. "Yeah. Aunt Emily accused Cathy and Harry, and they confessed. Boy, was Aunt Em mad. Peter, Diane, Jacob, and I admitted our part then, so Cathy and Harry wouldn't get punished alone."

"You didn't get punished really, did you?"

She grinned. "Nope. Uncle Harris gave us am—ames—"

"Amnesty?"

"Yup. He said what was done was done."

I vowed to thank Harris later.

ROMALA MCGILLICUTTY LEFT the hospital that morning, having spent nearly a week there recovering from malnutrition and exposure. She glowed with pride as she walked out with her baby in her arms and her two children at her side. Before the breakdown in society, which, of course had begun years earlier, she had been a seamstress working in a wedding gown shop in Minneapolis. Her oldest son had begun private school to avoid the horrors of public education at a time when it suffered so many cutbacks. But she had been on welfare the entire last year because she had no work, and her husband, a trucker, had been killed when his rig was hijacked. Harris, when he discovered her skills, had asked her if she'd consider making clothing for the many who had recently come to us with nearly nothing to their names. He had a fabric store's worth of supplies—cloth, thread, zippers, buttons—and a number of machines. She could even begin training helpers to assist her.

Others recently come to our doors found ways to keep busy helping with community needs. We had nurses and gardeners, dentists and counselors, more teachers than we needed, physical therapists, and a Jewish rabbi. Though none of the rest of us happened to be Jewish, he seemed willing to provide spiritual guidance in a non-denominational way.

BY THE EVENING BEFORE I was to leave the hospital, the partitions in front of me that separated part of the hospital from the donut were removed so that everyone could take part in the christening of Frank's and my son. We called him Noah. It seemed appropriate.

Later that next day, I was released from the hospital and could return to limited activity, most of which, both Marty and Jillian insisted, was the care of my son. I walked from the hospital with my family. I leaned heavily on Frank's strong arm. Andrea held my other hand. Beth carried her baby brother, and sweet little Jane paraded ahead of us with her little poodle in her arms. Our short walk across the donut seemed a triumphant march. I had survived a difficult birth with my life intact and a beautiful, healthy son in the bargain. I couldn't have been happier. At that moment, life was good.

Inside our slice, which had been carefully cleaned by Frank and the girls, I saw that the little crib at the foot of the bottom bunk had been decorated with ribbons and at least a half dozen cute little stuffed animals, gifts from family members. My side of the double bed was open, ready for me to crawl inside, which, after even so short a walk "home," was exactly what I needed to do. I was exhausted by that simple, well-supported trek across the donut from the hospital. I understood from that three-minute exertion that it would be some time before I felt any of my strength back.

I settled into bed, letting my family fuss over me—pile pillows at my back, remove my slippers and place them right where my feet would find them when I chose to rise. Frank gently put Noah in my arms and suggested that the girls give me privacy so that I could nurse him, something we had both struggled to achieve in that last couple of days since I had been off antibiotics. The girls each gave me a kiss, including Jane, and slipped out of the slice to resume whatever activity they were scheduled to be doing. Frank sat on the edge of the bed. As I worked to get Noah to take a nipple, which he still resisted after several days on a bottle, Frank said nothing. He just sat there and smiled at me. Finally, my red-faced, angry son realized what I was about and latched on, nursing hungrily and with considerable energy. He actually hurt.

"Strong little guy, isn't he," said Frank.

I winced at the pull of his little mouth. "He sure is."

Frank rested his hand on my foot. "I'm glad you're okay, hon."

I smiled at him. "We both knew a baby born in my late thirties could be rough. I'm just glad Harris did such a good job to get the hospital so well stocked. I've been wondering, though . . . blood doesn't keep long, a month maybe. Where'd he get the blood that was given to me."

"The blood supply had three days before expiration. That was a start. When they had to operate, though, they knew they'd need more. Jillian called for blood, and every person in the shelter with B-positive blood immediately formed a line. We formed then what Marty called 'blood partners.' For every blood type here, we know who has a match and who can be a donor. You'll be happy to know that B-positive forms the largest group, with eight partners. By vote we all agreed that, should anyone in a blood partner group need blood, all the other members will give a share."

I nodded approval. "That's a neat idea."

Frank nodded then looked down, but he was smiling.

"What?" I asked.

He gave a short chuckle then lifted his eyes to mine. "It's working. This place, this . . . 'Ark.' We're making a real community of this."

"Survival kind of made that mandatory, didn't it?" I said.

Frank shrugged. "You'd think so, but it might not have gone that way. You know that. So many people, so many different personalities and backgrounds and priorities and sensibilities . . . we could have dissolved into chaos. Mike and Wayne had me really worried for a while. Neither of them is a roll-with-the-punches kind of guy. You know that. Emily can be a pain in the ass, and Lori Fisk can get wound up so tight so damn fast, you'd think she'd snap. Mix all that with people like Max Gertz, who, for all his good points, is a little set in his ways, a little black-and-white in outlook, if you know what I mean. It could have gone a lot more sour than it did and just stayed there."

I heaved a sigh and switched Noah to the other breast. Again the determined little mite put up a fight, but not as fierce or long as before. When he had latched on and settled into tugging milk out of me by pure force, I looked up at Frank. "You're right. We had all the makings of disaster with the mix of people who came in here. But that disaster didn't happen isn't just a matter of luck. You know that, too, don't you. Flaky as Harris is, he's a good leader. So are you. People like James and Dewey and Donald look to the two of you for direction, you know."

He smiled. "And Melissa and Anna and Sissy look to you."

I huffed. "Me? I really doubt that."

"It's true."

"What about the new people? How are they getting along?"

Frank shrugged. "Activity is taking the place of tears, but I'm not sure the tears have gone. The one absolute they all really and truly understand is that where they are now is a hell of a lot better than being outside."

A LOUNGE CHAIR WAS SET UP for me outside our slice. For the next few days, I spent many of my waking hours sitting there with Noah either in my arms or in a bassinet next to me. Abby kept me more than adequately supplied in rich soups, meat sandwiches, and tall glasses of apple juice, milk, and water. She visited me often and insisted I eat or drink something almost every time she came by.

The activity of the shelter swirled around me. I watched the children troop into the classroom and listened to songs or lessons. I saw people file into and out of the animal room, the bathrooms, the kitchens. The children who had come in with Andy had made a rather remarkable recovery for the most part. All were attending school, playing in the donut, joking and laughing with our children, but some still grieved for families lost. Typical of children, much of what had happened to them in the days following the fall of the world had slipped from their memories. Jane, though she played Barbie dolls with Andrea, attended school and helped out with rudimentary chores in the kitchens as did all the children over the age of three, still had no memory of her ordeal or her name. She seemed perfectly content with being Jane. A time would come for her when she would have to face the hidden parts of her mind; that would come for many of the children who lost their families.

Mary Sanders, the woman who had lost her young son still had yet to take much part of daily life. She often responded angrily when Abby tried to include her in some activity and resisted the friendly advances of the rest of the women. Her poor husband, Brad, who seemed to have a better grip on things, struggled to help her. Helicopter pilot Dean Brewster's girlfriend, Hilary Cox, was a psychologist as was David Moos, one of the newcomers who had arrived with Andy. Both tried to talk to Mary with little success. After just such a futile session, which ended in Mary screaming her out of her slice, Hilary saw me watching and came over. She sat at the end of my lounge chair.

"I'm not doing much good yet," she said.

"She has to want to be helped, Hilary," I offered.

Hilary made a raspberry, double dimples showing in her freckled cheeks. "Please, call me Boopsie."

"Seriously?"

"I know it kinda leans toward my blonde hair too much, but anything's better than Hilary."

I laughed. "Sure, but . . . Boopsie?"

She nodded sagely. "I know. It's a little overly professional, but . . ."

I laughed, then sobered and asked, "So, what can be done for Mary?"

The pretty, young woman sighed. "I don't know. Poor Brad. He's not even getting time to grieve for his son, he's so worried over her."

"I know she has to be blaming herself for her baby's death," I said. "I don't see what she could have done differently, but you can't take that blame away from her either."

Boopsie nodded. "Dave and I think we might have to hospitalize her. Even that's going to be really messy. It's going to upset a lot of people and bring to the foreground a lot of their own feelings about what happened to them outside."

I knew that Boopsie had been practicing as a psychologist for only a few years; Dave Moos, in his mid-thirties, was still hardly a seasoned veteran in the profession. I hoped they had lots of experience with serious depression. They had been talking with Mike and his family and Jeannie, too, and, I had to admit that those individuals certainly seemed to have benefited from those talks.

I SAT ON MY LOUNGE CHAIR and watched the lives of those I loved and those I barely knew move around me. I felt almost invisible at times as I watched small dramas play out. I watched Abby in her domain of the kitchen, full of her purpose. She was a woman who loved to hover, to mother, to cuddle. Watching her simple honesty, I knew I would never find a more compassionate, kinder woman anywhere.

I watched Jeannie retape her twins' papers in more prominent places on the wall between the kitchen and the schoolroom. She skipped out on work Abby assigned her, gave multiple excuses when I knew she only returned to her slice and napped. Troops of little boys tip-toed to the bathrooms at least once a day to float boats in the sinks or the tubs. Sometimes I chose those moments to go to the bathroom and shagged them out of there; other times I ignored them, giving them a few moments of naughty play.

Rex, the airdale, who had attained his freedom and had the run of the animal room with Lassie the collie, often snuck into the living area when kids went in or out. The big dog had a smart head on his long, black-and-tan neck. He skirted the slices and made his way to the kitchen. There, he sat near the counter and waited. Eventually, Abby would come out and notice him. Though she scolded him mercilessly, her tone never matched her words, and she also tossed him choice bones and bits of meat. How that dog, never before in our company, knew who would give him treats was a wonder to me. As standoffish as he was with most of the rest of us, he acted the wiggly pup with Abby, making an utter fool of himself for a bite of pork rind or beef shank bone. Then he'd come and stretch himself out next to me, a black and tan sphynx and solemnly watch the goings on in the shelter, no longer the jester. I felt very protected in his company. I was a queen on a throne, and he my royal guard.

Once Lassie followed Rex out of the animal room. A bunch of kids saw them both begging from Abby and spent an hour playing with the two of them as if they were Lady and the Tramp, setting up a stool as a table and getting Abby to serve them on a plate with a sprig of rosemary as a centerpiece. It was cute, but the dogs didn't really cooperate. Rex grabbed the bone and took off with it, and Lassie rolled on her back to be pet. So much for canine chivalry.

Several of the children were tricksters. Harry, Jr., was one of the worst. For all he appeared to be nerdy and lost in his world of books, he had a mischievous side as well. One day, he and Donald Reinhart's Peter and David Moos' oldest boy, Brian, led one of the Jersey cows through the animal room doors into the living area and turned her loose. While the bawling cow wandered around, not liking the terrazzo floor, she caused several cases of hysteria. Jeannie backed out of her slice right into the butt of the cow, which leaped away, right into Lori Fisk's slice. Lori screamed at the top of her lungs, as if the wife of a veteranian hadn't ever seen a cow before. Bawling, the Jersy backed out and headed over to the kitchens, where she buried her muzzle in a large bowl of coleslaw Abby had just set out. Hearing the screaming, Abby came running from the kitchen, saw the cow munching down her slaw and snatched away the bowl with one hand. With the other, she caught the bovine by her halter and held on even when the animal backed away, pulling her abruptly into the counter between them. The slaw slipped and spilled over the counter, and the cow's hind legs slipped on the smooth floor, sliding under her. Abby held onto that halter even though the effort made her red in the face and she was heaved up onto the counter. So, there was the cow, sitting down on the floor and Abby, her feet kicking, swimming on the counter like a beached whale, both liberally dressed with slaw.

At this point, Harry, Jr., Peter, and Brian ran over and rescued Abby, acting the perfect little heros. They laughed all the way back to the animal room, while Abby cleaned up the coleslaw mess, and Lori and Jeannie hugged each other in mutual comfort. I tried not to pull stitches laughing.

Another time, all the dogs and cats, including the insane litter of fox terrier puppies were given access to the living area at the same time. This time, I believe the kids in the age group just older than Andrea—Ronald and Roland, my sister Anna's Lynn, Romala's Jamal, and Jim Stone's Billy—all six to seven years old, were the culprits. I saw them acting furtive one afternoon, just before the dogs started chasing some of the cats. Just to make it really interesting, several of Abby's big Orpington chickens, two hens and an impressively pompous rooster managed an "escape" at the same time. It took twenty minutes and most of the school and kitchen staff to round up the pets and chickens and return them to the animal room. A big Persian cat, which I think belonged to one of the Reinharts, required Paul Fisk and heavy animal gloves to extract it from under Connie's bed. The big neutered male hissed and spat and tried to claw anyone who came near. He had been chased by Rex, who couldn't fit under the bed. The cat wasn't about to come out again for fear the big, bad dog still lurked. Jillian and company had to bandage several bloodied hands. The kids thought the whole thing very exciting.

I suppose I should have ratted on the various groups of children who perpetrated this mischief, but I didn't. None of the incidents were terribly harmful or dangerous (Abby and those dealing with the cat might disagree), and the children had found ways to dissipate both the boredom that loomed in our future like a spectre and cement friendships among the new children recently come into our shelter. I really liked seeing this last part; there wasn't going to be distinctions between those of us who had paid so much to build the shelter and those who came to us in need—at least not among the children. I knew that this same acceptance would be harder for Wayne, Mike, Jeannie, even Jillian. That's also not to say that Mary Sanders didn't also resist, as well as a few of the others. And why not? They had not had much choice in where they went or how they would have to live. They had been thrust into an organization new to them and basically been told they must embrace our way of life. Only a blatant optimist, like Abby, thought this could be accomplished easily, and some, like Mike and Wayne, didn't want it to happen at all. Only a little over two weeks had passed since the newcomers had arrived with Andy and blending and mixing progressed at an uneven pace. From my vantage in the lounger outside my slice, I watched where success smoothed the edges between "us" and "them" and where gaps yawned.

I lowered my hand to the head of the airedale, who was now a permanent resident of the living area, a privilege earned both by his dignified good behavior and because that big persian cat caused holy havoc in the animal room when he was around. Three times a day, Noah and I escorted him to the potty area, then walked sedately back to the lawn chair. I might be his warden in that act, but he was my escort as well. Rex had made a place for himself, had made the transition from then to now.

With Thanksgiving just ahead, I had hope that we could find that impossible balance that would allow us to feel the gratitude we should in our situation.

18

THANKSGIVING

THURSDAY, NOVEMBER 28

═══════════

I T'S JUST NOT THANKSGIVING WITHOUT TURKEY." Jeannie pouted.

While some scowled at her and rolled their eyes at the obvious problem we faced since we had no turkeys, I was just glad Jeannie was actually at the general meeting and willing to contribute in terms other than insults. It really was quite the improvement. While several pointed out to her, for the sixth or seventh time, that the situation about the turkeys wasn't going to miraculously improve, I found myself eager to hear what solution would be proposed.

"I don't have no turkeys," Abby said with a deep sigh, "but I got several really big roosters to spare."

"We've seen those roosters. They're as big or bigger than many turkeys I've bought," Connie said.

"But how many?" asked Wayne. "Are there even enough to feed the masses?"

Always the slight slur, the innuendo of unworthiness towards those who came last and didn't pay—that, of course, was the rub for Wayne. His world had been all about net worth, potential earnings, material wealth. Jim Stone, a man of good humor and great patience, cast him a dark look even though Wayne couldn't see it. Then he slid his gaze to me and rolled his eyes at the man. I quite agreed.

Abby said, "Well, sir, I'm figuring we have half a dozen big roosters—"

"That won't be nearly enough," said Wayne, throwing up his arms. "Do you know how many mouths we have now?"

Abby squared her generous German shoulders. "We have near ninety. I do know that. I fix meals for all of us each day, three meals each day. I know how many I got to feed, and I know what it takes to feed 'em."

Wayne gave her such a patronizing smile I wanted to smack him. "If you know that, Mrs. Gertz, then how can you suggest that six chickens might feed this lot. Do we each get to lick a bone?"

Wayne and Mike laughed. Max Gertz stood, his face a mask of hatred. A half-second later, Frank and Paul Fisk flanked him, and Jim Stone and Dean Brewster readied themselves to step between the Deters men. Wayne was an ass, but a fist-fight wasn't really in the Thanksgiving mood either. I figured, even if they pummeled the man, he'd still be an ass.

Harris gaveled his podium. "Wayne, that was rude and uncalled for. One more interruption from you, and you'll be ousted. For now you may sit down. That wasn't a request. Abby, would you please finish what you were saying."

Wayne folded his arms and sat. Abby, flustered by the insults, had turned red. One hand pressed against her lips. But, empowered woman that she was, she inhaled deeply and took down her hand. "What I was trying to say was that six big roosters was the *start*. We have some wonderful fresh hams, big ones, beef roasts to melt in your mouth. We don't have no turkeys, and I can't do nothing 'bout that, but we can still have a really fine dinner. I've got sausages to make you think your mamas made them, recipes for six kinds of dressings, four potato dishes planned, yams and sweet potatoes both—and the marshmallows to make you remember every Thanksgiving dinner you ever ate. We've been saving the last of the frozen green beans, and I've fried onions and made a mushroom soup that's better than Campbell's. Got almonds to top it, too. We've got four kinds of pumpkin pie planned, plus pecan pies, apple and cherry. About anything any of you's ever had for Thanksgiving, we'll have this year and more than any family could prepare in variety."

"But no turkeys," Mike said. The brothers made an effective tag team.

"Nope," said Abby with finality, "there ain't gonna be no turkeys."

"What about a vegetarian entree?" Anna asked.

Abby nodded. "Oh, forgot about those. I have a recipe for spinach quiche, a pumpkin souffle, and two versions of veggie lasagna—"

"These are all *your* recipes?" Jillian asked, with a bit of awe in her voice.

"Well, no," Abby said. "I never meant that these were all my stuff or even my mom's and mine. I've been gathering recipes from everyone."

Jillian raised an elegant eyebrow. "Oh? You never asked me."

Abby blushed. "No, ma'am. I guess I thought you've been so busy with the hospital and all, you wouldn't have time for such things. I did ask Mr. Harris, though. He gave me your apple pie recipe. Hope you don't mind."

That put a very odd expression on Jillian's face. After a moment's thought, she said, "No . . . no, that's fine. I hope you use it."

"So what if we don't have turkeys," said James. "For me, the most important part of Thanksgiving has always been the stuffing anyway. I've been known to pass up on the meat and go for that alone."

Mom Quill agreed with that. "If we have lots of dressing, lots of potatoes, pumpkin pie and all the rest of the fixings, I don't see that not having turkey is that big of a problem. We have to have cranberry sauce though, and not that canned jelly stuff. I make the most delicious cranberry-orange dish—"

"Oh, but I like the jellied one," said Emily petulantly. "That's my *favorite*."

It was. Emily used to hog the cranberry sauce every year when we were kids.

Abby assured her that both the canned jelly and frozen berries had been hoarded just for this one feast.

Few of the newer people broke into the conversation. Mike and Wayne had seen to that. They remained in the classroom, however, so, in a sense, they were still part of the discussion. I hoped they felt they were, at least. I knew Abby. She hadn't been at all biased in whom she asked for recipes. Chances were better than good that the prized dishes of that segment of our population would be represented more completely than those of the original, paying founders.

Discussion continued, embracing the concept of six, and then eight, stuffing dishes, three coleslaws, four different recipes of pumpkin pie, three of sweet potatoes and yams—two with and one without tiny marshmallows—and at least three recipes of cranberry sauce that I could count. The only thing that bought no discussion was the one potato selection. Mashed with gravy. I was grateful to Abby that she didn't bring up the concept of what kind of gravy. That would have lengthened the discussion by about an hour, and it had lasted three already.

From the sound of the discussion and the vast variety of dishes that needed to be made, I figured it would take Abby's full kitchen staff about four months to make the feast. I was not prepared, however, for Abby in full-emergency-mega-food-catering mode.

Thanksgiving week arrived. The children of all ages had created turkey pictures and Puritan people pictures. Every space of wall and most of the curtain space had filled with these creations. We had multi-colored, rainbow turkeys, natural turkeys, big white butterballs and some so bizarrely shaped and colored I wondered if there had been a Picasso influence. Someone found a box of pine cones stored away. These soon turned up as more turkeys on little toothpick legs with pipe cleaner necks and wings and colored-paper tails.

Meals two days before Thanksgiving suddenly dwindled down to cold cereal in the morning, Campbell's soup and peanut butter and jelly sandwiches at lunch and Emily's burgers and fries for supper. These were served on paper plates with milk in paper cups. At the same time, the most delicious aromas wafted from the kitchen, causing a near riot in the lunch area on Tuesday night.

"How the hell can we sit here and eat soggy fries and plain hamburgers when we have such wonderful smells coming from the kitchen at the same time," said Frank.

"I think we should have a taste of what's to come," suggested Mike.

"Even if we have to share one pie among all of us," said Marty. Louder he pleaded, "Please. Can anyone in there hear us?"

Abby came out branishing a large wooden spoon. "You eat your supper and clear out, the lot of you. You've been fed well enough for now, and I ain't handing out no pies before Thursday. Don't nobody ask. And don't nobody get it in his little head to sneak into the kitchen for an early taste. I've set up a cot right inside and plan on staying right here in the kitchen until this here Thanksgiving meal's served."

She swiveled on her heels and marched back through the swinging doors.

Connie, Mel and I exchanged glances, then burst into laughter behind our hands so as not to bring out the kitchen general again.

Wednesday was even tenser in the kitchens, with shifts now around the clock making the salads and sauces and special condiments, plastic wrapping them and tucking them safely in the huge walk-in cooler. More pies, dressings, and spices teased our minds and watered our mouths even as we reluctantly filled them with Cheerios and, later, more Campbell's soup. Everyone's stomach grumbled with the tasteless fare when our noses drew in such lucious wonders.

Wednesday night was not one anyone living in the barracks carved out of the lunchroom or anywhere near the kitchens enjoyed. Pans clanged, oven doors squeaked, voices discussed, and more odors wafted. Now the rich scent of beef and pork melded with the dessert spices in apple and pumpkin and pecan pies. Steam rolled from huge pans boiling potatoes and yams, almost forming a cloud near the ceiling of the kitchen and lunchroom.

Early Thursday morning, Thanksgiving morning, the dinner bell rang. I looked at the little travel clock, surprised to see it pointing to six-thirty. The lights in the shelter hadn't even come up yet. Abby's clear voice rang out: "Breakfast is early, but it's over in half an hour. Come now or wait until dinner."

People knew better than to argue. They formed a sleepy queue and shuffled to the counter as their turn came. Instead of the usual cold cereal we expected, Abby had platters of sausage, hash brown potatoes, and large trays of caramel rolls. Eyes opened, smiles replaced grumpy frowns and paper plates filled quickly. After the long fast, we ate in near silence, savoring every bite. Though the tables and chairs clustered around the kitchen doors accommodated only about two-thirds of us, the rest seemed not to care that they sat cross legged on the floor with paper plates in their laps.

Abby, her hair in a scarf and her cheeks bright red from the heat of the kitchen, came out with Anna and DeeDee in tow. They looked almost as frazzled and a lot more tired. "Dinner will be served at two," Abby announced. "There ain't no food for no one from now till then, so if you're still hungry, clean up them sausages and rolls."

DeeDee looked up and said, "The usual rules of capital crime will apply. Anyone caught near the kitchen door between now and two will be shot—"

Anna guestured with a slashing motion across her throat, but then whispered in DeeDee's ear.

DeeDee corrected. "No, check that. Anyone caught at the doors will be chained to the sink until every pan shines, and, believe me, that should take to Christmas or Easter or the next Fourth of July, I just don't know. Misbehaving children get pine cones for their meal."

She said this with exaggerated venom as she caught the eyes of her students in the kindergarten class. The little kids squealed.

Being a holiday, no school classes were held that day. Several children had been selected from each grade level to present a "thanks" to the whole group, Beth among them. She sat up on her bunk reciting her lines carefully so as not to forget a word.

In so many ways, the day felt like every other Thanksgiving. Fragrances wafting through the air, the long wait to eat a meal we all knew bordered on the mythical in variety and proportions. People seemed to be in a generous humor. Kids tried hard not to be so difficult as to end up in a time out sitting alone somewhere. For me, one moment I was missing the cooking of my own feast and the next wondering what was wrong with me as I remembered sore backs, frantic preparations, and constant panic that something wouldn't be ready on time.

I had been more mobile during this week, more able to help out, and just sitting in the aura of the kitchen environment thrilled me. Though Abby wouldn't let me do much beyond scrape a huge bowl of home-grown carrots while sitting at the counter, I didn't care. I watched as she directed, supervised and encouraged the army of helpers, each with a narrow task that pieced one phase of a huge meal. All the ovens roasted, all the stoves bubbled and boiled. This woman could run a major New York restaurant, I realized. We were very lucky to have her.

After I finished the carrots, I continued to sit at the counter, just enjoying the scene and the odors and the cooperation in the kitchen. Not that it wasn't nine kinds of chaotic in many ways. Pots bubbled over, people yelled questions across the room, steam clouded part of the room like a rain forest, Connie suffered a minor burn catching a tumbling lid, and Abby shouted instructions to be heard over the racket of pots and pans and dishwashing. But I loved it and relinquished my desire to be in the thick of things. The sidelines worked much better. I couldn't help grinning at it all. I think that morning, for the first time since coming into the shelter, I forgot about the rest of the world, really forgot. We had earned our feast. We had gone through a lot to get to this point a month and a half after coming to this place. Mostly, of course, we had all come through a gate. In one way or another, each of us had been shaken apart at our roots and began the process of putting ourselves back together. With my sleeping son in his bassinet on the counter beside me, I felt we had all come through a birth of sorts and given birth to twins, ourselves and our community. Okay, I was reaching the maudlin, but that's the way I felt that morning. Then Brad Sanders came in.

In the brief moment he stood just inside the door, looking at all the activity but not seeing anything, I knew Mary would not be joining in our feast. Before anyone really was aware of his standing there, I motioned to Connie to watch Noah and slipped from my stool. I guided Brad out into the lunchroom and sat him down.

"Mary . . . Mary's . . ."

I wrapped him in my arms, and he bawled like a child. He had lost his infant son and now his wife. As he wept in my arms, James skittered into the lunchroom, saw Brad and paused. I met his eyes, and he slowly shook his head. He left, and I knew he went to fetch Harris and Frank.

"Why?" Brad said between sobs. "I just don't get it. I don't know what more I could have done?"

"It wasn't you," I said. "I've got a new baby. The bond that builds between a mother and infant is powerful, Brad. When it's broken and there's even the slightest hint of culpability, many mothers just can't take it."

"But they don't commit suicide," he wailed.

"Some do. Some go crazy. The problem with this place is that she maybe never had anything to hold onto. No home, none of the things about her she loved, no pattern she understood. From the way she reacted sometimes, I thought she hated us just as much as the bad stuff outside. She had nothing but you to hold onto, and, sad as it may seem, you weren't enough. Not after the loss of a child. To embrace this place, she would have had to get past the worst of her grief. I don't think she knew how."

He leaned back and looked at me with red, swollen eyes. "But now what am I supposed to do?"

I cupped his wet cheek in my palm. "You grieve. You've had a terrible loss. Two of them. You grieve. I hope, though, you'll realize that this had nothing to do with you. Mary got lost somewhere between her son and coming inside. That's not your fault."

Harris came in, followed closely by Frank and Marty. Marty crouched in front of the young man. "Listen, Brad. We tried. I thought when Mary allowed us to put her in the hospital last night that she was getting ready to make a change. I just didn't believe this would be it. I'm so sorry."

Brad had just soaked my shoulder, but he managed a smile and drew in a halting breath. "I've been expecting it, actually. She's been telling me for days that she saw no way to live without Steven. She's been telling me I should get on with my life, and that she was just holding me back. Nothing I said, no matter how many times I told her I loved her . . . she never listened."

"She couldn't hear you," I said softly.

Brad met my eyes with a little confusion, then it cleared. "No, she couldn't. She couldn't hear a word I said. Maybe . . . maybe this is for the best. She's suffered so much. She had four miscarriages before Steven. Even before he was born she was on shaky ground mentally." He heaved a jerky sigh. "Maybe this was the best way."

Everything in me ached for the young man, barely more than a boy. At twenty-four he and his young wife had been married since she got pregnant in high school. They had eloped. Mary lost her first child before they returned from their honeymoon. Brad had told us that both their parents had wanted the marriage annulled, but they wouldn't have it. They started college, but Mary got pregnant again, and Brad quit school to work to support them. By the time the second child died, Mary could no longer work. Brad had to struggle with nothing jobs to make a living for himself and his fragile wife. Two more failed pregnancies followed, and they sought professional help. When she became pregnant with Steven, she worried through the whole pregnancy. After his birth, Brad said, Mary was better, not the funloving girl he'd married, maybe, but better. She had been adjusting to Steven and cared well for him. Then the world fell apart. The night Steven died, they had found themselves wet and shivering in the lea of a barn near St. Joseph, trying with many mishaps to get to Brad's folks' home in Alexandria after leaving the Twin Cities. They nearly died themselves that night.

After the men took Brad to the hospital, convinced he needed a mild sedative and monitored sleep, I sat thinking. Brad was a mess. That was clear. He had struggled for a long time with his wife's difficulties, had suffered the loss of his son as well. As fragile as we all knew Mary was, the thought inkled at my mind that she maybe hadn't actually taken her own life. I hated the thought, despised the thought, but it came anyway. Then it seemed to fester there in my head.

Connie came out with Noah, who had awakened. I opened my blouse there in the lunchroom as we were pretty much alone. Connie sat down. "I saw Brad's face. Mary's dead isn't she?"

I nodded. "Do the rest in there know?"

"I don't think so. Too busy. Abby's working hard to get the meal ready right on time." Then she added, "It'd take an edict from on high to stop that woman."

"I really hate to see such gargantuan effort and this wonderful meal spoiled."

"Me either. Poor Mary. She just couldn't cope with any of this. When they all first arrived, she tried to go back up. She couldn't take this place even then."

"What if . . ." I hesitated. I resolved to table my suspicions. Completing the sentence differently than I had started it, I said, "What if we don't tell everyone until after the meal? Would that be bad?"

Connie sighed. "Bad? No. Possible? I doubt it. And some people will be really pissed off to know we kept information from them."

"You're probably right. Harris should do the telling, though. This is a major community occurrence. He should be the one to tell what happened."

"What happened?" Jim Stone had just walked into the lunchroom.

If I knew only one thing about this personable man, it was that he had good ears. And he paid attention. He knew more about the Quill-Deters-Dunn family history than probably any one of us. Now, with the influx of more people, he already knew more about them than I would in the next month. I turned to him and said, "Something bad happened. If you could wait with getting this information until after the meal, would you be okay with that?"

He sat down with us, instantly serious. He said, "Okay, the choice is eat a really great meal, then get bad news to spoil digestion or get the bad news first and not be able to enjoy the meal."

I nodded. "What would you choose."

"Me? I'd take the bad news if I had a little time to process it, then do the meal. The trick is to get that process time."

"How much time?"

He looked at his wrist watch. "We've got an hour to the meal. Depending on the news, I might be able to process that and eat. Unless it had something to do with my wife and kids."

"It doesn't."

He got up. "Then I think you ought to tell people. We're . . . all of us . . . a strong enough lot, I think. Let me be your test case."

I met Connie's eyes, and she shrugged. She said, "Brad's wife, Mary, committed suicide."

"Shit!" said Jim. "Really? Aw, shit. How's Brad?"

"Messed up."

"Damn. The poor guy."

"So, should we tell everyone before or after the meal?"

"I don't know. That's pretty awful news. I'd hate to be the one to spoil every-one's feast. But, Barb, how are you going to wait with this? When Brad and Mary don't show up for dinner, people will ask why. Then there's no process time at all. The news will travel like wildfire and everything will suffer, the people, the meal . . . everything." Jim turned and went to the kitchen door. He poked in his head and called to Abby.

She followed him out, flour on her belly and her cheeks bright red, and her hair coming out of her bandana. She met his, then my eyes. Jim said, "Abby, if it were really, really necessary, could you hold off on dinner for, say an hour?"

Abby's eyes flew open. "Hold off on—!"

Jim said again, "If it was *really* important."

Again Abby's gaze flitted between him and me. "I guess I could hold every-thing for an hour. Not much more than that without messing up that souffle. I was just about to pop it in the oven, but it could wait a bit. What's the matter?"

Jim looked to me and Connie then said quietly to Abby, "Mary Sanders took her life."

"Jesus, Mary, and Joseph," said Abby, this being about the first epithet I had heard out of her.

"We were thinking we should tell everyone and give them a little while to assimilate the bad news before we sit down."

Abby considered that. "When I was six, my cousin Tom fell off the barn roof. He was eighteen. It happened just at Christmas, day before maybe. He and my brother Cole and a couple other cousins had been up on the roof, messing around, daring each other to do dumb stuff, and Tom fell off. Hit the hay rake. No one said nothing at first, just hushed it up and let everyone come to Christmas and open gifts and eat a big meal, just like nothing had happened, and that's with poor Tom lying in the funeral parlor in town. His folks and sisters stayed home, of course. It still might have gone okay 'cept the cousins who'd been with him blabbed. They was upset and feeling nine kinds of guilty about the whole thing. They needed to talk and just couldn't keep Tom's death to them-selves. The rest of the clan, of course, noticed that Tom and his family hadn't come. When some of the talk came out, it twisted almost right away. Thing was that Tom had been drafted and didn't want to go to the Vietnam. Everyone knew that. With rumors of him being dead started around, some said he'd jumped off the roof. Before the day was out, the whole family was in a mess, everyone angry and hurt, and no one talked to each other for almost two years. They shoulda told everyone right up front. They should have said he slipped and tried to hang onto the edge, that he shouted to his cousins not to let him fall. Truth can hurt, but rumor can turn bitter. You get Mr. Harris to announce this, and I'll hold dinner *two* hours. That'll give everyone three hours before we eat."

Abby was my hero.

Jim Stone grinned at her, patted her shoulder, and ran from the room.

The announcement came from Harris five minutes later. Three hours later, we sat down to eat. I really don't think it was possible for us to come to terms with a suicide in our midst in three hours, not for us and certainly not for Brad, who didn't join us. The death hung over the room at first, and the array of amazing food didn't seem as impressive or tantalizing as we had thought that morning. Still, as people began to eat, the good food brought comments and pleasure. As we filled ourselves with mashed potatoes, vegetables, and a variety of meats and dressings, some of the rawness of the news of the death slipped. Smiles and pleasant chatter slowly began. If we had had any memories of Mary before she came to us, I'm sure those stories would have come out, but the truth was, we didn't know this woman. Though we felt her death more than that of a stranger, it didn't impact us as deeply as it would have had this been James Quill, my sister Emily, or even Jim Stone.

The children had it easier. Adults only had been told; Jim and James and Dewey had hustled all the kids to the animal room with the promise of a pony race. I heard they had put two kids to a Shetland and led them around the animal room with all the sound effects of a Thoroughbred derby, even as the ponies sedately walked.

As I watched family members and the others eat and talk, I could easily see the blanket of grief over everything. Yet, I also saw strength. We did justice to Abby's dinner and held a respectful quiet at the same time. Sure, it would have been so much more pleasant to have had the meal without the news of a death, but this was what our world had handed us. I mean, the meal itself was an act of defiance flying in the face of our current circumstances. On the other hand, on the first Thanksgiving, the Pilgrims basically said: We're not out of the woods yet, but we've had a little success, and, damn it, we're going to celebrate that much. We did the same in the shelter.

19

CHOICE

FRIDAY, NOVEMBER 29

═══════════

Mary Saunders joined Ma Anders and the plasticine expert Huey Broomfeld, who had died in the small plane that crashed just down the road. Everyone crowded in and outside of the room, listening to Ian Itkoft, our person of the cloth, trying to make sense of what had happened. But, there was no sense to make, no "better off" or "holy passage." I heard a few grumbles about suicide not being worthy of formal burial, but I didn't see who spoke, and this opinion was ignored.

I had hoped to come away from the service with something. I hadn't expected to feel relieved or okay with what had happened, but all I came away feeling was depressed and sad. Poor Brad bawled through the whole thing and lingered in the room after everyone else had gone, his head hung and his shoulders stooped. He had been defeated in a way, left behind.

The burial room was not near any place people went commonly. It was across the hall from the living area near one of the ubiquitously marked storage rooms. After we had completed the brief service, we all trooped back to the living area and filed down the stairs that Mary hadn't been able to descend alone. We returned to lunch preparations and activities. Black Friday, once the shopping day after Thanksgiving, would forever have new meaning for me.

The children still had no classes that day, so some of the adults set up a series of contests to entertain them and give the rest of us something pleasant to do. They had running races, three-legged races—all the usual church social kinds of things—but these didn't hold kids' interests for long. They started the "best trick" contests—which had to be halted when one of the little Reinharts wanted to jump from the top of the stairs— "Idol" contests where kids performed or sang, but the noise they made was unbelievable, best animal tricks, which seemed to be an excuse to let a goodly portion of the animals into the living area. By the end of a couple of hours, the kids were laughing and having a good time, but adults were running out of energy.

We didn't miss Brad until the kitchen crew began to bring out tasty leftovers for lunch. Abby laid out a lovely buffet of sliced chicken, beef, and pork for sandwiches, warmed dressing, fried potato cakes and what remained of the flaky, crusty pies. As usual, she hovered, making sure everyone got food. She asked me where Brad was.

"When I left the burial room, he was still there," I said. "He's had a horrible shock. I thought maybe he just needed a little time alone."

"He should eat. Grieving is hard work. He should get some food into him. He didn't eat yesterday at all."

I guess I agreed with her. When James came over to refill the plate of his adopted little boy, I asked him to see if he could get Brad to come to the kitchen for a bite of food.

I helped with the little kids, making sure they got what they needed and sat at their table with them to keep an eye on Jane and Andrea. Beth, of course, had elected to join her friends, and they sat way on the outside of the group of tables so they could talk and tease each other with impunity. I watched her for a time, marveling at how well she had adjusted to the routine and restrictions within the shelter. What really pleased me was that the burgeoning adult seemed to have submerged again. She was a happy ten-year-old doing what ten-year-olds did, and she and her cousins seemed to be bringing the children who had been outside along with them on their journey of innocence.

Andrea fiddled with her food as much as she always had. She wanted a chicken sandwich. I made her one. She wanted more mayonnaise on it. I opened the sandwich and applied another layer of mayonnaise. She wanted a pickle, then a little bit of mustard, then another pickle. I finally frowned and told her she was done. Jane didn't ask for anything, of course. She never did. I prepared her a chicken sandwich, putting a couple of bits of meat next to the sandwich on her plate. She looked up at me and said, "Prince really likes beef . . . and . . . and a little bit of pork."

I accommodated, hoping they would be satisfied and eat. Andrea lifted the bread off her sandwich and nibbled on the meat; Jane fed the bits of meat to Prince, giving him not only the pieces I set aside for him but most of the meat in her sandwich. She ate the bread, however.

"You know," I said as I cleared their plates, "I could make one sandwich for the two of you and not waste anything. Both girls thought that was funny. But, while at home I might have groused about the waste of throwing out good meat and good bread, in the shelter I didn't bother. Nothing went to waste. The meat would go to other pets, and the bread likely would be fed to the ducks or the pigs.

"Mom," Andrea said. "Who's that?"

I wiped my hands on a napkin and picked up little Noah, who had started to fuss. "What, dear?"

"Who's that?" Andrea said, her voice more insistent.

I turned to her to see that she pointed at the television mounted over the cafeteria door. I looked, seeing, as usual, the sweep of snowy countryside shown by the cameras. Then, far down the road, I saw the shape of a man.

The feelings that ran through me . . . I couldn't begin to describe them. At first a kind of fear washed through me. Someone was coming. Someone who might want to wrest our refuge from us. I banished that with a swipe of reason. We were too big a company now for one man to threaten, even if he were heavily armed. Then I felt a kind of joy. We could share our safety with some lost and hungry soul even after I thought the cold had sealed us away and probably killed anyone left unsheltered. All those feeling lasted for maybe a heartbeat until I realized that the figure wasn't walking toward the shelter; he was walking away. Only then did I recognize Brad.

I hollered to Jim Stone, across the room, pointed at the screen and shouted that he should get Harris and Frank. He looked and ran. At about that same moment, James skidded back next to me and said that Brad left the shelter. He had opened the door to the woodroom and walked out.

Harris ran across the room for the stairs, but Frank came over to us, looked at the television and asked James what he knew. "What's wrong with you?" he said.

Only then did I see that James was rubbing his jaw. "I tried to stop him, but he clocked me."

"Did he say anything?"

"Only that he couldn't stay, that he was glad Mary wasn't suffering anymore. He said, and he repeated this several times, 'I just couldn't see her suffer anymore.' He said he couldn't share our happiness, that he'd prefer to join his wife and son, but he didn't want to be buried in some little closet."

"Damn fool," said Frank. "We should go after him and bring him back."

"No," I said. "We shouldn't."

Both Frank and Jim Stone looked at me as if I'd just grown a second head. "How can *you* say that?" Jim asked.

I said quietly, "Because when Mary died, I suspected she . . . had help. Now I'm convinced of it."

Both men gaped at me. Jim Stone blinked rapidly several times and whispered, "You think Brad . . . killed Mary?"

I nodded tightly. "Mind you, I think he really did it out of love. I just think he's gone . . . a little over the edge."

Frank breathed out slowly. Then he nodded and rested a hand on my shoulder. "I'll go tell Harris."

He left, and Jim Stone, after looking at me a moment more as if I'd morphed into something awful, got up and trotted after Frank, catching him just at the edge of my ears' range. "You believe that?" he asked Frank.

Frank looked back in my direction, gave me a knowing if grim smile, nodded to the man and said, "You're really good about relationships, Jim. I've watched you get us all sorted better than we do ourselves, but you're missing something. Besides the relationships between people, besides what all of us do, what we did before coming here, there's this whole other level of knowing people. You don't usually tap into that, but Barb does."

"Because she's a nurse?"

That Frank could say that of me made me swell with love for him.

Then Frank continued toward the stairs leading to the steel doors, and I didn't hear the rest, though I could see that Frank continued talking until both men reached the top of the stairs. There they parted, Frank going through the doors to find Harris, and Jim Stone coming back down. He had a quizzical expression on his handsome dark face as he approached me again. He sat down and regarded me a long moment without saying anything. I couldn't stand it and asked, "So, did he tell you I'm psychic?"

Jim's eyes crinkled. "Not exactly, but close."

"What did he say, then?"

"He said you see into people's souls."

I gave an embarrassed laugh. "Into their souls? Me? I hardly think so."

He cocked his head to the side. "Describe me."

Now I could feel heat rising to my cheeks. I'd have to talk to Frank. "You're a very nice man, from what I've seen, and Beth's said you're also a wonderful teacher. She really likes you."

Jim was shaking his head. "No. One word. Describe me in one word."

Unfortunately, I had a word, though I was reluctant to say it. I looked away. He rested his hand on mine. I met his eyes again, my face burning.

He said, "Come on, Barb. You and I are friends."

I sighed, winced and said, "Player."

His expression froze momentarily, turned quizzical again. Then he laughed out loud and slapped his knee. "Damn. You're good, Barb."

"Look, I'm sorry," I said. "I shouldn't have—"

"You're right. I *am* an player. I always have been. I'm five-five and skinny. Every other guy towered over me in college. To get noticed, I had to use my looks and my charm."

"I should have said charming. I'm sorry."

"Charming doesn't look for angles, pressure points. I do. Player. Yup, I can accept that. And you saw Brad as . . ."

"Damaged. He loved Mary. I have no doubt of that, but he knew he couldn't save her any more than he could save his son. He'd lost control of every aspect of his life."

"In a sense, we all have."

I nodded. "But you have Angie and your boys. I have Frank and my children. Most of us have someone we depend on and who depends on us. When Brad came, he'd already lost Mary."

Jim said, "I think we all could see that."

"I don't think too many saw that he'd also already lost himself. He couldn't save Mary, couldn't make her happy again. He knew that. She had lost too much in the death of their son on top of previous miscarriages. He told me Mary was fragile even after the birth of their son. I think Brad knew he was going to lose both of them even before society broke down. That speeded everything up. He lost his son to the elements, and too much of Mary died then. He knew he couldn't pull her back from that loss. Nothing could. But he didn't want her to suffer more than her tortured mind would allow. She was on IVs that last night in the hospital done. Jillian assumes she got drugs from the medicine cabinet, but she couldn't have. Marty had given her a strong sedative so she could get some sleep. I think Brad gave her a little more."

Jim considered that. "I'd still call that more a mercy killing than murder."

I shrugged. "So would I. But the timing is the crucial thing. We've been trying to get Mary into some kind of treatment. Boopsie and Davis Moos have been counseling her since she arrived. Until that night when she finally went to the hospital, she'd been unable to ask for or accept help. The night she did ask was the night she died."

Expression drained from Jim Stone's face. "Wow. So it really was murder. Still, we can't just let the man walk away, knowing he's going to die out there."

"Each of us has the right to a death of our choosing."

"Yeah, but the man's not in his right mind."

"And what's not right in his mind would take years to put right. Unfortunately, during those years, he'd look pretty normal to the casual observer. He'd be able to function on a day-to-day basis, but, underneath, he'd be in constant and terrible turmoil."

Jim's eyes told me he was following my reasoning, though he didn't much like the journey. "Brad killed Mary because he loved her and didn't want her to suffer."

"Yes."

"And he walked out of here so he . . . wouldn't be a threat to us?"

"Yes. Brad is a very dangerous man on a very deep level. He knows this. What caused him to end Mary's suffering might make him end someone else's."

"Whew! You ever wrong with this stuff?"

I thought about that. "My own feelings can affect how I see things. Sure. That happens too often. Frank knows that."

"But not with Brad."

I shook my head. "I don't really have any feeling, other than pity really, for the man. I could see his love for Mary even as they walked down the stairs the first time. The rest didn't fall into place until I saw him walking outside."

"Whew!" he said again and rose. He gave me one of his charming smiles. "If you see me falling apart on some level, you'll tell me, won't you?"

I smiled back. "Sure. Your fly's open."

He snapped his head down only to see the zipper well closed. He grinned. "Ooh, you're a woman who requires watching."

When he left, I turned my attention back to the steel door. In a few more minutes, it opened, and Frank and Harris came in. Brad was not with them. Harris looked at me from across the space between us and gave a slight nod. Frank gave me the corner of a grateful smile.

That night, after dinner—more leftovers with the addition of a huge chocolate cake—Harris addressed the group. "You may have noticed that Brad is not with us tonight. He's gone. Earlier today, after the burial of his wife, Mary, Brad left through the woodroom and walked down the road. Frank and I went after him, but he refused to come back inside. I believe the death of his wife, following so closely the death of his son, had left him unable to continue to live. We could have muscled him inside, but the Ark isn't a prison. Each of us must choose to be here, choose to be a part of the community we're building here. If one of us can't make that choice, the rest of us must let that person go. We let the young man with folks up north go, knowing his chances of getting to Virginia, finding his parents alive and fine and returning to us weren't good. Still we let him go. Today we let Brad go. Though I fear that he'll die in the weather conditions out there right now, it's still his choice. For us to lose that, our free choice, is to admit that our world is dead. I don't want to admit that. I want to believe our world is . . . in transition, a correction, if you will. It's a harsh one, one that's already cost us a very high price . . . and I'm *not* talking about the cost of this facility. We have kids here who have lost their parents, parents who have lost their kids. Each of us has lost loved ones, friends, colleagues. But we've chosen life in these troubled times. That Brad Saunders has chosen death should sadden us, but it should never lead us to force him, or anyone, into actions not of their own choosing. We should think about that, come to terms with that. And, remember, we have been joined by Mr. Moos and Ms. Brewster, both of whom are trained counselors. If you have questions, please ask me or them as you see fit."

I smiled. Our little world was not perfect. How could it be when it was sliced from the larger, very flawed world we had left behind? No, not perfect, but we had a good leader who had a good vision and the articulation to express it. Harris had a lot of faults, but he did his most important job well.

20

CHRISTMAS PLAN

SATURDAY, NOVEMBER 30

W ITH THANKSGIVING OVER, mixed emotionally as it was, we tried to get back to a stable routine of classes, activities, and caring for each other and our animals, but everyone from the youngest child to the grandparents began to look to Christmas and wonder what that holiday would be like in our refuge. We'd pulled off Thanksgiving without turkeys, but Thanksgiving, after all, was mostly a meal. Christmas was a very different kind of event. Could we find Christmas in the walls of the shelter without gifts or secrets or the thrill of Christmas morning?

We had no malls to visit to buy gifts, and many of the items we might have found appropriate to give to family and friends before coming to the shelter no longer applied at all. I gave some thought to trying to make a doll with a variety of clothing for Andrea, maybe one for Jane as well, but Beth would surely be too old for that sort of thing. And what could I make for Frank? Warm socks? Internal temperatures remained the same day in and day out in our super-insulated refuge. I thought I could make Frank a bathrobe if Harris had included terry cloth in his material stockpile, but I was only a middling seamstress. I didn't have patterns even for the dolls I hoped to make, and I sure didn't know enough to just cut and sew. I thought to have Romala help me or at least guide me, but, what with the state of the clothing of some of the new-comers, her machines already whirred from dawn to dusk. I felt selfish asking her to help me with doll's clothes. It seemed so frivolous under the circumstances, and life in the shelter, comfortable as is was, really had no room for frivolity.

Connie and I had talked over the situation as we washed clothes together in the bathroom alcove set up with washers and dryers. She was at a loss as well. Sissy joined us with an overflowing basket of laundry, and she was actually depressed by the whole prospect of Christmas, afraid her children would be sorely disappointed when the day came. I resolved to bring the subject up for formal discussion after dinner that night.

Abby had served tuna-noodle casserole for supper, along with some boiled cabbage. After eating Thanksgiving leftovers for nearly a week, we welcomed the change provided by this crusty, cheesy casserole. With the dishes cleared away and some of the older children loading up the dishwasher in the kitchen and the younger ones playing out in the donut, the adults lingered over coffee and chatted. I was about ready to stand up with a topic for public discussion when Harris rose and said, "I have a few things we need to talk about. The first one is supplies. Anyone need anything to make their daily living a little more comfortable?"

A couple of the newcomers requested extra bedding, a rug for the floor of their slice. Another wanted to know if she could have a couple more pillows. Romala, looking much more fit and quite happy, checked her list of the clothing requests, assuring people her team would get to everyone's needs soon. I was glad I hadn't bothered her.

Carol Moos wanted to know: "Is the lighting in the living area adequate for plants? I mean, will plants grow in here?"

Harris pursed his lips. "It is, actually. All the lights are full spectrum."

"So . . . why don't we have some plants around, some greenery or, heavens, something with a little color to it?"

Sissy piped up and said, "Why aren't we growing edible stuff?"

"Like what?" said Abby, immediately interested.

Sissy said, "Salad greens, for example. They hardly take more than a month. I mean, I loved this boiled cabbage, but how much produce can we have left?"

Harris nodded to Abby.

"Well," said the chief cook. "I've been checking through the storage rooms, trying to use produce before it spoils. Haven't lost much yet. We've got quite a few cabbages, and them's good keepers, 'specially in our storerooms. Temperature and moisture are perfect. Got some carrots, lots of potatoes, a few yams I'm saving for Christmas, turnips, rutabagas, and lots of apples—I figure if we use what we have carefully, we've got enough produce to last us the winter."

"Really?" said Emily. "There's nearly a hundred of us now."

"I know," said Abby, "but I've counted and figured. And we haven't hardly touched the rooms of canned goods you folks brought, the commercial kind and what you home-canned. There, we have years of food, probably serveral. We sure have plenty of meat, too. Not wanting there. We also have a large supply of whole grains. I ran out of flour that was already ground just before Thanksgiving baking time, but Harris showed me this grinder machine that makes flour right out of the whole grains. I've been grinding flour for bread for a couple of weeks now, and the oatmeal you had this morning was also ground from stored oats. We have enough whole grain to last . . . probably two or three years unless we have to feed some to the beasts."

Harris turned to Max Gertz for an update on the animals.

"Animal room working well," he said. "They don't seem to care they's not runnin' around outside. The loafing pen we fixed up for the cows gives 'em enough exercise, and that concrete floor is real easy to muck out. We're gonna have a new calf in a couple of days, and the sheep and goats have been bred for spring babies. The cows and goats we're milking feed us and all the young stock plus the pigs. I'd like to make some cheese on a larger scale, but we'd have to slaughter a calf to get the rennet we need for that."

"No, no," said Harris. "I have a good supply in storage."

"That so?" Max Gertz smiled appreciatively. "Well, I'd like to try my hand at making cheese. We've got enough chickens for eggs right now, but when they go broody in spring, we'll have to let them have their eggs if we're to renew the flock. I'm thinking we could slaughter a few of them ducks, though. There's too many of them. Problem is those little Reinhart kids think pretty highly of them, got 'em all named and such."

"How many ducks are there?" asked Harris.

"There's forty-seven of them," said Max. "All the young ones are grown up, and they're messy. I can see a flock of twenty, but not more'n that."

Dewey said, "I'll talk to my boys about it. The ducks are mostly theirs. I'll get back to you on how Burt and Kurt take it."

"And a couple of those buck goats should be wethered," Max continued, "or we should just eat 'em. We've got a fine young Nubian buck and a good-looking alpine buck kid. That's enough. Those other two aren't needed, and they're getting old enough to start bothering the does. They should be butchered."

Donald Reinhart said, "Except for the little dwarf goats, which are Mary Sue Deters's, my two oldest raised all the rest. I know the two you mean, and I'm fine with that. I've already talked to Peter and Diane. They've purposely not named those two or the lop-eared nanny with the funny teats. I'll let my kids know the time's come."

"What I'd like to do is wether the two and move all three of them to their own pen to fatten 'em up. We have plenty of meat right now, but we might just want a bit of variety in a few months."

"How's feed holding out?" Harris asked.

"Good. We have plenty of hay and grain for the cows for the winter, and the pigs are getting so many leftovers and extra milk, they're doing especially well. We'll run into some trouble probably next spring. We could run out of hay for that many cows. I only put up in the barn what I needed for 'em for the winter, planning that they should go to grass come spring. Sold the rest. We might have to butcher some of the steers soon to keep enough forage for the rest of 'em."

"Let's visit this again when we can plan a walk-through in the animal room," said Harris. "So, our food's holding out and the animals have enough. Good. Good. Let's back up a step now. Plantings in the living area. It's a good idea. We have a good stockpile of garden seeds for next spring planting, but I think we can spare some salad greens, some radishes, spinach, maybe even a few peas."

That got a longing sigh from the group.

"Flowers and greens are a little harder. We have some flower seeds, but most of them will take a greenhouse to grow, but I'll look around. We might have some zinnias, maybe some cosmos and four-o'clocks. Would that work for you, Carol?"

Carol grinned widely. "Anything will work. Thank you, Harris."

When Harris didn't sit back down, we all waited. "I also wanted to talk about efficiency. Anyone have ideas how we could live here more comfortably?"

A man stood. Balding and mustached, he had a lean, hard build and bright-blue eyes. "Carl Hope here, if you don't know me well. I met up with Andy Quill in St. Cloud, but I came down from Grand Marais. Been a carpenter for more'n twenty years now. Sure am grateful you folks took me and my boy, Bobby, in." He spread his arms wide. "Quite the place here. Quite the place. I've been thinking, though, that the slices could be a bit more efficient. If the mattresses were set on a platform with drawers underneath, you'd have storage as well as sleeping space. I've watched some folks struggling to get stuff out from under their beds, and it isn't easy. Also, storage could be built above the beds. Same goes for the bunks. With a little lumber, I could build storage for the lower bunk just under the top mattress, and storage for the upper bunk above it. There's room, height-wise. I've measured. Then slices could be moved closer, and everyone'd have more room."

"We have some lumber for internal construction," said Harris. "Can you put together some numbers for me?"

The man shifted from foot to foot and pulled several sheets of paper from his back pocket. "Begging your pardon, sir," he said, "but I got a lot of time on my hands these days. I drew up several designs for folks to look at and got a count of the board feet for the lumber I'd need. Nails and other stuff are also listed."

Harris accepted the sheets and looked them over. "This is really impressive, Carl. I'll get back to you." He paused and looked around the room. I saw that he met James Quill's eyes, and his younger brother got up and slid the doors to the lunch-room closed. Then he winked and said in a low voice, "We need to start a new club."

"What's that?" said Emily from the back. "What'd you say, Harris? Speak up."

Harris rolled his eyes. In a voice only a little louder he repeated. "We need to start a club, a Christmas club."

Everyone suddenly moved closer to him. Obviously Connie, Sissy, and I weren't the only ones feeling awkward about Christmas.

Harris grinned. "While there's no way that we can duplicate the commercialism of Christmases past, nor should we, it's going to be our first Christmas here, and expectations as well as normalcy demand we do something for our kids. Maybe the teens can understand that Christmas has to be different now, but . . . well I look at my little nieces and nephews and ache to think their hearts'll be broken waking up on Christmas morning to . . . nothing. Regardless what we do in the future, we need to keep life as normal for our children as we can and still maintain life as well as making those changes that will improve our society and make it stronger. I have some . . . gifts stockpiled, gifts for each child I knew would be here and some in case others came. Truthfully, more people came than I thought would, but we'll manage. I have books, some puzzles and games, even some bikes. Romala has assured me that meeting all the newcomers' needs will be completed within the week. Then she'll turn her attention to Christmas items. I want each of you to think of what skills you can offer fellow parents for their kids, what skills you have that could be adapted to Christmas gifts and share them. We have, of course, a little less than a month to do this and make the day a happy one for our children."

Everyone started chatting between themselves, and the tone was improving. People were smiling, beginning to get eager about the prospects that, a few moments before had looked bleak.

Harris said, "But, we don't have malls full of stuff and everything under the sun available for us. There's nothing that requires batteries or electricity or a connection to the outside world. And," he said with emphasis, "we must refrain from making gifts for other adults or other peoples' children. Make gifts for your own children only. And no more than two gifts for each. We still are living with very finite resources and should not believe we can strip our futures for a few moments of pleasure in the present. Prepare your children that Christmas is going to be different this year, very different. Talk about the two-gift idea. See to it that they understand early."

We formed the Christmas club, dubbed the Elves' Club by DeeDee. We would meet in the closed classroom every couple of nights until we had good plans in place. Besides Romala, easily half a dozen women professed proficiency with a sewing machine, and a few had brought along machines, and Romala showed us some of the fabrics Harris had stockpiled. Among the sturdy corduroy, denim, and twill, of which he had dozens of full bolts, he had gathered hundreds of dollars worth of fun furs, gorgeous calicos, even some velvet and satin and drapery material. He had patterns for all kinds of clothes, in a wide variety of sizes, but also a large collection of patterns for dolls and dolls' clothes, stuffed animals, and children's fabric toys. For a man who probably didn't know that much about fabric, he had amassed an amazing collection of supplies. It occurred to me that someone had to have helped him, and I sure didn't think Jillian could have done so. When people started complimenting him on this, he just shrugged and said, "I was working on food, shelter, and clothing. This came under the heading of clothing."

Our carpenter, Carl Hope said he could make kids' toys out of the scraps of lumber used to improve the slices. He'd made wooden trucks and trains before, and said he could make an awesome set of blocks all the kids could share. Jim Stone had also worked summers as a carpenter and offered to help. James and DeeDee said they could hand letter cards if we wanted them, and Carol Moos said she knew how to knit and crochet really well, a skill others chimed in as having. Harris said he had lots of yarn.

As I watched the group of people, I felt my heart swell, both with the outpouring of proffered help and with the wonderful joy that grew among us. I had not seen such joy since Andy came, and that only lasted until the newcomers, clearly refugees, had begun to arrive. This joy of making things for our children and helping others make things might just sustain us all the way to Christmas.

I realized then that Harris had lied to us. He had said he wanted a semblance of Christmas for the children. That wasn't true. He wanted it for us, for the adults who had faced so much loss, so much change from their previous lives. We were the ones who needed Christmas this year, more than the children. If he had not provided a way for us to give something to our kids, we would have fallen into depression—I know I had been slipping down that road—and might not have lifted out of it.

Our lives in the shelter didn't need as much input from each of us as lives outside. I could spend an entire afternoon on my lounge chair outside my slice and not feel like I was playing hooky. Each of us had some kitchen duty, most had animal care chores, but none of it took as much time as on the outside because it could be spread out and because none of us needed to "make a living." Where the Gertzes had seen to their cows, chickens, and pigs in twice-daily chores of feeding and watering, now dozens more people shared those same duties while others cared for the smaller farm animals. What had taken them a couple of hours in the morning and a couple at night was accomplished by a cadre of workers in about half an hour. Boredom had visited each of us and loomed as a threat to the future of the shelter. Plans for Christmas evaporated that threat entirely. At least temporarily.

Then, in a couple of days, I noticed a growing excitement amongst the children. They were more chattery, more giggly than usual, and a lot more secretive. When I got wind of what had caused them to change, I smiled. Harris had spoken to the children in the classroom, away from all the adults, and told them his plans for a Santa's Helpers club, giving the children a way to make presents for their parents and grandparents or, in the case of the orphans who came to us, those who cared for them. He told them that, since their parents had lived longer in the outside world, we had lost more. They, the children, had to help us enjoy the season. All the kids had been sworn to secrecy, but I did learn that Romala and Carl Hope had been engaged by them for projects they planned.

Family secrets as demonstrated by Mike and Marie, by Jeannie, and even Brad Saunders had no place in our closed, communal society. They harmed the fabric of our lives. Secrets for Christmas presents didn't. In fact, it was so much fun meeting covertly, hiding gifts as they were completed and wondering what others were making and giving, that even the camera set up in the living area didn't see much attention anymore.

21

ASSAULT

TUESDAY, DECEMBER 10

H AD SOMEONE BEEN WATCHING THAT CAMERA, we might have seen what was coming. As it was, the white countryside, even stormy afternoons, didn't seem to change the landscape much anymore. Snow and more snow—it didn't make a difference. With Christmas projects well under way that second week in December, we almost forgot to mark the anniversary of coming into the shelter two months before. All we did was give a solemn toast that evening at supper. Two months wasn't much time, but it seemed like a lifetime. I had a whole other child—two of them really— that I hadn't had two months previous. We lived in a different way, in a different place, in a different world. And that maybe was the problem. We knew we had come through a gate, but we hadn't been watching the bridge behind us.

We had just finished our toast at the end of our meal. The cleaning crew of that evening set about gathering the serving bowls as the rest of us marched our plates and silverware to the counter, stacking them with our used glasses and cups. At that moment, a pulsing blare began, not loud or annoying enough to be a fire alarm, but it was close. Everyone turned to look at the red box above the door. Frank frowned and looked to Harris, who said, "That's got to be the woodroom door."

Dewey and James Quill ran for the radio room to check the monitor. On their heels, Frank, Harris, the Deters men, Jillian, and Jim Stone followed. The rest of us, concerned as to what was going on, headed for the classroom.

I guess I expected that someone would come down and tell us why that alarm had gone off, that maybe there had been a malfunction of some sort or, my hope, that someone had found us and needed our protection. But for nearly half an hour, no one came down, though I could hear a low rumble of a discussion bordering on heated. More people started to go up the spiral stairs. Emily, Connie, Carol Moos, and Carl Hope climbed to the radio room. That, surely would get a response. But, even that didn't happen for another ten minutes. Then everyone started to come down. Harris led the way.

When he reached the bottom of the stairs, his expression intense and hard, he stepped aside and waited until everyone who had gone up returned back down and had taken seats. Then he turned to all of us. "We have a problem," he said, his face utterly serious. "Outside in the woodroom are some armed men. Rather heavily armed from what we saw. We spoke to them. They want in."

Sissy said, "You mean they want to *share* the shelter with us?"

"No," said Harris, "they talked nothing of sharing. They said we have one hour to clear out and leave the place to them or they're coming in and taking it."

All around me, people gasped, held their hands to their mouths, gripped their children and hugged them to their sides. This sure wasn't the innocent outcome I had expected. I felt a wash of fear go through me like a tsunami, and I looked down at my sleeping son in the bassinet on the chair next to me. Mary Saunders' son had been three months old when he died of exposure. My son was only a few weeks old. The prospect of taking him outside terrified me.

"They said we can leave unmolested, but if we stay, they'll kill everyone."

Another wave of terror. I gasped for air. This wasn't happening.

"That's pretty strong," said Donald Reinhart. "*Can* they get in?"

Harris started to shrug, then said, "I don't know. The woodroom door is about as secure as a bank vault, but clever thieves get into bank vaults now and again. Only the steel door is closed now. We can lower the concrete door, too. In fact, I'm for shutting down all our doors at this point and being done with the outside world for a time. I'm all for hunkering down in here and thumbing my nose at these guys, but I can't really speak for anyone but myself."

"Could we offer them some food and blankets?" asked Melissa.

Harris kind of nodded. "Except that we'd have to open the woodroom door to give anything to them. We could put them outside one of the other doors, but then they'd know the shelter *has* other doors. They've destroyed the camera, and we didn't get a good head count. We've got the camera outside, of course, so we could see if some leave, but we wouldn't know if they all left. Easily they could leave someone inside to try to keep the door open while the rest of them run in to help. Or, they could booby trap the door, blowing it up when it opens and killing any of us just inside. The door is only safe while closed. I don't think our choice is whether we should offer them help and shelter or maintain our security under the circumstances. Our choice is how to handle this threat to our safety. These guys are dangerous."

"How do you know that?" asked Connie.

Frank said, "Those who came with Andy know how beaten down they were. Tired, hungry, suffering from exhaustion and exposure. Not one of them was out to make a fight of it. Most couldn't. The men outside, from what we could see before they shot the camera, all wore military fatigues, and four of them had on the same fleece-lined heavy coats, like they looted a store like Mills Fleet to get that stuff. They acquired guns and ammunition and are more than willing to use them. They probably have already. These guys are wolves. Letting wolves in here would be asking for them to kill us all. Feeding them would insure only that they'd come back."

Harris nodded vigorously. "The thing is they probably *can* get in if they really, really work at it—though not through the woodroom door. That's impregnable, but other avenues aren't. The outside walls are reinforced concrete. It'd take an earthmover to open up the hill enough to expose the skin and either a hell of a lot of explosives to do any damage or a massive wrecking ball. In a winter like this, with low temperatures—three days below zero already—opening up the hill won't be easy."

"I thought this place was supposed to protect us," said Jeannie.

"From the environment—from bad air, radiation, nuclear winter, disease—not people. That's always been secondary . . . and a concern. Our greatest defense against people has been secrecy and disguising the shelter in a hill. Somehow everyone and his brother seems to know about the shelter anyway. Secrecy hasn't been as good as I would've hoped, but we're kind of beyond that now."

"How much dirt would they have to dig through to get to us?" Andy asked.

Harris said, "Well, it varies a little. They know the woodroom's an entrance. I suppose they could dig right outside, trying to break into the tunnel. There they'd have to go through only a few feet of dirt. But I knew that'd be exposed, and there are safety measures there, a network of electrical conduits all through that area at different depths. They carry quite a charge. They'd have to cut through them all to get in, and that could easily kill them. That's one. I also have a way to collapse part of the hallway just inside the wood room. Getting past the 'electric fence' doesn't get one in. But then we can't use that exit ourselves, probably ever again. Some of the rest of the walls are buried over fifty feet deep, with a maximum of seventy-five, and then there's reinforced concrete with a few electrical conduits just beyond. I'd be happier if this were February. The ground would be frozen much deeper, but the back fill isn't just dirt. The shelter is surrounded with boulders and rock, lots of huge granite blocks buried in the soil.

"I think we can beat these guys, but we all have to agree . . . and quickly," he said, looking at his watch. "They're going to expect an answer in about ten minutes."

I said, "So, what're our choices?"

Harris met my eyes. I saw a flicker of annoyance, quickly hidden, as if he hadn't wanted to be reminded of this issue but knew it had to be discussed. "Our choice is to wait them out and hope for the best or do something . . . proactive."

People had started to discuss matters before Harris said this, but they shut up and turned back. James Quill narrowed his eyes and said, "Define 'proactive.'"

Harris shrugged and sighed deeply. "We have some defensive weapons."

"What?" Wayne shouted. "We've been here two months and only *now* you get around to telling us about this?"

"It's not something . . . it's not an area I felt comfortable with. We never wanted to kill people. We didn't want to be like those paramilitary survivalists. I wanted us to be safe but . . . benign."

"So," said Bob Quill, a little macho smile forming, "What've we got?"

With great reluctance, Harris said, "I have a way to release a gas into the woodroom. It'd kill them in seconds. In the walls of the woodroom are two machine guns we can fire with controls upstairs. They'd make a sweep of the room automatically. There's also a gun mounted just outside the woodroom entrance that'd sweep the yard. There are charges embedded in the road as well as all around the shelter."

We all got very quiet. When the students had come, trying to force their way inside and Mike had shot one, every one of us had condemned him for his actions. But the students had not been the threat these men were. The students were scared boys looking for shelter. On the other hand, I knew Harris was right: getting in was only a matter of "wanna." Humans had quite literally moved mountains before, destroyed buildings with far more concrete than we had in the shelter, dug so wide and deep as to create lakes. We'd cut continents apart after all. If these men wanted in, they probably could get in if they had the right machinery, and we didn't know they didn't. It all came down to a cost-reward ratio. It wouldn't be easy to get in the shelter, but the benefits would be survival. Pretty big. Lots of wanna there. Unless . . .

"Harris," I said. "Do they know what's in here?"

He looked at me, his brows tightening. "I don't know how much they know. Knowing where this place is is bad enough. What are you thinking, Barb?"

"You played a shell game with contractors. Right? Not many had any idea what they were building, what it was for, or how many it could support. Right?"

"I would've hoped not, but, again, I don't know what these particular men know. That they're here and want in suggests they know more than I'd have hoped."

"Yes, but I bet they have no idea how big it is or how many it can support or for how long."

"Your point?" Wayne said with, I noticed, less sarcasm than usual.

"My point is we're dealing with wolves. Personally, I'd rather not shoot them if we don't have to. If they could be made to believe that we're dying as is, they might go look for a fatter sheep farm."

Now I had everyone's attention, though, as soon as I stopped talking, everyone turned to Harris for his reaction. He stared at me a moment, then began to smile. "That's a good choice. One we all can get behind."

"What's it mean, though? What do we do?" said Jeannie.

Harris grinned his silly, wide grin. "Shadows and mirrors. We make them believe we're sick, starving, that there's not much point in their barging in here."

We planned quickly. There was no two-way camera for the woodroom, so the men outside had no real idea how many people and in what condition huddled inside. Harris would try to convince them we were almost as challenged in the Ark as folks outside it. He jotted down the best ideas and made his way back to the radio room with only Frank and Marty. The rest of us crowded the stage, waiting for word. Dewey got the idea to pan the outside camera, which was up on a high pole and hidden by trees below it, toward the woodroom to try to get a look at the men. He was just on his way to the stage when, apparently, one of the men upstairs also had that idea because the television in the classroom came on and showed the road coming up to the shelter. A pack of snowmobiles parked just at the bottom of the driveway showed how the men had arrived. All Polaris, all new. Stolen, I figured. Six machines. I guessed that they'd either ride singly, especially if the macnines were stolen, or double at most. No more than twelve men total, but I bet on six. The camera turned, revealing four men just outside the wood room. They had shotguns, rifles, and handguns at the ready. Two men had bandages on their arms, one on his thigh. These guys had fought others for what they had. Frank was probably right to call them wolves, though our northern Minnesota animal had a lot more dignity and nobility than these men.

I went to the stairs and called up to Marty. He poked his head down.

"Can the guns cut up their snowmobiles?"

Marty disappeared to ask Harris. He came back and gave me a thumbs up. Now we had a non-lethal weapon to discourage these wolves.

The camera watched. For ten more minutes, the scene didn't change. Men waiting outside armed to the teeth. Then one man came up the woodroom stairs. He shook his head. His compatriots didn't look happy. One of them had a lighter in his hands, and he flicked it open, revealing its flame. Then he closed it and opened it several times in quick succession while he talked with the man who had just joined them.

We could hear nothing, of course, but the man with the lighter seemed to get angrier and angrier, flicking open the flame and closing it more rapidly. It looked to me as if the one who had come up from the woodroom was explaining what Harris had told him. It also seemed to me as if he didn't want to pursue the work of getting into the shelter. He looked disgusted. Lighter Man swung his arm toward the woodroom and shouted at the first man. Whatever First Guy was saying didn't sit well. I don't think he believed the story of disease and starvation Harris likely had fed him. Finally, Lighter Man closed his toy and stuffed it into his pocket. Other men in the yard began to holster their guns or otherwise look less ready to fire. Lighter Man pulled on thick snowmobile gloves and started walking to where the machines had been parked. First Guy and the others, looking disgusted, started to follow. Two more men came out of the woodroom and joined them. Leaving. They were going away! Our plan of subterfuge seemed to have worked.

I heard the steel door to the hallway above the stairs clang open, and turned, with about a dozen others, to see the door close again. Someone, I couldn't tell who, had gone into the wood room hallway. All my alarms went off at once. Fortunately, I wasn't the only one to think this wasn't a good idea. James Quill, Jim Stone, and Dewey Reinholt bolted across the donut at a dead run and took the stairs two at a time. They swung open the door and disappeared into the hall.

While most of the rest of the people began to head in the direction of the steel door as well, I turned and watched the monitor. The men had now mounted their snowmobiles and were setting about putting gloves and helmets on. Suddenly, their attention swung toward the woodroom entrance as if all their heads were controlled as one. I wished I could hear what had drawn their attention. The six men slowly set down their helmets. Several drew weapons. Then one man in the back stood up and shouted toward the woodroom. That's when I saw Wendel.

Climbing up the steps, a head emerged—Wendel Morris, the seventeen-year-old boy who we found shivering in the Gertz's barn, the last to come to us. He seemed to be struggling awful hard. Finally, he came fully into view. He turned and kicked down the stairs. Then he scrambled up the last way and stood, his arms wide, walking toward the snowmobilers. Frozen breath poured from his heaving lungs. He kept shouting something over and over, his mouth making the same motions. I moved my mouth in the same way, but I didn't know what he had said.

Wendel had taken maybe two steps into the yard when Dewey launched himself against his back, bowling him over. Then James appreared, and he and Dewey pulled Wendel back toward the woodroom stairs. He fought fiercely.

The snowmobilers began to react. Rifles and shotguns had come up, and the man who had stood and shouted before, had dismounted his machine and was running toward the three at the top of the stairs. Other snowmobilers seemed ready to follow. Lighter Man had produced a pistol. He aimed it at the three struggling men, and, to my horror, fired. Dewey, whose shoulder was most toward Lighter Man, bucked as the bullet hit him. Then, almost in slow motion, all three men collapsed at the top of the stairs.

The snowmobilers were running across the yard, within a couple of seconds of reaching the woodroom stairs. The door had to be open, too. The entrance into the shelter had been breached by Wendel and stood wide. The wolves were closing in.

Their weapons were ready—so many weapons—pointing at the three on the ground. Then they stopped. Frozen in the horror of believing my world was about to change, I didn't see why. Something had shifted. Then I saw the gun over the concrete foundation. Jim Stone had once told me he was armed. Did he carry the weapon with him all the time? For this very moment, I was grateful if he had.

Outside became a stand off. Six well-armed men faced one handgun over the fallen three, who had started to sort themselves. James was shouting at the intruders.

Dewey had slumped down the stairs. But Wendel hadn't moved. Wendel lay in the snow with James crouched over him shouting at the men.

The man who had seemed to recognize Wendel, holstered his pistol and gave his rifle to another man, then walked toward the fallen boy with his arms held high. James withdrew as he reached him, backing down the stairs, Jim's gun still visible, covering him. Then the gun disappeared as Jim also backed down the stairs.

The man reached the fallen boy and checked him. Then he collapsed in the snow and gathered Wendel to his chest, rocking and screaming at the men in the yard. He pulled out his pistol again and fired it. Lighter Man crumpled. The others, some of whom had lifted their weapons, backed toward the snowmobiles. The man on the ground with Wendel shouted after them, his face twisted by anger and misery. The rest of the men fired up their machines and soon vanished down the road in clouds of snow.

My held breath—I have no idea how long I'd held it—began to leave my body, taking with it a lot of my energy. I sat in the chair next to Noah's bassinet and stared at the television screen. Just as I was about to lower my spinning head to my hands, the man holding Wendel turned toward the woodroom entrance, and his gun pointed in that direction. Slowly Jim Stone's head came back into view.

The man on the ground wrapped his arms around the boy. Jim was talking to him, but the man kept shaking his head. Jim rested his hand on the boy's face to close his eyes. He reached over to grasp the man's shoulder then, and the man leaned against him, weeping. James appeared, and accepted the man's weapons, a couple pistols and several huge knives, as Jim gathered Wendel's body into his arms. Jim disappeared down the stairs, and James assisted the man after him.

Next to me, also witness to the drama in the yard, Jeannie said, "They're *not* bringing that killer in here, are they? They can't bring him in here!"

Everyone headed across the donut to the stairs. In a couple of moments the door above opened and Dewey slumped in, holding his upper arm. Red had worked its way down to his elbow. Jim Stone followed, carrying the body of Wendel Morris, and James, his arm around the weeping man, brought up the rear.

Harris and Frank sprinted past me and parted the crowd to get to the bottom of the stairs just as Dewey reached them. Marty elbowed his way to Dewey. Melissa and he assisted him toward the hospital. Frank headed up the stairs—to check the woodroom door, I supposed.

Everyone was shouting, arguing, asking questions, demanding answers. Jim Stone, carrying Wendel, struggled to get to the hospital in Dewey's wake. James had even a harder time getting the man there as well. Harris mounted several stairs and shouted at us, "Everyone to the classroom. Now!" Then he followed Jim Stone and James to the hospital.

Some people returned to the classroom. Others milled about in the donut, pressing up against the doors to the hospital. Marty stuck his head out; his eyes found me, and he said, "I need a nurse."

I handed Noah to my sister Anna. Marty let me in the hospital, then barred the door. Wendel lay under a sheet in the first bed. Dewey, a grimace on his face, lay in the second. I helped Marty and Jillian cut away his shirt and get him settled.

"The bullet went right through Dewey's shoulder and into Wendel," said Marty as he sedated Dewey preparing to assess the damage and begin repairs. "Hit the kid right in the heart. He was dead before Dewey knew he was hit."

Melissa, tears streaked down her face and holding tightly to Dewey's other hand, said, "He'll be okay, won't he?"

Marty gave her a reassuring smile. "He won't have chores for a while, and he'll probably whine and complain more than you're used to, but he's going to be just fine, Mel. There's not a tremendous amount of blood, so the bullet didn't hit a major artery, which is very lucky, and, had it hit bone, it wouldn't have gone right through with enough force to kill poor Wendel. Yup, just missed about everything. Not all that serious."

"Yeah, well," said Dewey, "it sure doesn't feel that way."

Marty did a nice clean-up job, probing the wound to make sure no bone fragments, no serious bleeders remained, then packed and bandaged the shoulder, securing Dewey's right arm to his chest to immobilize it.

Then Marty approached the man who knew Wendel. "Are you hurt?"

The man shook his head. He was only average in height, but he had a thin, angular face that hadn't been shaved in several weeks.

"What's your name?" I asked him.

"Stewart Bohn," he said in a low voice.

"What's your relationship to Wendel?"

"He's . . . he was my sister's kid. She lived down the road a couple of miles. She left him in my care when all this mess started in October. Said she couldn't stay here and went to Georgia, but I've never even heard if she made it. Wendel wouldn't go. But he disappeared several weeks ago. Weather was bad. I thought he froze to death."

"We found him shivering in the barn just down the road."

"And took him in." The man gave me a pained look. "We wanted to rob you. Steve Johnson . . . the guy I shot, said some rich guy owned this shelter and didn't deserve to have it. The wealthy needed to die in the new order, their wealth redistributed to the masses. But you took Wendel in."

About then, Harris excused both Marty and me, saying he wanted to talk with the man and our people who had gone after Wendel.

Marty faced the crowd that had formed. "Dewey's going to be fine. Wendel died outside. Harris is talking with the guy. He's Wendel's uncle. It could take awhile."

Jim Stone came out of the hospital just then, striding across the living area. He called to Paul Fisk, Carl Hope, and Bob Quill. The men followed him up the stairs to the steel door and left.

I went back to the classroom. On the television screen, I saw Frank. He was checking the man who hadn't moved since falling in the yard. Then the four men joined him, and they conversed. Frank went with them to the two remaining snowmobiles. They stripped what they could from one of them and carried that inside. Jim Stone got on the other and made a wide circle in the yard, going entirely around the fallen man, and stopped the machine about in the same spot it had been but going the opposite direction. Then all four men heaved the machine up and carried it into the woodroom. Ten minutes later, they came back into the living area. Frank headed to the hospital, but the other men came into the classroom. Jim Stone sat down next to me.

"So," he said with his face crinkling, "Do I photograph well?"

I knew he was trying to lighten the mood, but it missed. "Two people died today," I said.

He sobered. Stress lines formed around his eyes. "I know. Sorry."

"What was the bit with the snowmobile?"

"Oh, well, we wanted it to look like Wendel's uncle left."

"What about the other snowmobile?"

"We're leaving it there. It's more serious than that, though. For a time we also *have* to leave the dead guy out there, too."

"What? That's horrible."

"Those guys could come back. Until the snow covers up all the tracks, we want them to believe Stewart Bohn left, that we wouldn't let him in. That's important. And why would we take in that dead guy? If we did, if the body was removed, it would indicate that we weren't so sick and near death, that we still had some civilized sensibilities. They could prey on those. We'll leave the body a few days, then move it, especially if the weather looks like snow."

"What are we going to do with Stewart Bohn?"

Frank shook his head.

I didn't know what I wanted to do with him. I had a new babe in my arms, I couldn't be absolutely certain I'd want him to leave or stay.

22

GLIMPSE

———

Wendel Morris was laid to rest in our cemetery room with as much honor as the others buried there. Four people had died in two months' time, even with our technologically advanced shelter. In a population our size, that was a horrific ratio, at least for any time before the shelter. Though Wendel and the plasticine expert had died from causes outside of the shelter, though Mary Saunders had been helped to death, and Mrs. Anders had died of old age and a lack of will to live, all those lives lost were the result of . . . well, it was like culture spinning backwards. Spinning one way tended to hold everything in place; a spin the other way saw pieces fly off at unpredictable times and in totally unexpected ways. Our world had reversed its spin to cause all this. The only difference between the shelter and the outside world was that the outside world was spinning a lot faster.

We were in transition between the world we knew and whatever lay ahead for us, but I had no idea how we were doing. There were no standards for this sort of thing. Big reorganizations of society didn't occur every generation. The paramilitary groups Harris contacted regularly on the ham radio certainly had done their share of killing in defense of their facilities, and a couple of those survival groups had admitted to internal deaths as well. I wondered if their front yards were littered with bodies killed and left to discourage anyone else from venturing too close. In that regard, Lighter Man was serving his purpose, I suppose, but I didn't like seeing him in the yard. At least so far, no one had died of a failed internal system or by an attack that breached our defensives. Who knew someone would leave our fortress to face armed adversaries? That wasn't something we could have predicted. Wendel's death galvanized us all to believe we were now in the shelter for the duration. How long was that?

Over the next several days, the snow covered over Lighter Man, so that he was just a lump of white in an otherwise smooth yard. The tracks on the road had been obliterated by snow and winds, but the stripped Polaris still sat at the end of the driveway, still visible above the snow.

For the most part, we returned to our activities of getting ready for Christmas, at least we tried to, but the innocent joy had gone out of it. David Moos and Boopsie counseled the children in the schoolroom on a daily basis, trying to help them deal with what had happened. Each night, though, some child, often more than one, woke screaming in terror of being attacked by vicious men who wanted to throw us out of our shelter or kill us. The kids who had come to us had it the hardest. They had memories, hidden or not, of recent bad times. Dreams had visited me, as well, and I woke more than once breathing hard and sweating. All Frank could do was hold me and promise that we were safe. He didn't know that my nightmares weren't about being attacked and displaced but about killing people whose only wanted succor and survival. With the machine guns in the woodroom and those about the yard, the mines and electrical conduits, I dreamed we killed neighbors and friends who had come seeking shelter. We had acted with honor with this first assault, acted honorably with the newcomers, but now, having been visited by jackals, would we jump at every shadow, every movement? Would we assume the next visitation to be an attack and strike out before we realized our error? That was the fear that tore me from my sleep and haunted me as I hid gifts for my children.

IN THE DAYS FOLLOWING the attack, we learned what we could from Wendel's uncle, Stewart Bohn. He and his band of marauders, led by Lighter Man (a.k.a. Steve Johnson), had spent the last month since they joined together taking what they needed from any place in the area that looked promising. They broke into houses, businesses, and farms. Most everything was deserted, had been from the first weeks, and people had left a lot of stuff behind. Food was easy enough for them so far, though the grocery stores, even the big ones like CashWise and Cub, had been pretty much cleaned out. People left their homes, however, with freezers full of meat and Hot Pockets and potato shreds. They had left behind pantries stocked with canned goods. The marauders helped themselves. They'd hole up in a house with a fireplace, burn chairs and tables and books—anything combustible—and loot the surrounding neighborhood, then move on. They'd been in "move" mode when they came to our doorstep. Stewart didn't think they'd be back, at least not until the whole area had been picked clean. The problem was that other groups were doing the very same thing. That was the reason his gang had armed themselves.

When asked if they had seen anyone else alive who had nowhere to go, he laughed bitterly. In the first month, he said, they sometimes found someone holed up in a basement, bent on sticking out the winter. Their group mostly left such places alone, but others didn't. Often, as they worked one end of a development, another group attacked from another side. He had heard shooting, and knew that, at least on one occasion, someone had been pulled from his house and killed. As far as their pack was concerned, the killing of Wendel and then Lighter Man were the only killings they had made, but they had displaced three people in the last several raids. What became of those people, he had no idea. He also said that he and Wendel had themselves been displaced by raiders. That's when he'd lost Wendel. How the seventeen-year-old managed to slog his way up to Gertz's barn, he didn't know. He thanked us for caring for him.

He seemed sincere. He clearly mourned Wendel's death and exhibited considerable remorse for his actions in recent weeks. But he had made some pretty terrible choices, had killed a man, and we didn't trust him. He knew that. After several days of good food and rest, he asked to leave. We knew he might just head straight back to what was left of his own pack or join up with another, one much more powerful, and sic them on us straight away. In a group meeting, one that, surprisingly, had little negative discussion, we gave Stewart our decision.

"It's not our policy," Harris told him while everyone listened, "to hold anyone in here against his or her wishes. It's our policy, for as long as we can maintain it, to uphold the best of human beliefs and rights. We realize that holding these beliefs and living under them might work against us before this time of transition in the world is over, before reason again overtakes insanity, and right weighs in heavier than might. But to dictate the choices for another human being, even one who poses a threat to us, is to fall more quickly into chaos than we're willing. You came here intending to harm us. Two people were killed in the process of that assault, and another person injured. If you had attempted to rob a gas station and the same results had occurred, you'd most certainly have been found guilty of murder twice over and deadly assault once. You would've spent the rest of your life in prison. But, while this facility has many facets, it does not have a prison, and we are not your judge and jury."

Stewart, standing before us, however, looked like a heavy sentence had already been levied. Head hung, he wept. But he wiped his face and asked to speak. His voice cracking, he said, "I've been punished for my actions. I loved Wendel like my own son, and he was killed. The only reason I stayed in the area was . . . well, I hoped I'd find his body and bury it next spring. Nothing holds me now. If you let me go, I'm heading south. I won't be your problem anymore."

He paused, and his jaw worked. Then he said, "I hope you guys make it. You've got a good start, and I hope you make it. But you need to know you won't make it alone, and a lot of the rest of those who survive this winter won't be nice people. When you guys come out and try to pick up your lives, men like me will be waiting. Right now there are a lot of packs of looters. There's shooting every night in St. Cloud, and I can only guess what the Twin Cities are like. There's plenty of booty still, but, eventually, they'll get hungry. The rest of the guys in my gang will remember that you guys are up here. They'll be back. When they come, you better have more than one little automatic on hand, or they'll chop your door open and get in here, and then you'll be dead."

We let Stewart Bohn go. We gave him back his snowmobile and loaded him down with food and blankets. He said gas still could be found, so he could fill his Polaris as he headed south, and sheltering in abandoned houses and barns wasn't difficult. We even gave him back his weapons, though the ammunition was packed away deep in the middle of blankets; no way could he arm himself quickly enough to keep us from closing our doors. We told him we would not let him back inside.

Snow started falling heavily, the day Stewart left. While some of us watched him go on the monitors, others repaired and replaced the cameras destroyed in the woodroom, but they were made less conspicuous. While before, the woodroom itself had been left open to allow people to get into its shelter, we now closed that cellar-door entry, barred it, and set up motion detectors just outside to alert us if anyone came into the yard. Then we watched as the snow erased the evidence of our endeavors and Stewart's trail as he snowmobiled away.

We knew we were taking a risk, but no more risk than letting some of his former gang leave us and probably less than letting him stay with us. All we had shown was that single gun carried by Jim Stone, which, it turned out, was a replica of a .45 Colt, but only an air pistol. He could shoot little plastic caps, though the sound of that shot mimicked a real .45-calibre pistol. He had defended Wendel and gotten our men back alive with, essentially, a toy. I shuddered to think what might have happened had anyone called his bluff. All three of our men could have fallen in seconds, and the rest of the gang would have found an open door inside the woodroom. With that door breached, we were vulnerable. The shelter could have fallen in moments.

"As you can see," Harris told us in the debriefing following Stewart's departure, "no one will ever be kept in here against his or her will. Even if there is a risk, we'll let them go. You've all seen that. I hope you believe it. And, though this instance is certainly the most dramatic and maybe even the most dangerous event we've experienced, it isn't the first time that people have gone out without authorization.

"You all believe you have a right to go outside anytime you want, but you don't. Not with so many other lives here. Staying here demands giving up some of our rights, some of the freedoms we enjoyed in a time that no longer exists. Each of you has to come to terms with that idea, and the world out there is a lot more dangerous than it used to be. Men like Stewart's gang are preying on what's left of humanity out there. Now it's just the leavings of people long gone from the area, but all who remain will eventually come under attack. They'll be back. For that reason, no one shall attempt to leave without the consent of the entire group, and measures have been taken to insure the safety of the rest of us remaining inside. To insure everyone's safety, I've lowered gates across the hallways of all entrances. Lifting those gates is not easy. It's not just pushing a button, trust me. No one gets out of here again without the approval of all."

Then Harris softened his tone. "Look, folks, this can work. We're as safe in here as we can define safe. We can survive in here and make lives that work. The shelter is working. We need to give it a chance."

"How long?"

People turned to my sister Emily. She didn't look happy. "You haven't told us everything about this place. Weapons? Who else knew? You need to make a full disclosure, Harris. You need to show us everything. You've never done that, and all our lives are as wrapped up in this place. I say you tell us everything right now."

A lot of voices chimed in. People wanted this, and I was one of them.

"No," said Harris.

Voices raised. Some people shouted at him, getting angrier as they did so. Wayne and Mike Deters shook their fists in his direction. People argued back and forth and screamed out questions and concerns. Harris held up his hands until a semblance of quiet gave him the opportunity to speak. This had taken all of ten minutes, and, when he opened his mouth to say something, voices started up again. Harris held up his hands again and waited. Finally, people calmed down enough for him to speak. "Will I make full disclosure to all of you?" Harris said. "Yes. I know you think that now is the time. I'd like the opportunity to explain to you why I don't think so."

We waited, tense and angry, but we waited. Mike said, "Make this good."

Harris said, "I've thought through this nine ways to Sunday. The Ark has been the focus of my life for a lot longer than the five years it took to build. I've been planning this and thinking about this for most of my life. And, against everything, I'm hoping to preserve our culture and society, not to mention our lives, but I couldn't think of a way to deal with full knowledge of the workings of this place before you're ready."

Several voices shouted that they were ready, long since ready.

When order settled again, Harris said, "Had we had full disclosure already, Wendel might've found out some things about our defenses that we can't afford to let fall into the hands of outside people. Had full disclosure already taken place, someone might have inadvertently given Stewart information that would allow him to come back with a large crew and ferret us out of here in a matter of days. We wouldn't have had the freedom to let him leave. He would have stayed our prisoner and never would've been trustworthy. We would've always had to fear him. And we would have had to watch him for fear he would sneak out to his buddies. Would you have wanted that?"

Harris had everyone's attention now, and he played to it. "We have people here, family members, who have challenges to their personalities and motives that could hold the rest of us hostage, and half our number now comes here out of need, with no controls placed on what they can know and where they can go any different from those of us original to the project and no investment in the Ark any greater than a hope for survival. We've made no attempt to assertain the moral fiber of any of these newcomers or take a history from them of their doings in the world previous to coming here—nor have we asked family members to submit to such a test. Only a fool might assume that everybody's motives in remaining here is the same, that everyone's commitment is the same. That coming to us in a state of need constitutes being a good person. To believe that each of us at some time or other will not wish to get out is to believe that people were always intended to live like gophers. To believe that no one of us will try to turn the shelter into some kind of profit is to believe everyone golden and good down to his soul. Living in the Ark is an unknown quantity to all of us. It's a hard life at best, and all of you will want to opt out before we leave as a group."

Some people weren't so happy with these remarks, but they listened. Harris was, if nothing else, a good orator, and some aspects of his speech began to make sense.

"In all my scenarios, in all my research and reading, the best chance we have as a group is to allow no one to know everything for the first winter. That'll do two things. First, because this is Minnesota and damn cold, much of the countryside will empty of people. That removes a huge risk for us. Only those who revert back to pioneer survival methods and the marauding gangs will remain after that time. By next fall, only the pioneers—if there are any left—will remain. And, yes, I knew that the gangs would form. They'll have headed south by next fall, becoming the problem of those who fled in the beginning. Second, and much more important, we inside will have formed a cohesive community. That's already well underway and progressing better and faster than I had hoped. Following the best plan I had worked out, I made captains of some of you, put people in charge of certain kinds of activities. That's worked beautifully. The cooperation of people under that structure is also working. We're eating well, caring for each other and our animals, schooling our children."

Emily said, "But not enough yet for you to trust us?"

"The shelter as a mechanical device never had hope of success in keeping us alive. You need to understand this. A machine can't save us. *We* have to keep us alive. All this place can do, all it ever could do, was provide the environment necessary for survival if we respect its limitations and parameters. In that, it's like our planet. Earth can't make people good or caring or respectful of themselves, others of their kind, or their environments. It just gave us some necessary elements for life. That's what it does. If we're to survive, we must become a community with one heart, one purpose, one . . . soul. And this comes at a time when all of our lives seem to be flying off in every direction. When we came into the shelter, 'community,' as we've grown up to understand it, no longer existed out there. Oh, yes, we lived in homes *next* to each other and in towns *near* each other, but each of us had separate dreams and aspirations and the moral frame within which we were willing to work to achieve our goals. What I did in my house didn't affect what my neighbor did in his.

"Well, now we live all together, separated by only curtains, a pretense of separation. What one does, everyone else knows. Secrets are harder to keep. Difficulties are harder to hide. Now we have to pay attention to the needs and wants of all the people we live with, that being the best way to satisfy our own needs.

"With interest, I watched as necessary duties were fulfilled, people rose to the challenge of putting our world into order. With great pride, I watched what happened when new people came to us. Orphans came, but they were orphans for maybe an hour. Without being told or asked, without complaint, every one of those children was taken into an existing family. Did I tell you to do that? Did I force you to open your hearts and cramped spaces to those children? Would you have been so giving, so open before we came here? If that were so, there would have been no orphans out there, but there were."

Tears fell freely down my cheeks, and I wasn't the only one moved by Harris.

"I know you don't think I have a right to hold things above you, to keep information to myself when so many of you contributed so much to the shelter. The fact of the matter is that money doesn't matter anymore. I have nothing monetary to gain by keeping stuff secret. But we have a lot to gain this way and a lot to lose if I don't. For a while. Please, I've devoted my life to this project. Being a lawyer was only a means to an end. For me, my life's work is this place, and I know how to make it work. I've never really asked this before, but I ask now that you trust me. You're doing what you need to do, building community, and you're doing it well. Let that process complete before we leap ahead. We have some trials ahead of us, some tests to our structure that aren't going to be easy. Once we've passed that point, everything will make more sense. I'm hopeful that you'll come to agree with my methods, not because I want you to, but because they're right. Please, trust me."

I don't know how many people could say that they did trust Harris at that moment. In so many ways, I had written Harris off as brilliant but flaky. I began to wonder if he hadn't cultivated the "flaky" part all along for a purpose of his own.

23

CHRISTMAS

WEDNESDAY, DECEMBER 25

J UST A WEEK BEFORE CHRISTMAS, Harris informed us that, since everyone wanted to
have a Christmas tree, he had a way of giving us one. A crew of four men—James Quill,
Donald Reinhart, my brother Marty, and Jim Stone—would be allowed to leave by one
of the most distant exits, just outside of which a suitable Christmas tree stood. That tree
and that one alone would be cut. The men would return to shelter in moments. Harris
led these four men, armed, out of the living area, not allowing anyone else to follow. They
would be trusted with the location of his long escape tunnel, but no one else.

The men left, and the steel door clanked shut behind him. While we had no
indication that any danger awaited them outside—there had been no sign of any
marauders and radiation levels had dropped—the mood of the rest of us hung on
their absence. Lunch had just ended, and the children returned to the classroom for
a couple of classes. I had Noah down for a nap and spent a few minutes cleaning up
our slice, but that didn't take more than ten minutes. I then had been assigned to
water the plantings we had made recently. Lettuce and radishes had emerged and
needed attention. Beans had just risen the night before on arching stems, and several
large planters of corn and squash also grew. The kids had been given a chance to have
a planter all their own, and they had chosen to plant sunflowers. Those already had
stretched to nearly six inches. Repeatedly I filled my watering can and sprinkled each
of the planters, being careful not to let the water overflow the trays beneath them. As
I pulled the wagon with the watering can from site to site around the living area, the
lunchroom and hospital, I thought I might weed as well, but I could find not one
weed in the dozen planters. Nothing we had not planted grew in the potting mix we
used. Somehow this seemed wrong to me. What was life without weeds?

This depressed me. It pointed out that ours was a hot-house life. Hot-house plants only had weeds when "contaminated" by outside soils. I surely could grow nothing in my own garden back home without a battle on my hands from several fronts: weeds, insects, rodents, and uncooperative weather. None of those factors existed here. Yet I doubted the plants I tended would be stronger for the lack of com-pitition, the lack of stress in their lives. I remembered the saying, "There is no art without suffering."

Still, it was such a wonder to see plants rising from the soil and putting out leaves, I forced my bad thoughts aside. I feared the plants would grow "leggy" because of inadequate light, but they didn't. In fact, they looked robust, with dark-green leaves and thick stems. I knew I would be eager to taste the first radishes, a bite of leafy lettuce, and the other produce emerging.

I had just wheeled the wagon and watering can back to its spot next to the bathroom doors when the steel door above me clanged again. I spun around, an instant fear in my heart, but it quieted almost immediately. The four men had returned. Grinning and cocky, they looked as if they had come home from a great hunt. Instead, they carried a Christmas tree—not a pine or spruce that had grown wild or in the Gertz's yard and had snow clinging to the branches. This tree, a fir, had been groomed for years for this one purpose. Moreover, it had not been cut. It came in a burlap ball.

The men proudly paraded the eight-foot tree around the donut and through the classroom and lunchroom before returning to the living area and setting it in a planter that Harris had not yet filled with dirt.

"You guys didn't go outside, did you?" said DeeDee.

The men laughed.

"Nope," said James. "Harris has been planning this for some time. The tree was in . . . storage."

Storage. In storage the tree would have turned brown and died. This tree had had the benefit of good lighting, waterings, and a place in soil. This tree had been groomed and tended. Harris didn't explain this, didn't say from which storage room it had come, and I could almost see the pact of silence between the men. They sure-ly weren't likely to tell us anything. I had to wonder, though, if producing this tree "out of thin air," didn't have its own purpose. I couldn't fathom what that was.

That evening we decorated the tree. Since it was alive and we didn't want it harmed, we only draped the strings of lights and garlands over its boughs. Hooks to suspend balls and family ornaments were left quite open. Harris had collected these furnishings from us at least a year before we came to the shelter, and when the girls' birth-year ornaments came out, tears sprang to my eyes. A little bit of each of us decorated that tree, and it looked magnificent. The barrel in which the tree was planted and about ten feet around it had a lovely red skirt. On this we began to bring out the gifts we had been squirreling away for the last couple of weeks. We were a large crowd; even limiting the gifts to children made for a surprisingly large pile, and the children squealed with delight each time they found their name. I could only give each of my children two gifts, but that didn't mean Frank couldn't do the same thing, and he had. I had also given gifts to my nieces and nephews—small things—though Harris had discouraged this. I wasn't finished yet as there was a week until Christmas, but I had planned a gift for each child in the shelter. I thought my idea was unique, but as the gifts were trotted out and placed under the tree, I saw that many other adults had done the same. In a way, of course, this was in total disregard to Harris's rule, but he didn't seem at all displeased with what he saw and he, himself, laid out gifts for considerably more than his one son. Gifts for adults also showed up, and these had a decidedly kid-designed aspect. Beth, with great pride, set out a box for Frank and one for me as well as one each for her grandparents. Many other children did the same.

Then we sang Christmas carols. It surprised me that, for a family a little light on religious fervor, we remembered so many Christmas songs, but one after the other we sang for nearly an hour. Ian Itkoff sang some Hanukkah songs, and he had a perfectly wonderful voice. Surprisingly, several were able to join him. Then Harris told us a story about one of his favorite Christmases, the one just after Harry, Jr., had been born. That started a round of stories from both adults and children that took everyone well past midnight. It was a memorable, wonderful, happy evening, and the entire community seemed to have had a good time.

I tucked my children into bed, and they were bubbly, talkative and happy. As I lay down to nurse Noah, I knew I'd never had such a wonderful holiday season. I found myself free of the fears that had nagged at me since the attack, free of the worry that all our effort was for naught. It wasn't. We had already build something wonderful and good out of the horror and harshness outside. Harris was right: the shelter was working.

CHRISTMAS EVE CAME QUICKLY, amid a flurry of wild activity. We brought in sheep and goats and one of the Jersey cows to take part in a play the children put on about Christ's birth. Noah, being the youngest baby, was to play the part of Baby Jesus, but he was fussy when the moment came, so Romala put her baby son in the manger. I still got to be Mary, and Frank was Joseph. Someone trucked out the *A Charlie Brown Christmas* DVD, and we all sat to watch it on the televisions in the living area, lunchroom, and classroom. That got us started, and *How the Grinch Stole Christmas* and *Rudolph the Red-Nosed Reindeer* were found and played.

Abby had made treats for the evening celebration, and we enjoyed sugar cookies cut into Christmas shapes, chocolate cake, and several fruit pies. Little gifts, like stocking stuffers, were handed out to all the children, and the adults enjoyed a delicious spiked eggnog. It was the most convivial evening we had enjoyed since coming to the shelter. Long after regular bedtimes, the children were finally ushered to the slices but, even then, talking and giggling continued for more than an hour.

The rest of us sat up in the lunchroom, chatting. When people finally headed off to their beds by twos and threes, they still seemed barely willing to give over the pleasant time to mere sleep.

I woke at two in the morning when Noah needed to nurse. With him so close to my side of the bed, it was easy to reach over to get him and snug him under the blankets with me almost in a single motion. I dozed as I nursed him, then changed him and put him back in his little bed. None of the girls nor Frank moved. I had barely moved. I got up after Noah had settled and headed to the bathroom. The whole shelter lay quiet as I emerged from my slice, but it wasn't the same place I had left. The tree and all the gifts were as I left them, but tinsel and garlands had miraculously appeared all over that end of the room. With the lights on the tree, the floor sparkled as if sifted with fairy dust, and a glorious star had been set on top of the tree. It was magical. Besides that, the gifts had multiplied by nearly a factor of two, spilling out over the floor in colorful wrappings.

I gaped at what I saw, disbelieving the transformation. But I needed to go to the bathroom and sidled past all the gifts and decorations to enter that space. Finished, I heard a sound as I neared the door. I peeked past the frame and saw Harris putting the finishing touches on his decorations, a wreath on each of the lunchroom doors. Already wreaths festooned the animal room doors, the hospital room and the classroom doors. Then Harris picked up two more wreaths and turned to the bathroom, seeing me before I could pull my head out of sight. He came around the corner and grinned that cheesy smile of his.

"What'd you think, Barb?" he asked.

"I think you're nuts."

"Probably. But will the kids be surprised? Will they still believe in Santa?"

I laughed. "*I* still believe in Santa after seeing this. You're a dear, Harris," I said and gave him a hug.

He kissed my cheek. "We're going to have a good day, Barby. It's going to be a very good day."

And it was. When we allowed the children to come out of the slices, they squealed with delight at sight of the presents, the tree, and all the decorations. According to our plan, no presents would be opened until after breakfast. While all the children knew about this rule had agreed readily enough to this in theory, with the presents staring at them in Christmas morning splendor, it was a lot harder to herd them into the kitchen. Harder still to get them to eat.

Breakfast was a feast, however. Several egg dishes, fruit cups, sausages made from our own pigs and cows, sweet rolls, even raised doughnuts. Our first experiments in cream cheese had been very successful, and tubs of it sat on the tables. We even had orange juice, though this was about the last of our frozen juices.

I doubt the children really appreciated the fare; I doubt most even tasted their breakfast, and a goodly number didn't eat nearly enough to sustain them through present opening. But, when the adult had finished their breakfasts, we allowed the children to sit in a wide circle around the tree. Presents came up to the height of the barrel in which the tree had been planted and spread out well beyond the skirt.

For a few moments there was considerable jostling as each child tried to sit directly in front of a gift with his or her name on it. The adults, most taking chairs or benches with them from the lunchroom, formed semi-circles around the children. Then, we waited.

The children heard the "Ho, ho, ho" and bells before we did and squealed with delight. Harris, who had somehow managed to disappear, came out of the classroom dressed as Santa and proceeded to hand out gifts. I saw the ones I had made for my children, the dolls for Jane and Andrea and the many outfits of clothing I had made with the help of Romala and the locking treasure box I had asked Jim Stone to help me make for Beth. I saw for the first time the gifts that Frank had made for them, obviously with help. He had asked Romala to made four stuffed bears, each a different size and color, one for each of our children. I would have thought Beth too old for a stuffed toy, but she hugged the bear and gave her daddy a big hug and kiss. Harris had added books and puzzles to the mix, gifts from Santa, of course. Commercial stuffed toys and boxed games appeared—card games and board games. He had comic books and story books, and adult novels enough to fill a small-town library.

Frank unwrapped the bathrobe I had helped make him with his initials embroidered on the breast pocket. He ran his fingers over those silken initials and grinned. He gave me my gift from him, which he said came in parts. The first was a pot he had helped the girls make for me. It had our whole family molded into the sides and painted. Each little figure held the hand of the ones on either side and was smiling. This had taken time and planning, and I spent an appreciative time looking at it. A plastic liner came next, along with soil. Then Frank handed me a little lump of a package, obviously wrapped with his own large, clumsy hands. I unwrapped it, revealing a dried bulb with a green shoot just showing at the tip of the brown onion-like wrapping layers. I stared at it.

Jeannie, sitting next to me, screwed up her face and said, "What's that, a rotten potato? Somebody wasn't too good this year."

I ignored her. With tears in my eyes I asked Frank, "One of mine?"

He shook his head. "What kind of a gift giver would I be if I gave you something that was already yours. I ordered this last September. It came the day before we left home. It's supposed to be the most fragrant, most robust, most beautiful one ever bred."

I was speechless. While Jeannie giggled over what she assumed was a lousy gift, I admired the tuberose tuber, amazed and moved deeply by Frank's effort. He knew I loved tuberoses for their exquisite fragrance and their spire of white flowers. Ever since we had married, I had grown them outside our kitchen door. I don't know how many times over the years I had asked him to smell them. In the first years, he had dutifully bent to sniff, but later he'd say, "Do they smell the same as last year?" and walk on past them. I never failed to draw in their fragrance. I even had a small weathered stool, not much good for anything except sitting next to the tuberoses among the fragrance that, for me, was the essence of summer.

As I carefully tucked the ugly little tuber into the soil of the liner inside my beautiful pot, Frank presented me with one last part to my gift. With a bow on top, I beheld my old garden stool. Another man might have painted it or sanded it down and stained it, but Frank knew me better than to try to mess with an artifact like this. That he had kept it at all was miracle enough.

I burst into tears and hugged him tightly, then hugged the children and thanked them all for giving me the best Christmas gift I could possibly have received. Jeannie, of course, looked at me as if I were crazy as I blubbered all over myself, then gave me a knowing look, as if I were making a big deal for the sake of the children. I wasn't. I loved this gift more than I could express with tears and hugs.

And so the gift-giving went. For well over an hour we unwrapped gifts and exclaimed over each one. All the paper and ribbons were saved for gift-giving at a later time. Harris had boxes set up to receive the smoothed out paper, another for the ribbons and bows. Then, all that was left was Harris's lumpy sack. He stood up, his beard hanging a little loose on one side by this time, and his hat set jauntily on his head. He raised a hand for quiet, then said, "What a wonderful Christmas!" and everyone cheered. When that faded away, he said, "I have a few more gifts, but I need to explain a bit about them. They come . . . with strings. In a community like ours where the survival of each of us is dependent on the survival of all of us, it's important that we cover those aspects of society and culture we hope to preserve. I am very proud to tell you that, in our moral fiber, we have exceded what I consider to be the median of our former society. The choices we have made in that regard, in how we've dealt with people needing our help and even those wishing us harm has mostly been noble and uplifting. I'm very proud of the distance we have come in so short a time.

"But our fledgling community needs to be maintained, to be monitored, to be encouraged at times and held to task at others. In our culture here, we are in as much transition as the outside world. We need to make choices that, previous to this, we didn't even think about. It's my feeling that culture is a very important aspect of what we're trying to preserve, but, since it, like us, is in transition, we need someone to monitor the process, to question, challenge and guide us in our decision-making of what we should be doing and how."

Harris pulled what looked like a child's Christmas garland made of paper rings from his sack. Everyone laughed. He said, "Like the jobs of being head of the kitchen and head animal caretaker, both roles taken on by the ambitious and generous Gertzes, I think we need someone in charge of Community Development." He ran the paper rings over his hand, looking at it. Made of colorful construction paper, it seemed an odd symbol. "Community is fragile, easily ripped. Like paper. One needs a gentle hand." Then he snapped the paper chair taut suddenly. "But it's surprisingly strong, too. The role of Head of Community Development, like the others, can be abdicated at any time if necessary, but for smooth transitions, I would ask that for anyone placed in "head" positions, finding a suitable replacement is necessary for giving up the role." He dangled the paper chain on his finger. "I've given this role a great deal of thought, and I'd like our Head of Community Development to be Connie Dunn."

Connie's eyes opened as wide as her mouth. "Me?" she said. "Why me?"

"Because you are a fair and generous woman," said Harris. "Because you have never wished ill on anyone and you pay attention to what goes on around you. You'll keep us all in mind as we live and work here, making sure no single link gets too much strain."

Harris tossed her the paper garland, and Connie caught it. "I'll give it a try, Harris. I hope you have some kinds of guidelines to help me, though."

He reached into his bag and brought out a *Robert's Rules of Order*, which he also tossed to her as everyone rolled with laughter. "This'll get you started," he said.

When everyone had settled a bit, Harris started again. "When we were gathering what should be brought into the shelter, you'll remember at one point I switched you all from food and supplies to art and books, DVDs, and CDs. I'm sure you thought me daft, but you responded. You brought me carloads of your favorite pieces, your most watched movies, and most listened to CDs. That's what I intended, too. But not all of you did that. I cataloged carefully what each of you brought, and I noticed that some of you stepped outside your own personal favorites and actually tried to bring into the shelter the best art and literature our culture had to offer. This person spent a tidy sum on museum art, classic movies, classical music, and literature spanning the best American and British authors and poets of the last three centuries. If nothing remains of the outside world after our stay in the Ark is completed, we will have preserved a small chunk of fine arts and liturature, the best our culture could offer. I would, therefore, like to appoint this person Head of Arts and Literature."

We, of course, were looking all around, trying to see who had done this, who we had to thank for preserving some of the best of our previous culture. I knew what Frank and I had brought, and it was just as Harris had said, *our* favorite things, which certainly didn't represent the highest and best of culture unless *Charlie Brown* comics and *My Little Pony* movies had a place there. We had brought a rather complete Dr. Seuss collection of books, though, some of which were pretty old, and I had brought all my Simon and Garfunkle CDs, but . . .

Harris pulled out a set of wings, the kind a little girl might strap on to pretend to be a fairy, and a knobby stick with the end a gnarled root clump. Again, we laughed. He said, "Every culture should have roots and wings, roots to look back on, to help weather long winters, to remind us how to grow, and we need wings to soar above the places where growth bogs us down to see the wider picture and the horizon at dawn. I bestow these as symbol of the Head of Arts and Liturature on . . ." Harris was nothing if not dramatic. "Paul Fisk."

Our resident veterinarian blushed deeply. "I don't know, Harris. Surely—"

"Fortunately, I do," said Harris, and he passed the short staff and wings to Paul.

Moved almost to tears, Paul nodded and mouthed, "Thank you."

He sat down and turned to his wife, but Harris whistled, and he looked up in time to catch the notebook Harris had tossed. "You'll want to know how to deal with Arts and Literature issues. This is a catalog of what everyone brought so you'll know how to use it all. Tell us when we're being thick or, heavens, *mundane.*"

Harris continued pulling odd items from his bag. He produced a large wrench and placed Frank as Head of Maintenance and Technology. Jim Stone accepted a jester's cap and became Head of Morale, and Marie Deters took the Superman cape to become Universal Advocate to make sure people's rights were always in the forefront of our minds. Romala became Head of Clothing and Fabric and had a macrame hanging to prove it, and Donald Reinhart, with the acceptance of several plant guides, became Head of Botany. The only placement I wondered at was giving Mike Deters Head of Justice. He grudgingly accepted the white wig and gavel that came with that placement. Jillian became Head of Health. She rolled her eyes as she took the the large outdoor thermometer as its symbol.

Harris looked down into his deflated sac and said, "Just one placement left. I know most of these headships have gone to the original members of this community.

I've had a lot more time to assess their qualities than those of others here. Please don't consider this a statement of value or worth. It's not. Just familiarity. As I said, all roles can be changed and moved on, and I expect they will as time goes by. And, probably, there'll be other offices.

"So, on to the last role, and it's an important one, which isn't to say that any of the others should be looked upon as in any way unimportant, but this one will chart our progress, give us perspective, and call us all to task when we fall down in any aspect of life here in the Ark. This is another part of the roots part of our culture, the counterpart to the wings Paul . . . is now wearing, I see. Our history gives us serious lessons about what not to do as well as when we, as a species, have made good choices, progressed, let us say, in the right direction. History is our backbone, our strength. Memory of what came before is vital to what comes after. I think you will all agree with this idea, which is not mine, nor, of course, new. And stored away, we have many fine histories of the time before we entered the shelter. That period is well covered, but not what we've done here, inside these walls. We might not be here terribly long, but even if we leave in mere months, I believe we should record what we do. It might be that our species will have need of our experiences."

"Oh, that's already covered," Mike said wryly. "It's called *Lord of the Flies.*"

Everyone laughed except Harris. "It damn well better not be," he said.

"Language!" Connie called out, holding up her *Robert's Rules.*

Again laughter.

When everyone had settled down a bit, Harris continued. "I've weighed each of these placements with considerable gravity, even if the symbols of them have elements of humor. But there really isn't anything funny about the symbol of this role nor its part in our society, and the selection of who should be our Historian was fixed in my mind for . . . well some time before we even came here. Since we tucked ourselves into this place, I've watched this person carefully, testing my choice. It hasn't changed. In fact, this person has proven to be an even better choice than I had hoped."

It had to be a family member, then. I looked around and wondered who he had left out, what couple had not yet been represented in his headships. Several had teaching or secretarial backgrounds. Likely it would be one of them.

"It is said that a culture is doomed to repeat its history over and over if it doesn't look at that history and heed its warning. Therefore, the role of Historian is important, very important, and requires a person with enough objectivity to write in a reasonably unbiased way as well as enough empathy to see through the surface actions into motivation and root causes. This Historian also must help chart for us a course based on the history written. Being a good writer is a benefit, being a clear thinker is a must." Harris reached into his bag and produced two large, thick journals with gold-edged pages and leather covers. He also produced a beautiful fountain pen with a whole box of refills. "As the shelter's Historian, I appoint . . . Barb Quill."

I felt a jolt go entirely through me. "Me?" I said. "My God, why?"

Harris walked over to me and deposited the two large journals and pens in my lap, "Because you'll do a good job. Write down whatever you wish to write about the shelter and its workings. From time to time, we'll have you read portions of it to remind us of our past to guide us in the future."

Shocked beyond words, I stared up at Harris. He was grinning that "I got Barby" grin of his. For a long moment, all was quiet. Then Frank began to clap. Marie took it up, and Sissy and Connie joined in. In a moment the room was filled with an applause that thundered through me, and still I stared at the beautiful journals and pen. I looked up, again with tears running freely down my face. Historian. I had no idea what Harris wanted me to do.

As I held those beautiful journals and the rather expensive pen, I didn't really know what to think. My mind had gone utterly blank. I know my face burned with embarrassment, stung with tears. Surely Harris had made a mistake. But the smell of the leather, its buttery softness, and the smooth quality of the paper overtook me. I opened the pen dramatically and on the line provided on the first page of the otherwise blank journals, I wrote, "A History of a Small Group of People in a Time of Madness."

I looked up to see Harris grinning down at me. Tears now glistened in his eyes. He said, "I knew you'd know how to do this. Do you accept the role of Head of History?"

In a small voice, I said, "Yes, Harris, I accept the role. Thank you."

AFTER THE GIFTS had been gathered and taken back to the slices, after a couple hours of quiet in the living room and holy Bedlam in the kitchen, we were called to a dinner that rivaled Thanksgiving. The stars of this meal were large fresh hams slow-cooked to unbelievable flavor and tenderness and platters of prime rib so tender as to melt in our mouths. All the fixings accompanied them. For dessert we had apple and pumpkin pies served with homemade ice cream and mounds of whipped cream.

Stuffed and happy, the shelter quieted early that night. As children were tucked into their beds with their new toys and stuffed pets, as adults relaxed and reflected on the day, I sat with a tiny light and began to write the history of our coming to the shelter. I wanted to get down what it felt like to leave my home, to leave the life I knew and understood, to face the fear of total global annihilation and come to a place so different for survival. I didn't write directly in the gorgeous books, however—I felt a little intimidated by them, to tell the truth—but on a legal pad with a rather dull pencil. I wanted to get the words right before I committed them to the official history of our lives. What we did, in a sense, was of little importance to the world. I knew that. But in another sense, in the smaller sense of our tiny community, what we did meant everything. It defined us. We were making global choices on a miniature scale. What we did in that sense defined the crafting of a new world.

Frank came in and smiled. He sat down and read over my shoulder what I was writing. Then he kissed my neck and whispered, "Harris told me he was going to make you Historian the first time he told me about the shelter. That was over fifteen years ago. We'd just gotten married. I thought even the idea of the shelter was nuts. It wasn't. I thought he maybe didn't know you well. But he did. He knew you'd do the job well even then."

I frowned. "How does he know when I don't. I've got a new baby to take care of. I probably don't have time for this sort of thing."

Frank sat down. "Those who fail to understand their history are doomed to repeat it."

"I don't think that's the exact quote."

"But the meaning is the same. You'll be the Ark's barometer, the beating of its heart, in effect, its soul."

I smirked at him. "Oh, good, *that* makes the job so much easier."

He gave me a hug. "Don't think about it too much, hon. Just do it. What comes out will be what it's supposed to be."

"You're so sure of that?"

"I'm positive."

"It was a lovely Christmas, though, wasn't it?'

"The best," Frank said. "It was memorable and amazing. In fact, I'm going back for a little bit more pie. Wanna come?"

Raiding the kitchens was, of course, strictly against the rules, but I grinned and bounced out of bed. Frank and I tiptoed to the kitchen and slipped inside, only to discover half the adult population in some stage of securing a piece of pie or consuming same. Everyone froze at our entrance, forks halfway to mouths, some in mouths, some just cutting a bite of pie; everyone paused in what they were doing. Everyone had been sure they'd been caught, then they laughed at us, recognizing co-conspirators rather than authority. DeeDee, her mouth too full of apple pie to actually attempt saying anything, handed each of us a plate and the knife she had just used.

I cut a generous slice of pumpkin, then added a sliver of apple. Emily grinned at me and shoved a vat of melting ice cream in my direction. I dug deep with the scoop and filled what remained of my plate. Then Jim Stone winked at me and pushed the Tupperware tub of whipped cream to me. *Ooo, whipped cream.* I deposited a large dollop on top and quickly made my way to a table before the whole thing overflowed.

"Six, maybe a seven," James Quill said with a sad shake of his head.

I dug in with my fork as Frank sat down next to me with his plate piled even higher than mine, if that were possible. James looked at his plate appreciatively and said, "Solid eight."

I laughed. "You're giving marks on dessert? Anyone get a ten?"

My sister Anna raised her hand and wiggled her fingers. I was shocked. My skinny kid sister almost never ate desserts in the first place. I caught a drip of ice cream before it hit the table and said, "How?"

Anna giggled. She sat with us and planted her elbows on the table. "The trick to achieving a truly ten-worthy plate is to start with two slices of pie, two *big* slices. You put them end for end on the plate. They hang over but create a base for the ice cream. I got here early, so the ice cream was firmer. Three scoops create a nice hollow where the whipped cream anchors itself well to allow a truly towering pile."

DeeDee came over. "It was a work of art, Barby."

"Probably weighed three pounds," Jim Stone said. "I had a nine and easily bow to her architectural prowess. Watching her eat it was almost as amazing, a perfect deconstruction. Watch that drip, Barb."

In truth, my plate was oozing everywhere, and I had a time of it—a really good time, though—keeping ahead of the melting. Before I finished, two more people arrived, and we played out the deer-caught-in-the-headlights freeze frame, followed by laughter as Dean Brewster, the helicopter pilot, and his fiancee, Boopsie, came in as if it was their original idea. I made headway on my plate as they built their own desserts, but they rated only a four and a three respectively. I had just shoveled in the last bite when the door opened again. This time we were right to freeze. Abby came in. Her mouth dropped indignantly open, and she planted fists on her ample hips.

"What's this?" she said. "Every last one of you knows the rules. No food taken from the kitchens between meals. You all know that."

It was really hard to look remorseful with my face full of pie, but I and everyone else tried. Abby was tutting and shaking her head. "And on Christmas, too. You all had your chance to fill up on pie at supper, and I seem to remember you did justice to them pies then as well."

James Quill started gathering plates. "We're sorry, Abby, really we are."

"I don't want to hear any of that," said Abby, her tone as German brusk as was possible even for a German woman. "I just want to know one thing," she said and paused, eyeing each of us critically in turn.

We waited (and chewed).

"I just want to know if you left enough for me and Max?" Then she grinned and let in her husband, who had been standing just outside the door. "If you kitchen mice ate all the spiced-apple pie and didn't leave me none, I'm gonna be *so* pissed."

We burst out laughing, which included Dean Brewster spewing whipped cream across the table. Jim Stone said, "We've got a contest going for the highest most amazing pile of pie, ice cream, and whipped cream. Anna DeSota here holds the record so far."

"That so?" said Max Gertz. "That little thing? No one that small and skinny could possibly build the record plate if any of you were trying."

He proceeded to build what I would have hardly believed possible on a dessert plate. Two huge slices of pumpkin pie, easily a pound of ice cream and several huge spoonfuls of whipped cream. It swayed and leaned like the Tower of Pisa as he carried it to a table. As I finished my dessert, feeling as if I wouldn't have to eat for a week, he calmly demolished his award-winning creation, spilling not a drop.

230

"Winner!" said Jim Stone. "Solid *fifteen!* Congratulations, Max. You're my hero."

An hour later, stuffed to the gills and just about as happy, Frank and I left the kitchen and returned to our slice. The kids slept soundly, all snug and happy in their beds. Frank and I crawled into ours. In mere moments, he started snoring, but I didn't fall asleep right away. I knew Noah would wake soon to nurse, and with all the sugar in my system, I wasn't sleepy anymore. I got up.

I was heading to the kitchen to clean up some before breakfast needed to get started, when movement across the darkened room drew my attention. I thought I saw Harris disappear into the classroom. Curious, I followed him. At the classroom door, I peeked inside to see him go up the steep stairs to the radio room. He was probably going up to radio some of the survival groups. He did that on a very regular basis. I almost turned around and left, except that I heard something that I had not heard since coming into the shelter. The hoot of an owl. Right afterwards, I heard a door close, then silence.

Now my curiosity was not only piqued, it set motion to my feet. I tiptoed across the classroom floor, up onto stage and climbed the steep, spiral steps to the radio room, which was darkened and empty. No Harris. There were lots of closed doors though. I started opening them. Some held huge breaker boxes, a number of them, which probably ran the systems in the shelter. I saw labels marked classroom, hospital room, kitchen, pantry, storage room, freezer, cooler, animal room, and many others with numeric designations. A lot of others. *What did that mean?* Another door led to a long closet with radios and computers and boxes of parts for them, most new and in plastic. The next door revealed a space even longer and wider than the computer storage room and was filled with boxes, shelves and shelves of them. I slid the lid up on one of them—paper.

Two more closets of more unlabeled boxes giving no clue as to their contents left me without another choice and no Harris. No owl either. It didn't seem to make sense. I looked up and down the radio room. One side had all the closets, which seemed to extend above the classroom. The opposite wall held all the radios and computers we used to monitor the outside world and our own internal functions. The end of the room nearest the stairs had a blank wall, and the other end had a bookshelf with ham radio manuals, computer manuals and the like. I walked to the bookshelf and tried to move it or find a mechanism that hid a door. Nothing. The other wall offered an equally blank and unmoveable face. What did that leave? I was almost believing that I had mistaken what I'd heard. Almost.

I looked again at the closets, wondering if a door opened from inside one of them. I started over, going into each and pushing against back walls and looking for mechanisms on and under shelves. In the first several, nothing turned up, but in the second last closet with all the shelves filled with boxes, I noticed that the floor looked dirtier than the other closets. I walked back, looking for side alleys and saw that the floor actually was getting dirtier as I progressed to the back. I started following that, even when the room started to branch out on either side with ever more stacks of boxes, I could clearly see the trace of dirt headed down the main aisle. At the end of the room, the dirt just ended at a wall. The light wasn't great at this end of the room because one lightbulb overhead had burned out, and, of course, I hadn't brought a flashlight or anything as useful as that. But I did have a small box of matches in my bathrobe pocket because I had helped light some of the Christmas candles, which Beth and her gang had missed in their "improving our air" sweep because they were in storage. I struck a match and held it up. For all of thirty seconds, I searched for something that could hide a door. Nothing. I lit another match and searched the other side of the space. Here I saw something, a kind of flap. The match went out before I could examine it. I lit another and looked closely. The stiff flap rotated to the side, revealing the end of a latch or lever. I pressed it down, and the end wall silently slid open.

24

SECRET WORLD

I LOOKED ONTO A SCENE I COULDN'T IMAGINE, something I had not thought I would ever see again. This space, unlike the one where we lived, had a ceiling about forty feet high, and it was lit as brightly as day. Trees! Grass! I heard the gurgle of a stream. Felt a gentle breeze. A pebbled pathway started at the door, quickly disappearing around shrubbery. I followed it, marveling at the sight of blue jays, bluebirds, cardinals among the branches of the trees—young oaks, sugar maple, ash, and basswood. I saw a cottontail zip into some longish grass, saw mice cross the pebbled path.

The walkway came to the stream, and I saw rainbow trout swimming in the current, saw crawfish sitting between rocks. I crouched down to look at them, and a school of minnows flashed in the bright light and disappeared into a pool out of the current bordered by cattails and bullrushes. I looked up to see a deer sip water from a pool futher on. It saw me and melted back into a thicket of hazelnuts. A small flock of chickadees flew over my head.

I continued along the winding path through a miniature aspen grove not much higher than my head. Beyond it, birches arched toward the ceiling, their nubile, reddish trunks showing white only in places. Several species of birch trees had clumps along the path, and the stream wound its way under and around the walkway and the small groves. At one point, stepping stones spanned its course. I glimpsed more birds among the branches of an oak: sparrows and finches and warblers. I saw squirrels sitting at a feeding station with cracked corn aplenty, and woodpeckers picking suet at another station. Several tall dead trunks of popple had been riddled with holes.

The path split. Off to my left the pebbles meandered invitingly, but to my right a dirt path led. On a hunch, I followed the dirt trace, and it took me toward the far wall. Here I found banks of cages each as generous as our slices down below and landscaped into something interesting. I saw wolves, wolverines, other species of weasels and skunks, badgers, cougars, martins and fishers, otters, raccoons. The stream flowed through some of these cages, obviously providing water and perhaps some entertainment. I saw huge snapping turtles, a tightly meshed cage with lots of frogs and salamanders, one with a variety of snakes, and tanks filled with fish—great northern, walleye, sturgeon. It looked like the Minnesota Trail at the zoo. Further on I saw large pens of elk and buffalo and pronghorns, and I could see these were very carefully selected individuals, a male of considerable size and maturity, several adult females, and a few youngsters. These pens—stoutly built of metal fencing—accommodated their occupants but didn't have the interesting features of the smaller enclosures.

Beyond these large herbivores, another bank of smaller cages contained foxes and coyotes, black-footed ferrets, prairie dogs, then grouse and prairie chickens, some varieties of ducks and a series of cages of owls and hawks.

As I came around a corner, I finally saw Harris. He had on heavy gloves and was in the process of putting a large great gray owl back into a cage. As he did so, he was saying, "Beatrice, I don't know how you keep getting out, dear, but you have to stay in the cage. You give heart attacks to the bunnies, and you can't fly. Get that through your fluffy head. You can't fly."

The big bird hopped to its branch, letting loose another series of loud hoots, matching the ones I had heard. Then Harris closed the cage door, wrapped a wire around the opener and twisted the wires around a bar. He taped the whole affair with black electrician's tape. Clearly Beatrice had bested him before.

He wore a kind of fanny pack or carpenter's belt around his jeans and reached into this and pulled out a dead white mouse, which he showed the owl. Her head started bobbing and weaving. He tossed the rodent, and the big bird caught it expertly in her beak and downed it in a single swallow. Harris shook his head at her and turned to go down the path, but just as he was about to take a step, he paused and turned entirely around. He looked at me with the strangest mixture of surprise and humor. I just stared back.

"Barb," he said. "You heard the owl, I suppose."

"Yes."

He shook his head. "That's Beatrice. An escape artist if ever there was one. She got out a few days before Christmas, but none of us could find her. She managed to escape this room and get inside the storeroom, almost got into the radio room, whyever she'd want to do that. Hooted up a storm before I could get the door closed. I was kinda hoping everyone was so full of pie that they'd all stay asleep."

"Potty run," I said, though it wasn't exactly the truth.

"Ah," said Harris. "Well, now that you've seen my little collection, how about I give you the grand tour?"

Without hesitation, Harris showed me everything, including places where precious wildflowers—several varieties of lady's-slippers, pitcher plants and sundews, wild iris, and marsh marigolds—had been planted. The inside area was a living park of wild wonders, and the perimeter of the circular area held pens and cages of Minnesota animals. He proudly pointed out the Blanding's turtles and the black-footed ferrets, both quite rare. "And these mountain lions were actually found in this very county as cubs, well actually, two cubs were found, both females, but I traded one for a female trapped in Lake of the Woods County. The male is western stock. Biodiversity, don't you know."

Truthfully, though Harris prattled on about his plants and animals, I was speechless. Finally I managed to get out, "How long . . . ?"

"Have I had this set up?" Harris finished brightly. "Several years, nearly three, which was really good because we had to replace some stuff after the first year. I hadn't provided a long enough winter. As you can see everything is in wind-down mode as in late fall. We discovered that we don't have to go to the whole thirty-below stage. In a few weeks, we'll lower the temperature down to freezing and hold it there for about a month, through, say the middle of February, with a few dips in temperature into the high teens. That satisfies dormancy. Of course, we'll have to catch all the warblers and migrants first. The hummingbirds were already removed to a special feeding cage. I haven't had the best luck with them in the winter months, but with those born in here this summer, I'm hoping for better results. The problem has been the migration mode. The poor things beat themselves against their cages. But we have a special formula for them now that includes minute traces of Valium to keep them calmer. It seems to be working."

"Harris," I said carefully, "this place is amazing, but . . . doesn't it take constant care? Who?" I'd heard him use "we" several times.

"Ah, Barb," he said with a smile. "A lot of this is automatic, the watering, the feeding, and most of the cleanup of the cages and pens. Had to be."

"So, you care for all of this?"

Harris grinned. "What do you think?"

"I think you're loonier than I ever thought. How do you justify the secrecy?"

Harris grew serious. "I want us to survive, Barb. Really, that's my only goal. But I know maybe a bit more about what's going on outside than any of the rest of you. It's bad, Barb, worse than any of us could have predicted. There's a band of radiation around the equator that's killing everything, and it's spreading both north and south. We're still hoping that, when it reaches this far north, it isn't so bad that we can't spend some time outside, but it could be. And while I've talked about staying in the Ark for the winter, maybe a whole year, the truth is it might be ten years . . . maybe more."

I was instantly very concerned, but also confused. It was hard to hear that the world was not doing well, hard to think about being inside the shelter for any time counted in years, but I hadn't asked about that. "Harris, what does this . . . this zoo have to do with either the state of the world or our survival?"

He blinked and stared. "Well, I . . . I wanted to . . . we have to . . ."

I rested my hand on his sleeve. "There's more to this place than even this."

He swallowed. Then his face screwed up. "Yes . . . but you can't tell anyone."

"That Christmas tree was from up here, wasn't it?"

He sighed. "Yes, and you have to keep *that* a secret, too."

"Why?"

"Because . . . because for right now our survival depends on it."

For a long moment I held his eyes. "Okay."

He shook his head. "Okay? That's it? No string of questions?"

"Would you answer them?"

He screwed up his face. "I . . . I really can't. Not yet."

"Then there's little point in my asking, is there?"

Harris slowly smiled. "You need to go back now. You need to return to your slice and not speak of this, any of this, until the time is right. When that time comes, I want everyone to be blown away by this place. The biblical Noah built an ark to preserve life while flood waters rose and fell. This ark was constructed to do that forever if need be and against way more than merely water."

236

"So . . . there *is* more."

Harris smiled. "Go back to bed, Barby."

Harris walked me to the door in the back of the closet. He pushed me through and closed the door between us. I stared at that wall a long moment, then made my way back through the radio room, down the spiral stairs and into the living area. The familiar dim night amid curtained off slices greeted me, and I padded quietly back to my slice and crawled into bed. Frank had Noah next to him. That meant the baby had awakened. I had been gone awhile. I lifted Noah. He stirred and whimpered, wanting to be nursed. Frank roused as well. "Where were you?" he asked sleepily.

"Upstairs," I said.

Frank didn't react right away. Then he lifted himself up on an elbow and regarded me carefully. "Why would you go to the radio room?"

"I heard something. I was following Harris . . . and Beatrice."

He blinked several times. "How far did you get?"

That set a series of conflicts in my mind. How much had I seen? Had Harris shown me everthing or just a tiny part of it. I had no way of knowing. It did clearly tell me that Frank knew of this place. "I saw a park, animals in cages."

Frank studied me, his eyebrows slowly raising. "What'd you think?"

"I think your older brother is seriously crazy . . . and thank God he is."

Frank nodded and smiled. "Harris is flaky, but he's smart."

"So . . ." I said, "what runs this place? What's the source of power?"

Frank took a deep breath, weighing what to say. "Hydroelectric. Harris harnessed an underground stream. An aquifer. Cutting-edge technology, that."

"You kept all this secret from me?" I said with some pique.

Frank rubbed my arm. "The psycological profiles of each of us have been studied for a long time. They had to be, you understand. We're the core group. We could have been the only group. Key people were pinpointed among us who had to transition well so the rest could use them as guides. You're one of those people."

"Me? Why me?"

Frank smiled. "Because a lot of the sisters-in-law look to you as a guide to how to react to the Quill-Deters' issues, because Jeannie and Marie and Jillian listen to you where they don't have time for some of the others—"

"Jillian doesn't even *like* me, and Jeannie *hates* me."

"You'd be surprised. You're a smart, thoughtful woman with liberal leanings, empathetic to the plight of others, free of strong prejudice, and generous of nature. That's a very important profile to have among us."

"Me?" I was started to sound like a broken record. "That's crazy."

Frank looked away, thinking. "Do you remember when Andy came?"

"Yeah."

"Everyone was cheering, giddy, right?"

"Well, yeah, but—"

"But what? Why did you stop? Why did you go quiet?"

"They had been through so much. I mean, we'd been worrying about them, but they had lost so much—"

"Yes. You sobered almost instantly. Connie told me. Others looked to you and quieted too."

"No, people settled down because they could see—"

"That you did."

I lay next to Frank, who had rolled over and gone back to sleep, but I stared up at the ceiling, wide awake. I was furious, but I couldn't react to that anger. Though I had been Historian only a few hours, I had begun to write some of my earliest impressions of the shelter, how I had hated my first sight of the inside, the squat, clauster-phobic space and the flimsey curtain walls. I remembered thinking, "Gees, what would a little drywall have hurt? Harris had money. Why couldn't we have solid walls at least?" But I accepted what we had been given. One communal kitchen. I accept-ed. Inadequate bathroom facilities, one small classroom, a tiny hospital. I accepted. I wanted to survive. I wanted my children to survive. And so I began to accept that prior planning to insure our survival wasn't bad.

Harris knew what our family was. He knew we scrapped like stray dogs at times, but he also knew we had the strength and fortitude to pull together and fight for our survival. Everyone who came in from the family had made a huge financial commitment to the project, and that was a binding force for us. Even Mike and Wayne had contributed small fortunes to the project. We had made a huge committ-ment to our common future. But . . . what I had assumed might have cost several mil-lion dollars now looked like it must have had a much higher price tag. Hydroelectric power from an aquifer? I didn't know such technology existed. It couldn't have been cheap.

The more I thought about what I had seen the more my anger seemed to lift. Harris alone had no hope of building anything like this place, invite in his huge, weird, dysfunctional extended family, and have a prayer at making survival viable if he hadn't had help. He had recognized this, sought out professionals early to assess the family. So often in the last weeks I had worried that we didn't have the wherewithal to survive in the shelter, that we didn't have the skills for living in this unique way. Harris apparently had thought of that as well. Perhaps he had manipulated some things in the shelter, but we had made the transition toward a unified community ourselves. Maybe we really did have to deconstruct what we'd known outside, the failing, damaged community we had known there, in order to built something decent up from scratch. Probably on the advice of many professionals, he had set up our inner world with care. But to embrace it came from our own free will. All Harris had done was give us the situation and tools to make that transition. We, together, had to make it work.

25

BOXING DAY

THURSDAY, DECEMBER 26

I KNOW THAT I WAS WITHDRAWN the next morning, quieter than usual and introspective. I wrote a fair amount in one of the journals I had been given, still trying to capture the feelings and impressions of our first days in the shelter. I tried not to allow all my unsettling new impressions to color what I felt and wrote. It was hard. It was also a way of avoiding those feelings. No one, not Harris or Frank, said anything to me about what I had learned, and none of the others looked any different or behaved in any way from what I thought normal. Why was I having such mixed feelings?

Minnesota threw an old-fashioned ice storm at us, starting late Christmas morning. These storms often showed up at the end of the year, snarling traffic—sometimes producing the first auto deaths of the year—and sometimes giving children a day or two more of vacation. I seriously doubted that there would be ice-related highway accidents this year in Minnesota, and the children began classes again the day after Christmas, Boxing Day, unhindered by the weather. The cameras iced up by noon, giving us little real view of what went on outside. Screens showed a bit of wind-driven snow flying past but little else except ice coating the camera lenses. By mid-afternoon on Christmas, no camera showed much more than the blurry waning of light falling quickly to darkness. The next morning, we didn't even know if the storm continued or had given way to blue skies and bright sunshine. Ice totally clogged the cameras.

"Why do we have to have classes between Christmas and New Year's?" Beth complained as she finished getting dressed.

"What do you want to do?" I asked in return as I changed Noah on my bed.

"Well, anything."

"That's why you have classes, dear."

Beth scowled. "That's not a reason."

"Okay," I said, finished with Noah and engaging fully with Beth. "Talk to your teachers and come up with a holiday week schedule that seems fair."

"What's fair is to have off between Christmas and New Year's just like we've always had outside."

"But this isn't outside," I said and laid Noah in his bassinet. "Time is given off after Christmas because people travel. We can't travel."

Beth gave that a moment's thought. "It's vacation time. Like summer." Then she got a shocked look on her face and said, "We're not going to—?"

I shook my head slowly. "No one's talked about it. Summers off came about because farmers needed their kids to help out. Again, we don't have that problem."

Beth had a look on her face that clearly telegraphed a total dissatisfaction with the direction our conversation had taken. She had put ideas in my head, and children hate to give their parents ideas, especially those that curtail their activities. With a deep sigh, she picked up her homework and stomped out of the slice.

I wasn't more than ten minutes behind her. I finished getting Andrea and Jane dressed, which entailed finding a lost shoe and one of Prince's topknot ribbons, which he had finally shook out. I arrived in the kitchens to an impromtu meeting in progress. Apparently, other kids had decided that some time off from classes was desirable.

"School never was meant just to occupy the children," Jim Stone said, probably in response to some question or comment.

I got breakfast for the two little girls from the buffet set up and sat them down at the end of a bench. I stood, rocking slowly from side to side to keep Noah content.

"Without classes," said Emily, "they'll just get into trouble. We'll have all the cows in here. It's not like they can go sledding. We could show them DVDs on one of the TVs, I suppose, but that's so pointless. I say they go to school."

Harris said, "Going out is definitely not an option, but movie day is."

Children started to cheer.

"As it turns out, I have a large screen projector that'll show DVDs almost as wide as a movie theater. We've got popcorn, and I bet we can find a enough candy to make all our kids sick."

The children, of course, went wild, but the adults didn't look too happy.

I said, "Are we talking only about today or all this week when, traditionally, kids don't have school?"

Jeannie and Emily gave me dirty looks, but Beth grinned and the kids certainly looked hopeful.

Harris gave that thought, and even the children quieted, eagerly awaiting his response. "Well," he said tentatively, "movies all week will get very old . . ."

The kids booed.

"And we definitely can't have the animal room turned loose in here."

The booing got louder.

"But," said Harris, "we can do non-school things. Contests, races. We have some reserve crafty supplies. Maybe we could paint a mural on the walls. How about this: today we have off, an official play day. We'll have movies in the classroom and provide popcorn and candy and maybe some drinks—I'll talk to Abby about that—but having off tomorrow and the rest of the week depends on you kids. Plan what you want to do, and, if it occupies all the kids and is lots of fun, we'll consider it. Beth, Harry, and Peter, you three brought up this topic. I think you should be responsible for coming up with activities for tomorrow. You also have the responsibility to find another kid committee to work out what we'll be doing on Friday."

The children cheered.

"Now," said Harris, raising his arms to get their attention. "Don't forget that everyday chores must still be done. All of them. The animals can't go hungry, and cleanup in the lunchroom and all other chores must be done as usual. Check your schedules. Failure to get all the chores done will absolutely cancel further days off."

There were some moans at this, but not so many. Harris left the lunchroom with a long train behind him. I hadn't eaten yet, but I followed as well. In the schoolroom, he lowered a large, white curtain across the stage, anchoring it on both sides so it looked relatively flat. From one of the usually locked side rooms, he wheeled out a DVD player with a projector and set it up in the back of the room. He opened another of the side doors, and ushered the three instigators inside. In a few minutes, they returned with about a dozen DVDs. Beth was grinning.

"Do you know how many movies Uncle Harris has?"

"No. Is it a lot?"

"A lot? It's like every movie that ever existed. He had us pick out some for the little kids and some for us. I made sure we had *The Lion King* for Andrea."

"It was very nice to think of your sister."

"And Harry wanted all the *Harry Potter* movies, but we told him only one."

"Which one did he choose?"

"The fifth one, I think. That isn't as scary as the sixth or the two sevenths."

"Do you think you can watch all the movies you brought out?"

"If we stay up to ten, we can, but I don't want to watch movies all day. I want to read my new book, and Wendy, Cathy, Diane, and I want to do somthing."

"Are there any new kids your age?"

"Molly's fourteen," said Beth. "I've tried to talk to her, but she doesn't want to. She doesn't talk much, and she cries a lot. It makes me feel uncomfortable."

Some children had yet to make full adjustments or forgot what had happened outside. Connie and my brother, with two kids already, had taken in Molly and Madeline. The two girls had no physical injuries, but neither was doing well yet. Boopsie spent a lot of time with them. Only in the past week had they started taking on a small share of the chores, helping with the meals a bit. In the classroom, neither had done more than occupy a chair. But Boopsie said she was seeing progress. Neither girl could accept normal yet, not when they both knew that everything else in the world was so far from normal. We didn't know anything of their parents, but we suspected they'd died. If the girls knew what happened, they hadn't said.

"That's okay, but ask her some other time," I told Beth.

Maybe that was my problem. I had accepted my former existence and gone on to accept our small community inside the shelter, but I was having a hard time knowing we'd have to rerout that again when everyone realized what Harris had upstairs. All of us had come to believe what we saw was the breath and width of our world. If Harris had a zoo of sorts, there had to be other suff, other levels. That breaker box proved that. I remembered those huge silos. The zoo level with its forty-foot ceilings added to our squat ten-foot-high living level, but left several hundred feet unaccounted for. Those silo-like structures had been the size of skyscrapers even if they started below ground. I knew Harris hadn't shown me everything, and my imagination ran wild with what might be on other levels. Would we find more zoos from other parts of the world? Did elephants and komodo dragons live somewhere above our heads? Tapirs and orangutans? Harris had willing referred to the shelter as the Ark, which originally had been a teasing derogatory. Did he accept the term because it really was what he had created? And while I applauded rescuing species, all of which likely endangered in the outside world, I worried that others would look at our habitations, compare them to the lovely park, and realize that humans had the servants' quarters. They wouldn't be pleased.

But, though this worried me, the fact that we might be inside for ten years bothered me more. How would that work? In ten years, Beth would be twenty, Andrea fourteen, Jane sixteen, and little Noah ten. Maybe Beth would have moved out . . . but to where? The others would be with us. How would our slice house teen girls and a ten-year-old boy? The extended family was young now with the oldest children being twelve. Ten years would give us a host of young adults, but many were first cousins. In our survival plan, we'd never considered what it meant to our children should we have to remain in the shelter for ten years. What would it mean to them if we stayed longer, much longer? I was slowly working myself up into a serious panic.

AT NINE THAT MORNING, movie day began. As each child also had chores to perform at some time during the day, the ticket into the darkened classroom was a slip of paper from the adult in charge of the work the child had to do. As we had a schedule on the classroom doors anyway, the person in charge of entrance—Beth, Harry, or Peter—knew if each child had duties only later or should have completed something. Presenting a ticket earned the child entrance into the theater and a small paper sack of hot, buttered popcorn or caramel corn and the choice of a candy bar from a bushel basket.

I had watering chores that day. I put Noah in a Snuggly and wheeled the water wagon around the slice and gave each of our planters a nice drink. Some of the kids had decided against the movie playing; three of the littler boys—Jim Stone's two and Romala's Jamal—had set up an obstacle course near the animal room and rode bikes around boxes and two of the planters. They made tire-squeal noises as they peddled back and forth and lots of vvrroooms in between. I called a time-out to get the plants watered and was summarily informed that in races stopping the action was called a "slow down," not a "time-out." I promised to remember this.

That emptied out my bucket of water, and I headed to the bathroom for a refill. Noah needed a diaper change at that point, and I switched a load of laundry—not mine—from one of the washers to a dryer and put on a load of Noah's diapers. When I was ready to head out to finish the watering on the far side of the donut, I came apon

Roland and Ronald trying to get into the obstacle course with the three other boys. Billy, Jim's older boy, was telling the twins they could play but they had to follow the rules.

"We can follow the rules," said Roland, with an innocent smile.

"Okay," said Billy. "Do you have bikes?"

"I thought we could share," said Ronald, though they had their own bikes.

Still, coming from these two, that sure sounded like a huge improvement in behavior. I smiled. Billy didn't seem adverse to this as he was telling the twins what the rules were, what the course was and how it was supposed to be run. The twins listened, then took over Billy's and Chuck's bikes.

At this point, I was wheeling away toward the hospital side of the donut. I didn't get far before Chuck was saying, "You had a turn. I want my bike back now," and Billy said, "Hey, that's not the course I showed you. You can't hit the box."

Ah, well, Jeannie's boys were still Jeannie's boys. I chose not to interfere just yet. Billy was a year older and nearly a head taller than the twins; he might have some sway in getting them to behave. I finished the planters near the hospital and school, then completed my circuit back at the kitchen area. As I was giving a further drink to the ever-thirsty sunflowers, I saw Jeannie cleaning tables from breakfast. She was scrubbing hard at a spot, looking angry. I left the wagon and went into the lunchroom on the pretext of getting a cup of coffee.

"Damn eggs, damn syrup," Jeannie said to me. "I hate it when Abby has pancakes or French toast and runny eggs. The kids always get it everywhere."

"I quite agree," I said. "How are you feeling?"

She scowled, then sighed and offered a bit of a smile. "Better, actually. I'm over the barf stage with this pregnancy, and that's wonderful."

She had just started wearing maternity clothes since coming out of the hospital before Christmas.

"I don't feel like I fit in, though," she said, and I could see her emotion.

"Give it a little time. Truthfully, we're all still adjusting to this way of life." *Yeah,* I thought, *and we were just getting started.*

She scoffed. "I sure hope this isn't a 'way of life.' The only way I can get by is thinking it's just temporary, like I'll be moving home next week."

"But—"

"Yeah, yeah, I know. I won't be. It gets me by, though."

"Then continue to tell yourself that. I just hope you don't get down about it when you have to readjust your thinking over and over."

"I see David every morning," she said with a sigh. "He's actually better that the psychologist I had. That one was all about the drugs. Got me started down that road."

I smiled. "I like David, too. Say, you'll be happy to know I just saw your little boys playing with some other little boys outside the animal rooms. Looks like they're doing a road race. It's nice to see them making friends."

Jeannie smiled, and I left the lunchroom. I pulled the wagon slowly, knowing Jeannie would go look at her boys. She trotted out of the lunchroom before I made the bathrooms with my water wagon. She intervened quickly as Roland and Ronald were not playing very nicely at all. As I headed toward the classroom to see how the movie was going, I passed Angie Stone. She stood just outside the classroom from where the delighted shrieks of children came in response to the movie being shown. Her gaze was directed across the donut, though, and I could see Jeannie trying to sort out who did what with her boys. Angie said, "Those twins are a handful, aren't they?"

"Always have been. Can't wait to meet her next one."

Angie sniggered. "My boys don't much like those two."

"Yet they did invite them to play, knowing Roland and Ronald most likely would disrupt rather than cooperate. Brave little boys."

"Yeah, well, Jim and I keep telling them to try to get along."

"You have lovely sons. Very patient. Billy does very well with Jeannie's twins, even if they want to be imps. I think it's good advice to suggest they try to get along, too. We all need that advice living in here." Maybe, just maybe, if we're deeply programed in "getting alone" we'll survive the additions upstairs.

As I crossed the living area again, needing to get Noah fed and down for a nap, I made note that the lettuce was almost ready to eat. I could see where a few people had plucked leaves already. No rules had been established to prevent this, so I wasn't going to mention it to anyone. None of the radishes had formed bulbs yet, but they were still seedlings. But all this was just pretend produce, make work and a way to beautify our living area. Heaven help us if we really needed to grow produce this way. We might get a handful of sunflower seeds from those few plants, maybe one skimpy salad serving for everyone from the planter of lettuce. Some of the other plantings—the beans and peas, for example—wouldn't even provide a serving to half our population.

I was making myself sick with worry and the festering anger. God, why had I followed that damn hooty owl? I'd have been so much better off just going to sleep stuffed with pie and whipped cream. Then I changed my thinking. When I first came to the shelter, first stood on the top stair above the living area and looked down with dismay at the squat, crowded area, the lack of privacy, and communal living being forced on me, I had told myself that this couldn't be the whole shelter, that what I was seeing wasn't everything. I counted on that, hoped that where we were wasn't the totality of this survival shelter we had sacrificed financially to build. I hoped for more. Now I knew without doubt that there was more. That was good, wasn't it? Why was I angry?

When Noah woke from his nap, I roused myself from the twisted thoughts and nursed and changed him. I then wandered back out into the living area. The Stone boys still raced their bikes, but Roland and Ronald had left—or Jeannie had taken them away—and Jimmy Deters watched. Jamal offered him his bike for a turn, but the shy, quiet little boy only shook his head. Bobby, Carl Hope's son, was using Billy's bike for a turn and making dramatic squeals as the bike took the corners.

I headed to the kitchen, hoping for a bite to eat. It was only eleven, but Abby always left healthy snacks on the counter. I picked up a couple peanut butter celery sticks. She came out with a platter of quarter-cut peanut butter and jelly sandwiches. I took one of those too.

"How's it going?" I asked her.

"Oh, fine, just fine. We had a good breakfast with French toast and fried potatoes and eggs, so I thought I'd go light on lunch, especially since the kids are filling up on popcorn and candy at their movies. What a nice idea for them. That Mr. Harris is a great man, a truly great man to have thought of everything so thoroughly."

I hope so, I thought. To Abby I gave a smile. "You said the other day that food stores are dwindling. How bad really?"

Abby took my arm and led me back to the storage rooms. She opened a door to reveal a completely cleaned out, empty room. "There's three storage rooms. Two are empty now, and we've made a big dent in the third. Apples'll go till spring, but this month we'll run out of potatoes for sure. That's pretty much the last of the celery," she said pointing the piece I had. "We still have some onions left, a few big cabbage heads and some squash, but it's going fast with this many people."

"What about rice, beans—?"

247

"Dried stuff? We got tons. Really. Tons. We got enough wheat for flour to last a year at least. Two more likely. I've been adding amaranth flour to it to make it more nutritious, too. Wouldn't'a thought Mr. Harris knew so much about grains. That stuff has its own storerooms with perfect conditions to keep for a very long time."

"So what's on the menu tonight. I forgot to look."

"We got red beans and rice with cornbread. It's a nice warm meal. Those who don't like that can have last night's soup. The last of the apples from storeroom two are getting a bit mushy and are only good for pies, so I thought I'd use 'em."

"Everyone loves your pies."

Abby grinned wide enough to show her gap. "I like pleasing folks. Lunch is canned tomato soup and grilled cheese sandwiches." Then she smiled. "The cheese is homemade from the Jersey cow's milk. Very tasty. The bread I baked yesterday."

We had arrived back in the lunchroom from the survey of the storerooms. Abby tutted and picked up the washcloth Jeannie had left on one of the tables.

"Is Jeannie working well enough."

"So-so. Her attitude's improved. She still turns her nose up at my cooking."

"She's still adjusting."

"Ain't we all. Right now I'm missing something I used to really enjoy."

"What's that?" I asked.

"Seed catalogues. I'd have a dozen in my hands by now. I liked to go through them all, circling varieties and such that I especially liked, then lay out all the order forms and start in to ordering. Before I was done, I'd have ordered a bit here, a bit there from each of the catalogues. I wanted the best producing, most resistant, most nutritious foods. The whole process took me about a week, four days if'n we had a blizzard and I couldn't get to work. After my seed orders, I started on taxes. Don't miss not having to deal with them. Each year, though, I'd have both done by the end of January. Then the seeds would come, and I'd set up my trays under lights to get a jump on the gardens."

"Gardens? How many?"

"I usually planted three. One for potatoes. One for corn and squash, and the third for the row crops. About half an acre total."

"Really," I said, thinking back to my last garden. It was big for me, about a hundred feet by twenty-five. I suspected that Abby's wasn't the weedy jungle mine had been at season's end. My carrots had been fingerlengths and spotty because of an infiltration of white clover, and the squash and pumpkins had to be hunted out in what became essentially a field of prairie grass nearly four feet high.

"How'd you take care of all that? How'd you get it all weeded?" I asked.

"I didn't have to be at the school until ten, and I've always been an early riser. I'd get up about five and work in the garden 'til nine. The boys'd till between the rows for me on weekends. Of course, when school was done, we all had more time."

Four hours of daily weeding. My garden was lucky to get four hours a week.

"Mr. Harris has a kind of vault for seeds just past the last storeroom. Your family brought a lot. I've been saving pumpkin, squash, tomato and pepper seeds all along. I've also set aside some of the nicest of the potatoes to use for seed. Thing is them little buckets out in the donut aren't going to do us much good with real crops. I must say I'm getting just a little worried about what we're going to do . . . later. We've got a lot of people to feed. And what if we can't get out and farm next spring? I'm thinking I should start rationing now. It could make a difference."

I gave that thought. In some ways, rationing wasn't the worst thing for us to do. We were eating very well, better in some ways than before coming to the shelter. I know I was having difficulty losing my extra weight following Noah's birth, and I also had noticed that Frank's paunch had grown. Mike looked nearly ten pounds heavier than before. We ate three excellent and varied meals a day, but our activity level wasn't keeping up with our caloric intake. Maybe when we got into the rest of the shelter, when we could walk the zoo, we would keep fitter, could utilize the nutrition we were receiving. Right now we were all just adding to our bellies, butts, and thighs.

"I think you should talk to Harris before you make a change," I told Abby, "but I certainly think a little rationing wouldn't hurt any of us."

"Not the kids, though," Abby said. "Little 'uns need good nutrition."

"Hmm, I agree with that," I said.

I wondered how many parents would voluntarily ration their intake. Those who came to us late had experienced privation and probably better understood the whole concept of rationing, but what about those of us who had been called in that October Tuesday? We'd worried together, made adjustments to the shelter, learned to live in tight, cramped quarters with no privacy to speak of, but we had always eaten well. Right from the start. Anyone who missed a meal did so by choice, and food had been in seemingly unending abundance from day one. We still had plenty of meat, but that alone would not sustain us. I really hoped that Abby would ask Harris about this. He had said food wasn't an issue. But why wasn't it?

Movie day went pretty well. Kids wandered in and out of the classroom as chores had to be done, and, in the case of Jimmy Deters, to throw up on the floor because he had eaten too much caramel corn. The fox terrier puppies were let in the living area, but they were rounded up before too many piddled, and James corraled a kid goat in the bathroom during the afternoon, but it hadn't caused any trouble. All in all, the kids had a great day. At supper, Beth stood up to announce that the next day would be an art day. While movies would still be offered in the classroom, lunchroom tables would be set up in the donut, offering paints, crayons, markers, and chalk for making pictures, modeling clay and Play-doh for sculptures. These materials had been used in the school setting many times, but now were set out for all to use. Harris offered that the wall between the kitchen and the classroom could have a mural painted on it. The kids cheered. Then Beth announced that she was "passing the torch" to three others to plan the day after that: Herman and Duane Gertz, along with Andrew Harkins, a college student who came into the shelter at the same time as Andy. These three young men (the Gertz boys were seventeen and fifteen, and Andrew was twenty) would likely have a different take on a vacation day than the younger committee.

As supper, Harris suggested that the adults get together at nine, an hour after the designated bedtime for most of the younger children. I suspected that Abby had spoken with him, and he was preparing a response.

The three girls settled into bed without any of the usual requests for snacks or water or eliptical long-answer questions like, "How does a bean know to grow up?" They'd had a full day and lots of junk food and were ready to go to sleep. I kissed Beth in the top bunk and then sat on the lower bunk to kiss Andrea and Jane, who had decided to sleep together that night, which probably meant an extra half hour of giggling. As usual, Jane insisted I also kiss Prince on the nose. I did this and was reaching for Noah to nurse him, when Jane said, "Prince has something to tell you."

The sweet little girl often used her poodle to communicate, and I easily responded, "Well, then, Prince, what can I do for you?"

"Nothing," said Jane. "He just wanted to tell you something."

"Okay," I said, "What would you like to say, Prince?"

"He wants to tell you my name."

I worked hard to keep my excitement at bay. "I see, Prince. So what is your friend's name?"

"He says to tell you my name is Caroline Huxley."

"That's a really pretty name, Prince. Tell Caroline that I'll be happy to call her that from now on."

"No," said the little girl. "Prince likes Jane Quill better. He asks that you continue to call me Jane."

"Why?" I asked gently.

The little girl pet her dog for the space of a full minute, not looking at me, then said, "Prince thought it would be better that way. He thought I might not be so sad if I stayed Jane. There's nothing . . . sad about Jane, especially if she doesn't remember."

"What do you mean . . . Prince?"

"Caroline was alone. Mom and Dad had gone away. They said they'd be back, but they didn't come back. Caroline was hungry and cold and scared. Jane was found. She has a family."

Oh, the simple, perfect logic of children. Tears burned at my eyes. This little girl, just six years old, had found a way to move out of her fear and loss by a simple change of name. Caroline had been alone in a hostile world. She had been afraid and cold and hungry. She had felt abandoned. Then Andy's party had stayed one night in her home and found her huddled in a closet. They took care of her. And when they all came here, she found food and warmth and comfort—everything she had lost except her family. Of course, she'd want to remain Jane. No child would want to go back to such fear and suffering. That was Caroline's world, not Jane's. All the counseling in the world wouldn't have thought of sloughing off the baggage of privation by taking on a new name that didn't have anything bad associated with it.

Then, since I tended to overthink everything, I began to wonder if this really were the good news I thought it was. I'd have to talk with Boopsie or Dave.

The girls were asleep by the time I finished nursing Noah, and he was down for a good sleep as well. I had already tested being able to hear him from the classroom. If I left the curtain open a little, I could hear him anywhere in the kitchen or the classroom. That gave me some freedom to interact with the adults. I headed to the classroom, where the adult meeting would soon start. I wanted to sit in the back so I could hear Noah if he cried and was pleased to see that Boopsie had also chosen the back row as well.

"Hi," I said to the pretty blonde.

"Kids all asleep?"

"Yup. I probably have several hours. I'd like to ask you about something Jane said tonight."

"What's that?"

"She told me her name. Well, actually, she had Prince tell me her name."

Boopsie brightened. "I think that's great. What's her name?"

"Caroline Huxley, but she wants to be called Jane Quill still."

Boopsie frowned. "Really. Did she say why?"

"Her exact words were 'Caroline was lost. Jane was found.'"

Boopsie sat back and blinked several times. "Wow," she said. "She's just six."

"So, you think this is still a good thing?"

"Oh, yeah. It's good . . . just a little . . . well, she'll have to deal with her ordeal later. It's not going to go away just because she changes her name, but, for now, it's fine. She's six. This is a really good solution for a six-year-old. When she's ready, she may take back her real name. That'll be when she's ready to deal with what happened, but that might not happen for years. I'd say go with it. Call her Jane."

As we talked, others had filtered into the room. The movie screen still dominated the stage, but the projector had been put away. Popcorn and candy wrappers littered the floor. There were thirty-eight adults total, and thirty-two had already arrived. Jeannie wasn't there, nor Connie, Melissa, nor DeeDee and James. All except Jeannie arrived before Harris took the mike at the front of the stage.

"Everyone here?" his magnified voice asked us.

Most everyone nodded. Having Jeannie missing wasn't that unusual, as she didn't participate fully yet.

"The question came up earlier about our food supply," said Harris. "Since we mentioned it a bit ago, a number of you have asked me about this. I need you to know two things: One, no one is going to starve in the Ark; and, two, we are coming to the end of some of the produce we brought in with us. What you need to understand is that we have a good supply of home-canned goods and an even larger supply of commercially canned goods. We're in no danger of starving. I don't want you to think that."

"Well, good," said Emily.

"Today the question was also brought up about rationing food, and whether I thought this was a good idea. Actually I do."

This caused a murmur to begin.

"The potatoes, squash, and cabbages are about gone. Carrots, beets, turnips, and parsnips have been gone for weeks. We've got some apples left. Abby's done a most remarkable job utilizing this fresh food to its utmost. I had hoped we could use about fifty percent of what we brought in before it spoiled. I'm happy to report that Abby has put over ninety percent to use."

A cheer rose up, and Abby blushed and hid behind her hand.

"Because she's used this food so well, we still have that store of home-canned goods and commercial cans. She reasoned, rightfully, that canned food would keep longer. Now they go into use. That's not the reason for rationing. We're fine for now, but I can't know how long we need to stay in here, and can't give the slightest opinion of whether we'll be about to grow any crops outside next summer. Radiation levels are fluctuating, still mostly in the okay range, but they've had a few spikes at levels that worry me. It's very likely we'll need to ration at some point, and maybe that should start before we're really low. If we then need to stretch our stores further than we have currently planned, we'll have that reserve. At the very least, I think we should learn how to deal with rationing before we seriously need to use it. It's also true that in this environment, where none of us are working particularly hard, we're putting on weight." He patted his own expanding belly. Some chuckled. "This will only serve to make our lives harder, less healthy. We've saved so much of the best of our society when we came here; to bring in obesity at the same time doesn't seem like a good idea. Our meals should be lighter. I ask that each of you consider taking smaller helpings, no seconds, and limit snacks. And while we do not intend for the children to be part of this rationing in any way, it would be nice if all adults took part."

"Wait a minute," said Wayne. "We don't *need* rationing, but you'd like us to ration *anyway*? Is that what you're telling us?"

"Yes," said Harris. "That's exactly correct. Thanks for restating it so nicely. We don't need rationing *now*. We have sufficient food, though we'll continue to run out of some things. I'm asking you to do this because we don't know the future. Should serious rationing be needed, I'd like to know we can rise to the challenge."

I could see what Harris was doing, and it made sense. Harris wanted to see our self-control and altruism, two very important commodities in our living so closely together. These were things I could get behind.

"So," said Mike, "you want us to *pretend* we need to ration."

"Yes." Harris gave him his silly, wide grin.

"That's nuts."

"Perhaps," said Harris equitably, "or you could look at it as an exercise in community spirit."

Andy eased himself to a stand. "I'm leaving the hospital wing tomorrow. When Ben and I go to our new slice, I intend to follow Harris's suggestion. Out there, waiting for rescue with very little food most days, I know how important it is at least to understand what privation is. I would ask, however, that, for those who already learned this hard lesson, they not have to take part."

"This is everyone's free choice," said Harris. "No one should do this if they don't want to. I do believe, however, that it is in the community's best interest to do this together. All of us. Those who have known true privation will easily see that what we're doing is only partial rations, not starvation rations."

Henry Maki, a retired physician who came in with Andy, stood. He was white-haired and had a pleasant, comforting smile. His wife, Helmi, stood with him. They held hands. Henry said, "Some days out there we didn't have enough food, when we didn't know if we'd find more. I always made sure my Helmi had something. We'd share if we could. When we couldn't, I wanted her to keep up her strength."

Helmi, tears in her eyes, said, "A few times, I just couldn't eat because Henry wouldn't. I'd rather go without food with him than eat and know he was hungry. We'll go along with Harris. It's good . . ." and she paused as emotion swept over her. Henry patted her hand. She cleared her throat and said, "Some events in life test people's souls. They test the basic beliefs and moral core of a person's life. What we went through out there did that for us, and I'm proud to say I liked what I saw. Everyone should know this about themselves, know that, faced with the worst, they can rise to the best."

Harris said, "Thank you so much Helmi and Henry. I couldn't have said it better. This is a soul test, if you will."

"How long?" said Mike, his voice sounding suddenly resigned, his objections blown away by Helmi's heartfelt words.

"If people know how long, if they can put a definite time frame to it, it's easier to accomplish. But when privation really hits, no one really knows how long it's going to last, in the same way we don't know how long we'll need to be in the Ark. Let's just say, it'll be as long as necessary. I'm hoping we can learn what we need to know in a couple of weeks, but if a month is necessary, so be it."

"A month!" said Wayne. "Gees, Harris. Give us a bloody break here. A month of starvation when we don't have to?"

"It's not starvation, just rationing. If we're in here for too long, it could be far worse and a way of life for us. I'd like to know we can rise to that challenge."

"What do we get out of it?" Emily asked, ever suspicious. I know her mind skipped quickly to cigarettes. *Nope, big sister.*

Harris said, "Get out of it? Hmmm. Well, having eaten less, we might loose a few pounds. That's a reward. We'll also have the knowledge that we do this if we need to. Do you need something more, Emily?"

Her mouth opened, her lips formed the S sound beginning of cigarettes, but she stopped. *Wow.* Big sister actually might have an altruistic bone in her selfish body. "Um . . ." she said instead. "Maybe . . . maybe let Carl Hope do some building for us, give us all more room."

Congrats to you, Emily. I was proud of my sister for maybe the first time.

Harris smiled. "Yes, that sounds perfect."

I felt an inkling of nerves. Did a little less food equate to readiness to accept the park above us? I wasn't so sure.

What was wrong with me? Why did I accept our cramped little world down here when I really hated it, had hated it from the moment I'd seen it spread out before me that first evening? I constantly barked my shins on the bed in our slice, and had to reorder the place every other day as the girls pawed through boxes or played there. I often found the days long and boring. Why was I holding onto this kind of life? True, I had enjoyed most of the aspects of community development and had written long pages about that in the journal, and I truly believed that community aced out private lives, but if there was a way to maintain community while we also enjoyed more space, I'd be up for that.

26

PRIVATION

FRIDAY, DECEMBER 27

———————

ABBY LOOKED DIFFERENT WHEN I CAME into the kitchens the next morning. She looked, quite frankly, shook.

"What's wrong, Abby?" I asked.

She looked furtive. "I don't want to talk about it." Her lips were tight.

I was completely taken aback. "What?" I said.

"I'm supposed to prepare plain meals," she said. "We're all supposed to do with as little as possible."

Abby, not one for subterfuge, had switched topics. Interesting. "Survival isn't about how much food. It's about community. Harris knows if we fail to build a strong, cohesive community, we can't make it even if we have all the food and comforts in the world. If we have to face real shortages, we need to know how. We have to be able to sacrifice. We've come a long way in this. I think Harris is testing his leadership, our community cooperation, and how we'll respond when some choose not to cooperate."

"Some won't. Jeannie won't," said Abby.

"Let's wait and see. Wayne sounded like he'd go along with it last night. Let's not count them out yet."

"Well," said Abby. "I'm making scrambled eggs this morning. I'm making about half what I'd normally do, and that's usually all eaten. There'll be no bacon or sausage with it and no fried potatoes. I've got some whole wheat bread for toast, but I'm not making enough for everyone. Mr. Harris told me how I should do this. It's going to be hard. After breakfast, people might just fight in line so they get something. I don't mind telling you, missus, I'm a little scared. It could go bad."

TYPICALLY, PEOPLE MEANDERED in for breakfast over a period of an hour between seven and eight. School started at 8:15, but most chores related to preparing breakfast and caring for the animals began at six. Chores related to cleaning and school and hospital duties began at eight or eight-thirty. The staggered schedule allowed parents to get kids ready for school yet still have crews up earlier to milk and fix breakfast.

Everyone came to the lunchroom at once, most arriving before Abby brought out the steaming platters. When she did, it was with averted eyes and mumbled apologies. "'S'it," she said. "We gotta share this lot. There ain't no more in the kitchen."

No one rushed to the counter.

"It's getting cold," Abby said. A tear coursed down her cheek. "That ain't no good either."

"It's not, is it?" said Mike. "Come on. No one said we had to starve altogether. And we might as well eat hot food."

He picked up a plate, which I saw was a salad plate and not a dinner plate, and spooned a lump of eggs onto his plate. He grabbed a couple pieces of toast and went to sit down. Others followed. Then a line formed. I watched. The children, who were never meant to be part of the rationing, never said a word or questioned what was happening. Not one complained about a lack of bacon or potatoes. Beth reached the line and took a small serving of the eggs and half a piece of toast, but she had Andrea and Jane next to her and gave them two slices of toast with their eggs. She lifted her eyes to mine just briefly, but a long ticker-tape of communication filled that glance. She was on board with this in a big way. Maybe too big.

Some took about a tablespoon of eggs; others nearly what they normally took. The line, however, consisted of all our young intellectuals—James, Jim, the Reinhart brothers, and a few of the newcomers. James, heading this group, asked if the kitchen crew had eaten. They hadn't. He insisted they get food as it seemed exceedingly cruel to have them prepare food, then go hungry. Melissa, DeeDee, and Carl Hope came out and served themselves small portions. James counted those behind him. He looked around to make sure no one was missing from breakfast, then divided the eggs into the six portions required to feed himself and the rest. Each scooped up the allotted portion of the remaining eggs, an amount that looked like about a teaspoon, and half a piece of toast.

The meal was consumed in silence. One by one, people returned their plate and silver to the bussing cart and went about their morning's work.

After breakfast, I tried to comfort Abby, who was weeping. She looked up through red, tearful eyes and whispered, "That was awful, missus. Terrible."

"What was awful?" I asked.

"It weren't fair. Them at the end got just a taste of eggs."

I smiled. "It'll be all right, Abby. Leave the toast. It'll get eaten too."

"Did you see them little kids. It was like they knew. I saw them take just little bits. And no one complained. Not one. But now I got another problem."

"What's that?"

Abby swept her arm over the cleaned out egg server and few pieces of cold toast. "What am I going to give the pigs?"

I laughed. Then Abby laughed.

"I think the pigs'll be fine with their mash and excess milk."

As I was turning to go to my slice to get the girls ready for school, Beth ducked out of the lunchroom ahead of me. She skittered across the floor and into our slice. I followed. I had just reached the curtain, when she bolted out, her school books in hand. "Got to go, Mom," she said and tried to get past me, but I stepped in her way. She might be able to communicate volumes in a look, but her actions talked too.

"Just a minute, young lady," I said. "I want you to answer one question. Where?"

She regarded me with innocence, blue eyes wide. "Um, where what, Mom?"

"Where do you and Harry and whoever else joins you hide when you eavesdrop on the grown-ups having a private, grown-up meeting?"

Her expression changed, becoming almost bored. "It's not like it's *hard*," she said with a touch of defiance. "It's always the same. You all pile into the classroom or the lunchroom, close the doors and think you are being so hush-hush."

"Where?" I asked again, screwing my voice down a little tighter.

Her expression turned haughty. "Actually, I never leave our slice."

I gave that a moment's thought. "A listening device, then?"

Beth's eyes flashed. "You're not going to stop us, are you?"

Not exactly an explanation, but it moved my reaction into a new area. "No, I'm not going to stop you . . . unless . . ."

"Unless what?" Beth had moved to the defensive.

I smiled and kissed her head, "Unless you stop making the most perfect choices based on what you hear. What you did in the lunchroom was very mature."

"Can *I* ask a question?"

"Why are we doing this?"

"Yeah, I mean, we still have plenty of food, don't we?"

"Yes. Harris wants to make sure we can act altruistically."

"For the good of everyone."

"Very good. It's important that those who came first don't consider themselves privileged over those who came later with nothing. This means that those kids who came without parents must be wrapped into families. Jane is your sister just as Andrea is."

Beth nodded.

"The shelter's too small to contain much trouble. Uncle Harris knows that we have to work twice, maybe three times as hard at community than we ever did outside. Out there, we might not go to city council meetings; we left education to the schools, and few of us took part in local government. It was easier to leave stuff to others, and, out there, there were so many others, we didn't need to worry that everything was being done. I had work, of course, and so did your dad, but we didn't worry that garbage would get picked up every week, or that our paper was delivered, that mail came, that someone had to bring groceries and clothes to stores to be ready when we went shopping. Community was much larger out there, multi-leveled, and many contributing to it were invisible. But we can see what happens when it all breaks down."

"It broke down really fast, didn't it?"

"Light speed. In the 1930s, we had the Depression. It was hard everywhere, and that was because one particular facet of world economy broke down. Just one. Now lots of areas have broken down, and the real question, the real challenge for us is to make sure we're not part of that. Harder, we have to build in the face of destruction. If our community fails, it won't be because of food. Uncle Harris knows this. For our community to succeed, it has to be a group effort, everyone contributing, everyone trying and thinking about the good of all. No one can afford to sit by and let others take up the slack."

"Aunt Jeannie took more eggs than she normally takes, and Uncle Mike and Aunt Emily took plenty. Aunt Emily even left some behind on her plate."

"It's okay, dear."

Her face screwed up. "No, it's not! They're selfish!"

"I know it seemed that way. It's more like they were testing boundaries. This was our first rationed meal. Let's see how it changes, how they change what they do."

Beth gave me a sudden hug. It lasted a long minute. I kissed her. When she broke away, she wiped her eyes. "Thanks, Mom," she said and headed off to school.

I thought about what I had said. How much of that had I really believed deep down? A good deal. Sure, we had to have a strong, very open community. So, why were we going to change what we were working so hard to build? I feared we were trying to recreate the outside world when it was, at best, a very poor model.

AFTER A MORNING of activity on a very light breakfast, the lunchroom was crowded and waiting when Abby brought out the food, a tureen of tomato soup and a platter of peanut butter sandwiches, no jelly. Again we saw the salad plates and, instead of our generous stoneware bowls, cups. Abby had stopped crying, but she didn't look any happier.

James spoke up from just outside the lunchroom doors where he stood with his cohorts. "How much do we have, Abby?"

She answered loud enough for him—and all the rest of us—to hear. "If'n everyone takes one-half sandwich and a cup of soup, everyone gets some."

Serving began. I noticed that all the bigger kids had littler kids, usually their siblings, around them. They helped them get their food. Ronald and Roland grabbed two sandwiches each and no one stopped them, but Connie and Melissa cut their half sandwiches into quarters and took only one piece. This time, when James reached the tureen and set out six cups for himself and those behind him, he had nearly full cups when he had evenly poured out the remaining soup. A couple of those people had only quarter sandwiches, but no one complained.

Supper consisted of mashed potatoes from dried flakes—one of the items Harris had tons of—commercially canned green beans cut into bits, and a couple fresh hams. Unlike the soup and sandwiches, this was a much harder meal to divide into equal portions. We all knew, however, that usually we saw twice as much food on the table at supper. What also made it difficult was that we had skimped at the two previous meals. My stomach growled loudly with the fragrant aroma of the pork. Typically, though we usually designated a carver, amounts were decided by each of us at the serving counter. Today, Abby sliced the meat onto a platter so that portions could be determined.

Again James called out, "How much is a serving, Abby?"

"One good slice of meat, this serving spoon of beans," and she held up the slotted spoon, "and one neat ice cream scoop of potatoes," and she held up the scoop.

Then she sighed and stood back. Rationing was coming easier. Fewer instances of larger portions occurred. Jeannie hesitated at the counter, turned to everyone and said, "I hate canned green beans. Can I have two scoops of potatoes instead?"

Abby stepped to the counter. "You can do whatever you wish, missus," she said. As Jeannie reached for another scoop of potatoes, Abby added, "but there's only enough mash for one scoop each. Taking two means someone'll get only beans."

Jeannie stared at her, then returned the scoop to the bowl.

THE NEXT DAY SEEMED HARDER. Oatmeal for breakfast, no sugar. Lunch consisted of Campbell's chicken noodle soup and those same peanut butter sandwiches. Two people at the end of the line had only soup, and not even full cups. For supper we had rice, fried chicken cut up onto very small pieces so that a breast piece was cut into three pieces and a thigh into two, and canned peas. When James asked the portion size, Abby blushed and said, "Mr. Harris asked I not say exactly. I'm sorry."

That night, James and Jim at the end of the line, determined to take the brunt of the privation. When Donald got to the counter, with ten behind him, he divided the rice and beans. There were nine pieces of chicken left. He took none.

The real difference this day was the attitude. Jeannie had started to complain. She, Emily, Wayne, and Mike commented: "How damn long is this going to last," "This isn't funny anymore," and "I'll go butcher a chicken, if this is all I get."

People seemed nervous, testier than usual. Kids were fussier, though they were probably responding to the atmosphere rather than the rationing.

THREE DAYS INTO THE RATIONING, and the ones at the end were getting pretty hungry. Five days into the program, DeeDee passed out in line. James shouted, "Look, we have to have food too. Take smaller portions."

By the end of the week, things were better. Rationing seemed usual now, and people weren't fighting it as much or trying to get more than their share. From all three meals that day, food remained on the counter after everyone was served. Abby then asked who might wish a little more. No takers. Our New Year's celebration had a few treats, little canapes and a sheet cake, but these were easy to divide into equal shares. We had firecrackers out in the donut—nothing bigger than sparklers really, but it was festive. The children were allowed to stay up until midnight, and we all counted down the last ten seconds. At the end of the countdown, when I was just beginning to move my two youngest daughters toward the slice, Harris called loudly to all of us.

"Happy New Year!" he said. "I've watched you this week, watched community tighten as a result of privation. I want you to understand what this week meant. We ate one fourth the food we normally consumed. You thought you were eating half the food, and you probably were, but we've been wasting way too much. Abby can save food left on the counter, but she can't clean off the plates and use that again. That's where the real waste has been all along. We'd been eating as if out of a restaurant, taking whatever we wanted and leaving uneaten portions behind as if it didn't matter. It most assuredly does. Sure the pigs and pets ate our leftovers, but we've got food for them. The dogs and cats haven't starved; they ate kibble. And the pigs got more of the skim milk than usual to make up for their missing scraps. This was a by-product from our cheese making and didn't take anything from our table."

Harris paused. "I need you to understand the limitations of this place. We're warm and safe and well fed. That's not true outside. And, it's difficult to remember that there are very real limits to what we can maintain. We can't waste food. There are no grocery stores inside the Ark, no truckers to resupply us when we run out. And we can run out. It's important that we adjust to our smaller circumstance, our narrower, very finite world. For the time we're here—and I can't know how long—that we're interred in this hole in the ground, we have to act differently than outside. To believe or act otherwise is to fail to understand the beauty and advantage of this life. 'Self' must be enlarged to include everyone all at once, our community.

"Outside, we had nuclear families, generational families, and extended families. Think about how different these were. As nuclear families, we fought a lot between ourselves. There's been animosity between the Deters and Reinharts for years, but when we got together for major holidays, those animosities mostly fell away. We had good times. And while it's eary to forget slights and bumps for a day or two, it's harder over time. Still, as one small community, we're dependent on each other in ways that even our extended family couldn't accommodate. Then there are those of us who are no relation. It doesn't matter. We're still one community. Everyone has to be equal; everyone has to share and cooperate for the one community to function."

Clearly Harris understood this. Clearly our circumstances had been designed to force community as much as such a thing could be forced. But, as I thought about this, I realized that Harris might just have thought deeply on this. Maybe he had a plan to push us further to solidify what we had begun on our own. I just hoped this tact didn't bring us to a breaking point.

"This week," Harris said, "we showed each other that we could share a much smaller portion of food without fighting or complaining or disrupting the community. It's good to know we can do that. Chances are better than good that, some time in the future, we'll be tested again, but not by our choice. If the Ark is attacked, if it's breached, we'll have to deal with that as a whole. If our cattle suddenly die, we have no way of getting more. We'll have to deal with that. It's good to know that we probably can.

"So, is this damn rationing over?" Wayne asked.

Harris regarded him levelly. "This is healthier. Rationing stays."

"Why?" said Mike.

"In the barely three months we've been in the Ark—less time, of course, for those who came later—eighty percent of the radio operators with whom we routinely converse have ceased transmitting. Some of these were individuals; some were groups as large as ours, and a few much, much larger. We don't know what happened to these people. In these few weeks, seven of the twelve large Western shelters run by paramilitary or religious organizations have failed. Some of those shelters housed over five hundred individuals, and, I need you to know that, when they failed, they failed catastrophically. People died. Lots of people. Children died. Three of the seven turned on themselves in Johnstown fashion, with every man, woman, and child wiped out by poison or gunshots. A few barricaded individuals reported this, one just as he gulped down his own cup of Kool-Aid, too despondent to continue living. Two simply abandoned their shelters and went up into the mountains to separate, mountain lifestyles with each family defending itself and its resources with shotguns and rifles. This was reported by the last family to leave. Two kicked half their membership out of the shelter. One, I just don't know, but I suspect it went the way of the first three, only no one survived to tell the tale.

"Understand, we're talking about thousands of people dying. Why? Did they run out of food? Not in three months. Not those folks. They each had food reserves for decades. Disease? Nope. Craziness brought on by inactivity? Not likely. Again it's only been three months. The real issue, the defining capability to survival as we have had to create it, is not in technology or food stores. Those are easy—easy to plan for, easy to maintain. Basically, it just takes money. Hand-picking who will survive within the Ark?

Not only was that not an option for us, but we really don't know exactly who we need in here to survive. None of these things can insure this place working. The real make-or-break issue is community. Community. And, of course, this makes sense. Those Western shelters failed because they failed in the test of community, and that's vital to understand.

"In the larger world, we all failed as a community, and the result is that the world as we knew it no longer exists. We cannot fail as community in here. And the defining necessity for community is common goals. In the case of some of the surviving Western complexes who had an inkling of what they needed to succeed, that sameness was longtime membership in the paramilitary community they built. As a community, we are less than three months old. Turning all of you into goose-stepping, regimented automatons isn't the point. That's control from without. It can only work for a time as long as the dictatorship lasts. The important control comes from within each of us. That's the lasting one, the one that can go the distance.

"We brought in diverse family members as well as random people off the street, so to speak, so we'll never have the kind of community built on like-mindedness. What we have and must work to maintain is a commitment to each other and to the Ark. Call it altruism, call it the same survival goal. The name's not so important. What is important is that we care, truly care about each other, even the ones who disagree with us. Without that, we're done. With it, we have the capability to survive for the long haul, for as long as it takes and more. Remember, at some point we need to leave the Ark and build lives outside again. That's our hope. Building community will sustain us in the Ark and support us outside when we begin to build a better world."

This was the most dramatic speech Harris had given to date. It brought tears to my eyes, and many others sniffled or wiped their faces. What he said rang true. In the beginning, I had thought Harris more of a default leader than someone we could count on. I remember thinking him benign. I had been so far from the mark, it wasn't funny. Harris wasn't benign, certainly not a default, interim kind of leader. He was, in fact, the Ark's perfect leader. I could see now that he had guided us through our maturing, keeping that concept of community always in front of us even if we didn't know it was there. And he did it without being the driving force orchestrating it. I could see now how gifted he was, and I was grateful for his knowledge.

Harris then said, "At Christmas I appointed certain roles. These are very important to our community, but we need to elect leaders to govern us. I've put this off as long as I could, but now's the time for that. Call it a court or council or, maybe, town elders. I think a leadership of five individuals would give good representation of our diversity without being ponderous. These five will be our officials with the appointed positions rounding out a full council. At least, that's my take on this. The actual configuration of this governing body is up to public vote. How you elect these leaders is up to you. We could elect a person from each of the major functions of the shelter, elect elders for their wisdom, use this as a popularity contest—well there are lots of ways to do this. We'll have to vote on that first. I also want officially to name the shelter—that will be the job of all our kids. And while kids that don't talk yet can't vote, I'd say any child older than five should. Younger than five, any child can still vote if he or she can get three other kids to vouch for that child's understanding of the task at hand."

The voting took place over the next couple of days. Since Christmas, we already had ten people appointed by Harris to serve in come capacity for the community. I saw these people as the cabinet for the officials we now needed to elect. We talked about representatives of major groups: food and farming, medical, educational, communications, housing, and resources. But that seemed like more advisory positions. Instead, we decided to have three at-large officials. After nominations were requested, we got several names, which seemed to be a good cross-section of our population makeup, some from the family, one of the cousins, and some of the newcomers. Each of these people had an opportunity to speak, but we decided this wasn't the time for debates or long lists of promises. At the end of the week, we had our election. Abby Gertz became the first representative, David Moos the second, and Harris rounded out the governing body. Harris was then elected our mayor with the vote unanimous. No real surprise there. The children decided that "Harris's Ark" should be the official name of our shelter. We decided on weekly community meetings to keep up with the workings of the Ark and the community, and everyone, including the children, could attend.

From that October Tuesday when we were called to the Ark until Andy and the final members of our community arrived, we had, of necessity, been looking outside, worrying what was happening to our family members out there and what the world in general was experiencing. Between our cramped housing, rationing, and elections, Harris was turning our focus inward, toward our community, away from the outside disunity, knowing that we needed to make that turn and pit our energies to the task of survival in this time and space with this small group of people.

For the first time since coming to the Ark, I felt a deep sense of relief and even greater hope that Harris's Ark would sustain us and that we would survive together. Not even seeing what was upstairs had given me quite this much pure hope. But now, the idea of incorporating what was up there into our community seemed to be something we had to embrace to fulfill our destinies. If we were to join the larger world any time in the future, we had to come at least halfway back to that world with the strengths we had learned down here in the slices.

27
JANUARY

AND SO WE WORKED OUR WAY into January 2014. We were eating less, and finally, those excess pounds from pregnancy began to slip off my hips and belly. I liked that. But that was probably the only highlight of the month. In years past, January had always been problematic—the holidays were over, and it was a long time to spring. January was the month of endurance. Outside I'd have to contend with digging out snow to get to work, cold, problems with the furnace, worrying about the sewer system freezing. All that had been lifted from my shoulders, leaving . . . nothing to worry about.

Kids got fussier. Andrea and Jane squabbled over dolls and books, and Beth lost patience with both of them. Cousins throughout the shelter shifted alliances almost daily as one upset another, who became "best friends" with a different cousin. Everyone seemed sick of each other's company. We had entered the after-holidays grump that January often was. I felt directionless. I couldn't plan for spring, couldn't plan a vacation or trip to the cabin, found myself listless and a little down.

Mealtime became a battleground again, as if food were the only interesting part of our days. Some, like Mike and Jeannie, were altogether sick of rationing and started filling their plates as they had done before. People at the end of the line began to go hungry again. In response, the rest of us chose to eat a bit less. Then David Moos had the bright idea to have everyone except the hold-outs queue for supper ten minutes early. When Jeannie and Mike discovered that they were at the end of the line, they started a loud complaint.

James, just ahead of them said, "Doesn't feel good to believe that your own family might let you go hungry, does it? You've let some of us go hungry, but, take heart, we're not as selfish."

When they reached the counter, nothing was left on the platters. Nothing. Then DeeDee brought out two plates with fair portions for them. Red-faced, Jeannie accepted hers and sat down. Mike stood at the counter staring at the plate and nodding as if he were talking to himself. Then he snatched up the plate and left the lunchroom.

I wasn't hopeful this example had made any impression on him, but, as I headed back to my slice, I passed his. With no front curtains to their space, I could easily see in. Mike sat on his bed, his back to the open front, the untouched plate behind him on the bed. He was weeping. I could have just continued on, ignored what I was hearing, but I didn't tend to do that. Like Jillian said, I was pushy.

"Mike," I whispered. "Can I help?"

"Go away," he snapped.

"Okay," I said, and stepped away from the opening. Being pushy didn't always win me friends.

"No, wait," he said and turned around.

I waited.

"I don't know if I can do this," he said.

"Do what exactly?" I asked, stepping into the slice.

He spread his arms and looked up. "This. This whole communal thing. I mean, geez, I'm used to having control over my life. I headed my firm, for crissakes. Senior partner. Now . . . here . . . no one needs my skills at all. An accountant? I'm redundant, useless. I take my turn feeding cows, mucking stalls, cleaning tables and mopping floors. God, I had minions to do that kind of grunt work. I paid them shit and fired them regularly. I don't know if I can stand all this . . . equality shit."

"Harris made you the Head of Justice."

He made a raspberry. "I got a gavel and a white wig. Did you hear the laughter at that presentation? It was a joke. I'm set for next Halloween. Great."

"Is that all that it means to you?"

"It's what it is. A pretend title and a costume to make me feel stupid. You got a couple books. Tell me you've written anything in them, Ms. Historian."

"Actually, I've written about fifty pages."

He laughed. "Well, you're an idiot. I thought you were smarter than that, Barb. Harris gives out some stupid roles and people buy the gambit? I don't know."

"Mike," I said carefully. "What is real is that we're here and the world we knew is absolutely gone."

"No, it's not. It's right out there," he said, pointing to the stairs leading to the woodroom hall. "Sanity will reign again. Governments will pull it altogether again, fix the economy, call us all back out. The world we knew is just a few hundred feet away."

"You believe that?"

His cock-sure expression faltered. "I have to. I understood *that* world. This one I don't get at all."

"And you think you'll just go back to work, take up where you left off? You'll move back home, clients will come back, and everything will be fine?"

"That's my hope. You're a nurse. You've worked as a nurse down here. Jill's a doctor. She can still be that here. But I had an accounting and investment firm. I don't exist down here. I've got to get back to *my* world."

I stared at him, seeing how fragile he was. I wanted to point out that, having shot someone, outside might not be his best bet, but I refrained from that. "Mike, if that's your hope, you should hold it. You should also use it. Be the judge Harris made you. Help us make this place work so that you can return to the life you knew and loved. I mean, we might be here for a while, sure, but, eventually, we'll all go home. I think about my little farm all the time. I think about working at the hospital. Good times. The whole point to the shelter is to keep us safe until this insanity is over so we can go home."

Mike studied me. "You believe that?"

"Yes," I said with conviction. "I have to. This is a hot house, meant to allow delicate plants to survive Minnesota's harsh winter. But I long for spring when I can be set outside again to grow as I was intended."

For a long moment, he said nothing. Then he nodded. "And I've been a white fly, an aphid. I need to join the effort."

"It'd be nice. Consider this: you're an accountant. Dividing meals is math."

Marie came in at that moment, and I quickly bowed out.

As I put Noah down that night, I realized that, regardless of my sensibilities, I was committed to the Ark. It wasn't a perfect place, but it was the only place I had.

THE NEXT MORNING, Mike was already waiting for breakfast before anyone else, before the kitchen crew started work at six. When breakfast was served, he took up a bowl and approached the steaming pot of oatmeal. I was about ten back in line, just inside the doors, so I could see him and hear him when he spoke.

"Abby," he called. "Could you come out here a moment?"

Abby came from the kitchen, wiping her hands. "Yeah?" she said warily.

"What do you consider a portion?"

"Half a bowl of oatmeal, one pat of butter, a quarter cup of milk."

"And the fruit?" Mike asked, pointing at the platter of sliced apples and canned peach slices.

"I figure each could have two slices of peaches. I'd put them on the oatmeal, but that's me. There's two slices of apple each as well."

"Thank you, Abby," he said. He set down his bowl and walked to the end of the line.

We all watched him walk out, confused about what he was doing. When about halfway through the serving, Jeannie reached the counter, she filled her bowl.

"Jeannie," Mike called. "Do you really intend to starve your brother-in-law? Did you not hear the portions?"

"I'm pregnant," she snarled. "I deserve more."

Mike said, "Then I go hungry." With that, he turned and left the line altogether, heading to the radio room to take his shift.

Jeannie stood open-mouthed, staring after him. Then she swore and shoved her bowl across the counter. "Shit. How selfish can you get?" and she, too, walked out.

That was the end of difficulties with food. Thereafter, when each meal was served, a little card describing portions was set on the counter as well, and that's what people took. Our waste dropped to nothing, and we ate lovely meals.

ONE MORNING TOWARD THE MIDDLE of January, I found myself sitting outside my slice. Noah had just nursed and was slipping off to sleep. I glanced up at the television screen. Though the cameras still had a good coating of ice from the early-month storm, we could do nothing about it without going outside. With the concrete doors closed behind the steel doors at all entrances, it was determined that we had to just let it be. Still, some of the ice had melted a few days earlier, and I could see a corner of the panoramic scene we had previous enjoyed. As I expected, the snowy valley hadn't changed much. Winter had set in solidly, and it looked cold out there.

I smiled to think I wasn't dealing with ice dams on the roof of the house, trying to stuff Noah into a snowsuit, or worrying about how to get to work on icy roads. That gave me a moment of cheer. But, just as I was looking back at Noah to see if he had fallen asleep, something brown moved at the edge of my vision on the screen. I snapped my eyes up and looked for it, hoping I'd seen a deer wandering through the yard. Nothing. I studied the screen, seeing a trail of steps going to the woodroom door. But these weren't delicate deer tracks; these looked like the trail made by someone wearing bulky Sorrels.

The camera had panned away from the woodroom, and I tensely waited for it to turn back. When I did, I all but screamed, and my sharp inhaling made me choke. The entrance to the woodroom, which had been locked from the inside was broken open. A gaping hole of broken wood and twisted steel.

Noah woke with a jolt as I jumped up. I was yelling, calling to anyone, and people came running. Coughing, trying to quiet Noah's lusty cries, I pointed at the screen. The camera had panned away again.

"What?" said Wayne. "Are you having a fit or something?"

"Someone broke in," I choked out.

"Don't be ridiculous," he said. "That's a steel door."

I was still pointing, and the camera was finally making its swing back to the woodroom. "Look!" I said, waggling my hand at the screen.

Wayne looked, as did James and Jim, who had come from the schoolroom, and Abby, who had come from the kitchen. Others were crowding around. The camera, after what seemed an endless wait, finally showed the ruined woodroom entrance. People stared. Abby's hand went to her mouth.

As we watched, two men bolted from the woodroom and ran through the snow past the camera. We felt a shudder through the shelter and heard a heavy explosion. The camera jolted; then we lost the picture.

"They're breaking in!" yelled Connie.

A blare started, and red warning lights began flashing all through the shelter. In that same moment, everyone was running and yelling. Children startled and alarmed by the adults' behavior joined Noah in crying. I was on my feet, yelling for the girls, panicked that I didn't know where they were. I held Noah to my chest protectively, and I wanted to take him somewhere safe, but I didn't know where.

Men were running toward the stairs now, and I saw rifles and handguns. Frank and Harris and both the Deters brothers, the Reinharts, Carl Hope. Their faces looked grim. Before the door closed behind them, I already heard shooting.

We were about to be breached. In the middle of January, we were going to be killed or thrown out into the cold. I hadn't brought any winter clothes and didn't have anything for Noah. He'd freeze in minutes. I was nearly hysterical when I saw Jane. She was just outside the schoolroom doors, sitting on the floor. She had a death grip on Prince and was rocking her little body. Her eyes were pressed shut.

I stopped running in circles, stopped crying. I stopped panicking. Jane needed me. I walked over to the child, amid the running adults, amid the panic that so quickly filled the Ark and crouched down in front of her. "Jane," I said softly.

She rocked harder, making strangled sounds in her throat, her eyes closed.

I rested my hand on her knee. "Jane," I said again.

She looked up.

I smiled at her and said, "It's going to be okay. Where are your sisters?" My voice was so calm, it didn't sound like mine, didn't fit with the panic all around us.

Jane held my eyes, then pointed into the classroom. At that moment, Beth, her hand firmly holding both Andrea's and Lynn's. "What's happening, Mom?" Beth asked, her voice high but under control.

"Someone's trying to break in. We have to get everyone someplace safe."

"We should go up into the radio room," Beth said. "I sent the rest of the kids up there. Uncle Dewey said one time that the stairs can be pulled up."

I handed her Noah. "Go up. Figure out how the stairs move. Get ready."

She took her little brother and Jane's hand and herded the other children ahead of her back through the classroom.

I turned back to the living area and started to grab everyone I saw, sending them to the school. Romala was on the far side of the room, trying to get hysterical children calmed down, and Abby was standing at the kitchen door, looking catatonic. I ran to her. "Shut down everything and go up into the radio room."

With direction, she responding immediately, heading back to the kitchen. I helped Connie, then Mel and Sissy in turn, hustling a mixed group of their kids to the school. Sissy's daughter Diane tried to bring an armful of dolls. I took her by the upper arms and looked into her scared face. "Di, you have to leave the dolls."

"No!" She clutched them tighter.

"The dolls will be fine on your bed. Go help Beth with the little kids."

Diane was Beth's favorite girl cousin, one always a part of her "enterprises" since coming to the Ark. She shared Beth's convictions. Diane met my eyes, and her chin came up. She nodded and dumped the dolls just inside her slice. Then she grabbed her little sister, Lisa, and Mel's screaming Gertrude. As Mel and Sissy took this bunch of kids to the schoolroom, I started going from slice to slice, yanking back the curtains and calling out to make sure no one was left behind. I found Jeannie huddled in the back of her slice with her whimpering twins.

"Jeannie, come on," I yelled.

She shook her head in panicked jerks. I took maybe two steps into the slice when another explosion shook me to my knees. It sounded as if the whole shelter was under assault and the rumble of the impact lasted agonizing seconds. The living area was suddenly filled with dust. I didn't know what had happened, but it couldn't be good. I heard the steel door on the top of the stairs clang and knew I was out of time. There was no way I could get Jeannie and her boys to the schoolroom and up the stairs without being seen. Still, I had to try.

The explosion had shaken books and boxes to the floor, and Jeannie was screaming, trying to free her boys from the mess. I clambered over fallen jewelry boxes and toppled lamps to reach her. I pulled Roland up by one arm, got him free and set him on the bed. He was white-faced and scared. I helped Jeannie move a box that had fallen on Ronald, and it looked like his ankle could be broken. He was too upset to cry. Jeannie was having no trouble screaming, though. I pressed my hand to her mouth and crossed my own lips with a finger. With my other hand, I pointed toward the steel door. "Quiet," I husked. "The door opened just now, but I don't know who came in."

She stopped yelling with an insucking of breath, and her eyes went wide.

"Do you have anything in here to use as a weapon?"

She shook her head, then started gesturing toward the head of the bed. I took large steps over fallen mess and reached under the bed at that end. A flashlight about a foot long with a metal shank met my fingers, and my fist closed around it. It had heft and weight. I nodded to Jeannie and crossed my lips with my finger again. Soundlessly, I slid the curtain closed over the front of the slice. Then I tried to calm myself enough to figure out who had come in. I didn't hear anyone on the stairs, didn't hear any voices. In fact, with Jeannie and the twins hushed behind me, I heard nothing.

Dust had clouded the air, turning everything murky. After the heavy explosion and the thunder-like rolling afterwards, it had gone quiet, but I had no idea if that was good or bad. Where were our men?

I desperately wanted to get Jeannie and the boys up into the radio room. It seemed the safest option. In order to do that, though, I had to see what was going on.

Jeannie's space was just a couple slices down from the base of the stairs. Theoretically, if someone had come down, I should have heard something. I hadn't. To get to the schoolroom, we'd have to cross the entire width of the living area, and that was risky. I had to know what was happening.

I eased aside the curtain and looked to the stairs. The door above was closed, and no one was on the stairs. That didn't mean that someone hadn't tiptoed down. But I felt it was better to take the risk and get Jeannie and the boys to a safer place. I came back into the slice and gathered Roland into my arms. He curled around my neck and wrapped his legs around me. Jeannie took the hint and struggled to her feet. She picked up Ronald, who whimpered in pain. I waved her toward me and held out a hand to assist her over the debris clogging the path.

I took the flashlight before we left. The dust in the donut made Jeannie cough. I forced her along, looking all around. We were just at the schoolroom, when a man stepped in front of us. Armed with a handgun. I didn't know him. Balding, thin, and with glasses, he looked about forty years old. Our eyes met the moment he appeared, so there was no way I could attempt to hide. Instead, I set Roland down and stepped ahead of Jeannie. I raised the flashlight over my head as if it were a bat.

"Get out of my way," I said ominously.

He stared, almost shocked. Then he looked down at the gun in his hand. "A .45 aces a flashlight, don't you think?"

I heaved the flashlight. It struck him in the shoulder. He dropped the automatic. It slid close enough to me that I reached down and grabbed it. Then I held it out in front of me, my finger on the trigger. "I don't think so," I said.

Now his expression was filled with both pain and shock. "Don't shoot. I'm Jeff Cocoran. I . . . I'm from upstairs. I came down to help."

I stared but didn't lower the gun. From Upstairs? There was a zoo upstairs. "How do I know that's true?"

He seemed at a loss. He was rubbed his shoulder. "I'm . . . not wearing a coat?"

He wasn't. He had on a T-shirt, jeans, and slippers. Hardly outer wear in January in Minnesota. And who would come into the Ark, carefully take off his coat and boots and bring along a pair of slippers to change into. "Harris has . . . *people* up stairs? You're one of the . . . zookeepers?" My mind was racing. No, not a zookeeper. Something else. I lowered the barrel of the gun.

He winced. "I'm the head of the staff. Is the boy hurt?"

Staff? I could feel shock solidifying my mind. I fought against it. "It's either a break or a bad bruise."

He took two steps to Jeannie and lifted the boy into his stronger arms. "Come with me," he said and turned.

"No!" yelled Jeannie. She tried to pull Roland from Jeff.

With one hand, I pulled her away. "It's okay, Jeannie. He's been in the Ark all along. He and . . . others run this place." And as I said the words, I knew them to be true.

Jeannie looked at me as if I were crazy, but let go of Jeff's shirt. He ran into the schoolroom. "Go with him," I ordered Jeannie. I didn't follow. I continued where I had left off searching the slices for people who had decided to hide instead of go to the radio room. I was glad I did this. Mom and Dad Quill were kneeling in the back of their slice, praying silently. I got them up and escorted them to the school-room, telling them to go up to the radio room. Henry and Helmi Maki were cowering in the corner of the lunchroom. I had just gotten them to their feet when Abby again came out of the kitchen. She held a long kitchen knife. Her head was bleeding.

"Are you okay, Abby?" I yelled as I guided the Makis toward the door.

"A big fry pan fell in that last explosion," she said. "Knocked me to the ground. I think I'm okay, though."

"Good. Get the Makis to the radio room. I've got to check the animal room. Some people had to be there when this started."

Abby nodded, smeared blood out of her eyes, and took Helmi by the arm. Henry took Helmi's other arm and the three hurried away.

I had looked in every slice now, and made a check of the bathroom before I ran across the living area to the animal room. Inside the heavy door, I found Abby's younger son, Herman, branishing a pitchfork and looking terrified. He rushed at me, yelling.

"It's okay, Herman," I said. "It's me, Barb. Barb Quill."

He lowered the pitchfork and started to weep.

"Is anyone else in the animal room?" I asked him.

He shook his head.

"Okay. Go up to the radio room. Everyone's waiting there. It should be safe. Where's your brother?"

"I think he went out with the men to fight. Is he okay?"

"I don't know."

Herman, still holding the pitchfork, ran for the radio room, and I peeked into the animal room. No dust. The animals looked perfectly fine. The cows chewed their cud, and the little goats were playing their endless game of king of the hill in their manger. Rex the airedale stood just inside the door, and he seemed happy to see me. I decided to take him with me. He'd warn me if someone he didn't know showed up. Together we made a quick circuit of the animal room, but no one was there.

Feeling certain that everyone had been sent to the radio room who was not already in the hallway fighting, I turned and made my way back through the mud-room, pausing at the steel door to look out. Nothing had changed. The dust didn't look as heavy anymore. "Come on, Rex. We've got to get out of here."

I started back around the donut, trying to look everywhere at once. The quiet of the living quarters—usually filled with conversation, kids giggling or whining, the sound of bikes and skates—was creepy. It made me more frightened than at any moment before. It was as if something were about to happen. Rex began to growl, and that set my heart beating at an even higher tempo.

"What is it, boy?" I whispered.

Jeff Cocoran appeared at the schoolroom doors. "Barb," he called.

Rex showed his teeth, and a large male airedale has some pretty impressive teeth. Jeff looked at the animal and said, "Is he safe?"

"I sincerely hope not," I said. I tucked a finger under his collar.

"There's two children missing," Jeff said.

"Who?" I said.

"Ah, Molly and Madeline . . . being cared for by your brother and his wife."

276

I already had turned. "Come, Rex," I said and set off to Connie's slice. I'd checked this space, but went in again. A variety of books, lamps, and games had fallen from shelves with the explosions. "Where are they, Rex?" I asked the big dog. I didn't expect him to understand, but he seemed interested in something under the bed. I lifted the quilt. Two very scared girls looked back at me with huge eyes. Madeline started screaming.

"Come now," I said. "Hurry. The radio room."

The sisters scrambled out from under the bed and bolted for the schoolroom, skittering to a halt at the sight of a man they didn't know. They spun around, but I spread my arms and herded them in. "He's okay. Move it."

They sprinted between the desks and up onto the stage. We all climbed the spiral stairs, the airedale right behind us. At the top, Jeff went to the control board and lifted a plastic cover off a switch, which he toggled down. The stairway, like a cork screw, began to turn and moved upward. In just a few seconds, it had turned up into the ceiling above the radio room. At the same time, a round metal plate reached the floor of the radio room, completely separating us from the schoolroom.

And for the first time since I had seen the streak of brown in the television screen, I could take a deep breath. My thought immediately turned back to Frank and the brave men gone to fight. "Are they dead?" I asked Jeff.

"What?"

"Are all the men who went to the woodroom dead?"

He stared at me. "Probably."

My knees went weak. It was all I could do to stay standing. Tears burst into my eyes, and I couldn't hold back the sobs. The dread that had been held at bay by emergency was unleashed. We had had casualties. Frank, Harris, both the Deters men, the Reinhart twins, Carl Hope, and Duane Gertz had gone to defend us. In the space of the ten minutes between seeing the snowy footprints on the screen and now, I had become a widow. I heaved a ragged sob. I reached for my girls, folded all three of them into my arms.

"Barb."

A hand rested on my back, then wrapped around my shoulders.

"Barb."

I took Jane's and Andrea's hands. "Leave me alone. I just lost my husband."

"No, no, no. Hey, sweetie—"

My head popped up, and I clawed tears from my eyes. Frank stood next to me. I stared up into his face, trying to understand. "He . . . Jeff said . . ."

Frank wipes tears from my eyes gently with his thumbs. He smiled. "Not me, sweetheart, not any of our guys. The men in the woodroom who were trying to get in. They did a rather effective job of blowing themselves up. One hundred cords of firewood make very lethal projectile weapons."

"What? Our . . . backup fuel?"

He laughed and gave my shoulders a hug. "Didn't it seem odd to have all that wood when the Ark has its own heat source?"

I knew I was stammering but I didn't care. "Well, I don't know. Harris said it was back-up fuel."

"Yeah. Back-up fuel . . . for defenses. After the last assault we armed it. If someone tried to tamper with our door, it could set off charges under the wood, and it did. Those were the same guys who came before, and they were setting their own explosives trying to get in. They had C-4, too. Who knows where they got that."

"So . . . the explosions . . . was that the guys coming in . . . or us?"

"Both actually were us. The first one was the woodroom going up. The second was when we collapsed the long tunnel from the woodroom to the living area."

"But you and the others were in the tunnel."

Frank was being very gentle, knowing I was feeling confused and that understanding would help me settle down. "Yes, dear, we went out into the hallway, but we didn't stay there. We couldn't. The amount of rock and debris that fell into the hall to block it would roll all the way down to the steel doors at the end."

"That's what I heard. I thought the intruders were breaking in."

"No, they never got in further than the woodroom."

"But . . . but I heard shooting. I thought—"

Frank let out a hiss and cut a look to his brother James standing just off to the side, holding DeeDee. James shrugged. "James is really bad with weapons. Really bad. It's a wonder he didn't hit something, didn't kill one of us. We may have to institute classes in the uses of weapons at some point."

Jeff Cocoran said, "You'll be happy to know your wife is pretty good with them."

Frank spun. "Jeff! What're you doing here? And how's that?"

The balding man shrugged. "I came down to help."

"So what are you talking about?"

"I had a gun, and she had a flashlight. Still she disarmed me in about three seconds and took the gun." He rubbed his shoulder.

Frank looked at me, impressed. I almost didn't remember doing what Jeff said, and I certainly couldn't have duplicated that defensive move on a bet.

My emotions had had a huge workout in the last few minutes, and my mind was stretched from concern and fear. I desperately needed to find some place where I could finally feel safe. I looked around. Stuffed into the radio room was our whole group. The faces looked a little shell-shocked and scared. Families—some original, some made up since coming to the Ark—held onto each other. The children who had come to us clung to the adult now their parents. Little Jane held my hand just like Andrea did. Beth had a hand on each of their shoulders.

"So, we're all here and all okay?" I asked.

"Yes," said Frank.

I took a long, deep breath. "But . . . I don't see Harris."

Frank held me tighter. "Relax, hon."

"Harris has gone ahead," said Jeff. He gave me a sheepish look and added quickly, "And that's not a euphemism, either. Sorry about before."

I looked down in the general direction of where the stairs had wound down to the school-room stage. "We can't live there anymore, can we?"

"Well, the wall cracked between the hallway and the living quarters," said Frank. "That messed up our air-filtration system. It can be fixed, but . . ."

Just then I heard a motor sound, and a panel of wall next to us opened. Harris stood inside a large elevator box, his hands on the control panel. He looked around, grinned at Jeff Cocoran. Then his gaze settling on me. He winked. In a loud voice so that everyone could hear him, he said, "Come aboard, everyone. I believe it's time to move upstairs."